RIP TIDE

Also by Colleen McKeegan

The Wild One

RIP TIDE

A Novel

COLLEEN McKEEGAN

HARPER

An Imprint of HarperCollinsPublishers

RIP TIDE. Copyright © 2024 by Colleen McKeegan. All rights reserved. Printed in the United States of America. No part of this book may be used or reproduced in any manner whatsoever without written permission except in the case of brief quotations embodied in critical articles and reviews. For information, address HarperCollins Publishers, 195 Broadway, New York, NY 10007.

HarperCollins books may be purchased for educational, business, or sales promotional use. For information, please email the Special Markets Department at SPsales@harpercollins.com.

FIRST EDITION

Library of Congress Cataloging-in-Publication Data has been applied for.

ISBN 978-0-06-330554-0

24 25 26 27 28 LBC 5 4 3 2 1

For my Leahey ladies. Always.

Her stockings are torn but she is beautiful.
—ADRIENNE RICH

1

Beach Week 2022

DAY SIX

Peter Cameron had been missing for a few hours when they found his body floating near the 97th Street Jetty. A fisherman spotted him just before 5:30 a.m., one sleeve of his teal gingham button-down caught between two rocks, the other fluttering with the current, his limp and bloated body bathed in early morning sun. "We got lucky," the detective tells Tess Cameron when he calls her an hour later. "He must have fallen into the marina. The rip tide pulled him toward the jetty. It's the only reason he didn't sink, and then we may have never found him."

"Lucky," Tess repeats, her voice hopeful. She's in the kitchen of their vacation home in Rocky Cape, New Jersey. They bought it three years ago—before the world shut down and prices ballooned, their foresight a point of dubious personal pride. This is their first summer living in it after two years of gutting the insides, the scent of new paint clinging to the walls like an old habit. She runs a hand along the counter, made from a tree that fell during a thunderstorm in the backyard of their home just outside of Philadelphia. Peter spent countless weekends at the Shore house during the renovation, making sure that it was all perfect for her. It had, in fact, come together perfectly, her dream retreat for her beautiful family of four. She rubs a thumb across the fresh ding in the wood at the corner of the island, where she had thrown a baby monitor at Peter less than forty-eight hours earlier as he revealed all the secrets he'd been keeping from her. The monitor missed his head by an inch, but left its bite and a reminder of Tess's anger in the butcher block.

Still, even now, as she cradles her cell against her ear, she can't help but appreciate the serenity the space encourages, the way it taunts her to relax, despite the situation. She's been worried since 1:17 a.m., to be precise, when she groggily rolled toward Peter's side of the bed and realized it was empty. Tess checked her phone, three missed calls from him, her heart pounding as she opened her voicemail inbox. *Tess*, she listened to Peter say, his voice distant, slurred. *I'm so, so, so, so sorry. I don't deserve you. I don't deserve the twins. I love you. I love you. I love you.* She felt annoyed at first. He had promised not to drink, to come home with a clear head. She listened more closely and heard some rustling, like he was walking and carelessly holding his phone. *I'll fix this*, he said. *I'll fix it.* He said nothing else, but the call didn't end. Tess flipped her phone, pressing her ear near the speaker, hoping for some sort of clue, some hint of where he was. After a minute of jumbled white noise, she heard a quick gasp and—well, she wasn't sure. A splash maybe? Then the line went dead. She immediately called 911.

"So he's okay?" she asks the detective. She pulls her phone from her ear and presses "speaker," noticing it's a little after 7 a.m. The twins are still sleeping, their chubby fifteen-month-old limbs curled in their cribs, each of them snuggled cozily in matching sleep sacks. "Thank god." She sits on a rattan barstool and takes a sip of her espresso, her fourth of the morning. Her hand shakes, from either caffeine or fear, she's not sure. All Tess can think about is the thousand ways she wants to apologize, to sit down with Peter like the reasonable partners they are and talk—not scream, just talk—about their problems, about the ways Peter messed up, yes, but also the ways she didn't listen to him, didn't see his cries for help. She wants to erase yesterday's fight, erase the things she spat at him just before he left for the Devines' party. She wants to hold Peter in her arms and never let go, to drag him to Uncle Joe's Pancake House for breakfast with the twins, laughing as all three stuff their faces with stacks of chocolate chip goodness. "Is he there? Can you put him on?"

There's a pause on the other side of the line, and Tess's stomach drops. "Mrs. Cameron, I'm so sorry for the confusion." The detective gulps, and she hears him take a deep breath. "Your husband's dead."

Tess stares at her cell phone on the island counter, the entire act feeling detached from reality, like she's watching a movie of someone else's life. Because this can't be hers. She can't have a life without Peter in it. She collapses to the floor, the noise escaping the deepest parts of her like a deer bleeding out. The twins' monitor suddenly lights up and they're crying too. *Mama mama mama*, they shout. *Dada dada dada.* But he's not coming. Not for the twins, or for Tess.

She knows only one thing for certain. Somehow, this is the Devines' fault.

Blocks away, the Devine sisters sip freshly poured cups of coffee—black for Kimmy, with oat milk and honey for Erin—on the back deck of their childhood home. It's off the kitchen and family room; like most waterfront houses in Rocky Cape, the floor plan is inverted, so they loom above their backyard, quietly taking in the glassy surface of the bay, the only disturbance the occasional mullet or bluefish leaping toward survival. "So," Kimmy says, breaking the silence, "would you rate last night a disaster of major proportions, or a disaster of epic proportions?"

Erin laughs, but she's missing her signature lightness, her eyes still puffy from crying herself to sleep. She takes another sip of her coffee, then pulls her legs up to her chest and looks back toward the bay. "Do you regret coming back?" she asks, not able to meet her big sister's eyes.

Kimmy reaches across the table, her hand on Erin's. "We all make mistakes, Er."

Erin turns to her sister, her hand retreating like Kimmy's is covered in muck. "That's your sage advice?" Her brows vee in irritation, and Kimmy realizes she's said the exact wrong thing. *"We all make mistakes, Erin. Except me, because I'm perfect and can do no wrong."* Erin pitches her voice and flutters her arms, her impression of Kimmy like a prissy brownnose tattling on the class cheat.

"Is there a reason you insist on acting like a ten-year-old every second of your life?" Kimmy rolls her eyes. "You know that's not what I think." Because she's made mistakes too; fifteen years ago, when she left this place and swore she'd never be back—and this past week, when she found herself hypnotized by the steady crash of the ocean's waves. Their calm reassurance, their soothing siren call, made her think this town had softened like a piece of glass washed up with the tide. How easily she was lulled back to the past, slipping it on like a pair of last year's sandals, broken in and comfortable, forgetting about the blisters they gave her when worn too long. "To answer your question: It's weird to be home. I don't regret it, but I feel like my body's fighting between rationality and muscle memory." *And want*, she thinks. Fifteen years of ignoring it, only for it to explode with a sudden and spectacular speed.

"I am glad you're here." Erin's expression lightens, and Kimmy thinks of the night before, the way Erin's wails bounced across the freshly cut front lawn of the yacht club, her body shaking in Kimmy's arms with each sob. How she ushered Erin into an Uber before anyone could see her, the drama hidden from the crowd of everyone important to the future of their family's business tipsily gossiping inside. "Seriously, I couldn't get through this without you. Who else will keep the Peeping Tom that is Carissa Devine out of my business?" She nods toward the sliding glass door between the deck and the eat-in kitchen, where their mom stands, her hand on the handle but unmoving.

"Oh god." Kimmy stands and opens the door for Carissa. "Hello, Mother dear," she says with a playful curtsy. "May we help you?"

Carissa stands there, her face pale and her eyes looking past them at the water, as if in a trance.

"Mom, what's wrong?" Erin asks, also rising from her chair.

"Peter Cameron." She pauses. "He's dead."

"What?" Erin asks, her face confused. "What do you mean?"

Carissa shakes her head, as if to snap awake, her shocked expression replaced with one of motherly duty, the type she only wears during the most serious conversations. "Ben Lamb just called. You know he's a detective now? Peter never came home from the party last night, and Tess called the police."

"This doesn't make sense," Kimmy says. "He was just with us. Literally hours ago. This can't be true."

Carissa looks back at the bay, her eyes fluttering as she talks. Kimmy and Erin's dad, Bill, is circling it, his arms splashing against the navy surface as he completes his morning swim. "They think it was a suicide."

Erin drops her mug and it shatters, creamy coffee and ceramic shards scattering across the deck. The phrase "happy place," etched into one side, is now in pieces, the letters as disjointed as the thoughts in her head.

"Oh, honey." Carissa rushes inside to grab a towel. Erin crouches to pick up the fragments, her motion mindlessly robotic. It's not until she slices the tip of her finger, the blood dripping against the wood of the deck, that she looks up to see Kimmy crouching next to her, her hand wrapping around Erin's finger to pressure the cut, but it's too big, too deep to stop, and now both their hands are bloody.

Kimmy looks up at Erin, her mouth tight. "Er, what did you do?"

2

Beach Week 2022

DAY ONE

Kimmy pulls up to her childhood home, the familiar crackle of the crushed seashell driveway rumbling under her car's wheels. Erin runs across the front lawn, wrists covered in bangles and charm bracelets that sing like wind chimes as she waves, her sheer cover-up floating with each skip.

"You're here!" Erin says. "Here, here, here! And damn, did you travel in style." She bounces as she opens the driver's-side door and bends over the front seat of Kimmy's white Tesla.

"Oh, stop. It's just a rental." Kimmy breathes in Erin, the blend of jasmine and sandalwood from the Love Potion essential oil she ironically started using during her (still pending) divorce.

"Sis," Kimmy says, closing her eyes as she holds Erin. They squeeze tighter for a second, the tips of Kimmy's fingers indenting her sister's back. "God, I missed you. Let me take you in, you little beam of sunshine." Erin lets go and steps away from the car, twirling again.

She's fitter than she was three Decembers before, the last time Kimmy saw her in person, when they both visited their parents' house on 114th Street in Rocky Cape for Christmas. Erin was there with Kent, her husband at the time. She seemed off, malnourished and disengaged. Kimmy had been in town for less than thirty-six hours, so she never got to press Erin on what was up. And then, during the height of early COVID, she announced she was getting divorced and moved home. A few months later, their mom told Kimmy that Erin had a miscarriage after two rounds of IVF and three failed embryo transfers, and it had been the final straw in her marriage to Kent; Erin never told Kimmy because she'd been embarrassed, not wanting to burden Kimmy with her problems. Seeing Erin, the bright smile and tanned skin and full figure—which she'd lost in the months leading up to her divorce, when she'd cut out almost anything that wasn't organic and green and recommended by a fertility influencer—Kimmy lets out a sigh of relief and clicks off her seat belt. Their mom had been right. "You're glowing, Erin. Really, truly glowing." She crawls out of her car and opens her arms. "Come here and give this sap one more hug."

It seems being home cured Erin, the sun and sand and salty air doing what it has for so many others: giving her a new start, or at least the promise of one. "Mom's waiting," Erin says, transitioning from a hug to a sideways embrace, her arms still around Kimmy as she pulls her toward their house. A single step past the threshold and Kimmy teleports to the late 2000s. Familiarity kicks in as she slings her flip-flops off to the shoe bucket to her right, the ceramic tile in the circular foyer cold under her feet. The storm-blue walls, which had been a light shade of butter all through Kimmy's high school years, are still covered in framed photographs snaking the stairwell. Kimmy takes them in as they walk upstairs: she and Erin sandy on the beach, their toddler thighs like four croissants; Kimmy with her prom up-do, Erin beaming next to her in a T-shirt; their senior photos airbrushed to two-dimensionality. Above, a hand-blown glass chandelier hangs, the first big purchase Kimmy's parents made after opening a second Devine's Hardware and Home store in Oceanwind two decades ago. Kimmy had been embarrassed by the fixture for most of her teen years; it screams nineties, its multicolored glow like a jellyfish explosion. Now, though, she understands the pride it represents, the hard work and planning and saving. Of having Made It. After building a career that is solely hers and closing the biggest deal of her professional life a few months ago, she can finally afford a Made It purchase of her own. She's still not sure what, exactly, her chandelier is, but she thinks, *This is mine*, every single time she checks her bank accounts. *No one can touch it. I will never have to go back.*

Yet here she is, in her childhood home. Kimmy was in London for the bulk of 2020, only able to FaceTime with her family, and then she was wrapped up in a career-making deal that kept her away even after COVID flight restrictions eased. When her dad started complaining of back pain this past April, Erin joked to Kimmy that he had the man-cold version of long COVID, and they both laughed about it until he came in from a five-mile run in May and collapsed on the kitchen floor. Carissa called Kimmy with the news of his heart attack—he was stable, going to be fine, totally fine, she added—but in a straight tone Kimmy hadn't heard before, said, "It's time to come home, Kimberly. The stress of running Devine's is killing your father. We need you." Her mom's call gave her the push, but in truth it was the emptiness of her daily hustle that made her leap. What was the point of working to live if her life had so totally and completely become all about work? She quit her job at her private equity firm the next month, wrapped up the polished world she had spent over a decade curating, and moved back to Rocky Cape—to be with her family, and to take over the business.

Already, she feels the pull toward the past, everything about this place like a revisionist tidal wave, knocking out all the bad and leaving the good untouched, vivid and grasping at Kimmy's most ancient longings. Her mind wanders for a moment to him, wondering if he'll be at Beach Week. She wants to ask Erin if she has any new gossip, nudging her to spill whatever she's heard about his whereabouts, but she shakes the thought. One minute at home and she's already reverted to a boy-crazy teen with a heart-pounding crush. She inhales, her rib cage expanding. *Stop being desperate*, she tells herself. *You are better than that. You have bigger things to worry about.* Exhale.

"If it isn't my long-lost daughter." Carissa walks toward Kimmy with her arms open and hips sashaying. Despite the humidity, her hair falls in a perfectly straight line just below her chin, the gray invisible, edges smoothed from keratin—and despite the hours she spends on the beach weekly, her forehead is unwrinkled, hardly moving under the weight of her thrice-annual Botox treatment. "Oh, my sweet girl, I've missed having you here in my arms." The top of Carissa's head brushes the bottom of her oldest daughter's chin, her petite frame giving her a pixie vibe.

"Hi, Mom." Kimmy pats Carissa's shoulder as she pulls away. "It's not like I don't call you multiple times a week. You act like I'm coming home from war or something."

"No mother should ever go more than two years without holding her daughter. I've hated that I see you more on my phone screen than I do in person," Carissa says, going in for a second hug. "And now, after all this time, I finally get both my girls under the same roof for good." She places her hands on Kimmy's upper arms and smiles, her happiness brimming.

"Kimmy, come look in the kitchen," Erin says. "The club sent over some cocktails and apps for us to test before your homecoming party on Saturday and OMG are they to die for." Kimmy follows Erin into the kitchen, the quartzite island covered in plates of hors d'oeuvres and two pitchers of sparkling orange liquid.

Kimmy picks up a short rib and takes a huge bite, the sauce dripping down her chin. "Oh yikes," she says, dabbing her face with a napkin. "Apparently I'm starving."

"Try this one." Erin pushes over a pulled pork slider topped with coleslaw. Kimmy stuffs the whole thing in her mouth, crossing her eyes at Erin as she chews and swallows. Something about being under this roof with her baby sister brings out her inner child, which feels like it's been hibernating for far too long.

"That was impressive," Erin says, laughing. Kimmy beams back; it's so good to hear her sister laugh again.

"Or obnoxious, if you'd like my opinion," Carissa says, her penchant for Emily Post–approved etiquette never tired. She slides two martini glasses full of bubbly Aperol spritzes to Kimmy and Erin. She picks up her own, her eyes already welling. "To my girls. Finally, finally, finally all together."

"Jeez, Mom. We've been reunited for, what? Five minutes? And you've already brought the waterworks," Erin says, but the three look at one another, smiling, as they each take a sip.

There's a minor lull, then Kimmy asks, "The club isn't serving spritzes in these, right?" Her drink sloshes up the rim of her glass. "That would be a hot mess. And super nineties, which I understand are back, but not like this; these glasses scream mashed potato bar unless you're serving martinis or Manhattans." She takes another sip. "Also, let's pass on all the sloppy comfort food? I don't want to have, like, a barbeque beard while catching up with Mr. and Mrs. Wilson."

"Are these better for you, princess? God, you are annoying." Erin turns around and pulls out thin juice glasses, setting them on the island near Kimmy. "Obviously the club knows what it's doing. Only, what," she says, looking at her watch, "two minutes at home and Miss Bossy Pants has already emerged. Sometimes it cracks me up that you were such a shit show at the end of high school. Like, who even was that girl?"

Kimmy wants to avoid that particular walk down memory lane; she turns to her mom. "How's Dad? Is he home?"

Carissa waves her hand in the air. "He's at the boardwalk setting up for the auction. And you know how he is. 'Everything's fine! I'm fine! I don't want to talk about it!' I think he's convinced if he ignores it, his hypertension will just go away. He hasn't told anyone he's planning to retire, just so you know," she says, trailing off with a warning eye.

"Who am I going to tell?" Kimmy laughs. "Besides Erin, Nikki's the only person I talk to from here, and she's not even coming back for Beach Week."

Carissa nods, holding eye contact a beat longer than normal, then points to a console table off the kitchen where vases with mixes of peonies, parrot tulips, and gloriosa lilies sit in various combinations. "These are all for you, by the way. Aren't they stunning?" Carissa says, walking to the display and petting the edge of a vase.

"Oh, wow," Kimmy says, following Carissa. She picks a card up from an arrangement. *Welcome home, Kimmy! We're so proud of the amazing woman you've become.* "Aw, look—this one is from the Camerons. How are they?" Kimmy hadn't heard their name in years, save the occasional update from her parents. They had been the Devines' neighbors for a few summers. Peter was their only son and Erin's teenage crush—and, if Kimmy remembered, he seemed to enjoy her adoration a touch too much. Kimmy once caught Erin carving a heart with PC at its center inside her desk drawer; Kimmy promised she wouldn't tell their parents that Erin had vandalized their property if she did Kimmy's chores for two weeks.

"In Florida most of the time," Carissa says. "They sold their house a few years ago, but Peter—their son, remember him?—he and his wife bought a place on Ninety-Ninth Street. They're the sweetest couple with the most adorable twins. Erin's seen Peter a few times since he's been back. He RSVP'd that he's coming on Saturday."

Kimmy looks over her shoulder at Erin, giving her a what-am-I-missing look, but Erin just nods her head, then takes another sip of her drink. "You know, Stevie grows the peonies in this tiny, sheltered greenhouse she built herself," Erin says, changing the subject. "And obviously she still remembers your favorite flowers. I swear I didn't even mention it to her."

"Stevie? As in, Stephanie Long?" Kimmy puts her drink on the island, her lips suddenly pursed. She doesn't want to make it a thing, but how could it not be? The last time Kimmy talked to Stevie, they were both newly eighteen, slinging insults at each other as they watched their once impenetrable friendship crumble in real time.

"Yes, duh. The Flower Box is still the best place here unless you want, like, a total granny bouquet. And you know they have the best prices. That hasn't changed, even since Stevie took over."

"You talk to her? To Stevie, I mean?"

Carissa looks at both her daughters, raising her hands. Shortly after Kimmy and Stevie fell out, she would poke and prod during her conversations with Kimmy to see if there was any hope for reconciliation. But all Kimmy did was shut down, telling her mom that she could never understand. So Carissa stopped, and now it's an unspoken rule that they don't discuss Stevie. "I'm going to call your father and check that all's okay with the auction prep." She backs away, nearly scurrying out of the kitchen. Kimmy looks to Erin for an explanation.

"Yeah." Erin's gaze turns to the floor, not wanting to see the shock crossing her sister's face. "We do a morning walk about once a week. Honestly, Kimmy, I thought enough time had passed. I was so alone when I first moved home. And Stevie has always been like a second sister to me."

Kimmy's throat catches. Her saliva turns sour, the memory of it all like bile she thought she had expelled. "God, this town is so fucking small." She presses her temple with one hand, the other pushing against the counter. "Erin—" She stops when she sees her sister's expression, the worry that Erin's done something unforgivable sparking a disorienting déjà vu. "It's fine," Kimmy says suddenly, picking up her drink and taking a sip. She licks the mustache of orange kissing her top lip. "Fine. Totally fine."

Erin puts her hand on Kimmy's arm, the warmth a reminder of the love Kimmy will always have for her. "Are you sure? Because I can stop the walks. It's different now that you're home."

Kimmy's watch suddenly vibrates. "Shit, I need to get ready for the auction." Kimmy gives Erin's right cheek a quick pat. "We're good, Erin. Always."

"Always," Erin says with a smile, humming as she turns to the sink to pour out their drinks.

3

September 2005

Their legs push against the sand like pulled taffy, stretching then hitting but never breaking, over and over, the cycle mesmerizing as the tension forms the perfect shape. The afternoon air is fresh, the beach hardly marked, minus Stevie and Kimmy's footprints. They run in silence, pacing each other to push a little harder, churn a little faster. There's a shadow over the beach, that friendly fall light that looks like it's out of a movie, hopeful yet sentimental. When they pass the Windbreaker Hotel, the two-and-a-half-mile mark, Stevie pauses, hands on knees, eyes facing the ocean. Kimmy jogs in place, her weight shifting from left to right.

"You okay?" she asks, still bouncing.

Stevie lifts her chest, shaking her arms, her hips, her legs. "Fine, I think." She massages her right knee, then kicks her leg behind, holding her ankle against her butt. The stretch doesn't help, the slight pain in her knee tenacious. "Actually, can we walk back?" Stevie sees the annoyance in Kimmy's face, just a flash, before she says okay.

They take the first few steps in silence, Kimmy pressing pause on the tiny iPod shuffle attached to her bra strap and pulling out her headphones. "Your knee again?"

Stevie nods, giving her leg another kick. The feeling persists, a stab that keeps thrumming. She limps for a few steps, then feels it calm, her walking pained but not impossible. "My dad thinks I'm overreacting, but my mom wants me to go see a doctor about it. I think she's afraid it's serious." Kimmy bites her lip. They both know a serious injury isn't a possibility; Stevie's legs are her ticket to an out-of-state college. Her parents got divorced two years earlier after her dad lost his fifth sales job in three years; they're still negotiating his alimony payments, the only reason he's stayed in Rocky Cape. The Flower Shop, which her mom solely owns, pays the bills and puts dinner on the table, but it doesn't provide oodles in extra cash each year and definitely won't cover much beyond a New Jersey public university tuition. Her dad is adamant Stevie should have bigger dreams than taking over the family business, and says if she doesn't want to end up like him, she needs a private college education. So there can't be problems with her knee, as he repeatedly makes very clear, never owning his own measly contributions to her education fund. Stevie doesn't know what she wants, what she should want; she just knows she doesn't want to let anyone down. "Honestly, I'm sure it's nothing."

Kimmy grips her shoulder. "It'll be totally okay." They take a few more steps in silence, then Kimmy gently punches Stevie on her upper arm. "You better ice that before we go to Nick's." She smiles, knowing the mention of his name will make Stevie completely forget her knee.

"Ugh," she says, the slightest hitch in her walk. "Am I pathetic? I'm totally pathetic."

"Stop." Kimmy hops in front of Stevie, grabbing her hands as she walks backward. "He'll come around. I mean, you started reading the Bible for him, for Christ's sake. What more does he want from you?"

Stevie says nothing, loosening the tie holding her frizzed hair, letting her curls fall before scooping them again, pulling her pony tighter and tighter until it nearly gives her a facelift. Kimmy's hair is in a single French braid, the sections even as they weave toward the nape of her neck, her highlights—painted on at the fancy salon in Philly her mom drives her and her sister to every six weeks—like woven gold. They're about the same height, but Stevie always feels like Kimmy is inches taller, her bones elvish compared to Stevie's denser build. The one plus: Stevie's boobs are way bigger, a point she secretly relishes. She doesn't fault Kimmy for the easy way things seem to come to her— good grades, excellent race times, attention from boys; it's part of what makes being her friend so fun, the proximity to a way of life Stevie craves, the proximity to being the best. But a part of Stevie is always a little happy when she hears the guys make fun of Kimmy's flat chest behind her back.

"Want to get ready at my house?" Kimmy asks, her hand cupped over her eyes as the sun sharpens overhead.

"Ooh, cool beans. Race you back there?" Stevie says, then tries a slow jog again. Her knee still hurts, but not like before. She doesn't want to miss today's workout, so she pushes past, her trot turning into a run. Kimmy, a few feet behind, fumbles to put in her headphones. She presses play, and within seconds she's next to Stevie, dots of sweat collecting on Stevie's upper lip. Kimmy picks up the pace and Stevie sprints to stay by her side.

In Kimmy's room, Stevie splays her body in an X on the queen-size mattress, her head surrounded by jewel-tone throw pillows embroidered with shiny beads and tassels. They wear flared jeans and chunky white sneakers, topped with oversize sweatshirts (Kimmy's borrowed from her boyfriend, Brian, and Stevie's, ripped in a V at the neckline, from her collection of XC team gear) with tight camis underneath, their weekend uniform. Stevie adjusts the hot-pink push-up bra she got at Victoria's Secret a few weeks ago, not thinking anyone will see it, but just in case. Kimmy goes braless, for the exact same reason.

"Here," Kimmy says, throwing Stevie an assortment of lip gloss in metallic packaging. "My mom just ordered these for Devine's. She's trying to find new ways of getting people into the store. Cute, right?" Stevie pulls a tube from the box, screwing off its clear cap. It smells like a cotton-candy-injected strawberry, the taste tickling her tongue as she shellacs her lips. She hops off the bed and stands next to Kimmy, cocking one hip and putting a hand on the other.

"Ooh, pretty!" Kimmy says, turning to face Stevie for a second, then turning back toward the mirror, mascara wand in hand.

"That's hot," Stevie says, doing her best Paris Hilton and pursing her lips into a kiss. She flips her hair, strutting in a circle.

"Oh my god, Stevie. You kill me." Kimmy isn't actually laughing, too concentrated on separating each lash as she bats her lids, her face inches from the mirror, but she gives a small smile. Stevie is always doing impressions, her way of deflecting compliments. Sometimes Kimmy thinks the guys would be more into Stevie if she wasn't always trying so hard to be funny. Over the past year, she noticed they increasingly prefer when they, not the girls, are the ones making everyone laugh. Like her boyfriend, Brian; he's called Stevie "quirky"—code for weird—more than a few times.

She grabs the tube and puts some on her lips too. "Twins," Kimmy says, her arm draped over Stevie's shoulders. They look nothing alike, complete foils in many ways, but have been inseparable since they were five, when they both sat at the Orange Table in kindergarten.

Stevie looks at the gloss on Kimmy, a ping of envy hitting so fast she almost doesn't notice. The gloss settles better on Kimmy's lips, of course, but she swats away the thought and puts her arm around Kimmy's waist. "Twins," she repeats, the evening light spilling through the bedroom window, landing so Kimmy's profile slightly shadows Stevie's face.

The door flies open, Erin bursting in, knobby knees poking out of a frayed jean skirt, her lanky legs barely filling her Uggs. "Um, knock much?" Kimmy says, chucking the tube of gloss at Erin's head, missing by an inch.

"Psycho," Erin says, her hands Ferris wheeling around her ears as she looks to Stevie, her audience. Laugh, her eyes say, plead, her need for validation the scarlet letter of teenhood. Erin was a bit of a disjointed bloomer, all her features developing at different times, a confusing Picasso until this past summer, when it all came together. So long as she isn't slouching, her big lips and doe eyes and frail collarbone make her look more mature than Kimmy, who's only fourteen months older but two grades above Erin. "Where are you guys going tonight?" Erin asks, sinking into the bed.

"Young Life at Nick's," Stevie says, referencing the weekly evangelical club Stevie attends because it's hosted by Nick, and Kimmy attends because Stevie needs a wingwoman. She plops back into an X on the bed, her dark hair falling into a halo around her crown. Erin takes a few strands, starting to braid them as she asks more questions.

"Ooh, Nick's," Erin says, batting her eyes at Stevie. "Are you still Nick Rolland's biggest fan?"

Stevie picks up a pillow, throwing it at Erin, missing and instead hitting Kimmy's back. The mascara wand in her hand slips, a streak of black trailing across her cheek.

"Can you two not?" she asks, muttering "children" under her breath. Stevie turns on the bed, belly down, her body between Erin and the pillows. "Do you like my new look?" she asks, mouth smooshed in a fish shape, slurpy sounds rolling off the thick sheen. Erin grabs the pillow from behind Stevie and smacks her face.

"Freako," she says, her vocabulary of late composed of reductive words that all end with o. Though not sisters by blood, Erin and Stevie have a bond that's nearly as close as Erin's with Kimmy, Stevie almost as consistent a presence in Erin's life. A softer presence, one without the fighting and competition and occasional resentment, the normal stuff of teenage sisterhood that, despite its banal commonness, always feels impossible in the moment. Sometimes, when Stevie's over for sleepovers with Kimmy, she sneaks into Erin's room to ask about school or boys or dance, then launches into a complaint about Kimmy, like the time Kimmy wouldn't talk to Stevie for twenty minutes after Stevie beat her in a game of gin rummy. Erin loves when they complain about Kimmy; Stevie's the only other person who understands what it's like to know someone so well, so deeply, you both adore and detest them with all your heart.

"That looks ridiculous," Erin says, smearing her finger across Stevie's lips. "What is this goo, anyway? It smells like Rainbow Brite barfed all over you." She lifts her finger, covered in pink gloss, to her nose and makes a face.

"Don't hate me cause you ain't me," Stevie says, hopping up from the bed and looking out the window. "Ooh." She points to a huge moving truck parked in front of the house next door. "New neighbors? They have to be shoobies, right?" The three girls huddle by the window, their noses nearly pressed against the glass. A woman with bright pink readers propped atop a sleek blond bob motions the movers toward the house, a conductor leading her symphony. The furniture and décor are shades of candy pastels, hues embraced by vacationers in the area who don't have to worry about everyday wear.

"Oh yeah," Kimmy says. "Carissa already got the scoop. She said their last name is Cameron and they live in the Philly suburbs. They're planning to come for part of the summer. It doesn't sound like they'll have a ton of renters. The dad's a doctor or something, I can't remember exactly."

From behind the woman, a boy—no, a man, maybe a few years older than them, appears. "Mmm, well okay, then," Stevie says. "At least they're hot shoobies."

Erin presses her nose harder, her breath fogging the glass. "Drool much?" Kimmy says, walking away to finish her makeup. Erin closes her eyes, imaging a life where her sister isn't such a bitch.

Kimmy's phone, charging on her nightstand, pings, and Erin, the closest, picks it up to pass to Kimmy, but pauses, and unable to re-sist her little sisterly urge, she flips open the phone to snoop. "Um, Kimmy," she says, "why are you texting with Justin Fitzpatrick?"

"Oh my god, random. Let me see!" Stevie crawls on top of Erin, grabbing for the phone. They wrestle a moment, the phone bouncing between their grasps. Kimmy runs over, grabbing it midair, and clicks the text open on her keypad.

los3r u going to YL tonite

She's surprised. Justin is not the Bible-thumping type.

Of course, it's at Nick's. You going? Didn't take you for a Jesus lover

He answers almost immediately.

down wit g-o-d, u kno me

cya there brah

Kimmy pauses for a second, a flit of illicit energy jolting her body, then startled, she shuts her phone, tossing it into her bag. "Stevie, you ready?"

"Um, so you're just going to ignore my question?" Erin asks, her tiny frame curled against the edge of the bed as she stares at Kimmy. "What would your precious boyfriend, Brian, say?" she adds, a mis-chievous grin springing to her lips. Brian Accardi is co-captain of the soccer team, the only junior ever to earn the title. A member of the National Honor Society. Class president. Kimmy is also a proud member of the NHS, as well as vice president of their school's Key Club and captain-in-waiting of the cross-country team, just biding her time until senior year. They've been friends since freshman year of high school; she knew of him, had seen him play against her school's soccer team during middle school and junior high district matches. Brian always seemed to have a girlfriend, usually a cheerleader or field hockey player or dancer, their common trait performing athletic feats in skirts. Kimmy was taken too; she had a long-distance boyfriend she met over the summer, who lived in Morristown. He was two years older, and since both of them were inherent homebodies, they fit into one another's social lives perfectly, rarely seeing each other in person—until his senior year, when he started going out more and Kimmy felt him drift, which led her to hang out with Brian and his friends more and more throughout her sophomore year. By the summer before their junior year, Kimmy was single and so was Brian. They shared a first kiss in Derek Kasanaar's hot tub, walking their towel-clad bodies into Derek's living room to applause from him and his longtime girlfriend Katie Ray, Stevie, Nick, and Ben Lamb, the fourth and oft disregarded wheel to the Brian-Derek-Nick trifecta. Kimmy felt like she'd not only been initiated into the Rocky Cape Club of Golden Children, but named its queen.

"You really are a psycho, you know that?" Kimmy says, throwing her phone in her purse. "We have American history together, so Justin is a friend. Am I not allowed to have those? And he's friends with Brian. So stop being a loser." Still, she feels her cheeks warm, hopes their flush goes unnoticed.

Stevie shrugs, jumping off the bed. "Do you want to come to Nick's tonight, Erin? It's mostly juniors and seniors, but this get-together is technically for whoever."

"Stevie," Kimmy starts, "she can't—"

"That sounds like a wonderful idea!" Carissa is in the hallway, full laundry basket cradled against her stomach. She's in workout clothes, her hair swept into a high pony, post-powerwalk flyaways springing near her temples. "Erin, I think it would do you good to spend a little time with the Bible." Carissa isn't religious, but she's spiritual, something she told Kimmy every Sunday growing up when Kimmy asked why they weren't going to church, why they had to miss out on what, in the years before parties and licenses, was the highlight of social activity on the weekends. These days, building an entire evening around worship is far less appealing to Kimmy, but Young Life at Nick's doesn't usually feel religious. His dad is an assistant coach on the soccer team, so most of the players attend, plus friends and girlfriends and Nick's groupies, who pant when Nick, with his dark wavy hair and Crest commercial smile, follows his Bible passage reading with an acoustic rendition of the Wallflowers' "One Headlight." Stevie had thus far avoided being clumped into the groupie crowd by becoming Nick's best girl friend, but anyone with eyes knows she is, without a doubt, hoping to be his Mary Magdalene.

Kimmy wants to tell her mom Erin can't join them because she doesn't want to deal with a tagalong sibling, but really she doesn't want to deal with the gawking. Erin had become undeniably beautiful over the summer, and people—random sales associates at the mall, a modeling scout in Philly, and worst of all, Kimmy's guy friends—were starting to notice. The attention made Kimmy feel both protective of her sister and jealous, not ready to surrender her role as the Devine sister making heads turn. Instead, she's quiet, never one to talk back to her mom; that's Erin's role. She folds her arms across her chest, glaring at Erin.

"Sure." Erin shrugs, like she isn't turning what was supposed to be a super-fun night into a babysitting adventure for Kimmy.

"Just don't embarrass me, okay?" Kimmy watches Erin glance at her reflection, smoothing her jean skirt, tucking her hair behind her ears, running her fingers underneath her eyes to perfect her makeup. She sees her little sister in her kindergarten dance recital, their mom plopping bright blue eye shadow on her lids, curling her hair until she looked like she was shipped straight from a southern beauty pageant, Erin's eyes unsure, yet her demeanor acquiescent, seeking Carissa's favor. Kimmy almost hugs her, but the feeling flits away as Kimmy's mind drifts to her own issues—like having to babysit her clingy little sister at the night's social event. "Can we go? Now?" Kimmy snaps her fingers in Erin's face, rushing out the door of her room, brushing past her mom, who's grinning like a fool.

"Have fun, babies!" Carissa calls down the hallway at Kimmy's back, tense with bottled irritation. "Cherish these moments, girls. I would have killed to have a built-in best friend!"

Erin crawls into the rear row of Stevie's Accord, the fabric worn from years of her older brother's friends piling in. The front seats and wheel are covered in faux leopard fur, Stevie's attempt to personalize the tired gray interior. Kimmy pops a tape adapter into the cassette player, plugging the auxiliary cord into her iPod. Corinne Bailey Rae blasts, both Stevie and Kimmy hand-cranking their windows down, the chilly fall air whipping their hair as they sing the words at the top of their lungs. Erin only knows the chorus, but rolls her window down too, letting the air sting her face, savoring the feeling of being one of them.

They pull into Nick's driveway, and Erin suddenly feels small and unwelcome, a leech grasping on to her big sister. She gets quiet, folding her arms across her chest as they walk up the front steps, her slouch, which she worked to get rid of all last summer, returning.

"Come here, little one," Kimmy says, putting her arm around Erin as they walk to Nick's front door. "It's just people from school. They don't bite." Erin nods, appreciating Kimmy's sisterly protection while also feeling vexed by her condescension, their power imbalance always obvious, always irking Erin while somehow pushing her to mimic Kimmy more deeply.

They're inland, on a half-acre slice of green lined with pristine landscaping, parked at the end of the line of cars snaking the driveway, some spilling onto the street. The front door is unlocked, wafts of pizza and Axe body spray lingering in the entry hallway. In the kitchen, a few people graze around the island, stuffing their faces with cheesy bread and snacking on plates of snickerdoodles and platters of crudités, ranch bucket in the center. Erin eyes the scene, looking for someone, anyone she might know.

"Oh my god, Fitzy's here?" Erin asks, spotting the first familiar face to come into the kitchen. She elbows Kimmy in the side, who pulls her arm back and gives a scolding look.

"What did I say about not embarrassing me?" she whispers, no louder than a hiss. Stevie has already wandered off, likely searching for Nick like a lost puppy. Erin tightens her lips.

"Sup, Legs?" Justin Fitzpatrick says to Kimmy, using the nickname Kimmy picked up when she came in first in the 13 and Under category in Rocky Cape's Turtle Trot 5K—at age eight. The whole town still talks about it, their parents bringing it up at every dinner party they can. Erin doesn't have a story like that, a small moment of precocity or excellence in her childhood. She was—is—average, unspecial. Normal. "And sup, Little Legs?" Erin whimpers hi, shrinking the tiniest bit so she can slip under the radar, watching her sister watch her. Justin cradles a piece of celery in his hand, crunching down as he looks back at Kimmy. His jawline sharpens and Erin sees Kimmy notice, her eyes on him like he's Brad Pitt in *Ocean's Eleven*.

"I can't believe you're here," Kimmy says, a smirk spreading across her face. Her voice is different with boys. Lighter, fizzy. Usually Erin makes fun of it; this time she observes, watches its charm ooze in real time. "So was I incorrect in assuming this isn't your usual Saturday night scene?"

"Si, chica," Justin says, swallowing what's left of the stick. "But bonding with the team, you know? Not that Mr. Rolland gives any of us much choice." He plays soccer with Nick and Brian, and Mr. Rolland, in addition to being the assistant coach, is the team's biggest booster. "This shit could get real boring, but seeing your polished li'l face makes it a touch better."

"Oh, just a touch?" She jabs his shoulder. "Sorry I couldn't be more satisfying, Justin." Minus teachers, Kimmy's one of the only people at school who calls him by his actual name. To everyone else, even Erin, he's Fitzy. Erin feels uncomfortable, a third wheel. She can't be the only one who sees this, who senses the naked flirtation, the electric hum, but no one is looking, her eyes the only two on them. It doesn't matter, though; her sister, she knows, will never do anything about it, not one to deviate from the yellow brick road she's laid toward her future, especially with someone she considers to be on a vastly differing path. Justin's mediocre grades and love of weed would never pass the Devine parents' approval gauge, Erin knows.

"Don't temp me, Legs." Justin fake-punches Kimmy's stomach, never making contact. She laughs, but her gaze quickly floats over his right shoulder.

"Brian!" She walks right past Justin, their flirtation evaporating in an instant, Brian's hands immediately on Kimmy's waist, his lips on hers. She pulls away, but his grip on her waist only tightens, her upper body arched back and her pelvis mashed into his, leaving Erin and Justin alone. Justin watches Kimmy and Brian, a new piece of celery dangling from his lip, forgotten, like him. Erin recognizes his expression, his longing. She's felt it about so many things, especially when it comes to things in Kimmy's life.

She clears her throat. "I'm gonna head outside," she says. Justin snaps out of his daze, crunching down on the celery.

"Aight." He wraps an arm around Erin. "I'll escort you, Li'l Legs."

"It's Erin," she adds, looking up at him. He smells like smoked apples, a twisted orchard on the cusp of being overripe.

Justin shakes his head. "No shit, I know that." He tsks, pulling her closer for a second. "You're friends with Reid, right? I've seen you with my bro and his crew when they do their dumbass skate tricks in the parking lot." He laughs, his embrace loosening as they walk down the steps of the back porch to the yard, clumps of kids splattered throughout. Erin doesn't recognize some—they must be from Oceanwind, their high school's soccer coach is Nick's dad's best friend—but smiles as they walk toward a group of players.

"Erin?" A girl in tight jeans, which Erin later notes have bedazzled logos across the back pockets, with a slouchy stud-lined leather bag perched on her shoulder, charges toward her. Her hair is so blond it's nearly white, its crimpy length like a mermaid's. Fall weather has started to creep in, but her tan is dark, and Erin bets she permanently smells like Hawaiian Tropic. "Erin Devine? Oh my god, it's been so long!" Her arms are open, going in for a hug. It's not until they embrace that Erin realizes it's Madison Jensen, whose family owns a small chain of hotels along the Jersey Shore, their clout almost as feared as Mrs. Jensen's snobbishness. Kimmy's parents know the Jensens from the club, and Erin and Madison had a few dance classes together as girls. Their parents had hosted one another for dinner a few times when Kimmy and Erin were little, all three playing together as the adults had stilted conversation. Erin still remembers Madison's room, how it was lined with a shelf near the crown molding where Collector Edition Barbies still in their boxes perched in a row like a wallpaper border. She told Erin she got them at the Barbie store at King of Prussia, the one with pillars filled with floating pink high heels at its entrance, the same store Carissa rarely let Erin visit, and even when she did she was never allowed to get a Collector Edition Barbie. *Not until you can show me you're responsible enough,* Carissa said, referring to the piles of burnt-hair Barbies, their skulls half exposed, Erin had experimented on while playing salon. As Erin looked around Madison's room, she thought, *She has everything I've ever wanted.*

"Madison, hi!" Erin says, slowing her pace. Justin stalls, his eyes on Madison. A sliver of her stomach shows, the rest hidden by a glittery tank top and velour hoodie with a shiny *J* zipper. "What are you doing here? I thought you were at boarding school at Lawrenceville?"

"Not anymore!" she says, flipping a chunk of her near-white hair over her shoulder. "I'm starting at Rocky High on Monday. Which is why I'm here, not because I've turned into some church girl. No offense, I mean." Peter's parents own the local Toyota and Lexus dealerships; it makes sense that the Rollands and Jensens are friends.

"None taken," Erin says, raising her hands. "I'm just here because my sister's here." She doesn't acknowledge her excitement at being invited, instead agreeing that the event is decidedly uncool.

"Okay, phew." She flips her hair over her shoulder again, her hands doing their own dance as she talks. "Honestly, since I was gone last year I know, like, zero of the Cape kids," her eyes suddenly moving to Justin. "Speaking of, hi." Her smile shines even in the dark. "I'm Madison, a soon-to-be junior at Rocky High and in desperate need of friends." She speaks with an ease that intrigues Erin, her tone enticing rather than desperate.

Justin sticks out a hand. "Justin Fitzpatrick." His fingers lace her smooth palm, their hands lingering. "Happy to be your personal tour guide, should you find yourself needing an escort."

"Yo, Fitzy," someone yells, breaking the moment. He looks over her shoulder, then back to her face. "Very nice to meet you. I guess I'll see you on Monday," he says with a wink.

"Um," Madison says low, moving closer to Erin as they watch Justin walk away. "What is his deal? Totes a babe, wow." She rests her head on Erin's shoulder dreamily, the move familiar despite the fact that they hardly know each other. Erin takes another look at Justin through this new lens, the combination of his long hair, which he's always flipping with a left swing of his head, and his wiry build suddenly more surfer boy than unkempt gamer. Still, she doesn't find him traditionally attractive, his style far from her type, but she gets it; Justin carries himself with a confidence that follows him like a potion, his casual flirtation with anyone and everyone he meets oozing swag.

"Justin Fitzpatrick. Junior. Soccer player. I think a stoner? Or that's what my sister says. I don't really know him that much, just his little brother." She sees how misplaced Madison is among the Birkenstock-wearing Bible lovers at Nick's, the frayed edges of her designer jeans soggy in the grass, how much cooler she is than them all. Erin decides she wants Madison as her new best friend. Needs, really.

"So he's single? Interesting," she says. "God, I am so effing lucky I ran into you. It is so good to have a friend before starting school. Are you still dancing? I was thinking of trying out for the team this fall. Here." She pulls out a rhinestone-encrusted BlackBerry from her purse. "What's your cell? We should go shopping together. I need, like, a totally new wardrobe before starting. Boarding school kids dress like nuns, I swear to god."

And like that, Erin's in, with a partner in crime to help her craft a new identity all her own.

4

Beach Week 2022

DAY ONE

Beach Week is the Shore's most sacred tradition. Always in the thick of August when temperatures and tourist numbers are at their peak, the event draws thousands. Restaurants and bars spend the days before blasting their slimiest corners with pressure washers, the novelty T-shirt shops stock up their hoards of merch with ill-advised slogans, and the five-and-ten stores push piles of beach chairs and buckets to their front windows. For tourists, the week is about forgetting their humdrum reality for a few relaxing—or, depending on the group, debaucherous—days. For locals, it's about making as much money as possible off the tourists' desire to escape.

The entire ordeal launches with a few small events and the Cape County Lifeguard Championships, the beach patrols from across South Jersey's shores racing one another for glory while the audience downs lukewarm Miller Lites in koozies and vodka-spiked lemonade from Igloo thermoses. Growing up, Kimmy always spent the day of the kick-off race readying the Rocky Cape and Oceanwind stores, *DEVINE'S Hardware and Home* emblazoned on the front of her turquoise T-shirt, which was usually speckled with sweat. For the past fifteen years, she's managed to avoid Beach Week, mumbling about a crazy schedule or traveling for work when her parents pressured her to come home, just for a few days.

When she transferred from Rutgers to Pepperdine after her first semester of college, lugging all her baggage to the West Coast, she had no plans to return to the Shore. With each degree (Pepperdine, Stanford), stamp on her passport (every continent except Antarctica), and work visa (Hong Kong, United Kingdom), she felt her old self shed, the painful memories and shame blurring with distance. But this year, instead of managing to avoid a visit home, she's leading Oceanwind boardwalk's annual Devine's charity auction. The 2022 benefactor is the boardwalk itself, still recovering from last fall's ferocious hurricane, which barreled into the amusement park and caused a slew of electrical blowouts as it flooded most of the oceanfront stores.

Kimmy drives her car into the Oceanwind Beach Patrol lot and flashes an email on her phone at the attendant, the lot's spaces reserved only for OWBP and a select few working events during Beach Week. She wonders if high schoolers still use the lot for impromptu car parties on Saturday nights in the dead of winter, popping open their trunks as they pass 40s and vodka-filled water bottles with gloved hands, noses red with cold, cheeks flushed from hormones. "Ma'am," a college-age kid with a salty mess of hair interrupts her thoughts, "over here." He's wearing an orange tank, OWBP bold and blue across his front, and pointing toward a corner spot, the silhouette of the boardwalk's roller coaster visible in the background. Kimmy nods and slowly drives her car between the lines, moving the gear into park. She turns around, and the kid's staring at her Tesla.

"It's not mine," she says, unbuckling and climbing out, her smile an attempt to be relatable. She did own one, part of her wants to add. And a Land Rover, both recently sold back to their London dealerships before Kimmy's return to the States. That impulse—to shrink herself so she's more palatable, more pleasing—is one she's never quite curbed when she's home, etched in her personality like a fossil refusing excavation. Always apologizing, accommodating, never intimidating, the way so many men in this town like it.

"Oh," the kid says, pretending he wasn't looking. He shrugs, his sudden indifference and disinterest further evidence that little in Rocky Cape has changed. A comfort and, in a way, a warning.

Kimmy takes a deep breath, smoothing the front of her linen Bermuda shorts and white sleeveless blouse, the combination Erin spent about twenty minutes making fun of Kimmy for, saying she looked like a couture version of Steve Urkel. Kimmy's stylist, whom she hired after her 2015 review included a not-so-subtle hint that her "presentation" could use work, had recommended the pairing during their Summer '22 session a few months earlier, before Kimmy knew she'd be back in Jersey for good. *It's a clean summer look*, she'd said, but as Kimmy watches the sandy-haired boy walk away, his tank top worn and guard shorts sun-washed, she sees herself through his eyes and wonders if she should have taken Erin's advice and borrowed one of her flowing floral maxi dresses. She glimpses her reflection in the window of her car and suppresses her insecurity, remembering who she is, what she's accomplished, how she's lived beyond the borders of New Jersey. Her sunglasses pushed onto the bridge of her nose, Kimmy walks to the closest boardwalk entrance, the wood planks' grayness on full display in the bright sun. The auction is taking place near the amusement park, a good ten-minute stroll, and Kimmy looks to her right as she walks, her Grecian sandals clacking with each step. Halfway, she pauses at the boardwalk's rail to stretch out a burgeoning cramp in her calf, the intensity of a week of packing followed by sixteen hours of traveling by plane and car catching up to her. The sky is a crisp blue, a few white wisps painted across the pristine canvas, and the air has the perfect amount of wind, each gentle gust sweeping in just as the heat feels it might suffocate. Bright umbrellas dot the wide swath of beach, the sun-crisp locals and beer-bellied tourists just like the ones she remembers. She smiles, the comfort of familiarity tugging at her again. "Is that my Kimmy?" a voice interrupts her reverie. A thin man with a swimmer's stature holding a clipboard approaches her. "Honey," he says, wrapping his arms around her, his embrace like a time machine, a reel of cross-country finish lines and Christmas mornings and robe-clad graduations suddenly playing. She holds him tight, as if her grasp will keep him healthy, safe, and with her forever.

"Dad," she says, flipping the bottom layer of his hair, which has grown long and now curls at his ears and neck. "What's up with this flow?"

He laughs. "Midlife crisis, according to your mother." He poses like a toy soldier, knees bent as he flexes one arm up and the other down. "You like it?"

She tilts her head, assessing the look. "You know what, I do. Though it does scream, 'I'm about to retire and hand over my entire business to my daughter.'" She winks, hiding the concern she feels creeping up. That's how their family functions; they cover the serious stuff quickly, then move on as best as possible, not wanting to bog down life with all its crushing realities. Especially her dad and Erin. They are the same, bathing their worry with humor, laughing through hardship and pain until they're on the other side. It's probably why their go-to movie night pick is always *Patch Adams*. Bill Devine looks tired, worn, like he's aged in 2x speed since she's seen him last. But Kimmy knows better than to acknowledge that, especially in these early moments of their reunion.

"And thank god for that." He beams, his eyes proud. "And for your return home. Your sister's been a huge help since she moved home. Did you know she set up our e-commerce store last year? Impressive stuff. But I need the big guns for what's next. I need you." He puts his arm around her, turning toward a white tent in the distance. "But for now, my little shark, it's time to sell some ridiculous décor to the Cape's finest."

"Let's do it," she says, ready for the challenge. She hasn't helped lead the auction since she was a tween, when she and Erin would flash their cutest smiles while holding local artists' canvases and driftwood sculptures and her parents acted as the auctioneers, pointing to all the familiar faces in the crowd as they raised their paddles. This is her first time as a co-auctioneer with her dad; he suggested they do it together as a way of easing her into her role before she formally takes over. Erin had run it with their dad the past two years; it surprised Kimmy that Erin didn't mind that she's doing the auction this summer, since Erin had always been the performer of the family.

The corners of the tent are fitted with misting fans, a huge stage flocked by speakers at the front facing a sea of about a hundred and fifty folding chairs. A group of five middle-aged locals are near the front, one of whom looks weirdly familiar to Kimmy. "I'm going to check in with the mayor," her dad says, nodding toward the group. "Why don't you get your microphone, and then I'll debrief you backstage."

She nods, her palms suddenly sweating. Kimmy isn't that comfortable with all eyes on her; she much prefers the kind of power she had in her finance job—backed by numbers and data and well-rehearsed presentations. This is what her parents asked her to do, though, and with everything that's going on with her dad, she's not one to ignore their requests.

She waves, and one of the guys running tech, a stout bearded man wearing cargo pants and a ratty concert shirt, comes over. "Kimmy, hey," he says, his hand raised. His voice transports her to tenth-grade Spanish, when he was about fifty pounds lighter and the class clown taking the course for the third year in a row. Drew, maybe? "Man, you look exactly the same. Wild." He nods to a few familiar faces. "You remember the guys?" Their names also escape her.

"Oh my gosh. It's been a minute, huh?" She pulls away, giving them all a small wave. "Seems like you're doing well for yourself," she says, gesturing toward their setup. She means it to be a compliment, but it comes out like a dig.

"Not like you," the guy says, his smile genuine. He smells earthy, a mix of sunscreen, sweat, and bud. She'll ask Erin to look him up on Facebook later, a memory of them smoking a joint around a beach bonfire suddenly floating across her mind. Had they made out once? She's not sure, the lack of memory tensing her neck. "I read that article in the *Wall Street Journal* about that huge deal you closed. You gotta be worth, like, a zillion dollars now." She smiles tightly. Four million, to be exact. That made her a modest success in her industry, a blip to the men with an extra zero or two at the end of their bank statements—and far from enough never to work again and retire anywhere besides the middle of nowhere. But he didn't have to know that, because she knew she was rich—richer than most people in this town, richer than most people in the world, rich enough that it felt okay to completely upend her career and return to her hometown to help her dad, at least until his health isn't such a question mark. It makes her feel some semblance of control, like she has an escape hatch if her homecoming goes sideways. She says none of this, instead grabbing the lavalier microphone on the table.

"Thanks." She holds out the microphone. "It was sort of embarrassing." That's not a lie. She didn't like having her portrait taken, being the center of attention at the firm for a solid week. But they wanted to show that they had not only female employees, but female leaders—and she wanted to make sure she got all the credit for her work. She turns, her back to maybe-Drew. "Can you attach this to my belt?" she asks, her finger pointing toward the center of her back. She's done enough finance conferences to know the drill. He nods, taking the holster and clipping it to her waistband, then clips the wire to the collar of her shirt. She flinches at the touch of his hands, the act so intimate yet distant, strange fingers tracing their way across her skin. She thanks him as she pats the tiny microphone. "I'll do a test now." She looks at the guy at the table, who gives her a thumbs-up. "Test one, two, three." Her voice is grainy on the speakers, the slightest bit pitchy. "Mmm. Let's try that again, shall we?" He moves the base lever a hair, enough to clear the audio. "Test one, two, three." Kimmy returns their thumbs-up with her own, then clicks off the power to her headset. "Well, I'm gonna go check in with my dad. Thanks," she says, not wanting to linger. She doesn't like small talk, especially with people she only vaguely remembers. What if she has to say their names? Or if she did, in fact, make out with maybe-Drew and he brings it up? She feels her chest tighten and massages her cheeks, already achy from all the fake smiling. She turns without saying bye, so different than the guys remember, her underlying coldness a stark contrast to the girl who had spent the end of her senior year loving everyone.

"Dad," Kimmy says, walking toward the stage. The entire group turns and Kimmy squints as she makes eye contact with the tallest person in the group, a man with messily parted copper hair. Why does he look so familiar? She smiles at them all. "Hi. I'm Kimberly Devine, Bill's oldest." Her smile is big, pleasant, professional.

"Wow, you've grown up!" says a white-haired man, his cheeks red and sagging from, she's sure, hours on the water without any SPF.

"Kimmy, you remember, Mr. Kasanaar?" Her dad nudges her forward, a habit of his in these networking situations.

"Derek's grandfather? Oh my gosh, hi!" She's genuinely excited to see him, putting out her arms as they hug. When she was in high school, they often hung out at the Kasanaars' campground, huddling around bonfires as the guys strummed on guitars and the girls pretended they had talent. Before Kimmy drifted away from Derek, from the group, she remembers how simple, how happy those nights were—and Mr. Kasanaar always interrupted their hangs with a plate of his wife's famous M&M cookies, using the treat as an excuse to chat with his grandson's friends and figure out what they were all about.

"You have grown into a beautiful woman," he says, giving her a kiss on the cheek and then holding her upper arms as he takes a look. She laughs, used to old men with no shame gawking. "And Kimmy, you're quite the success, so your father says."

She blushes, tucking her hair behind her ears. It's amazing how no matter the level of success she's achieved, these men from childhood can still turn her into a bashful mess with just one sentence. "Thanks, Mr. Kasanaar," she says. "I actually go by Kimberly now."

She glimpses her dad swatting his hand in her peripheral vision. "Nonsense. You're home, you're Kimmy." He ruffles her hair, she forever his little girl. "None of this fancy-schmancy stuff. Kimmy, Mr. Kasanaar is Rocky Cape's mayor," he adds, giving Kimmy a look she knows well. *He's important*, it says.

"I had no idea I was in the presence of royalty," she says, her business side kicking in.

"Oh, you flatter me. Please," he says, finally letting go. "Meet my deputy, James Langley."

She puts her hand out, and James does the same. As they shake, her dad and Mayor Kasanaar start to talk separately, something about trying to get a meeting with the governor's team. James says quietly, "We've met before. A few times, actually."

Kimmy furrows her brow, trying to remember. "Did you do cross-country?"

He laughs. "Lisa's Diner. New Year's Eve 2007." He smiles, his expression kind.

Kimmy's jaw drops in surprise. "Oh my god. Diner James!" Reflexively, she pulls him in for a hug, her excitement clouding any professionalism she was trying to exude. "Erin and I randomly talk about you, I'm not kidding. We have absolutely wondered what Diner James is up to over the years." Leave it to Erin not to put two and two together and realize the James in local government is the same James who saved their New Year's Eve all those years ago.

"I'll admit, that's flattering to hear," he says, his dimples as pronounced now as they were when he was a teen. She didn't remember him being this striking, his looks more Marvel superhero than *Superbad*'s McLovin. That's what fifteen years will do, though, the most unexpected ducklings transforming into swans. Kimmy opens her mouth to ask a question, but before it comes out, she finds herself yawning.

"Oh," she says, her eyes wide with mortification. "I swear it's the jet lag, not you. I think I may have just hit a wall." She looks at her watch, then back at James with an apologetic face. "It's almost nine p.m. my time."

"Anything I can get you? A water? A seat? A Shirley Temple? If I recall, that was a Devine sister favorite." She smiles, taking in his broad shoulders, clear skin, the way he's grown into himself. There's an arrogance to him, like he knows she's looking at him with a new appreciation—or maybe even for the first time—but it's gentle, earned, the kind only a kid who was bullied in high school for his cystic acne can understand. Kimmy has been single for a long time, her male dates either as busy as her or intimidated by her dedication to the partner track, their breakups including phrases like "too ambitious" and "sort of intense." Maybe it's the travel exhaustion, or the fact that she hasn't slept with anyone in months, but James embodies small-town charm, and she finds her interest piqued.

"Kimmy, can we debrief quick?" her dad interrupts as he walks up the stairs of the stage, and James motions for her to go follow.

She walks toward her dad, looking back over her shoulder at James. He's helping Mayor Kasanaar get set up in the front row; there's an ease to the way he moves, his obvious comfort with himself stirring a surprising thirst in Kimmy. He gives her another wave and she smiles back, biting her lip.

Maybe coming home wasn't such a horrible idea.

About twenty minutes later, the entire tent is swarming with Lilly Pulitzer–clad summer renters, true locals with leathery skin, and a handful of shoobies who very obviously wandered into the tent out of curiosity with zero intention of buying a thing.

"Ready?" her dad asks. Kimmy nods; she feels a dryness in her mouth as she plasters on a smile. The tent's fans are helping with the heat, but sweat dapples the back of Kimmy's shirt, the humidity dizzying. Her calf starts acting up again, the ache creeping toward her toes. *Ugh*, she thinks, *I should have drunk more water.*

"Good afternoon, Oceanwind!" Her dad has his most professional voice on, showman CEO on duty. "What a beautiful day, and we at Devine's are honored to be here with you all today raising money for the very boardwalk we stand on right now." He pauses, waiting for the applause to quiet. "I'm especially excited this year because our prodigal daughter, Kimmy, has made her triumphant return home and agreed to help her ol' dad with this year's auction." Kimmy gives the audience a little wave as she stands next to her dad, her heart racing. She's hated public speaking ever since the end of senior year, the feeling that everyone is watching, judging, impossible to brush off. "Today is about community. About coming together to lift this wonderful place, a home to so many of us, whether permanent or for just a few weeks every summer. And what better way to do that than by celebrating some of the Shore's finest artists?" More applause. Bill nods at Kimmy, her cue to unveil the first item being auctioned. Kimmy pulls the curtain, and the audience lets out audible oohs and aahs. It's a bookshelf made from a repurposed Rocky Cape Beach Patrol rowboat. "We're starting off with a very special donation. As you know, Reid's Rehab has become one of Manayunk's most beloved sustainable furniture stores. And we're fortunate enough to have Reid Fitzpatrick, a local himself, in our audience this afternoon," her dad reads from the paper. The name. Kimmy's stomach does a flip. She looks at her dad, trying to sense if he's made the connection himself. If he realizes who Reid is related to. She doubts it; at this point in his career, Bill outsources the event planning to a local firm, trusting them to tackle the weeds. "Reid, where are you?" Bill puts his hand over his eyes, scanning the crowd. Reid stands, necks craning to get a glimpse of him. As applause breaks out, Kimmy also turns toward Reid, who's waving to the audience, and she sees a fist punch his side. She recognizes that arm, the scribbled *pb* tattoo etched on the inside of his left bicep, the match to the *j* she has on her rib. He looks different, his beard thick and his hair short, the locks she used to love running her hands through shorn close to his scalp. He also looks the same, his presence enough to completely knock her out. As their eyes meet, she feels the familiar ache in her chest, the zing all over her body. The want. The need. The exact feeling she desperately hoped to avoid.

Justin Fitzpatrick.

Here, at the auction, smiling at her like he has no idea he broke her heart all those years ago. The audience is still applauding, but Kimmy stares at Justin. He mouths "Hi" and she feels another wave of dizziness, the air too heavy, her body too dehydrated. Still, she smiles back in an almost delirious way. She can't help herself. She never could with him.

She brings the back of her palm to her forehead, the edges of her vision spotty, and takes a deep breath. It's not enough, though, her body giving up on her. The room blurs and she hears a gasp, then everything goes black.

She says he never says he loves her. Isn't that messed up?

He's her father. Of course he loves her.

But it's the way she told me. There was this emptiness. Like she had just accepted it.

Honey, he is very proud of her. He's always at the finish line at every meet.

With a stopwatch in hand and a lecture about her time ready to go.

There are so many different ways to show love. That's just his way.

I'm not sure it's working.

5

October 2005

The path to the Point vibrates, singing crickets hidden among the untamed dunes lining the walk. Brian leads, a small flashlight in his hand, a few of the other soccer guys, including Justin, trailing. Nick is asleep in Brian's car, so passed out he didn't even wake up when they pelted a soft pretzel from Wawa at his head ten minutes earlier.

Kimmy, Stevie, and Derek's girlfriend, Katie, walk a few feet back, arms linked, steps in sync. "Honestly, this is so much better than that party," Kimmy says, throwing her head back. The sky is clear, the constellations twinkling overhead. It had been her first time at Aaron Roop's house, despite his reputation for hosting legendary parties whenever his dad is out of town. He's a grade older, quiet, into harder drugs than most, but managed to maintain popularity thanks to Mick Jagger cheekbones, a natural gift for goalkeeping, and absent parents. Girls were drawn to his bad-boy vibe, but as far as Kimmy knew he'd never been attached to anyone, his romantic reputation drifting just below Rocky High's clouds of gossip—minus one ancient rumor that he got Becky Lawler to send him nudes in eighth grade—making him all the more aloof and mysterious. The property was shrouded by trees, located in thick woods on a strip between Rocky Cape and Oceanwind. His house, a white cottage with chipped shingles and a creaky front porch, patches of crabgrass poking through the front lawn, was filled with a different crowd than they usually hung out with, her classmates laughing and mingling and clinging to one another with a drunken desperation. She'd never been into big parties; she preferred one-on-one hangs, especially when she was with Brian. It took Kimmy less than a minute to turn to Brian, raise her eyebrows, and almost run with him to the trunk of his crossover SUV, their hearts racing as they grabbed each other's clothes and their bodies crashed. They had a limited window without parents, without their stomps up the stairs to the Accardis' attic or down the stairs to the Devines' movie room to announce their presence before entering, Kimmy and Brian fumbling to get their clothes back on. That meant sex, even if it had to be in the small, cramped trunk of Brian's car.

"Not that either of you would know, you little skanks," Katie says, pushing her hip into Kimmy, her lips pursed. She's not offended, because Kimmy knows she's having sex in a way that Katie deems acceptable: monogamously, with someone Katie considers a good guy Kimmy loves and who loves her back. She can still feel Brian's breath on her neck, his hands in her hair, the golf umbrella he stows in the back of his car digging into her shoulder, limbs jumbled and tongues tied. They've been together for about three months, versus Katie and Derek's three years—they became official in eighth grade—but Kimmy is the only one who's gone all the way, her virginity shed on the scratchy taupe couch in Brian's finished attic two weeks earlier. She loves being first, possessing a level of knowledge her friends don't. Still, she isn't one to pour out specifics; girls who talk about penis size and the way some guy's jizz tastes make her uncomfortable.

She ignores Katie, turning to Stevie. "Who were you with?" Stevie stumbles with each step, still drunk from the party. "Wait." Her eyes agog, Kimmy asks, "Nick? Oh my god, you didn't." She clasps a palm over her mouth.

"Shh," Stevie says, her faux shame not enough to keep her secret. All three huddle, their heads in a small conspiratorial circle. "We kissed," she says, her nose scrunched. "And did a little more." She looks down, kicking the sand. Katie and Kimmy scream in unison, their shrieks echoing in the dark. They're all relatively inexperienced, curious and crazy with lust, relying on one another's stories and triumphs and mishaps to inform their own bedroom behavior. Kimmy has so many questions, not sure where to even begin. This is huge, life-changing news. Stevie has been hunting for a sign that Nick feels the way about her that she feels about him. She would do anything for him, and he knows it.

"Girls, come on!" Brian shouts, flashing the light toward them again. The boys mumble, looking over their shoulders a beat too long, acting disinterested but their attention a sign they desperately crave the gossip.

"We are so not done with this conversation," Kimmy says, Stevie giggling to herself as they chase after the boys. The beach is deserted, the masts of land-bound sailboats lined against the dunes looming over the sand, soldiers protecting the beach from intruders. Brian and Ben lay two blankets before popping open a cooler of beer. Derek sits next to the cooler, Katie immediately relaxing between his legs, her back against his chest, the two of them morphing into one unit. Sometimes Kimmy thinks they look so similar they could be related, but maybe that's just what happens when a couple spends such intense amounts of time together. Stevie sits by Justin, passing him a beer, her body glowing with accomplishment.

"Is anyone else ready to totally pass out?" Kimmy pirouettes to the first blanket, where she crumples to the ground. Brian follows, lying on the outside edge while the others get their drinks.

"You're so beautiful, you know that?" He props his head up as he lies on his side, gazing at Kimmy. Whenever he compliments Kimmy, whispering sweet strings of romantic words, his voice pitches up, a lithe coo. Its softness, the babyish way his sentences tingle against her ear, nudge some deep irritation in Kimmy. She worries something's wrong with her, this vexation a sign her heart is unable to fully commit, to lather itself in the love Brian is so clearly giving her. She smiles through, though; he is the type of guy she's supposed to be with. In Rocky Cape, there's no one better.

She turns onto her side, their bodies parallel. "You always know what to say." She inches her face toward Brian's, his hair curling in the humidity. He kisses her, his lips chapped from all his hours playing soccer in the fall air.

"Oh, come on, guys." Ben throws a beer can at Kimmy's butt. "Too much fucking PDA going on at the party. And here. Is nowhere sacred?" Ben is hopelessly single, a romantic with absolutely no game and a taste for unrequited affection. He pulls out a portable speaker, hooking up his iPod. "Farmhouse" by Phish plays and they all fall onto their backs and look at the sky, the quiet of the night swallowing their energy. They should be worried about being caught since the Point is closed to the public after dusk, but Ben's dad is the sheriff. The worst he'd get is a grounding, and each of them calls to their parents. The waves are calm, this section of the channel rising and falling each day without fuss.

The peace is disrupted by a weird squawking, like someone stepped on a skunk. "Oh no." Brian hops up, a stream of sand spraying Kimmy in the face. "No, no, no." He runs toward his car with no explanation, until they hear him scream, "Nick, are you fucking kidding me?" from the path.

"Shit." Ben turns off the music. "That kid is the definition of a two-beer queer."

"God, Ben. Offensive much?" Katie says, her arms draped over Derek's knees, the heat of her judgment cutting through the fall dusk. She thrives on the moral high ground.

"What do you mean?" Stevie asks Ben, hopping up only to collapse back on her butt. She laughs to herself, her feet stretched in front, then shakes off her sea legs. "What's wrong with Nick?"

"Uh, you dumb, Stevie?" Ben asks. "He's ralphing. Chundering. Tossing his cookies. Puking." She stands quietly, the explanation like a scold. Her lips shape into a worried line, a line Kimmy has seen before. After bad races, difficult tests, just before her parents divorced. She's analyzing her night, her moments with Nick, what they mean in the light of their equal states of fucked up. Ben, who notices nothing, keeps talking. "Kid has the worst stomach in the world. Like, he fucking puked when he had three slices of meat lover's pizza a few weeks ago. Pizza." Ben rolls his eyes, hopping up. "Imma go help Brian." He pours his leftover beer into the sand and turns off the music, the soundtrack now one of lolling waves, their refrain suddenly overpowering. As Ben trudges toward the path to the parking lot, Stevie runs after him.

"I guess we're the scrubs." Derek chugs what's left of the can in his hand. He grabs the cooler and walks ahead with Katie.

"Come on, Legs," Justin says, brushing off his thighs, then hopping to his feet.

"Noooo," Kimmy whines. "Don't make me leave. It's too pretty to leave." She's exhausted, the day's run and night's backseat escapades catching up to her, her body buzzing from the heat of it all.

"Okay, stargazer." He holds out his hand, pulling her to her feet.

She spins, ending with a curtsy. "Why, thank you, kind sir."

"You're a little weirdo," he laughs. "You know, I always thought you guys were goody-goodies. Brian and those guys are my bros, don't get me wrong. But you all just seemed a little too perfect," he says. "Like straight out of a Polo ad or some shit. But tonight was fun. You're fun."

"Way to judge a book by its cover, Justin," she says, picking up the blanket.

"Please." He grabs the blanket from her. His eyes look glassy, like they're coated in dew. *Probably high*, Kimmy thinks. "I know when someone's out of my league."

"Who's out of your league?" They're walking on the path now, lazy feet sinking in the sand. The fall air bites and Kimmy wishes she still had the blanket in her arms, suddenly feeling vulnerable.

"No one." Justin avoids the question, something unspoken floating between them as the parking lot and headlights come into view.

"Fuck," Brian is muttering. Nick, curled by the side of the car, pukes as Stevie rubs his back, looking like she herself might vomit.

"Well, I'd say the night's over, huh." Derek grabs Katie's hand, shielding her as they move toward his car so she can't see the vomit, as if its acid might burn her. "Come on, babe, I'll drive you home. Stevie, you too." Stevie's house is a block away from Katie's. Stevie looks torn, knowing she can't do much to help Nick, but afraid to end the night like this.

"Yo, Fitzy, you mind giving Kimmy a ride home?" Brian asks. "Ben's gonna help me with this idiot." He looks at Kimmy and mouths "Sorry."

"Yeah, no prob, man." He turns to Kimmy, asking quietly, "If that's okay with you?" He's a touch awkward.

For a moment, she feels alone, the atmosphere frozen. There's something about tonight that is different, a little dangerous, the air of their innocence slowly dissolving right in front of her eyes. She shivers, the chill enough to jolt her body. "Yeah, of course," she says, following Justin to his car.

"Thanks," she says as she shuts the door, burrowing into the velvety cushion of his Oldsmobile, which she remembered him once telling her was his grandparents' before they passed it down to him. "Tonight was"—she breaks, the engine humming as they cruise—"a lot? Do I sound lame saying that?"

Justin shrugs. "Nah, I guess. Clowns can't handle their shit. It sucks." He turns up the volume on his stereo, a harmonica plays.

"Who's this?" Kimmy asks, the music soothing her back to calm.

"You're fucking with me, right?" He turns to her, then moves the notch louder. "It's G. Love and Special Sauce. 'Baby's Got Sauce,' 'Rodeo Clowns,' 'Cold Beverage.' Nothing?"

She brings a finger to her chin, thinking, none of those songs ringing a bell. "Wait, wait," she says, the band name coming back to her. "Are they the guys who do that 'Milk and Cereal' song on eBaum's World?"

"You are seriously killing me, Legs," he says, laughing. "How is that all you know them from?" He shakes his head, looking at the road. "You're not lame for thinking tonight sucked, though. Sometimes I can't wait to get out of this fucking place."

Kimmy's never heard him talk like this. "Really? I thought you were all about Shore Pride. Like, your whole family has that live-here-forever kind of vibe." Justin's dad owns a small lawn service in Rocky Cape, which his dad had owned before him. His mom helps organize the town's Halloween parade every year. They are the types of people politicians refer to as the backbone of the community.

"Nah, that's more my brother's thing." He drums his fingers against the wheel. "It's just, like, people get stuck here."

She understands, because she worries about that too. Her parents have planned her whole future: Rutgers, an MBA, then a few years of real-life work experience before returning to Rocky Cape to help run Devine's. She's not sure why she's about to be so free with her words, blaming the comfort of the warm air spilling out of the front vents and the soft fabric against her legs. "I hear you. I mean, imagine the amazingness of living in a town that doesn't get every new movie, like, six months after they originally came out in most theaters across the country." He bobs his head. She swallows, then says, "I mainly applied to schools in New Jersey and Pennsylvania, and my dad definitely expects me to go to Rutgers like him, but sometimes I dream about applying to a place in, like, Florida. Where it's warm all the time and you can always go to the beach."

"Damn, Legs," Justin says. "I was thinking, I dunno, like, Philly?" He runs his fingers across the edge of his seat belt. "Florida, huh. That's mad cool. Maybe I'll look into some schools there too. Are you gonna run at Rutgers?"

"I don't know," Kimmy says. "I've talked to their coach a few times, but I don't even know if I'll get in. PSATs suck. I am so bad at tests."

He laughs, his eyes on the road. "I highly doubt you're bad at anything." They're both quiet for a second. "I want to get out of here, but growing up sucks. And the money all that shit requires. It's criminal."

Kimmy pauses, unsure how to respond. The money part has never been a worry for her. "What if we just escape to Neverland?"

"Neverland?" Justin asks.

"Yeah. Like Peter Pan style. That way, we can get out of here, but we never have to grow up. I can bring the fairy dust."

"And I'll bring the booze and weed," Justin says, his grin the tiniest bit wicked. "All right, Legs, it's a deal. You can be my fairy girl." His hand held up for a high five, Kimmy brings hers to his. He wraps his fingers around her palm, his skin warm against hers. For a moment, the world seems to pause, the only movement their blood rushing as they touch. The feeling is confusing, new. She looks at him for a second too long, her hand breaking away as she points to a street sign.

"Right here," she says, watching his face as they pull up to her house. His sudden look of awe and the way he tries to hide it is something she's grown used to, how people change their perception of her when they spot the columned porch wrapped around the entire house and the shiny chandelier glittering through the window above the front door.

"Thanks," she says, bowing her head down as she gets out of his car. "You're—" She turns back to him, their eyes locking. She's not sure what to say, landing on: "I guess tonight wasn't all bad."

As she walks around the side of the house toward their back door, her back to Justin, she can't stop smiling. It's confusing, this fizziness— like sipping a freshly poured soda a touch too fast. She pulls open the latch of the pool gate and sees her sister on a lounge chair, her face glowing from the screen of her phone.

"Hey," Kimmy says, pausing in front of Erin. "What are you doing out here?"

"Dad's watching *Top Gun* at, like, volume eighty. I just needed some peace." Kimmy laughs, Erin's sensitivity for noise one of her most pronounced quirks. "How was your night? Out with Brian?" Erin nods toward the street.

"Um, no. Actually, Justin drove me home," Kimmy says, and Erin raises her eyebrows.

"Is it just me, or does his name keep coming up lately?"

"What do you mean?" Kimmy asks, feigning ignorance.

"He's texting you before Young Life. He sits at your lunch table. I've seen him waiting by your locker more than a few times." Erin won't let up, a dog chasing a bone.

Kimmy shrugs. "It's not like that. Brian had to drive Nick home. It was sort of a mess." She looks off toward the bay, the moon shimmering against the water, its current slowed with the chilled air. "He's just a friend."

Erin raises her hands. "I'm not judging. Madison thinks he's hot. And Reid said he talks about you a lot too. That's all."

Even in the darkness, Erin can tell Kimmy's cheeks are turning red and she's suppressing a smile. "Well, whatever. Tomorrow's my long run day, so bedtime for me. Don't stay out here too late, okay? It's starting to get cold."

Erin nods and looks back at her phone as Kimmy walks inside. Madison wants to drive to the King of Prussia mall tomorrow, which normally would be way too much of a day trip, but with Madison the plan seems exciting. After they shop, Erin's sleeping over at Madison's so they can practice the latest routine for dance team. It's been ages since Erin's made a new friend, felt the tickle of excited butterflies that comes with meeting someone you know, just know, will be a future confidante. And she's become that for Erin already. That fact that it's Madison, a grade older and gorgeous and brazen, makes it all the more exhilarating. They're texting about what stores to go to tomorrow when, next door, Erin hears OutKast playing, the lights to the neighboring house suddenly on. A group of guys, all in pastel polos and baseball hats, spills out of the sliding door, hands gripping beer cans, voices loud and sloppy. Erin stays in the shadows as she moves to the fence between her yard and theirs, trying to get a better look.

"Hi." A head pops up, nearly knocking Erin over with surprise.

"Oh god." She brings her hand to her chest. "Sorry, I didn't—" she stammers, caught.

"You live here?" He motions to her house. His hair twirls as it falls past his ears, a ragged mustache resting above his upper lip. She nods, biting the sleeve of her sweatshirt. He grins, his lip curling to the side. He's preppy in a way that's rare among most locals in Rocky Cape, his pressed, collared shirt and air of elitism as appealing to Erin as her friends' sun-worn skin and bleached hair is to vacationers. "My parents just bought this place. Me and some of my buddies are here for the weekend." He flips a piece of hair out of his eyes. "We go to Penn, I guess we're neighbors now. I'm Peter," he says. She feels his eyes take her in, the oversize sweatshirt she stole from her dad's closet cascading past her thighs. He's attractive, but in an attainable way—like manager-of-the-basketball-team hot. Blushing, she gnaws harder at the sleeve, realizing how childish she must look.

"Dude, you are relentless. Is there any place you won't try and pick up chicks?" one of Peter's friends yells from far away. A guy next to him adds: "What would Tessy-poo say?" Another friend humps the air, his hips swiveling back and forth as splashes of the beer in his hand splatter all over the pool deck.

"Please ignore my idiot friends." Peter looks over his shoulder and flips his middle finger at them, then turns back to Erin. "What's your name?"

"Erin," she says. "Erin Devine."

"Devine. Like the hardware store everyone goes to in town?" She nods again. "No shit. Wow, who knew our neighbors were local celebrities. Now I get why the property values around here are so high." He grins again, charm snaking through his teeth. "You want a beer?" he asks, reaching his arm across the fence and taking Erin's hand to help her hop the fence, his grip firm, committed. Interested, she is sure. She nods yes as he pulls her toward his side.

She can't wait to tell Madison about him.

6

Beach Week 2022

DAY TWO

The heat is merciless, the kind that anchors your limbs and lungs in place. The sun slinks toward the reedy horizon, the growing shade starting to cool the air, but the temps are still high enough to drive anyone wild, to blur their understanding of rationality and madness. So instead, they drink: Painkillers, Mind Erasers, and Tipseas, three of Bluefish's specialties. It's Kimmy's first time at the place, its planked walkway and sand floor new to north Oceanwind only two summers before. As she nears the entrance, she sees the restaurant is already packed, dusty footprints covering the ground, rows of frosted blondes and trucker hats lining the outside bar, which is centered on a patio overlooking the bay.

"Hi Kimmy!" a smiling redhead says, a Sharpie in one hand and a name tag in the other. The event is for locals, those with ties to Rocky Cape, a massive high school reunion of sorts, the event their equivalent of the night before Thanksgiving. Kimmy immediately recognizes him. Wes Michaels. He graduated a few years before her: class president, homecoming king, Most Likely to Be a Millionaire, and now the founder of a local empire that mixes music, event planning, social media consulting, and real estate. He's the town's true mayor. "Your auction yesterday was great. So glad you could make it tonight!" he says. She hadn't realized he was there, and her face turns pink.

"Oh gosh." She puts a hand to her forehead. "Please tell me you didn't see me faint." When she had come to, Kimmy was flat on the ground, her dad, Mayor Kasanaar, and James all standing above her. As they helped her up, the audience clapped and she gave a weak smile and wave. Justin's face was obscured by the crowd, and frankly she was relieved. James held her elbow and walked her down the stage stairs, guiding her to the makeshift backstage area. He grabbed a bottle of water from a foldable table and pulled a pouch of electrolyte powder from his pocket, mixing the two. *He must be a runner*, she thought, but said nothing, still too frazzled to talk, too woozy from fainting, too in shock over seeing Justin after fifteen years, too flooded by the strength of his gravity, to remember she had been crushing on James moments before. She spent the rest of the day stuffed in the corner of their family room's sectional, Erin by her feet force-feeding her Pedialyte freezer pops and bottles of water while they watched a handful of their nostalgic favorites: *Clueless*, *Aquamarine*, *The Devil Wears Prada*, and *Hairspray*.

"Remember how deeply obsessed you were with Zac Efron?" Erin asked as Kimmy's phone vibrated.

"Uh, okay." Kimmy tossed an M&M at Erin. "Like you have any room to talk. Remember how you were Team Dawson?" She picked up her phone and her stomach dropped as she was confronted with ten simple numbers, ones she'd long buried in her mind when she deleted his number. Justin. She swiped open.

You always did know how to make an entrance, Legs.

Will you be at Bluefish tmrw?

Kimmy felt the sides of her lips curl. "Who is it?" Erin asked.

"What?" Kimmy shook herself back to reality.

"Who are you texting with?" Erin asked, inching closer to Kimmy. "No one looks at their phone like that unless there's someone they want to see naked on the other side."

Kimmy twisted her face, shifting her lips to the side. "Do not freak out. Because it's random. And I'm not even sure I'll do anything about it." Erin flops onto her stomach, facing Kimmy, her body language pure anticipation of Kimmy's big reveal. "It's Justin Fitzpatrick." Kimmy pulled a pillow over her face and sank into the crack of the sofa.

"Shut the front door," Erin said, slowly sitting up as her expression of excitement turned into apprehension. "How the hell did that happen?"

"Shh," Kimmy said, looking toward the stairwell off the second floor. "Mom and Dad cannot hear. They'll lose it." Both Kimmy and Erin know the Devine parents would never be fans of Justin Fitzpatrick, not after the hell he put Kimmy through, the swirls of rumors his games caused. They all blamed him for Kimmy's disappearance these past fifteen years.

"Okay, sorry," Erin said, her forehead crinkling. "So what's the deal? Did you see him?"

Kimmy nodded. "At the auction. Right before I fainted." She sank deeper into the sofa, cupping her hands against her face in mortification.

"Oh my god, who cares what he thinks." Erin pulled Kimmy's hands back to her lap. "I feel like he's who people were thinking of when they came up with the term *fuckboy*."

Kimmy nodded, but didn't fully agree. No one understood the depth of what they had, how it had always felt like so much more than a fling. Even now, after all this time.

"He doesn't live here, right?" Erin said as she yanked her hair into a messy bun on the top of her head. "And you're single. And in need of a good hookup."

"That's not true," Kimmy started, but Erin shushed her.

"Miss Work-Is-My-Personality, puh-lease. You need to get laid. And sessions with your vibrator do not count." Kimmy was about to interrupt, but she had no comeback, her sister's prescription stingingly accurate. "Normally, I would be the first to tell you to stay the fuck away from Justin Fitzpatrick. But revisiting the past might not be as terrible as you think." Erin paused, breaking eye contact with Kimmy before looking at her again with a wicked smile. "A hate fuck, if you will."

"I don't hate him," Kimmy said, and made a pained face.

"You should," Erin said with a laugh. "But people change. And you deserve a little hedonism, Kim. Stop letting the cloud of your past over this place keep you from your womanly right to pleasure. You're home now. You gotta make the most of it."

"Jesus, how many self-help books did you read after you split with Kent?" Kimmy asked, making a grossed-out face. "You sound like a holistic influencer or something."

"Glennon Doyle is my god." Erin raised her hands, smiling. "We're going to Bluefish tomorrow night. You have no choice. It's a sisterly order."

So now she's here, at Bluefish, scribbling Kimmy Devine under the "Hello, my name is . . ." line on a flimsy sticker, but without Erin, who bailed an hour earlier because her lawyers called. She had to go to Philly for the night to meet in the morning and finalize a few items in her divorce from Kent. Kimmy had been looking forward to their time together at Bluefish. Erin so rarely opens up—she's quick with a one-liner, but not a heart-to-heart—unless she's stricken with guilt or a little tipsy. Kimmy wanted to be mad at her, but she sensed this pending divorce was making Erin a touch unsettled, her attention never fully there since Kimmy had been home. So she let it slide. Kimmy peels off the plastic backing, pasting the white rectangle on her light chiffon spaghetti-strap top. "Drinks are on the house tonight," Wes adds, his eyes darting behind her, already calculating his greeting for the next person in line, always on, always ready for a new partnership, before looking back to her. "We're so glad to hear you're the future of Devine's." Kimmy flinches, not realizing the news is public. But of course it is, this town so small nothing stays secret for long. She plasters on a smile, sharing an effusive "Thank you" as she smooths the tag against her top, reflexively tightening her stomach as she walks toward the bar propped at the end of a pier floating ten feet above the water on a few solid wood pilings. The silhouette of the Oceanwind bridge is to her left, black against the warm sunset, the buzz of the bar's patrons humming in the distance. Within seconds, a couple stops Kimmy, friends of her parents, the owners of Christmas shops down the Shore. This becomes a trend: acquaintances, friends of her parents, even strangers stopping her as she makes her way toward the bar. Her parents rarely come to these things. They prefer no-shower-happy-hour on the beach with a small crowd of their closest friends—or glossy drinks at the bar of the yacht club. ("They're the only ones who make a Manhattan the way I like it," her dad always says.) Kimmy feels her anxiety swirling in her chest again, the walk right into her past, into her small hometown more suffocating than she expected.

"Kimmy?" she hears, then sees Tess Cameron, Peter's wife. She recognizes her from meeting years ago, but more so from LinkedIn. Tess had thought about getting her MBA and picked Kimmy's brain by phone once, though seemed to have quit corporate life altogether once she got pregnant with twins. "Hi!" Tess says, her floral sundress swaying as she walks toward Kimmy. "What are you doing here? I thought you were in London." She gives Kimmy a kiss on the cheek.

"I'm home for good, actually," Kimmy says, pulling away. "The Camerons may have mentioned it." Her parents and the Camerons still get together every few years when the Camerons are in town. "They're ready to retire, so the whole succession plan has begun. I think my mom said Peter was coming to the party on Saturday. Are you?"

"Oh wow. No, Peter didn't mention any of that," she says, rubbing her eyes, her eyelash extensions unmovable. "He's been in Philly a ton for work conferences and dinners and all that. And we have two little ones now, so things are"—she motions her hands in a spin—"like two ships passing, I swear. I'm sure he'll tell me when he gets here tomorrow. I can try to look into a babysitter—"

"Oh," Kimmy says, something in her brain clicking. "He's not here yet?"

"Nope." She nods back toward the older couple walking toward them, each holding a sleepy-looking baby in their arms. "My parents are here saving my sanity but have to head home later tonight. And, as you can see, we're crashing toward bedtime." She grabs the toddler in blue from her mom, the movement so swift and natural it pulls at something inside Kimmy. "Everett, say hi to Kimmy! Oh, and, of course, this is my mom and dad. And Evelyn." A pink-cheeked little girl is curled against Tess's mom's shirt, already snoozing. "Mom, Dad, this is Kimmy Devine. Peter's summer house growing up was next door to her family's." Tess's parents give polite hellos, all of them knowing it's unlikely they'll see one another again. "We have to go, but so good seeing you. Give Erin a hug for me too. We should all do drinks soon.

It would be so good to catch up, especially now that I'm finally starting to feel human again."

Kimmy nods, her stomach suddenly uneasy. She politely excuses herself and turns to the bar, leaning her elbows against the lacquered wood top slippery with condensation rings. "Oh shit," she hears, and turns around to see Derek Kasanaar's arms open wide. "Kimmy Devine! I can't believe you're actually here in the flesh." His face is pink with sun and drink, the roundness of his stomach showing that he still has a thing for six-packs.

"Derek," she says, hugging him back, the tacky logo on his Sixers Jersey cool against her chest. "I saw your grandfather today! So good to see you," she says, not really meaning it. They haven't talked since the few years after high school. Maybe even longer. "How are you?" After years in private equity, she has plenty of practice small-talking with midtier men who have a permanent chip on their shoulders.

"You know, I'm good," he says, adjusting the flat brim of his baseball hat. "We're on the water sorta," he says, his Philly accent pronounced. "Jenny and me, I mean. My wife." He raises his left hand, wiggling his fingers as he shows off a black rubber ring. "Over at the campground, near the pond. We're helping my parents run it since Pops is all about town business now." He shrugs, swigging the cold beer in his hand. "It's a good life, you know? Can't complain." The sun continues to lower, a shadow pouring across the bar, across Derek's face. "It's kinda crazy you're famous now," he says, sidling up next to her, his arm almost touching hers.

"I'm not famous," Kimmy says dismissively, then waves down the bartender. "Tequila and soda, please, with a dash of lime." She doesn't have to wake up at 5:00 a.m. tomorrow to squeeze in a run before work, or the next day, or the next, her first time in almost a decade not needing to work out to manage her stress over the market and office politics and making partner. Her worries in this town, she hopes, can be easily calmed with a few shots of tequila. So, for tonight, self-medication it is.

"Damn, you going for the hard stuff already," Derek says. The bartender moves quickly, practiced in the art of mastering the happy-hour rush, efficient and no-nonsense, the way Kimmy likes it. He pushes the glass toward her and she lifts it and gulps, the cocktail filling her entire mouth like a dose of propranolol. *Much better*, she thinks, Derek's presence more palatable with the glass in her hand. "But seriously," he says, leaning closer. She smells the beer in his sweat, the only reason she can think of as to why he's acting so chummy. "We had some finance guys from New York stay at the campground for a bachelor party the other week right after your *Wall Street Journal* article came out. I asked if they knew you; told them we go way back," he says, as if they're still close.

Kimmy lets out a small laugh, raising an eyebrow. "You do know my industry is pretty big?" Finance bros on a bachelor party; she was glad she had built her career overseas and not in New York, where Wall Street was, in fact, far too small. "And do we?"

"Hey, I'll admit I was a dick to you senior year. You know, I've forever wanted to apologize for all that. I see Erin out from time to time and always want to tell her to tell you. Katie was just—well, you know how she was. And I just fell for it all," he says, absolving himself of responsibility. Erin's never mentioned seeing, let alone talking to, Derek; Kimmy assumes it's hot air. "I mean, I haven't talked to her in like ten years."

Kimmy shrugs, not wanting to get into this sort of conversation so early in the night, at a bar full of emotional land mines. "It's cool, Derek," she says, patting his arm. "It was a long time ago." She bristles, taking another sip, and turns back toward the bar, leaning again, when her eyes land on a familiar face. Brian is across the way, in the beer garden–esque area, a baby strapped to his chest in a carrier. Across from him, there's a woman with a cute bob, a toddler on her lap.

Derek watches Kimmy's eyes. "They got married a few years ago," he says. "She's nice. Sort of basic." He doesn't mention what either of them do, leaving Kimmy with a craving to sneak away and look them up on LinkedIn, her competitive nature impossible to squelch.

"They look happy," Kimmy says, and she means it. She knew she wasn't right for Brian, their personalities constantly trying to one-up each other. Still, something about seeing this made-for-HGTV tableau stings. In London, she was practically a child—a thirtysomething wunderkind with an entire future ahead of her. Here, she feels behind, like all her professional accomplishments mean nothing unless she has a baby on her hip and a husband by her side. She has to remind herself she is happy too. She's melded the life she wants with sheer ambition and hard work—and it is enough.

"Yo, man." That voice, so distinct. Her back straightens. She looks over, her eyes meeting Aaron Roop's. "Oh whoa, Kimmy. Hey," he says, giving her a small wave. In his wake is Stevie, and Kimmy finds herself frozen with surprise. She gulps, trying to keep her composure.

"Hi guys," she manages to get out with a shred of normalcy. She slurps the rest of her cocktail through two skinny straws until the bottom gurgles. "It's nice to see you," she says, her eyes on Stevie, the tug of nostalgia, of longing to reach out and scoop her into her arms so strong it almost knocks Kimmy over. Stevie's still so petite, her frame helpless against the sea of big bodies surrounding her. Her crow's-feet are deeper, her skin more tired, the fact that she lost her mom a few months earlier apparent. But otherwise she looks the same, her hair untouched by dye, almost in the exact same cut she wore it when they were teenagers. It's disorienting, a time machine of sorts. Kimmy takes a few steps back from the bar, regaining her balance. "Can I get you guys a drink?" she asks, gesturing toward the bartender. "It's on me. Or, technically, Wes Michaels. Erin said you two have been hanging since she moved home, and she really needed a friend," she adds, looking at Stevie. "It's the least I can do." They lock eyes again, so much to say after all these years, but all they do is smile. Has enough time passed for friendship, or at least cordiality, to reemerge?

"Sweet," Derek says, his presence a continued annoyance. How does he not see Kimmy doesn't want him around, that he reminds her of all the shitty things people did, said, all those years ago? She can still remember exactly what was said, having gone over the words again and again trying to make sense of it. How Katie made vague status updates about desperate girls and Madison posted about slutty bitches, neither of them ever naming Kimmy, but everyone knew who they were talking about. Derek repeated the updates whenever he spotted Kimmy, like he was Rocky Cape's own Gossip Girl and the sole defender of Brian's honor, laughing in Kimmy's face as if he were telling her about the weather, not about the terrible reputation she'd gained. But that's the thing about gossip; no matter how salacious, it's careless, a passing flutter to everyone except its subject. "Hit me with another brewski."

"Derek, no one has used that word in, like, a decade," Stevie says, her mouth turned down. She walks past Aaron, past Derek, to Kimmy's other side. "I'll have a Landshark," she says, her shoulder smushed against Kimmy's arm. Aaron gives them both a look, cautious, wary. "You too, Aaron?" she asks, ignoring his expression. He nods, looking ahead when his eyes meet with Kimmy's for a millisecond. Derek asks him something, the two diving into regular banter, their friendship solidified by geography. Kimmy orders the drinks, turning back to Stevie, not sure what to say.

"So—" she starts.

"I got your letter," Stevie interrupts, her conversational cadence unchanged, still blunt and earnest. "When my mom died, I mean. I got it."

Kimmy is unsure where this is going. She was still in London last year when Erin called with the news that Stevie's mom had a heart attack early one morning while opening the shop, had been found by an employee two hours later, her skin already cooled. Kimmy wanted to fly home for the funeral but wasn't sure it was appropriate. She wanted to call Stevie, to dive into memories of her mom, who had been such a light throughout Kimmy's childhood. But something, their past, the years of silence between them, manners, really, held her back. She used work as an excuse, and instead, she handwrote a lengthy letter on notebook paper, her love and memories tucked between each line. She never heard from Stevie after, never even knew if she'd received the letter. And here it was, the confirmation that she received it but didn't reply. "Oh," Kimmy says, Stevie's delivery straight, no inkling of her feelings about it.

"I appreciated it. Really," she says, angling her body to face Kimmy. "I didn't actually open it until a month ago." She pauses to take a sip of her beer. "When Erin told me you were moving home, it felt insane I hadn't opened it." Her lower lip slightly trembles. "Right after my mom died, I was angry about everything, obviously. And didn't read anything from anyone. Like, I still have a box of untouched letters." Kimmy nods, not sure what to say or how to react, this conversation diving far deeper more quickly than she could have imagined. "Well, I don't know, maybe it's weird with me dating Aaron and all." Kimmy gulps, this fact like a slap in her face. She clenches her fist by her side, taking a deep breath as Stevie keeps talking. *It's also weird*, Kimmy thinks, *that we haven't talked in fifteen years.* "I'm just sorry for everything. Because when I read your letter, I suddenly felt okay. Just like how you always used to make me feel okay. I have missed you, really. I was just so immature then. We all were."

Were we? Kimmy wants to scream, but she feels the fragility of this too-perfect moment, not wanting to break it. *Am I being pranked? Is Stevie drunk? Did the pandemic and being isolated with her thoughts, with her memories, both good and bad, mess with Stevie's perception of the past too?* She's grateful for Stevie's olive branch, truly, but something about it makes her anxious, nervous, like it's all some big joke. She doesn't voice any of this, though, instead putting her hand on Stevie's shoulder, the warmth surprising. There's a connection, a surge for a moment, that feeling of protection, of sisterhood they'd both been missing from each other. And Kimmy knows, with certainty, the only way to protect Stevie is to forgive their past.

"Yeah," Kimmy agrees. "We totally were." She flags the bartender, ready for her next round, anything to quench her nerves. "You want another?" she asks Stevie.

She nods and the two clink their half-empty glasses.

7

April 2006

The nail polish display gleams under Devine's fluorescent lights, the latest OPI collection sparkling at the front of the "Beach Essentials" rack, pop music showering each aisle, mainstream yet harmless, expletive-free crooning about love and heartbreak set to soft guitars. Kimmy picks up a bottle of Tijuana Dance?, her mind wandering as she stares at the rose-pink vial, the title a stark contrast to the reality of her life. Certainly no glamorous travel that requires a passport, or the all-night dancing the polish name evokes. Just running. And studying. And waiting for her boyfriend to text her back. She drops the bottle in the basket hanging from her forearm, her final restock haul for the day, and pulls her phone from her back pocket. The tiny screen glows, a picture of her cuddled against Brian's chest, both sweetly smiling. No new messages from him. He's at a soccer tournament, she knows, but her fingers itch to follow up on her "how'd it go?" text. She wills them to stay still, to not make her look desperate, eye twitching as the uncertainty lingers. Nothing had happened to make Kimmy question their relationship, but it was the nothing that seemed to pick at her insecurity. Over their ten months together, steamy hallway make-outs and late-night phone calls divulging deep dreams and deeper anxieties had morphed into have-to-get-to-class pecks and quiet snores on the other side of the line. She felt her discontent growing, an itchiness to take a break, date around. But then Brian would go MIA, and, like a magnet, his absence lured her back in. Why wasn't Brian responding? Was he about to dump her, bored by her stick-straight hair and booblessness and 10:00 p.m. bedtime? When he broke up with his last girlfriend, he told Derek she was clingy and gave bad head. Derek then told their entire class. But they had only dated for two months; he wouldn't do that to Kimmy—because he loved her. Right?

That goddamn song, Kimmy thinks as the piped-in music taunts her from the ceiling speakers, the singer droning on about a bad day. She thrusts a middle finger at the sky before catching a glimpse of herself in the warped plastic mirror next to rows of bug spray and sunscreen. The bottom of her teal Devine's T-shirt is knotted over her right hip, the rest billowing from her shoulders, her legs lean and tight and tanned from miles and miles on the road. She shakes her head at her reflection. No, she refuses to believe it's anything she's done. She's perfectly followed the unspoken rules of high school dating: loyal but not clingy, sexy but not slutty, conversational but not confrontational. As she looks back down at her phone, her insecurity shifts toward indignation. The heat in her temples, the blood on the edges of her tongue as her grinding teeth rub, her body teetering on the edge of insanity. She texts Stevie, a distraction, but also a salve for her simmering resentment.

Movie night tonight? I could so use a girls hang

Kimmy presses send, knowing Stevie won't see it for at least an hour, her workout pain recently diagnosed as full-blown runner's knee and her Friday evenings occupied by a weekly physical therapy session. But that single text calms Kimmy's thoughts, her sense of control, however little, realigned. She really could use some girl time with Stevie, whose moods had been less predictable ever since her one-night fling with Nick. He told people at school nothing happened between them and ignored Stevie for about two weeks until she finally confronted him in the lobby of his church, the sadness in her voice echoing across the glistening tile floor as she shouted, "What did I do?" He hadn't been planning to go that far with anyone until marriage, he said. She tempted him, took advantage, seduced him, his whisper hissed as his eyes went round, begging to be viewed as the victim. Stevie was still in shock when she told Kimmy about it hours later, the rims of her eyes salty from tears. "I don't get it, Kimmy," she said. "He wanted it. He's the one who kissed me. He's the one who unbuttoned my shirt first, who unzipped his pants. Who pushed my head so hard I gagged." Kimmy held her writhing body, whispered "It's okay" over and over until it became a rhythmic chant, soothing Stevie back to life. She said she didn't want to talk about it again, wanted to pretend it never happened. So they didn't. But Kimmy saw it, the way the shame ate her sense of self, turned her inward. Nick started dating Rachel Walton, the pastor's daughter, three weeks later, breaking from their friend group unless it was soccer related. Neither Kimmy nor Stevie went to Young Life again.

A girls' night was just what they both needed. Kimmy slides the phone back into her pocket, pivoting on her heel without looking up, her body slamming against another. Dolce & Gabbana Light Blue smothers her nose and she knows, before looking up, it's Nikki Ritter. The basket on Kimmy's arm shakes at the collision, the nail polish bottles vibrating so much that Kimmy's sense of stability is once again suspect.

"It's cool," Nikki says breezily, before doing a double take. "Ah, shit, Kimmy! Duh, I should have known I would run into you here." They have physics together, Nikki's lax view on both schoolwork and authority a fascination of Kimmy's. There's a lightness to her, never tied too tightly to anything or anyone, besides rumors. They always seem to follow her: that her mom, who owns a local surf shop, almost went pro but got pregnant with Nikki in her teens; that she's distantly related to Tony Hawk; that she modeled for Roxy as a kid; that she grows her own weed; that she's dating a college swimmer who trains with Michael Phelps. Evasive when asked, Nikki laughs off the gossip like it's nothing, but never gives a straight answer. She's one of Kimmy's favorite class friends, the two hunched together giggling over the time Kevin Flannerty accidentally glued balsa wood to his butt, the sticks clinging for the rest of class, or when Corey Gordon's bottle rocket launched sideways, landing right in Mr. Focht's stomach. "How are you?" Nikki asks, tilting her head at the basket. "Working all night?"

"Thank god, no," Kimmy says, rolling her eyes. "Honestly, though, I wouldn't mind. Brian's out of town this weekend so no plans, like, at all." She thumbs another bottle of polish, her nail digging into its label. "God, I'm boring." Kimmy laughs, looking back down at the basket.

"Kimmy Devine, free from Brian Accardi for a night? This is an opportunity I am not missing." Nikki plunges her hand into the basket. The bottles jangle as her fingers swim, eventually landing on a light peach color. "How late are you working? I'm about to meet up with the guys at the baseball game. JV's playing now, but then varsity. Come with?" She reads the bottom label of the bottle in her hand. "'My Daddy's The King!' Who comes up with this shit?" She looks at Kimmy, her brows tilted in a plea. "Come. We never hang out outside of school. Promise it will be fun," capping her sell with a bright smile.

Kimmy's eyes drift to the office tucked just off the corner of the stairs to the second floor. Her dad is in today, handling end-of-the-month payroll. He won't ask questions, won't ask who she's going out with or when she plans to be home. Not like her mom, always poking her nose in Kimmy and Erin's business. Not that Kimmy has anything to hide. "Sure," she says. "I'm off in, like, ten minutes."

"Sweet," Nikki says, running her hand along the steel frame of the makeup display, green and tan string bracelets crowding her wrist. "I'm parked out front. The Jeep." Kimmy already knows; Nikki's yellow Wrangler, named Beverly, is famous in town, she and her mom's neon orange and pink surfboards perched against its roof at the first sign of warming temps. She once told Kimmy that Beverly had been her mom's; it broke down once a year, at least, but "its soul," Nikki said, her smile wide. "That's why we can't get rid of her. The things that car has seen. We sure as hell couldn't keep a pet alive, so Bev is the best we got." She walks backward toward the registers, waving bye with the polish in hand.

"Don't worry about that," Kimmy says, her voice an octave higher than normal. She clears her throat, recalibrating her excitement, forgetting all about the cozy proposal she sent to Stevie minutes earlier. "I got it."

Nikki tosses the polish into the basket, raising her arms in touchdown position. "You rock," she says as the bottle clashes into the others, the noise sharp enough to make Kimmy jump. She gives a weak wave, turning to hide her anxiety that the whole basket of polish might break and spill, that she'll have to work an extra shift to offset the inventory, that her dad will ask her too many questions about her plans for the night, that there's something risqué about them. *But there isn't*, Kimmy reminds herself. It's just a baseball game. Her weekends, though, had become a blur of predictability, the height of excitement hanging out in Brian's attic, devouring cheesesteaks and bagel bites as the guys jump on one another while singing Tenacious D's "Fuck Her Gently." (This, despite 90 percent of them being virgins.) An invitation from Nikki, it's something new. Kimmy hadn't realized how much she craves new.

She takes a deep breath, trying to calm her jitters as she knocks on her dad's office door. "Hey," she says, her head peeking from the door. "Can I come in?" she asks, already walking to the aged leather couch off to the side of his desk, each cushion sagging at the center from years of wear. The whole room has a tired vibe, her dad preferring to invest in expanding his small chain of hardware stores rather than in redecorating.

"What's up?" he asks, looking up from his laptop for a moment, his hands still on the keyboard, glasses resting on the bridge of his nose. He rarely has his computer at work—he once read that Warren Buffett doesn't believe in that sort of technology, so he decided he doesn't either—but payroll isn't an area he likes to mess up, pencil and paper and human imperfection far less trustworthy than shiny software. Kimmy can tell he is in the thick of some intense accounting, his expression like he's trying to untangle an impossible knot. The perfect time to get permission without a multitiered inquisition.

"Is it okay if I sneak out a few minutes early?" she asks, her tone forcefully nonchalant. "There's a baseball game that starts at six."

He nods, his eyes back on the screen. "Is Brian driving you, or do you need a ride?" More typing, more distraction.

"Yep, I have a ride." She's not sure why, but she avoids mentioning it's not with Brian.

"Have fun, kiddo," he says, putting his finger to his cheek, his gaze still locked on his laptop. Kimmy hops up and walks over to his desk, pecking him goodbye the way she's done for as long as she can remember. He still views her as a kid, she knows. As his prized baby girl. She loves his pride in her, the way he celebrates every one of her accomplishments. Yet the rush she felt telling him a half-truth, the tingling the lie ignites. It's new too.

There's a bin of pastel Rocky Cape sweatshirts next to the door, just outside the office. She grabs two, pulling one over her head and rolling the other under her arm. Normally, she'd ask whoever was working the register to charge them and the polish to her parents' account. Today, though, she walks right out, and she realizes no one's going to stop her.

Nikki's in front, back slouched against the driver's-side door of Bev, eyes glued to her phone. "Hey," Kimmy says, her voice quieter than she anticipated, unsure.

"Nice sweatshirt," Nikki says, looking up. The rush of audacity, the taste of rebellion Kimmy felt moments before shatters, replaced by the shame of feeling like a dweeby tourist. The weather is the early spring kind, warm and cuddly until the sun disappears and the air swallows you whole. "Um, actually, do you have an extra? I can already tell it's gonna be cold as balls tonight."

Kimmy smiles, her footing regained. "Already got ya," she says, tossing the sweatshirt she's carrying at Nikki.

"Knew I could count on you. Has there ever been a day in your life you weren't on top of your shit?" Nikki laughs, pulling the shirt over her tank and cutoffs. "Twinsies." Nikki moves her hand under her hair as she flips it over the sweatshirt collar and slinks into the driver's seat, Kimmy on the passenger side, her crouch on the seat precarious, like she's trespassing. *The things that car has seen*, Nikki had said. Kimmy's hand pulls the door shut, fingers grazing its armrest, the car's shabby fabric itching the backs of her legs. She yanks her seat belt across her body, the friction against the polyester of her sweatshirt producing a tiny spark, its heat glowing.

"Making a quick pit stop at Wawa, if that's cool?" Nikki turns right instead of left. "The guys snagged some vodka, so we're just grabbing a few chasers."

"Oh," Kimmy says, calculating what it all means. She wants to ask so many questions, but stays quiet, afraid they'll highlight her penchant for prudishness, for rarely drinking, for following the rules. "That sounds fun," she says instead.

"It will be chill, don't worry. No one ever notices at these games." Nikki slides a pair of shield shades up her nose, despite the overcast puffs crowding the sky. "You're cool with Justin, right? And, like, his whole crew."

"Yeah, of course," Kimmy says, gripping the edges of her sleeves. "It will be kind of weird to see Justin out of school. I feel like he's my class husband. We have, like, a zillion together this semester."

Nikki's hands weave over each other as she turns Bev left. "Well, at least he's someone's husband." She looks directly at Kimmy. "Commitment isn't his thing." She says it like a warning.

"Oh, I didn't realize—I mean, it's not like that, obviously. I'm with Brian." Every word feels dangerous to Kimmy, the wrong one capable of obliterating whatever fun they were planning to have. "I didn't know you two were hanging out." She doesn't want to be interested in Justin's love life, knows she shouldn't. That's not her personality: nosy and intrusive, the person people spill their secrets to. Maybe because she never shares hers. At least with anyone besides Erin and Stevie, and even then it's an edited version of the truth.

Nikki snorts. "God, no. I mean, like, yes, we used to make out now and then, but it's not like that." The casualness of her comment alludes to a breadth of experience Kimmy lacks, jealousy pinging like sonar searching for its target. Minus make outs with her ex, Brian was her first everything, the concept of careless flings and meaningless kisses foreign. Scary, even. "Like, I meant that he's married to World of Warcraft or whatever stupid-ass game they're all playing this week." She pulls into the lot of Wawa, Justin and his best friends—Chris Atwood and Ryan DeRose—sitting on the hood of Justin's car in a row, spitting blue-and-red slush, high-fiving when Ryan's spit goes the farthest. "This is why Fitzy is just a friend. A bunch of losers," she laughs, pulling into a parking spot. "What's it like dating someone who's not a total freak?"

Kimmy remembers Brian, her fingers moving toward her phone again. She opens it, the inbox still empty. She debates sending him a text right then, maybe telling him about her plans, a petty part of her wanting to make him green, when her car door is ripped open. "Oh shit!" Justin shouts. "Kimmy fucking Devine. This combo is not something I expected. You corrupting the Cape's most pristine student, Nik?"

Nikki rolls her eyes. "Fuck off, Fitzy. As if I'm the degenerate of the group." Kimmy climbs out of the car, giving them all a small wave. Justin looks her up and down, then at Nikki, then back at her. "All right, am I tripping or are you two dressed in identical outfits? This is like all my Olsen twin dreams coming true." He wraps an arm around Nikki, and the other around Kimmy, pulling them close. "My two favorite ladies."

Kimmy laughs nervously. "We didn't do it on purpose." The intimacy of his touch beyond the school hallways is unsettling, his attention making her self-conscious, like she accidentally tucked her dress into her underwear, her rear exposed.

"Been there, done that," Nikki says, breaking away as Justin laughs. "How much did you already toke, man?"

"It's the freakin' weekend, baby. Don't hate your dude for kickin' it," he says, his arm still around Kimmy. She can feel her cheeks heating. "You in to get a little loose tonight, Legs?"

She hesitates, looking up at him, then at Chris and Ryan, then Nikki, who's about to walk into Wawa, all of them like a massive undertow pulling Kimmy in, submerging her in a world where she's a novice swimmer.

"No turning back now, babe," Justin says, wrapping his arms around Kimmy's waist and flipping her upside down and over his shoulder. She shrieks, swatting at his back, but Justin's touch is confident, like he knows she won't really object. It's different from everything she has with Brian, a series of familiar motions and "are you sures." It's disorienting, this lack of control, of boundaries, of caution. She hates it, yet craves more.

"You're riding with me," he says, carrying her to his car. For the first time all day, she's not thinking about her latest run, her PSAT score, or Brian. She's present, with Justin. For the first time all day, she feels light.

8

Beach Week 2022

DAY 2

Her car in park, Erin glimpses her reflection in her rearview mirror. She left her hair wavy—a little wild, like her, he once said—and makeup minimal. She flips her curls over to one side, rubbing some rosy salve on her lips, and takes a deep breath. The parking garage at the Bellevue is dark as day approaches night, the fluorescent lights already on. She locks her bright red VW Beetle, a relic from her high school years. It followed her to college in Savannah. To her first apartment in Austin. To her small studio space there, where she painted custom portraits of pets for locals and her Etsy customers. To early dates with Kent, whose passion for courting her matched only his passion for work. At first, she loved how he rushed into things, breaking them and asking for forgiveness later—but when it came time to try for kids, her struggles and subsequent diagnosis with PCOS were a surprise to them both, and his impatience proved lethal to their marriage, the three embryos they have left sitting frozen in a lab in Texas. He wants them destroyed, and she wants total ownership of them. So he remains her almost-ex, refusing to sign paperwork until he gets his way, their interactions relegated to back-and-forth with their lawyers—Erin's paid for by her parents. And now her Bug drives her to this hotel, which she's been visiting every few weeks for almost a year. It's the most haunted hotel in Philadelphia apparently, and that comforts Erin; there have to be souls lurking these halls that are worse off than hers. *Don't chicken out*, she tells herself as her espadrilles slip along the glossy lobby floor, sandy rubber sliding across smooth marble. It would be so easy to avoid the elephant in the room, to just dissect her complicated feelings about Kimmy's return, the excitement she had that her sister is finally home, mixed with the annoyance at her parents for not thinking she—despite all the ways she helped them weather the pandemic by launching an online store, adding a touch of personality and wit to their social media pages, visiting renovation sites to talk to contractors to help inform their buying strategy, for starters—is enough to lead the store into the future. But she has bigger goals for tonight's conversation. Her fingers twitch with each step, nerves streaming through them. Tonight is the night, she's decided. Tonight, she will give him an ultimatum. He has to pick: her, or his wife.

Erin walks past the reception desk and smiles at the clerk, who she's sure recognizes her face by now. There's one other person waiting for the elevator, and Erin feels the woman's eyes scan her body. She turns her head, but the woman is already looking forward. *Paranoia*, Erin thinks. All the more reason to make him choose, to put an end to this sneaking around, to worrying that someone will sniff out their secret. Erin wants to control the narrative, to have her hand in his when they make their big reveal, to start their future the right way, even if its foundation was wrong. Because what they are doing is wrong, so wrong. She knows this, even as she knocks on the door to his room. Almost immediately, the door handle turns—and the moment she sees his face, her guilt is replaced by a gluttonous desire. It devours reason, confuses her conscience. All she wants is him, no matter the cost. Her Peter.

He looks tired, the bags under his eyes darker than normal, but his face lights when he sees her. She loves her power, the way she can brighten his world with her mere existence. "God, I missed you," he says, pulling her into the room, his arms around her. She inhales the cologne on his neck, a thick musky scent that evokes some of her favorite memories. Her mouth is already on his before the door shuts, the two of them like rabid teenagers releasing two decades of sexual tension. He turns her around, his chest against her back, and they face a full-length mirror in the room's entryway. His hand trails toward the hem of her minidress, his mouth on her neck as he catches Erin's eyeline in the reflection. Erin wants to lean into him, to let him continue, but she puts her hand on his wrist, pushing. She needs to keep a level head tonight, to have the conversation she practiced over and over and over as she drove toward Philly. *Peter*, she will say, *I want you. All of you. A real life together. If you want me, you need to choose.*

She breaks away, turning to see a spread of small plates, lit candles, and a bottle of champagne on the suite's coffee table. "What's this?" she asks, her hand loosely gripping Peter's as she pulls him toward the couch. Maybe she wouldn't need an ultimatum after all.

"My ErBear deserves the best," he says. "And I know the past few months have been tough, between my work and the kids and Tess—"

"Don't." Erin holds up a hand. She remembers when they reconnected, in September 2020. She had been home for a few months at that point, the store a bit of a mess thanks to the world falling apart. They had furloughed most employees once the summer season was over, and Erin was sitting at the register tapping her nails on the counter when Peter appeared, Tess by his side. "Erin," he said, "I didn't realize you were visiting."

Her mask hid the embarrassment splattered across her face. "I'm back," she said, making sure she looked at both Peter and Tess, not wanting to make things weird. "Divorced." She held up her bare ring finger. "And living at home, working for my parents. The dream, right?" She shrugged, laughing to make it seem like she was in on the joke. "But honestly, I'm happy." This, she knew, was obviously not true. But if she didn't say it, she would be greeted with two looks of pity—and she couldn't handle that, not from him. And definitely not from her. "How are you two? I thought your parents sold their house a few years ago?"

"They did," Peter said, looking at Tess. Erin could feel a smile under his mask, and it made her stomach turn. "But we just bought a place on Ninety-Ninth and Fourth. Last winter, luckily. We hope to start demo in a few months."

"We better," Tess said, looking at Erin with a hand on her stomach, "because we have two little ones on the way!"

"Congrats," Erin said, feeling her eyes well as she thought of her own empty uterus. "That's exciting." The truth was, she hated the families who came in and tore down cottages that had sat there for decades, only to build impersonal monoliths cluttering the already crowded blocks between the ocean and the bay. She didn't want to think of Peter as one of them, as a shoobie ruining the Shore. She let out a sigh of relief when they walked out the door, the bell jingling. But six months later, in the depths of March, she was walking to Devine's, snow from the previous week's storm shoved in piles near the curb as flurries swirled with the wind. It reminded her of circling her and Kent's apartment block with her mom the day after she got her D&C, Austin's temperate winter disrupted by a snowy cold front that week. Her hand instinctively clutched her stomach, her lower lip trembling. Erin thrust her hand back into her pocket and pivoted toward Ninety-Ninth Street, anything to keep her from thinking about the dream she'd lost. There was a pile of stark beams propped up like a massive dollhouse midway between Third and Fourth avenues. It had to be Peter's, Erin thought. She tilted her head as she took it in, and for a fleeting moment envisioned herself next to Peter within its walls, a baby cradled in her arms. She was being ridiculous, she knew, but what was the harm in a little daydream? She Googled him that night and saw he had taken over his dad's dental practice—and looked very hot in a white coat on the home page of the practice's site. *He will be a great dad*, she thought, and the thought lingered even after she closed the search window. Two weeks later, she walked by the house again. A few days later, again. She started making the block a part of her daily walk to the store, checking out the progress as the insulation was added, the windows secured, the beeping trucks and griping chain saws suddenly soothing background noises to her daily stroll. In September 2021, they started working on the interior, the drywall and appliances arriving in massive trucks. And that's when Erin took a picture of a slab of beige wood being delivered through the front door and sent it to Peter.

Looking good. Though I'm personally partial to a more colorful kitchen.

She didn't even know if his number was the same. She tucked the phone in her back pocket and kept walking to work when she felt it vibrate almost immediately.

I expect nothing less from the shore's most vibrant gal

She smiled, just seeing his name on her screen bringing up feelings she didn't realize she still had.

I'll be in town next week to handle some of the deliveries. Want to come by for a tour?

Erin knew she should say no, knew this wouldn't lead anywhere good. Yet five days later, she was on all fours on the unfinished kitchen floor in the Camerons' new Shore house, Peter behind her. She looked at his Facebook that night, his cover photo a professional shot of him and Tess with their babies swaddled in their arms. She threw up, the betrayal so toxic it had to be expelled. She dreamt about Peter that night, gauze-like silhouettes she hardly remembered in the morning—but she did remember the warmth those dreams enveloped her in, the blind fervor she felt when she thought of him. She texted Peter: *I don't think I got to see the second floor. We'll have to do another tour soon.*

He was in town every other week for a night or two. Peter ordered takeout from Clay's by the Bay, one of the few local spots open throughout the winter, and Erin would sneak into the house once it was dark. On one particular night in February, the temperature dipping below freezing and the HVAC still not installed, Peter decided they needed a new plan, especially since the house was almost finished. That's how they ended up at the Bellevue. Peter used work conferences and breakfasts as an excuse to sleep in the city, telling Tess it was much easier than fighting the commute traffic from their house in Villanova. And Erin blamed her divorce, which was still not finalized, and meetings with lawyers to get it over the finish line. There was more freedom at the hotel, fewer reminders of the life and family Peter had beyond the walls of their treachery—but Tess's presence occasionally found its way out of the shadows.

"Sorry," Peter says, knowing he'd committed a misstep by bringing up his wife in this sacred space they'd declared free of Tess. "I just wanted to do something special for you. You've made my life worth living again."

Erin walks to the other side of the table, picking up a flute of champagne. "Same," she says as they say cheers. She sits on the edge of the couch, looking up at Peter. "You broke my depression. You know that. And that I've been embarrassingly in love with you for, like, half my life." She gives him her cutest eyes, her head tilted. She knows he loves hearing her say that. "It's just been a weird few days, with Kimmy back and all. I'm so in my head."

"If only you'd been a little bit older when we first met," he says, sitting next to her. He puts a hand on her upper thigh, her dress hem creeping up. "Then we wouldn't be in this mess."

The mess, Erin assumes, being his marriage. When he did talk about Tess, which she only allowed by phone, when they weren't physically together, it was all complaints. About how expensive her taste was. How demanding she was. How all she did was drain their bank account while trying to keep up with the Joneses and tell him everything he did with the kids was wrong, wrong, wrong. Anyone could see he wasn't in love, but they had children. He had a life with her.

"I did want to talk to you about that," Erin says, taking a deep breath.

"Of course." Peter swigs his champagne, his tone suddenly changed. Erin hates these moments, when she brings reality into their perfect bubble. But how else can they make sure there is something beyond this little world of theirs, that it isn't just the thrill of secrecy keeping them together?

"What are we doing?" she asks, the cliché of the question so obvious the second it leaves her mouth.

"What are we doing?" Peter repeats, his lips turning up into a smirk. He puts his glass on the table and kisses her neck. "This." He kisses her cheek. "This." He kisses her lips. "This." She hums, her neck arching, but pushes him away.

"Peter, seriously." Her eyes plead. She hadn't planned to sound so desperate when she broached the topic of him leaving Tess, to trip over her words like she was one of Peter's patients, brain scrambled from anesthesia and cheeks numb with lidocaine.

"Erin, I haven't seen your gorgeous face—or any other part of you," he says, tugging at her dress strap, "in two whole weeks, and I am starving. Starving, I tell you." He pulls her onto his lap, her dress inching up around her waist. He once requested she not wear underwear during her visits, and she's obliged ever since. "Can we talk about this later to-night?" His fingers are already inside her.

"Okay," she says, pressing her cheek into his. "Okay, okay, okay." She rests her lips against his ear and ignores her prepared speech—her ultimatum—at least for the moment. She shakes her dress off, tossing it toward the bed, and unbuttons the top of Peter's shirt, one of the preppy plaid ones he always wears to work. She grabs the collar, leading him off the couch.

"Whatever you want," he says, his face pressed against her chest as she walks backward toward the bed and sits while he stands. "I will literally do whatever you want." He unbuttons the rest of his shirt as she undoes his belt, his pants shimmying to the ground, and wraps his arms around Erin, lifting her into his arms, her legs tucked around him. He turns so she can rest her hands against the dresser, his grip on her ass as he thrusts. Over his shoulder, Erin sees the city twinkling through the massive windows lining one side of their room. She catches their reflection in the glass, her arm muscles flexed. Peter's back is toned but aging, skin loose atop his muscles from hours of running but a disinterest in lifting. She usually doesn't mind, but tonight it irks her, this imperfection. She closes her eyes, erasing the thought with the memory of the first time they slept together.

She was a sophomore at the Savannah College of Art and Design, and he was in his last year of dental school, engaged to Tess. He was in Savannah for his bachelor party, drunk out of his mind, when he texted her late on Saturday night. She had been asleep but answered in the morning, making a joke about how nice it was to hear from him. He called her at noon that day, saying his flight wasn't until dinnertime, and he was on her campus. She told him where she lived, and within ten minutes he was at her door. Within fifteen, in her bed. The sex had been hungover, lazy, nothing particularly memorable—except for the fact that it was with Peter, the boy she had loved since she was sixteen. To feel his breath on her neck, to feel him inside her, was like a fantasy come true. It was Erin's first time, no one ever appealing to her except him. "I'm marrying Tess in a month," he said not long after he came, Erin's head resting on his chest. She felt her eyes watering, a tear dripping onto his chest.

"I know," she said. Her parents were invited to the wedding.

"You mean so much to me." He kissed her forehead. "But Tess—"

Erin put a hand on his mouth. "Don't ruin this moment." She looked at him. "I want to remember it forever."

Ten years have passed, and now she wants more than tastes. She wants all of him. A life—a real life—together. "You're so fucking tight," he says as he thrusts. She hates when he says things like that, knowing he's comparing her to Tess, to the other person he fucks, to the one he gave two babies to. She lifts her hips, hoping the new position will help her refocus, forget about the tiny red flags—were they red flags?—flapping in her peripheral vision. She digs her nails into the wood of the dresser as he pushes one final time, throwing her head back like she's coming too, squeezing her muscles so it's believable. Peter's body convulses, a low moan releasing. He wraps his arms around Erin's waist, holding her up against him, his glasses scraping the side of her face; he insists on wearing them during sex so he can "see all of her." They both fall onto the bed, her on top. She rests her head on his chest, sweat sticky on his neck, and kisses his cheek, rolling to the side, curling her body against his. "Peter," she whispers, the words she had practiced during the car ride finally finding their way to his ear. "We have to tell your wife. It's time."

He turns to her, their bodies curved in a lopsided heart. "Er"—he holds her hand, pulling it near his heart—"I love you, really. But it's complicated. You know I would leave Tess in a heartbeat if I could."

Erin refuses to let Peter, just like Kent, try to defer her desires. She spent eight years with Kent, three of which were riddled with ovulation sticks and blank pregnancy tests and probing ultrasounds and too many needles. By the end, Erin was a hormonal mess, she knew, but she still had hope—and she was determined to keep that tiny speck of it afloat. Kent, on the other hand, was done; he said quite simply one night: "The science isn't on our side, babe. It's time to move on." Erin didn't fight, didn't think Kent was worth it. She just packed up and moved home, and now she's tangled in legalese over her future babies, all their possibility on ice until she and Kent can find a way to get on the same page. So this time, with Peter, she has her fists up. A future with him is her new dream, and she will make sure he's on the same page as she is, whether he's ready or not. "If you don't tell her," she says, putting a hand on his cheek, "I will."

"Woah." Peter sits up. "Can you calm down for a second? I mean, this will tear apart my family. My kids . . . ," he says, his voice trailing.

Erin stands up, walking toward her crumpled dress. "Then we're done, Peter. I can't keep doing this if it's not going somewhere."

"Okay, okay." He rushes to her side and scoops his arms around her. "I'll talk to Tess this week. Before Kimmy's party. Okay? It's time. I know it's time."

Erin's cheek is pressed against Peter's chest, and she smiles. Her ultimatum worked. But that night, as Peter's breathing turns to soft snores, she stares at the ceiling, her stomach in knots. She wants to trust him, to believe he's telling the truth. But can you ever really trust a cheater?

Do you think I'm fat?

                                                      Of course not.

But that Philly scout did.

                              He doesn't know what he's talking about.

I guess it's good he said he could see a little bit of my hip bone. Ten pounds isn't that much to lose.

                    Sweetheart, modeling is not the only future for you. It was
                              supposed to be a fun thing, that's all.

Maybe if I take another dance class this year, my hip bones will show more, and he'll be happier at the next open call.

                    There won't be another open call. There's no way I'm letting you
                                                            go back.

Oh. So you don't think I'm good enough either?

9

May 2006

"What's that smell?" Madison asks, pinching her nose as she sits on Erin's bed. Erin follows her up the main stairwell of the Devines' house to the second-floor kitchen, which is overwhelmed with the scent of something burning.

"Oh my god," Kimmy yells, running from the family-room couch. "Bri, how long did you put the popcorn in for? It's on fire!" She pulls the bag out of the microwave like a hot potato, juggling it between her hands.

"You set the timer, Kimmy, not me," Brian says, defensive, slowly walking in behind Kimmy. "Though nothing wrong with popcorn that has extra crunch."

"Uh, this is more than crunch." She opens the bag, a plume of smoke billowing up. "This is straight-up toast."

"What are you guys doing tonight?" Erin asks, watching Madison watch them. Something has shifted between Brian and Kimmy since their early days, when their hands were always on each other. Erin equated it to comfort, routine—but she wonders as she watches them argue over such a dumb thing whether it's something more.

"Movie," Brian says. "I have a scrimmage tomorrow morning, so can't go crazy or anything."

"Ah, yes," Kimmy jokes, "because that is something we do so often." She sounds annoyed, but defuses the moment by making a face at Brian, who laughs, their dynamic completely healthy, Erin tells herself, but maybe a touch too platonic. "Er, tomorrow's my long run day. You know that. In case you want to join?"

"God, I would rather die," Madison says, inserting herself into the conversation. Kimmy turns, her back to Madison, and Erin watches her beam at Brian, like they've talked about Madison before. She doesn't respond—Kimmy once asked Erin why she liked Madison so much, saying she seemed "shallow and fake"—then snakes an arm around Brian's, and just like that, with a single touch, they're back to their romantic selves.

"Come on," Madison says, her eyes on Kimmy's back. "Let's go to your room."

Instead, when they get downstairs, Madison opens the door to Kimmy's room. "Madison," Erin whispers, her eyes big. "We cannot go in here."

"Relax. Her and Brian are probably, like, sucking each other's faces right now," she says as she walks toward Kimmy's closet. Erin knows every nook of it. The T-shirts and blouses dangling above dark pants and crisp jeans, each category hanging from its respective color-coded hanger. White for shirts. Pink for blouses. Purple for pants. Teal for dresses, which are pushed to the back, rows of A-line and sweetheart cuts waiting to be worn, though they only make an appearance at year-end banquets and parties their parents force them to attend. Erin has been eyeing a cream-colored lace mini, hoping Kimmy will eventually toss it her way. The shelves on the other side hold perfectly folded running gear and sweatshirts, sneakers and flip-flops crowding the bottom. The closet's plush rug folds under Erin's feet, her tiniest movement documented in its threads, which is why she feels sweat building under her arms as she watches Madison messily sift through Kimmy's stuff, her French-manicured nails grazing every piece in the closet. "Why does Kimmy always wear such boring clothes when she has stuff like this?" Madison asks, holding up a sequined tank. "I mean, even the preppy stuff is cuter than her whole tomboy look."

Erin takes the shirt and hangs it back where it came from, smoothing the cloth. "I dunno," she says. "They're more my mom's thing than hers, I guess." Erin can't imagine Kimmy in anything overtly feminine, her boyish body built for spandex and graphic tees and low-rise denim. Not like Erin's, her curves growing each day, her hips and boobs pushing against the edges of her old clothes, their scream for release the source of constant internal embarrassment. "Can we go back in my room?" She looks toward the closet's doorway, waiting to be busted.

"Why are you freaking out? Kimmy's occupied." Madison tightens the ponytail pinned to the top of her head, both their hairlines speckled with dried sweat from dance practice. Erin hadn't even taken off her tights before Madison forced this raid of Kimmy's room on her. Something, she tells her, she never had the chance to do as an only child.

"I know," Erin says, sheepish. "She's just, like, super particular about her things and the way they're organized."

"Mm-hmm," Madison says, nodding. "She has OCD?" *Grey's Anatomy* is her new favorite show, each episode adding fodder to her canon of medical ailments and pseudo diagnoses.

"Um, no," Erin says. "I mean, I don't think so. She's just type A or whatever." Erin walks out of the closet, seeing Kimmy's room through Madison's perspective. Everything has a place, clutter hidden by baskets, headphones organized in small circular cases, pencils and pens and neutral-tinted folders propped up in matching acrylic holders. It's a microcosm of the way she lives her life. Neatly, without excess, everything assigned a purpose or thrown out. Erin's is a mess, clothes in piles all over, glitter and bronzer streaking her rug, misplaced homework assignments crumpled beneath her bed. She has tried to keep her room as clean as Kimmy's, but it never lasts more than a few days. She just ends up hiding things—under the bed, in the corner of her closet, in one of the three junk drawers she uses as catchalls. The illusion of tidy, but nothing more.

"Do you think Brian ever gets mad that she's so close with Justin?" Madison asks, walking over to Kimmy's desk.

"Uh," Erin says, not sure how to answer, "I think he just comes with the territory of hanging with Nikki." Which Kimmy has been doing more and more of, Erin doesn't add.

"They're always together at school. And I just saw he has a little 'p, b, and, j' in his AIM profile. That has to be about her, right?" Madison walks over to Kimmy's desk, a neat stack of papers on the left, an oversize Apple desktop angled on the right.

Is Madison right? Erin honestly has no idea. "That could just be some best friend lingo he uses, or could be about their entire group? I mean, Kimmy has stupid Dashboard lyrics in her profile dedicated to Brian. Why do you care?" Erin's voice turns a touch defensive as she watches Madison run her fingers across the chair, a white ergonomic one that cost their parents a fortune but was worth it to ensure Kimmy's studies didn't cause her body an injury. Good grades don't come naturally to Kimmy; she works hard for them. The same focus and determination that make her an excellent athlete make her a decent student. Not on honor roll every quarter, but in a spot where she's attractive to coaches at near-Ivies. Erin doesn't have that same gift, a clarity of knowing what you want and how to get it. She flounders, excelling in subjects like painting and English, flailing in those founded on numbers. When her first set of midsemester report cards came back in seventh grade, she once bragged to her parents that she had received one of every letter. They just patted her on the head, like they didn't expect more. Erin lingers near the desk, not touching, afraid to mess up Kimmy's sanctuary. "I don't, god. Touchy much," Madison says. "Is this a diary? Juicy." She holds up a plain blue notebook she pulled out of a desk drawer, its spine cracked from use.

"Madison—" Erin reaches for the notebook as Madison pulls it away. "Kimmy will lose her mind if she finds out." Erin feels her palms sweating again, temptation mixed with fear. "Please. Let's just go back in my room."

"Stop being such a wimp." Madison opens the notebook, flipping through pages covered in Kimmy's tight cursive.

"What's it say?" Erin inches closer, her curiosity unavoidable. Of everyone in the world, she knows her sister best, but what does it even mean to know someone like Kimmy, so tightly wound, her walls high, her focus narrow, every part of her life constructed in a way that propels her toward success, or at least the traditional kind. For most of their lives, Erin had always assumed that perfect future was what Kimmy wanted. As they got older, and Erin began questioning her own path set by her parents, she began to wonder if that was true.

"Oh my god, snooze," Madison puts the notebook back on the desk. "It's, like, a bunch of numbers and foods."

Of course, Erin thinks. Kimmy wouldn't scribble her guts, all her feelings, onto the pages of a flimsy notebook, a place anyone can peer into. She walks over and picks up the book, dates and distance times and food items stacked in Kimmy's flawless penmanship. Just looking at it stresses Erin out, another reminder she will never be like her sister. She places the notebook back where they found it.

"This was a letdown," Madison says. "I have a way better idea." She runs back through the bathroom connecting Erin's room to Kimmy's, Erin close behind. Madison plops on Erin's desk chair, a plush furry thing, the teal iMac behind her glowing. "Password?"

"Smile123," Erin says, her cheeks flushing.

"Oh my god, no." Madison flattens her hand under her chin and cocks her head to the side. "You are honestly the cutest. Like, no joke. So cute."

Erin smiles, but can't help feeling that, once again, she's the little sister no one seems to take seriously. She would change that. *I am changing that*, she thinks. Madison would see. Everyone would.

The dial-up sounds as Madison logs online, her palm on the mouse and fingers on the keyboard moving with impressive agility as she pulls up Erin's AIM account. "Please don't message anyone from school," Erin starts to say before Madison shushes her.

"No shit," Madison says. "We're chat crashing." She wiggles her eyebrows and pulls up a chat room box, the colors and design way different from the last time Erin used one of those. In sixth or seventh grade, maybe.

"Oh my god." Erin grabs a hot-pink pouf and perches on it next to Madison. When Carissa let the girls redecorate their rooms two years ago, Erin went loud, everything a bright happy color that reminded her of a sunset. Kimmy chose various shades of whites, pops of color via changeable pillows and décor. It was practical, she said, her face disgusted as she took in Erin's pink ceiling and shag rug. "I haven't done this in ages," Erin says. "What room?"

Madison doesn't answer, instead scrolling through the categories.

Friends. Interests. Games. Romance. She clicks on the last one, closing her eyes as the mouse floats over the available rooms. "Started Out with a Kiss," she says, looking over at Erin with pursed lips. "Sexy." Her smile widens, the room full, names floating as people enter and exit.

Love2feelgood: *ladies show me ur piercings*

Blowyamind69: *ill show u mine if u show me urs*

Dogdad62: *ne1 wanna chat 1on1*

It is chaos, each person pretending they're talking to the room but really having conversations with themselves, the whole thing on speed. "This is so effing sad," Madison says, a cackle pouring out of her mouth. Erin shifts in her seat, watching this car crash she can't look away from. "These people are all prob, like, living alone in their thirties with a zillion cats," she says, a grimace. "Or cheaters. The scum of the earth, basically." Erin had learned a few months after Madison's reappearance that her stint at boarding school ended when her dad discovered her mom's affair with their hotel's head of fitness, the fact that she was "slumming it," as he told anyone who would listen, such a bruise to his ego that he launched a campaign to gain sole custody of Madison while making millions in assets conveniently disappear, which meant she had to be closer to home. Madison had taken her dad's side, despite the way the move impacted her life and her relationship with her mom. *She's such a ho*, she often said about her own mother, Erin never fully knowing how to respond, never bringing up her own parents' whispered conversations about Madison's dad's rumored improprieties over the years.

Again, Erin says nothing, the silence filled only by Madison's clacking. "No," Erin starts to say, but Madison already hit send. "No!" she squeals, a message from Erin's screen name appearing in the room. "Ah, ah, ah!" Erin pushes Madison so she spins around on the chair's axis.

ErBear1001: *id luv 2 chat u sound like sex on a stick*

Immediately, a chat request from Dogdad62 pops up. "You're a psycho, you know that?" Erin says, digging her fist into Madison's shoulder. Madison clicks accept, a grainy image appearing in the chat box. "Holy shit," Erin says, covering her eyes. "That's not—"

"Kind of small, don't you think?" Madison moves her face closer to the screen, squinting like a scientist trying to cure cancer. Erin peers between her fingers, the penis tall and ready. She's never seen one, unless you count the flash screen in *Fight Club*. She tries not to scream. With excitement, that she's actually seen a real dick—and in horror, because it's actually sort of weird looking and why did no one warn her? Still, she sits more upright, repositioning herself on her chair to calm the heat she feels between her legs as she thinks of one person in particular she hopes to see without pants. Soon.

Madison can't stop laughing, harder and harder and harder, the frantic cadence capturing Erin, who joins at equal intensity, both feeling above all these ancient losers, not thinking they could ever be so pathetic, so low. Erin can hardly see through the tears in her eyes when Madison asks, "Who's Cambam85?"

"What?" Erin says, her giggle slowing.

"I don't know. They just IM'd you." Madison opens the box, clicking open his profile. Nothing in it except a single quote: "The question isn't who is going to let me; it's who is going to stop me." Erin's stomach drops, and she throws her body between the computer and Madison. She clicks the conversation closed, but not before she sees his message.

Cambam85: *See you in exactly 27 days ErBear*

She smiles to herself, almost forgetting she promised not to tell anyone about their conversations. They had only hung out in person that one time in the fall, Peter's school schedule keeping him away from the Shore until the summer. They hadn't talked about much, Erin slowly sipping a can of Natty Light as Peter and his friends beer bonged, ball tapped, and got in fights over who the hottest Victoria's Secret angel was. But Peter kept looking at her, making a face every time his friends said something stupid like she got it too, like together they were in on the secret. She snuck away a little before 1:00 a.m., and Peter, at that point fully wasted, begged her to stay, said she could sleep in his bed, promising he wouldn't be a creep. Erin knew she would be grounded for all of eternity if her parents woke up and she wasn't in her room, so she turned him down. "Can I at least have your number, then?" he asked. Of course she gave it to him. She told Madison about his existence, but nothing more.

"Cambam," Madison says again, putting her finger to her chin. "Cameron. Like, Peter Cameron, the hot neighbor guy? Isn't he, like, thirty? I didn't realize thirty-year-olds used AIM."

"He's not thirty," Erin says, her smile turning into a defensive line. He is twenty-one, a junior in college. Not that much older than her, really. And she was old for her grade, although she didn't know how Peter would know that. Originally, they texted. Casual "how are yous" and "how's the beach?" turned into longer threads about the stress Peter is feeling as he nears his final year of college, and the ways Erin can't stand her sister. After a few weeks, Peter said he was at the library on his computer more often than on his phone, so their conversations shifted to IM. After another few weeks, Peter told her he'd actually downloaded the service just so he could talk to her all the time while he was at school. "You're like my Pasithea," he'd typed the other day. He's currently taking a Greek mythology class. Erin loved when he referenced things he learned in his college courses during their talks, like she was smart enough, old enough to keep up. "Our talks keep my mind clear." They both agreed to keep their conversations to themselves. Even though they were just friends, Peter said, people might get the wrong idea. Erin didn't want to stop talking to him, so she said of course. She hasn't even told Madison, which is why she immediately changes the subject.

"Want to do a photo shoot?" They had spent the past week messing around with the code on their MySpaces to revamp their pages, the last unchanged offenders their profile pictures.

Madison pushes herself away from the computer, shrugging. "Sounds perf," she says, not asking Erin more about Peter, maybe because she knows the limits of squeezing info out of your best friend, or maybe because she doesn't care, the inbox of her own MySpace page similarly active thanks to one user in particular. Like Erin, she smiles, their secrets deepening as they grab their respective makeup bags, contorting their eyes with liner and taming frizzies with straighteners until they look far beyond their years, their pursed lips and arched brows enticing. *Want me*, they say.

And for both girls, it seems to be working.

10

Beach Week 2022

DAY 2

"Stevie." Bluefish's bathroom door swings behind Kimmy as she grabs for Stevie's arm. How, in a matter of forty-five minutes, had they gone from reconciliation to this again? "I didn't mean to—"

Stevie glowers at Kimmy, a vein snaking the center of her forehead. "Stop." She shakes her arm away from Kimmy's clutch. "I just need a minute, okay? This is bigger than you." She turns, walking back toward the bar, toward Aaron. Kimmy's heart is racing, her sensibility blurred by the stream of cocktails coursing through her veins. She had promised herself she wouldn't make the same mistakes she did fifteen years ago, but already she feels she's stumbled, her attempt to course correct with Stevie mishandled. She watches as Stevie whispers something to Aaron, who's obviously drunk. His brow crinkles, a hand on Stevie's shoulder, and Kimmy reads his lips ask, "Are you sure?" Stevie nods, then walks away. Just as she's about to disappear in the crowd, she turns her head, looking back at Kimmy, her expression unreadable.

Why had Kimmy said anything? She feels her chest tighten again, the three tequila sodas not enough to calm her anxiety as she looks toward the bar, Aaron's eyes on her. There are rows of people between them, buzzily swaying to the cover band playing beachy alt rock, but still he feels too close. She dodges through the crowd until she reaches the edge of the deck, her hand shaky on the wood railing. *Breathe*, she reminds herself for the umpteenth time since returning to Rocky Cape. The sky is streaked with color, purples and oranges and pinks smeared with the clouds. This is why she came home, she remembers. This beauty, this contrast to London's ever-gray atmosphere, this natural reminder that her problems are small in the grand scheme of things. A handful of people in Rocky Cape may stress her out, but the place itself is like atmospheric Ambien. Kimmy takes another breath, and feels the knot against her sternum relax.

"You hiding from someone?" Her body reacts before her brain, a queasy spring of elation bursting in every cell. She beams, looking over her shoulder to see Justin. He looks so damn good, his shoulders curving into toned biceps, ones he hadn't fully developed in high school. His beard makes him look all the more rugged, the Paul Bunyan vibe a refreshing contrast to the manicured finance bros she's dated over the past decade. A few new tattoos bleed past the edges of his sunbleached tank, and Kimmy has to keep herself from ripping it off to see what they say, to explore all the grooves underneath. "I hope it's not me." Justin takes off his hat, the rim tattered from wear, and runs a hand over his shaved head.

"Hi," Kimmy says shyly, her stress over Stevie a distant memory. Justin always had that effect of intoxicating amnesia on her. For a moment, both of them seem unsure what to do. So much has gone unsaid these past fifteen years, their distance essential for Kimmy if she was to have any semblance of a normal life. Still, it's also like no time has passed, his pull on her as strong as ever. She opens her arms to give him a hug and he draws her in, his chest broader than she remembers, everything about him bigger, brawnier. She saw on LinkedIn he works as a marine engineer for a handful of ships near a port in Jacksonville, Florida. She senses the physicality of his work as his arms tighten around her. She breathes him in, the familiarity of his body soap taking her back to their senior year, his body behind her and his elbows locked against her sides, her fingers gripping his rough denim comforter. She takes a quick breath and breaks from his hug. "I am so embarrassed about yesterday." She takes a step back and places a hand on the rail of the deck, steadying herself. There's that dizziness again, but this time she doesn't mind. It's simply the allure of unexplored history. "I'm sorry I didn't text you back. I was pretty much on the couch all day being force-fed electrolytes by Erin."

"Well, glad to see you're here now. And upright, at that." Another memory of being horizontal with him flashes, and she blushes. She feels him taking her in, hoping he sees all the ways she's changed too, but also all the ways she's the same.

"I am," she says, their eyes meeting. "Justin, I regret so much—"

He stops her. "I know," he says. "I know, trust me. We were just kids. Real wild kids."

Who were in love, she wants to add. But maybe it's too early to dive into that. Instead, she agrees with a laugh. He has two beers in his hand and he passes one to her. She takes a sip, its carbonated fizz making her wince—she has long outgrown her cheap beer phase—but she swallows and gives a strained smile.

"Let me guess," Justin says, his eyes on her lips. "Beer is no longer your drink of choice."

"Was it ever?" Kimmy places her hand on her hip. "I'm pretty sure I exclusively drank flavored Smirnoff and Mike's Hard Lemonade in high school." She shudders at the memory of sickly-sweet sour apple vodka slipping down her throat.

He wraps his hand around her drink, their fingers grazing, and Kimmy feels her cheeks turn pink again, the familiar heat of being around him rising. "Once a princess, always a princess." Normally, she would be offended by such a comment, but not with Justin. Nikki used to theorize that he was attracted to rich girls because a taste of them might elevate his own status. "You wouldn't get it since you were born into a different world than us," she said to Kimmy, "but he can be a materialistic little fucker." Kimmy knew Justin was into brands in high school—he had Lacoste polos and Armani cologne and those bright red Supreme x Nike sneaks—and he talked about money a lot, but to Kimmy his vibe always felt more Johnny Knoxville than David Beckham. Still, she leaned into the whole princess thing; if it was a turn-on, who was she to deny him? "You sit your fancy little self down over there"—he looks to an empty table—"and I'll get you a drink. I don't think they serve champagne here, and I assume you've graduated from Vodka Crystal Light?" His eyes sparkle in the dusk.

"Tequila soda, with a splash of lime." He walks away; her palms are sweaty. This is what she feared when she came home, Justin like a mirage that might actually be quicksand. But part of her, maybe, hoped for it too. She sits at the table and rests her cheek on her palm, staring out at the bay, when she feels a tap on her shoulder. "What'd you say to Stevie?" Aaron is towering over her, a cigarette stuffed behind his ear, which he grabs and pops in his mouth.

"What?" Kimmy asks, her heart rate picking up. She does not want to look at him, to talk to him, to be alone with him. She hates Aaron. She really, really hates him.

"Fuck, Kimmy. What did you say to Stevie?" He bends toward her, the unlit cigarette sagging against his lip from a mix of heat and sweat. "You're home for less than twenty-four hours and you've already caused fucking drama."

"That's not true," she says, unable to look Aaron in the eye. She had never really been the one to start drama, at least not intentionally. She just wants Stevie to know the truth. But she can't say that to him.

"Right. So you two go to the bathroom together, come out, and she takes off saying her stomach hurts and she wants to be alone. And you're gonna sit here and tell me somehow it's not your fault?" His nostrils flare and his teeth grit as he talks. She can see why some people are still into him; it's like someone picked him from central casting for a brooding bad boy. But Kimmy doesn't think he has the appeal he used to, his cheeks hollowed even more, a rock star aged by too much partying.

It's enough to remind Kimmy of what a loser he is, how she doesn't have to take any of this from him. If he were ever in her old boardroom, she would have eaten him alive. She's thought about this confrontation for years, various versions of what she'd say running through her head late at night. She wants to curse him out, to tell him to eat shit and never talk to her again. But something about him still makes her feel small, intimidated, powerless. "I didn't say anything, Aaron." Kimmy looks around him to see if Justin's on his way back from the bar, avoiding eye contact. "I don't know why she left either. She's probably just tired. It's a big week for her."

His shoulders calm, his body less tense. "Yeah, maybe." He pauses, lighting his cigarette.

"Can you not do that right here?" Kimmy asks, her patience minimal. She hates cigarette smoke—more so when it's coming from Aaron's mouth, the memory of the way it tastes on his lips impossible to shake.

"You're kidding, right?" Aaron is incredulous. "We're at a bar, not a fucking wellness retreat. Sorry, corporate solider. Didn't mean to offend." He takes a drag and blows the smoke just over Kimmy's head.

So he's kept an eye on her, his comment a giveaway. It jolts her confidence. "That's rich, coming from the guy who's the tobacco industry's number one fan." She looks Aaron up and down, her eyes cold as she stares at his cigarette and gaming T-shirt. "You've punched way above your weight with Stevie."

His eyes go soft for a moment, enough for Kimmy to know her insult landed, but then they turn daring. "What about you? Did I punch above my weight with you?" He takes another drag.

"Fuck you," Kimmy says, the words sharp as they leave her lips.

"But you already did," he laughs, smoke floating from his mouth. And again, he knocks her on her ass. Justin walks up just then and sits across from Kimmy.

"Sup, man," Justin says, his obliviousness as evident as it's always been. She's sure Justin and Aaron hung out earlier this week, an alumni pickup game of footy one of the Rocky Cape soccer team's annual Beach Week traditions.

"You're shitting me," Aaron slurs, and Kimmy realizes how drunk he really is. He looks back at Kimmy. "You pissed off Stevie and you two are together. Hey, everyone," he shouts, a few people turning toward their table. "It's 2007 again!"

"Nice to see you too, bro. You still mad I scored that goal on you yesterday or something?" Justin asks, putting the drinks on the table as Aaron turns around, walking away shaking his head. He looks at Kimmy and pushes a drink toward her. "What was that about?"

She shrugs. "It was weird." She feels like she's telling a lie. "I guess some people can't get over old shit."

"Well, let's hope we can." Justin lifts his drink, giving Kimmy a hopeful look. They're young again, their past erased, their future just beginning. She's not thinking about Stevie, about her dad, about all the work she has ahead of her. She always feels stress-free with Justin.

She lifts her drink too, the plastic smooshing as she clinks her cup against Justin's. "I was hoping you'd say that." She takes a sip. "Listen, about everything I said back then—"

"How long are you here for?" he asks, interrupting. "I'm here all week, at the very least."

"Permanently." She raises her eyebrows. "Never thought I'd be saying this, but I quit my job in London. The plan is that I'll eventually take over Devine's so my parents can retire."

"Damn." Justin brings his drink to his lips. "Reid told me you've been girlbossing all over the globe." She smiles. Reid has always been on Team Kimmy, even in high school. Like her, Justin's not on social media, at least according to Erin, both of their lives something of a mystery to most; Kimmy will have to thank Reid for talking her up to Justin. "I'm glad you're home." Justin puts a hand on her hand. *Me too*, she thinks, surprising herself. "I gotta say," he adds, "when I booked my flight I didn't expect to be sitting here sipping on a cold drink with a beautiful woman by my side, living out all the what-if dreams."

"You've had 'what-if' dreams?" Her biggest fear was that he hadn't thought about her in all these years. To hear that he's not only thought about her, but dreamt about her—just like she has about him—topples every wall she's ever built between them.

"Of course," he says. "Haven't you?" Suddenly he looks shy, like maybe he read the situation wrong.

"I just figured you knew that." Hadn't everyone known she was desperately, pathetically in love with Justin, including him?

They both look at each other, the moment pulsing with tension. "I was a fucking idiot." He edges closer in his chair, his empty hand on Kimmy's leg, the heat rising again. "That's all I knew. Or at least all I know now."

The band starts a new song, "Amber" by 311. She smiles at him. "How much does this song remind you of high school?"

Justin smiles back, standing. "It's fate," he says, his hand out. She takes it, rising, lacing her hands behind his neck, his arms circling her back. They sway, her head against his chest, their bodies hardly moving, just clinging to each other. *Don't let me go again*, Kimmy's grip says.

As the song nears the end, Justin whispers in Kimmy's ear. "You wanna ditch this place? Pretty sure I still have a DVD of *Green Street Hooligans* somewhere in my room."

She pulls back, looking up at him, laughing. He remembers where it all began. So does she, always. Both staying in their childhood rooms, his house a much better option than hers. She could hear her mom now. *This is the first thing you choose to do after moving home? What are you trying to do, give your father another heart attack?* She looks up at Justin, smiling. "Do you have room in your trunk for my bike?"

He grins, his teeth glowing in the dark air. "I'm not sure if you're making a *40-Year-Old Virgin* joke or a pass at me." He raises one eyebrow. "But whichever it is: Fuck yeah, Legs. Fuck yeah."

They walk out of the bar buzzed and holding hands, just like old times.

11

June 2006

Kimmy stares at her phone, its screen blank once again. Her veins are warm, raspberry Smirnoff and Crystal Light swimming upstream as she clicks on her phone's menu, checking the inbox for the hundredth time that night. The voices around her blur, bouncing off the cold cement floor of Aaron Roop's basement, the setup so odd there's little to do but ignore it. It's all futons and mismatched sofas, the pillows soggy with teenage sweat and spilled beer, fabric softened from hours of bong rips and lethargic butts. Does Aaron's dad ever check on this room, question the stashes of liquor under the IKEA coffee tables or the dank scent soaked into the drywall? It's like one of those movies where the kids seem to be adults, living on their own with no real supervision besides a well-intentioned coach or an overachieving best friend. The basement's crowded—there are more faces at the party than Kimmy recognizes—but lonely, unfinished, and emotionless. A chill tickles the nape of her neck as she takes it all in. No one notices, though. Or cares, maybe, their bodies slack with drink and weed and god knows what else.

"You good?" Nikki's eyes are splattered with red, a by-product of the long hit she just took off Gus, the stout bowl with swirls of red and yellow they named after a *Willy Wonka* character. "I'm about to toss that thing into the ocean," she says about Kimmy's phone, sinking into the cushion seat next to her. Kimmy and Nikki had been hanging out more lately, mainly at Kimmy's house. Carissa had been surprisingly excited about the friendship, going on and on about how much respect she has for Nikki's mom, who had Nikki when she was seventeen. "She didn't have to have Nikki, you know," Carissa always said, "but

she did and you can see she raised her with endless amounts of love."
It surprised Kimmy, who was initially worried her parents wouldn't
approve of their friendship—but that was Carissa. No one ever fully
knew what was going on inside her head, her views a mottled mess
of contradictions. (Pro-Kerry, anti-Clintons, pro-weed, anti–her kids
smoking it, pro-Botox, anti–putting anything but organic foods into
her body, to name a few.)

Kimmy brings her Solo cup to her lips, gnawing on the edge, phone
clutched in her palm. They'd started hanging out more regularly, especially once the school year ended and Brian's string of soccer camps and
summer tournaments and kids' coaching gigs picked up. He was a ghost,
popping up when convenient, regarding any sort of consistent presence
in his girlfriend's life a low priority.

"Hello?" Nikki says, pushing her forehead directly into Kimmy's,
her movements slow but fluid. "Tonight is not the place for feeling
sorry for yourself. Or obsessing over a total snoozer." She says it not
unkindly, her words more like encouragement than criticism. It makes
Kimmy flinch, though, this outside perception of her relationship. Because she sees it too; last week, Brian came over to watch a movie and
they didn't even kiss because he bruised his lip during a soccer game.
When she offered to have sex with him *Pretty Woman*–style, he still
turned her down, claiming he was too tired. "Come." Nikki stands
facing Kimmy, her hips swinging like a Newton's cradle, their rhythm
hypnotizing. Kimmy shakes her head, but puts her hand out for Nikki
to grab, to pull her onto this impromptu dance floor.

"Stop thinking," Nikki says in Kimmy's ear, the music rising. "Stop
worrying so fucking much. About all of it. Just fucking dance." Nikki
backs away, whipping her head around as she twirls in a circle. When she
stops, facing Kimmy, her expression is feral, her shoulders shimmying
and eyes big as she mouths the lyrics to "Promiscuous Girl." She slith-
ers all over Kimmy, arm on her shoulder, hand on her wrist. Jumping,
dragging Kimmy with her, each bounce a release, shaking loose pressure
and stress and nerves. Kimmy throws her head back, eyes closed, hands
rising, hair floating like ribbons. They dance with abandon, reflections
of each other.

Someone whistles, then they hear Ben shout, "Take it off." He swigs from the opaque bottle in his hand, blue syrupy liquid spilling from the corner of his mouth.

"Gross, creep." Nikki slows her dancing and flicks him off, her tongue sticking out. She's not intimidated, his Smurfish buffoonery nothing more. The attention, Kimmy sees for the first time, isn't wasted on her. She recognizes that look: bright eyes, twisted lips, the bring-it-on stance. It's the same one Kimmy gets when she crosses the finish line first. The knowing that you are being watched. Admired. Maybe even adored. After all, what's the point of a performance if no one's looking?

"A guy can dream." Ben holds his hand up for a high five, another guy meeting it with his own. Kimmy doesn't see who at first, the room shaking as she slows her jumping. Until they lock eyes, Justin's gaze meeting hers, her stomach rolling like she's on the Slingshot at Six Flags. She knows she should feel ridiculous, should be embarrassed by her careless arms and pseudo moshing. Instead, she feels seen.

A chime interrupts the moment. Kimmy's phone, wedged between two cushions on the couch. She leaps past Nikki, her heart racing. She's already thinking through her response, how long she'll wait to answer Brian. Because it has to be him. Has to.

But no. It's Stevie. And for some reason, this bugs Kimmy.

Wanna do din at Ocean View with me n my mom 2morrow then sleepover?

Kimmy snaps her phone shut, not wanting to answer, to commit to Stevie's plans despite their familiarity. It's what their summers have long been made of: working at their families' respective shops, lounging on the beach for hours lathering each other in tanning oil until their skin has the ideal crisp, and staying up way too late talking about everything and nothing in each other's beds. Kimmy's gut churns as she looks at her phone again, the guilt of avoiding Stevie enough to slightly sober her up. She isn't this person, this flaky girl who blows off her best friend, this insecure shell of herself begging, pleading for her boyfriend to call her back. But deep down, she wants more than that life, a safe cocoon of sleepovers and marathon *Titanic*-viewing sessions. That unspoken reality—betrayal, really, of Stevie, of Brian, of the whole life she's felt she's supposed to maintain—hits, the tension pooling along her lower eyelids. She shakes her head, sliding her phone back into her pocket so she can wiggle away these thoughts. It's exhausting, this tightwire act between behaving and experiencing, between people-pleasing and doing what she's starting to realize she actually wants—at least sometimes. Her phone rings again.

"Well, aren't you Miss Popular?" Nikki says, still twirling, still preening for the guys.

Brian, Kimmy's phone screen says. Finally.

She sneaks away from the music, outside under a flimsy porch roof, the rain beating against the asphalt driveway with anger. "Hey," she says into her phone, trying to act composed. "How's the camp tourney?"

"Um, it's good." Brian sounds distant, like his phone is resting on his chest. She knows the position, his way of casually lounging to recoup his muscles. "I'm tired. We won. I scored twice, Derek once. So we'll be in tomorrow's final. I dunno." She hears his head hit the pillow, the speaker smothered for a second. "This tourney kinda rags. Like, it's just the B team this round." There's a lull, his sigh taking up all the space on the phone. "What are you doing tonight?"

The question isn't uncommon, just a standard conversational cue. But for some reason it feels weird this time, too direct, like he's trying to catch Kimmy doing something she shouldn't. Or maybe it's all in her head. She scrunches her nose, trying to wring away any lingering drops of alcohol in her system. "I'm actually at a party at Aaron Roop's house. Random, I know." Her tongue is thick, her mind working extra hard to make sure she doesn't slip over any words.

"I heard." Brian doesn't say anything else, once again letting his silence do the lifting.

"Oh." And like that, she forgets that he ignored her for the past few days, that she was ever mad at him, instead fumbling over her own guilt to make sure he's okay, that she hasn't upset him. "What do you mean?"

"Ben just texted me a pic of you dancing with Nikki Ritter. It was all blurry. Are you drunk?" The question is pointed, the judgment drip-ping. He has never approved of their friendship, of the crowd Nikki hangs with.

"No," she lies. To be fair, she's only had one drink. But then she re-alizes what it means if he received a picture text of her. "Wait, so you've been getting texts this whole day?" Again, he's quiet. "What, you can only pick up the phone and talk to me if I'm doing something you disapprove of? Are you fucking kidding me?"

"Cursing, Kimmy—really? See, you are drunk." His tone is conde-scending and avoidant. "I'll be home tomorrow night. We can catch up then." Kimmy hears someone shout in the background on Brian's side, making kissy noises, the speaker muffled as a pillow is thrown. "I'll call you when I'm home, okay?" She nods, knowing he knows she'll pick up. "And Kimmy, be careful. That crew isn't like you and me, know what I mean?" He pauses, silence on her end. "I love you," he reminds her, hanging up before she can say it back. Kimmy feels her breath catch, the lump of frustration swelling into a full breakdown, a loud whimper escalating into sniffles, her body quietly convulsing with each sob.

"Hey," someone says. She turns. Aaron is hunched in a rocking chair smoking a joint. His voice is gravelly, a deep bellow with an uneasy power, cigarette perched behind an ear, his hair falling across an eye. She has never talked to Aaron before, at least without Brian by her side. All she knew was that the guys considered him deep, a little introverted, and most of the punk girls at school wanted to sleep with him. He has a reputation for being smarter than the rest of them, mostly because he read *On the Road* two summers ago and has taken to sharing quotes instead of answering questions.

Kimmy wipes her eyes, suddenly feeling ridiculous. She looks at her feet. "Oh, hi, sorry," she says, a whisper. "I didn't realize—" She stumbles over her words, her hands grabbing her hair, twisting it in a knot at the back of her skull before she lets go, strands spilling across her shoulders. "I know it's your house. Thanks for having us, by the way." She rubs her eyes again.

"'Follow your inner moonlight, don't hide the madness,'" he quotes, holding up a joint, smoke willowing from its tip. "Wanna hit?" Kimmy pauses, not sure what to say. She can't imagine smoking, her lungs dragged down, her runs belabored by tar. For a moment she thinks, *What would it be like to be someone who said yes?*

"Nah, princesses don't toke, dude." She feels a hand on her shoulder. Justin's.

"She's not some fragile little girl, Fitzy. Shit, you guys sometimes. She can speak for herself." Nikki has a bong in hand, leading Chris and Ryan toward the weather-worn patio furniture around Aaron.

Kimmy thought she had regained her balance, yet she finds herself leaning into Justin, who's still behind her. He cranes his neck to look at her face, the trail of Kimmy's mascara across her cheek a giveaway. "Hey," he whispers, his cheek against her hair. "You okay?" He squeezes her shoulder and she shrugs him off, then looks out at the rain. "You know what, Legs?" he asks loud enough that the whole porch looks at them. "None of this emo shit." He tugs her hand, then lets go as he runs off the porch directly into the downpour—his arms wide, face looking at the sky, mouth open, catching the droplets and signing the theme song to *Laguna Beach*, his voice off-key and muffled by the downpour.

"Justin!" Kimmy shouts, laughing. "I'm not going in that!" She looks back at the group for guidance, or maybe reassurance. Ben isn't there, likely passed out inside from too much Hpnotiq. Nikki raises one brow as she places her lips at the rim of the bong, her inhale glowing the bowl embers against the cloudy night.

"Fitzy, you pussy. Bet your skinny ass gets hypothermia in two minutes," Ryan shouts as Nikki passes him the bong, smoke haloing both.

"You coming, Legs?" Justin asks again, ignoring his friends, his grin taunting.

She looks back one more time, and Aaron shrugs. "You heard the man." He takes another drag of his joint, the early summer air making his exhale all the more dramatic, looking off into the distance, Kimmy already an afterthought. Nikki gives her a wink before leaning into the patio cushion, her head lolling back, eyes closed and mouth curled, the weed tingling through her limbs. So Kimmy follows, droplets pelting her face. Before she gets to Justin, he sticks his tongue out and runs, spinning past the cars parked out front, hurdling over the split-rail fence lining the neighboring property, a not-yet-opened vineyard, its grapevines in their infancy. Kimmy had heard the family that bought the land a few years ago were still growing their backlog, the property mostly unwatched at night. She shivers at the danger of getting caught. The grass soaks her toes, the soles of her feet muddy and slippery against her Rainbows. Barely visible, Justin weaves through the rows of trees, winding until they reach a covered concrete patio, a folding table with buckets underneath the only furniture. Kimmy is breathless, her runner lungs thrown off by the surprise sprint, the shaky weather. Leaning her hands against her thighs, bent over as her breathing steadies, she looks up at Justin, sitting on the table with his legs swinging. He pats the spot to his right, empty and inviting. This time without hesitation Kimmy follows.

"Spill." He shifts his shoulders to face her. "What's the deal? Why are you spending an otherwise awesome fucking night all teary?"

"I wasn't crying," she says, defensive. She pushes off the table, about to run back to the house when Justin grabs her shoulder, his touch tender.

"Come on, don't freak." She turns back around, his features hard to make out in the night air, but she feels the sincerity, the dopey apologetic eyes. "I didn't mean that. I meant"—he sighs, his hands clapping his thighs—"I meant Brian's shitty, okay? I know, I know. Everyone says he's smart. And dreamy. And soooo perfect. Blah blah blah. But I saw you eyeing your phone. You're always eyeing your phone these days, Legs. You shouldn't be. Dude's being a dick if he's not calling his girlfriend, calling *you*, every chance he can."

A misty gust swirls under the covered patio, its drizzle seeping through Kimmy's tank top. She wraps her arms around her chest, rubbing her sides to stay warm as she walks back to the table, back to Justin's side. Just thinking about Brian, the layers of frustration, the guilt of ignoring Stevie, the confusion she feels about everything, brings back the tears. Kimmy sniffles, rubbing her eyes, the wet sleeve of her zip-up doing little to help the matter. "I feel crazy." Her hands grasp the edge of the plastic tabletop, fingertips pressing its underside. "Like, desperate. Not like myself. Unstable, I guess. I hate it." She burrows her head into her hands, suppressing an exasperated growl. "Like, what did I do? Why doesn't he want me?"

"You're not crazy, Legs." Justin's hands are still on his thighs, his fingers twitching with uncertainty. "He's the idiot, get that? You are a fucking prize. A prize. If he doesn't realize that, the kid's mental." He looks out at the vineyard, then back at Kimmy. "I have an idea."

"Oh god." Kimmy laughs, wiping her sleeve under her nose. "I'm scared to even ask." But she isn't scared. She is distracted. Relieved. Justin's presence shaking her tightly wound coils, adding surprisingly welcome detour signs to her rows of well-placed dominoes.

He doesn't answer, running back into the rain. And then he shouts. Screams, really—a massive call into the darkness.

"Justin!" Kimmy shouts as she runs toward him, pulling his bicep. "What the hell are you doing? You're insane!"

"Come on," he says, grabbing her wrist. "Let's have a little *Garden State* moment."

"Since when did you become such a pop culture connoisseur?" His hand is still around her wrist, the two facing each other as the clouds keep pouring out their insides.

"Let's just say a lady friend may or may not be very into this shit."

Kimmy pulls her hand back, an unconscious response. "Again I find myself saying: Do I even want to ask?"

He grabs her wrist again, twirling her so her back's against his chest, both looking up at the moon glowing amid the angry clouds. Kimmy blinks, the droplets falling on her face, Justin's warmth enough to make her forget the air's edge. He puts his hand on her other wrist, elevating her arms until they're outstretched against his, her skin thrumming as it touches Justin's, the energy dissolving her anger. Insecurity. Age, even—this moment forever a snapshot of youth.

"She doesn't mean anything," Justin whispers, lips brushing her ear. "But you know that." His fingers graze her wrists, steaming skin to skin against the foggy dusk. Frozen, wanting to be still in this moment, Kimmy closes her eyes, rolling her neck, her head, into the crook of Justin's shoulder. She pauses there, the lust almost painful, then keeps rolling, spinning herself away from his grasp so they're face-to-face. And she lets go.

Her scream isn't a shriek, a defenseless girl crying for help. It's loud, brash, ugly, a fossil from her wild toddler days when she was allowed to be messy, encouraged even, to jump and fall and scrape her knees. She feels it all go, the pressure of perfection she's spent her most recent years chasing. Justin's smile is so big it shines against the moonlight. "Hell yeah," he says. "That's my girl."

And when she runs back to the house, her face wet but tears dry, he follows.

12

Beach Week 2022

DAY 3

Justin lies next to Kimmy, his eyes droopy with sleep. The sun spills across the bed, streaks of gold striping their bodies, so different from when they were eighteen but immediately familiar, ancient patterns kicking in. Kimmy smiles sleepily as she looks around, taking in the room. It hasn't changed much—there's still a futon nestled between a desk and a closet, a pile of clothes messy in one corner, and a dresser with a TV at the foot of the bed littered with trophies, ancient bottles of cologne, framed photos of their high school friends. But there's a bareness too, a reminder that they've long moved on from this place. It's dated, but feels like home. It *is* home.

Justin stirs, his eyes blinking as the sun rises higher, its beams pushing against the window's blinds, but he settles again, his soft snores whirling in the peaceful morning air. It's a dream, this gauzy version of reality. Still, Kimmy can't shake her conversation with Stevie. She wants to blame the tequila, the transportive quality of being back in Rocky Cape and seeing so many past faces in such a short spurt, like the salt in the air suspended time and preserved all of Kimmy's emotions and vendettas. She doesn't want to be this girl again, the one drama always seems to follow. She rolls to her side, picking up her phone from the ground.

Sorry about last night. I really didn't mean to upset you. It was so so good to see you

She hits send, holding her phone above her head as she rolls to her back. It took Kimmy years to understand why everything went down the way it did—and why it didn't have to if she had just stood up for herself, if she knew the words. Now she does, and one of the things she promised herself when she moved home was not to let this town stomp all over her with its misconceptions and gossip and judgments. She wants to right the wrongs of her past. To make sure they never repeat. So much of that starts with Stevie, with stitching the broken pieces of their friendship back together. She closes her eyes, unsure if the burgeoning headache tapping her forehead is the result of a looming hangover or a dark cloud threatening to ruin her morning, her lazy lounging with the one that got away. She shakes her head, then takes a quick selfie, neck up, and sends it to Nikki.

Guess where I am?

She knows she's up, probably in the kitchen of her shingled craftsman just outside of Stowe making vegetarian mush for her two-year-old son while her wife flutters about as she rushes to get to the mountain, where she's the head of operations. Nikki is likely stretching, gearing up for the yoga classes she'll teach that day, her life filled with love and happiness and stability, more traditional than either of them could ever have imagined for her. When Kimmy ran away from Rocky Cape all those years ago, Nikki refused to let Kimmy give up on their friendship. She invited herself to Pepperdine, went to Stanford football games with Kimmy (and met her now wife, a classmate of Kimmy's, at one), and named Kimmy the maid of honor at her wedding. She forced friendship on Kimmy and Kimmy is forever grateful.

Oh my god. I would recognize that ugly ass headboard anywhere. HOW?! I NEED THE DEETS. Kimmy looks behind her at the wood bookshelf headboard Justin made himself as a freshman in woodworking class all those years ago. *I bet the reunion sex was fucking off the wall*, Nikki adds, followed by a string of eggplant emojis. Kimmy thinks back to the night before, the heat of being in Justin's car, the anticipation almost unbearable. They tiptoed into his house, right past his parents' room, just like they used to in high school, Justin ahead, one of Kimmy's hands in his and the other trailing the stair banister, taking in the gallery wall stacked with pictures of Justin and Reid at the various stages of their lives, nothing changed. The way, when they finally got to Justin's room, the air-conditioning unit blasting at full power made Kimmy's skin prickle just like it did years ago, a chill running up her spine, Justin took her in his arms and kissed her, all of it so slow and passionate she almost melted. "Damn," Justin said, pulling back. "You've gotten better at kissing."

She swatted him, rolling her eyes, remembering all their sweaty, sloppy make-out sessions throughout senior year, including the one time they emerged from a bathroom at a party and her shirt was inside out. "I could say the same about you."

"We were babies." He ran a finger down her neck and under the strap of her shirt. "But not anymore."

"No." She pursed her lips, taking a finger and pressing it against his chest. "Not anymore." She shook her head, pushing him toward his bed, where he fell onto his back, propped up by his elbows as he watched her pull her shirt over her head and shimmy out of her jeans before she straddled him. The sex wasn't wild, wasn't rushed and chaotic the way it had been so many times before. It was patient, deep, both of them watching each other the whole time, rising and falling in rhythm. The next three times were the wild ones, their hunger for each other resulting in a bite mark on Justin's shoulder and a handprint on Kimmy's ass. Ravenous. There was no other way to put it.

Kimmy sends Nikki the speak-no-evil monkey emoji. *Fucking beach week*

Fucking beach week is right, Nikki answers. *So sad I can't be there this year. Keep me updated the whole time, pls. I need to live vicariously through your teenage sexcapades*

Kimmy pauses, not sure how much she wants to share. She lands on a small update.

Aaron was there last night. He's dating Stevie.

Shut up, Nikki responds, typing, then deleting, the dots ebbing and flowing. Finally, she sends:

FUCK THEM

Nikki has always had Kimmy's back, was always ready to fight her battles when it came to those two. But this round, Kimmy doesn't feel it's a them. It's just a him. He doesn't deserve Stevie, doesn't deserve that sort of happiness.

Off to day care. Send me all the hot gos this week. My mom doesn't know shit that goes on. So glad you can be my spy. xoxoxo

Kimmy puts her phone down, then looks at Justin again, her whole body aching with happiness. She rolls over, kissing his ear. "I'm starving. Gonna go to Lisa's. You still a breakfast sammie guy?" He groans, his eyes closed but lips smiling, a small nod.

Kimmy hops out of bed, stretching her arms as she looks for her clothes. Her shirt is dangling on the desk, jeans piled at the foot of the bed, her underwear still inside. Her bra is MIA, but she's sleepy, careless, so she just pulls a T-shirt from the pile on Justin's futon. It would be a quick run anyway.

As she creeps downstairs, she tiptoes toward the side door, not wanting to wake anyone, but it's too late, Justin's brother, Reid, is sitting on a stool at the kitchen's breakfast bar that backs right up to the back door, the counters still a muddy shade of tan. "Whoa," Reid says, his eyes big. "Did not expect to see you here." He drops his spoon into his bowl of cereal, the neck of it crashing against the white edge.

"Reid," she says, her arms out. He's staring, his shock obvious, and she is irredeemably mortified. "Thank god it's you. If it was your parents, I might actually pass out."

He hugs her back, his embrace a touch standoffish. "Twice in three days. That might be a Rocky Cape record."

"How are you?" she asks, taking a seat on the stool next to him. Kimmy runs a hand through her hair, the knots from last night catching her fingers. "I loved your piece at the auction."

"Actually, in a rush." He shovels a spoonful of Raisin Bran into his mouth, then grabs a messenger bag near the door on his way out. "I just stopped by to see Justin quick, but you beat me to the punch." He doesn't say it unkindly, but Kimmy senses some sort of annoyance in his voice. She's about to apologize, but his back is already turned, his hand on the doorknob. He turns around, giving Kimmy a close-mouthed smile. "It's good to see you, really." She can tell Reid means it, but there's a sadness in his eyes.

"You too." She rubs her arms as he shuts the door, waiting a beat until the hum of his car engine is in the distance, then walks out the door. The sun is brighter than she expected, the sidewalk reflecting its heat as Kimmy strolls to Lisa's Diner. This part of town is quiet, about a mile from the tourist-filled Main Street and its surrounding summer mansions. Most of the houses out here are still cottages, though that's changing each year; Justin's parents have been in their house since the eighties and would rather die than sell to a Main Line yuppie. Kimmy loves that type of Rocky Caper—even if they don't like her family's local influence—their insistence that nothing change part of what keeps the place so charming. Kimmy brushes the mascara crumbs collecting along her eyeline and pulls her hair into a high messy bun. She spots the awning at Lisa's, the yellow hue like a warm hello. Walking inside, Kimmy's taken back to postrun hangouts with Stevie, their hairlines frosted with sweat as they devoured omelets and home fries doused with ketchup. She smiles to herself, pulling out her phone reflexively to snap a pic of the donuts lining the glass case, their tops sprinkled with rainbow wax and drizzled with chocolate syrup. She almost sends it to Stevie, but stops herself when she sees the unanswered text from thirty minutes ago. "Can I help you?" a man behind the counter asks, and Kimmy snaps back into the moment.

"Can I have a bacon egg and cheese?" Her eyes are still on the glass case as she talks. "And two of those." She points to the marble iced chocolate-and-vanilla donuts, Erin's favorite. She'd bring them to her when she got home this morning. "And two coffees, please. Both black and iced." She looks up and sees James, an amused expression on his face. He's in a hairnet and yellow apron, his hands covered in loose plastic gloves. "Oh my god, Diner James," Kimmy says, without thinking. A few days ago, she would have been embarrassed, both because of James's stature in local government and because when they re-met at the auction, she felt a flicker of a crush—or at least the hope of one. In the aftermath of her night with Justin, though, she just feels hungover and in desperate need of caffeine; she doesn't care who provides it.

"You are looking charmingly disheveled this morning, Kimmy

Devine." His smile grows bigger as he picks the donuts from the case and places them in a small white box. "And here I was worrying you were stuck at home nursing your jet lag." He says it in jest, no hint of meanness in his tone, but Kimmy breaks eye contact as he subtly calls out her walk of shame.

She crosses her arms against her braless chest. "How many jobs do you work? I thought I was the town's greatest overachiever," she says, trying to change the topic.

"I help my aunt on weekend mornings in the summer and over the holidays. I have since high school." She has a quick flash of James serving her when she was at Lisa's with Justin one August morning after they went on a long run. She had hardly remembered, now wondering how many other times he'd been around and she'd completely ignored him. "You know, the breakfast rush and all that." He tilts his head to the growing line behind Kimmy.

"Oh." She realizes she's holding everyone up. "Here." She passes James her credit card; he still looks amused, but doesn't say anything else as he rings her up. There's an awkward silence as he flips a tablet toward her, the tip page bright. She awkwardly presses *30%*, signing as quickly as she can, and mumbles a thanks as she backs away toward the waiting area, her arms crossed again. Just as she's finally settled, her eyes averted, she hears her name.

She looks up and sees Tess again. "Hi!" Tess says, her enthusiasm that of someone who's on their third cup of coffee by 8:00 a.m.

"Uh, hi," Kimmy says, slightly startled in her state of dishevelment. "I guess we're on the same social schedule these days," she jokes as Tess walks toward her.

"Peter mentioned ages ago that this was, like, your family's go-to coffee place, so I figured I'd try it since the locals must know where to get the best caffeine." She sees Tess's eyes linger for a moment on her shirt, and Kimmy remembers her lack of a bra, her sex hair. "Is Erin with you? I haven't seen her in ages." Tess's eye contact makes Kimmy shift her stance, crossing her arms tighter.

"No," Kimmy says, looking back toward the counter. "She's still sleeping," she lies.

"Oh." Tess pauses. "Too bad." Ever the diplomat, she shakes her re-action before Kimmy can fully process it. "Wait, did you know Madison Jensen? I always forget how small this town is." She turns back toward the table where she was sitting, and just behind a double-decker stroller filled with Everett and Evelyn, Kimmy sees the shock of platinum hair, the tight scowl greeting her.

Kimmy forces a smile, nodding. "Hi, Madison." She swallows. "How are you?" This town is, in fact, not just small, but too small. Madison gives a polite wave and smile, then looks out the window. *Still a petty bitch*, Kimmy thinks. Tess pauses a moment, then seems to decide to ignore whatever tension she's sensing.

"Madison is helping me find a babysitter! She runs this great service. One of Peter's partners used it and raved." Tess brushes a wisp out of her eye. "The twins are going through a brutal sleep regression and I'm dying for some help. And sleep."

"Oh," Kimmy says, looking back at Madison. "I thought for some reason you worked for your dad."

Madison gives her a grim look. "No, I do not." Kimmy, of course, knows this. Six years ago, it was the talk of the town: Madison was a midlevel executive learning the ropes of her dad's hotel chain when she decided to use her corporate card to buy a Birkin, which she told her dad she needed to own to be taken seriously during meetings with clients, and besides, it was secondhand. He promptly cut her off until she could prove she was responsible enough to fund her own life and career. She's been nannying ever since, Nikki sending Kimmy the occasional screen-shot from her ridiculous influencer-wannabe Instagram. "Some of us prefer to make it on our own," Madison adds, her lips pursed. Kimmy lets out a small laugh, looking at Tess with big eyes, as if to say, *Who's going to tell her?* But Tess, quite obviously and understandably, has no idea what the look means.

"Kimmy," James says, placing her breakfast sandwich and coffees on the counter.

"Coffee for two, huh?" Tess wiggles her brows.

Kimmy tightens her lips. Does anyone mind their own business in this place? "It's for Erin," she lies again. "Good to see you. Good luck with the search." Kimmy speedily turns and feels Madison's eyes on her back as she turns to pick up her order. "Thanks," she says, making eye contact with James as she grabs their coffees.

"Enjoy," he says with a friendly smile. "May you and Fitzgerald have a wonderful morning."

"What?" Her cheeks burn.

"Your shirt." He points to it. And it's only then she realizes she grabbed an old soccer shirt of Justin's with his last name blaringly printed on the back. Kimmy near sprints out of Lisa's so she can jump back into bed with Justin, tucked away from the outside world and all its commentary. On the walk home, she spots a small alley between an organic soap store and a home décor shop that don't open until noon; she slides between them, placing her drinks and donut bag on the ground, her back to the street, and peels Justin's shirt over her head, flipping it inside out before putting it back on. She cannot risk someone else she knows—or, worse, her own parents—spotting her with his name on her back. Not yet, at least.

When Kimmy gets to Justin's house, she sneaks through the back door and up to his room. He's still in bed, the scrunched sheet covering only his feet. It turns her on, the whole image, how comfortable and ordinary it is, like they've been doing it every day for an entire lifetime. He stirs when she slips into bed, propping his head up on his hand. She passes him a coffee, and he sips, both of them grinning. He puts his coffee on the top of his headboard and she does the same, his hand on her waist, pulling her closer. She's about to tell him about seeing Madison but pauses, afraid to open a Pandora's box of all their past drama. Instead, Justin says, "Why did we wait a whole decade for this," his coffee breath lingering. It doesn't bother Kimmy, though, his warmth against her euphoric. His hand snakes up her shirt, her bra still forgotten. "Shit," he says as his palm cups the side of her breast. "What are you trying to do to me?" Kimmy laughs, the memory of her recent embarrassment wiped. She looks down; he's already hard, hands wrapped around her. She melts into him, ready to be totally taken.

What are you girls screaming about?

You'll never believe this. Bradley Fisher told Kimmy she has the potential to be hot! He said maybe once she gets her braces off.

Isn't that amazing?

Oh, girls. You know you're already beautiful, right?

God. Gross! Like you would know.

Excuse me. Sorry for just trying to remind my precious angels that they are worth more than whatever some dummy named Bradley Fisher thinks.

We love you too, Mom.

13

August 2006

Peter's hand grips a stopwatch, his thumb lightly resting on the top left button. Erin's eyes scan a sentence about Group 1 of the periodic table, the side of her pinky gray with graphite. She rests her chin on her free hand as she narrows the multiple-choice answers from four to two. Is the group alkaloids or metalloids? She looks up at Peter, hoping for an assist, but he tsks, his tongue pressed against his teeth. She pouts, then turns back to the empty bubbles taunting her. "Thirty seconds left," he says, scanning her paper.

She presses the tip of her number 2 pencil into the paper, the bubble next to metalloids darkened. "Done!" she says when she fills it in, tossing the pencil onto the table. It bounces and hits Peter's chest. "Sorry," she says in an embarrassed whisper as he passes it back to her, his fingers purposely on the eraser, no possibility of their fingers grazing. Erin grabs it back and pushes her finished practice test toward Peter. "I totally dominated this one. I just feel it."

"We'll see." Peter reaches for the red pen behind his ear. Erin stands as he starts grading, walking toward the kitchen fridge, Peter's back to her as he hunches over the kitchen table. The stripes on his polo shirt hug his shoulder muscles while he writes; how badly Erin wants to sneak behind him, to hug that gorgeous back and nestle her cheek against his. She's stuck in her daydream, staring at Peter, when Kimmy flicks her forehead. "What the—" she says, snapping out of her daze.

"Earth to Erin." Kimmy breezes past and hip checks Erin so she can open the fridge. She pulls out a Diet Coke, cracking it open and taking a guzzle. "How's the nerd squad doing today?"

Peter turns, Erin's practice test in his hand. "Great, actually." He looks right at Erin, his smile wide. "Erin just got a ninety-three percent on her latest practice test."

Erin startles, unprepared to do so well. She was going to be in college prep chem this fall—unlike Kimmy, she wasn't in any honors or AP classes—and after her near-disastrous run with freshman biology, her parents were determined for her to do better. Over Memorial Day happy hour, shortly before Peter was arriving to visit his parents for the summer, splitting his time between his dad's dental office in Blue Bell and the Shore, the Camerons mentioned his stellar GPA and predentistry class load. Bill Devine couldn't help himself; he asked if Peter would tutor Erin over the summer, citing her trouble with numbers and memorization. That was how Peter found out Erin had just finished her freshman year of high school, and subsequently treated her as such. She knew she had maybe tricked him a little. She never told him her age, avoiding the subject whenever it came up. But he never pushed it, like he didn't want to know. She IM'd him a few days after, asking, "Are you mad I didn't tell you my age?" He responded, "Why would I be?" and Erin, confused, logged off. Now every Tuesday and Thursday at 3:00 p.m., before Peter's shift at the local tavern began, the Devines pay Peter a hundred dollars per session to tutor Erin for an hour.

"Oh my god," Erin squeals, her excitement genuine. "No way, let me see!" She rushes toward Peter, grabbing for the paper. During their early sessions, she would dress up a little, wearing her tiniest jean shorts and tightest camis—but after weeks of him actively avoiding looking at her, she started to give up, throwing on a cover-up after lying by the pool, her hair ratty and knotted from the sun, or strolling into their sessions still in her Devine's T-shirt after a shift at the store. Today she's in an oversize tank dress, the strings of her bikini pulling at her neck, the skin underneath stark white. She looks at his marks, the lack of red feeling new. She beams, throwing her arms around him, surprised when he reciprocates.

"I'm proud of you, kid." He pats her back and she feels her entire body tremble.

She steps back, realizing Kimmy is watching, and Erin walks toward her, waving the paper. "Take that, sissy. Devine family genius coming through."

Kimmy rolls her eyes, swatting the paper. "We'll see"—she looks at Peter—"if you can keep up your grades when boy wonder over there is gone."

That reality stings Erin more than she expects. Peter is leaving for his senior year at Penn tomorrow and she has no idea when he'll be back to visit. She isn't sure how to say goodbye to him, if they'll restart their IM sessions like they'd done the previous year now that he knows how young she is. But she does know one thing: She loves him. She is sure of it.

"Where are you off to?" Peter asks, taking in Kimmy's Rocky Cape Soccer T-shirt.

"First soccer scrimmage of the season," she says, and takes another sip of soda.

"You're going?" Erin asks, her eyes wide. "But I thought you and Brian were over?"

Kimmy shrugs. "We said we'd be friends." She looks at her feet for a second, then back at Erin. "And, I mean, I'm still friends with the whole team."

"You mean with Justin." Erin wiggles her eyebrows.

"Stop." Kimmy's voice is disarmingly serious. Erin senses her insecurity, her uncertainty about the whole situation. She senses her nerves, on edge in this new phase of singledom, of vulnerability. Kimmy has never done well with being vulnerable.

"Who's Justin?" Peter asks, piggybacking Erin's teasing. She loves when he does that. It makes it feel like they're a team, a real couple.

"He's no one." Kimmy glares at Erin. Peter understands the cue and turns, putting papers in his knapsack, rustling and zipping, his back to the sisters again.

Erin looks over her shoulder, then back at Kimmy, and puts her hand on her sister's arm. "Just tell him how you feel."

"Easier said than done, no?" Kimmy glances over at Peter. She gives Erin a pat on the head and walks down the stairs toward the back door.

Erin lifts her chin toward Peter, his backpack tight against his shoulders. "I can't believe you leave tomorrow." She crosses her arms against her chest.

"Yeah." Peter's hands grip the straps of his backpack. He's awkward; Erin can't tell if he's stalling saying goodbye or desperate to leave.

He looks young, so much so it emphasizes in Erin's mind that in a few more years their age difference would be a nonissue. "Can I walk you home?" She's surprised by her own forwardness—but he says yes, and she's happy she asked.

They're quiet as they walk down the stairs to the Devines' front door. Erin is ahead, and she holds the door open for Peter. He walks past and she breathes him in, freshly showered compared to her scent of sunscreen. She suddenly wishes she had dressed up a little more, done something special so his last memory of her isn't of the disheveled kid next door he tutors. His house is close, their walk less than a minute. When they get to his front door, Peter stands awkwardly, unsure what to do. Before she misses the chance, Erin gets on her tiptoes, puts her hands on Peter's cheeks, and kisses him. For a moment, she feels him kiss back, his hand rising to her cheek, and she feels like an adult, like the star of a romance movie about star-crossed lovers, her fantasy finally becoming reality. But then he pulls away, pushing her back gently.

"Erin." He has a scared look on his face and shakes his head.

"Just promise me we can still IM." Her fingers twist the bottom of her tank.

"Sure," Peter says, but he sounds noncommittal. He pats her on the top of her head, just like Kimmy did minutes before, like she's little more than a toy poodle in need of a scratch, then walks inside.

"This is weird." Kimmy's arm is twined through Nikki's. She sees Brian's parents in the stands, their eyeline on the field and not on her, thank god. "Like, do I say hi to the Accardis?"

"He's not fucking dead, Kimmy," Nikki laughs, brushing her hair behind her shoulders. Brian's parents are sitting with the Kasanaars, the Rollands, the Lambs, basically all the families with financial or political clout in Rocky Cape. They all wear crisp golf shirts or performance material tees, the wives in pristine visors and brightly patterned skorts. A few rows ahead, Kimmy spots Justin's parents, his dad's signature mustache impossible to miss. He's still wearing his Fitzpatrick Lawn Service T-shirt, proudly. The parents surrounding them are all more casual, in worn Rocky Cape Soccer shirts and cargo shorts. Nikki waves to the Fitzpatricks, and Mrs. Fitzpatrick gives a big whistle, with a wink. The noise grabs the Accardis' attention, and Kimmy makes eye contact with Brian's mom, giving her a weak smile. Nikki made Kimmy take off the oversize Rocky Cape Soccer shirt she was wearing and change into a similar ribbed tank top, just like Nikki's, which stretches tight against her stomach. She can't help but feel exposed, especially as Brian's mom watches her; she plays with the dangling iridescent shell earrings Nikki also lent her. She tells herself she doesn't care if his parents hate her now. But of course she does.

"Don't worry," Stevie whispers. "She has always been a little judgy." Stevie flanks Kimmy's other side, her two best friends providing both physical and emotional support. This is the first soccer game in a year she's been at not as Brian's girlfriend.

The field is nestled between the Oceanwind boardwalk and rows of houses, the outline of the famed Ferris wheel looming in the distance, the ocean waves just beyond. They grab seats on a stadium bench, the heat of the metal shocking the bottom of Kimmy's thighs. The stands are packed, parents smooshed on one side and students on the other, mostly organized by class. She sees Madison Jensen a few rows back, sitting with some girls from the dance team. She averts her eyes, not wanting to say hi; Erin told Kimmy that Madison was visiting her mom in Florida for the past month, so Kimmy's been able to avoid the occasional run-in at their house. Kimmy's not a fan of Madison, of the influence she's had on Erin; how vain they are together, taking endless photos and giving each other makeovers and talking about celebrities and designers nonstop. She hoped Erin would have realized how vapid Madison is by now, but her sister has always been too innocent, too generous with her evaluations of people's flaws.

Behind Madison, a handful of Kimmy's fellow soccer exes sit, the girlfriends of last season. Kimmy should be with them, clustered like widows, but she feels no connection to their sadness. In fact, she feels sorry for them. Despite all the ways the boys on this team have hurt them, they still come, still cheer them on, still hope maybe the sun will shine on them again. And that's definitely not why Kimmy's here.

Katie, wearing Derek's jersey, walks up the stadium stairs. "Hi," she says to Stevie, avoiding eye contact with Kimmy and Nikki. Kimmy knew Katie didn't like Nikki. *Her mom's a total floozy*, she told Stevie and Kimmy during a sleepover a few weeks ago. *I don't know why you want to associate with that.* But now Kimmy is part of that too, all because she broke up with Brian? Katie hadn't approved of Kimmy and Brian's breakup, had thought Kimmy was expecting too much of Brian. *He's an athlete*, she had said. *Soccer is his number one priority, but you're number two and that's all that matters.* Kimmy was also an athlete, she reminded Katie, and a better one than Brian. Katie dismissed this and told Kimmy she couldn't wait for her and Brian to get back together. That was two weeks ago; they still aren't together, and apparently that means Katie no longer wants to be associated with Kimmy. She pulls at the hem of her shirt again, covering a slice of bare belly as Katie walks by.

"God, what a fucking priss," Nikki says, her jaw jutting as she watches Katie's back.

"She's not so bad," Stevie says, convincing no one. "I think she's taking your breakup with Brian hard, Kimmy. We're, like, her only girlfriends."

"Wonder why," Nikki mutters, crossing her eyes in faux shock. Nikki understood it, how bored Kimmy had been near the end, how tiring all the chasing and preening and being available whenever Brian wanted was. How Kimmy craved a little adventure. "I don't think that girl has ever had a single original thought. She just repeats whatever her parents say, or Derek says, or whoever she deems socially acceptable. You're better off, if you ask me."

Kimmy laughs, resting her head on Nikki's shoulder. "Honestly, I never really liked her." But beneath her smile there's worry, her comfortable slot in the high school social hierarchy now shaky.

"Is that Aaron Roop?" Stevie changes the subject, pulling her sunglasses on as she looks across the field, actively avoiding any part of the green where she might accidentally make eye contact with Nick. Aaron is sitting on a bench by an assistant coach, his usually messy hair freshly shorn.

"Yeah." Nikki scrunches her eyes. "I think he started dealing once he got to campus last month and wants to tap into the high school market. He's more ambitious than he lets on, but greedy as fuck."

"Ugh, don't tell me that"—Stevie stares at him harder—"because honestly he looks sort of sexy? I don't think I realized before."

"Ooh," Kimmy teases, "suddenly she's a senior and she only wants college boys."

"Careful with that one," Nikki says, concern in her voice. "I've heard he's already gotten into some dark stuff on campus. Like opioids and shit."

Stevie ignores Nikki's warning and nudges Kimmy's side, shaking off the notion, but Kimmy sees she can't take her eyes off Aaron, his sharp features making her mind turn. Stevie always does this, turns what should be a small crush into an all-encompassing fixation. Kimmy knows to brace herself for at least four months of her talking about Aaron. It's the minimum timeline in Stevie's obsession cycle.

The game starts and Kimmy finds her eyes glued to Justin, to the numbers on his jersey, the ways his spandex clings to his thighs as his shorts ride up with each stride. The shape of his muscles makes her mind drift to one week earlier. They had spent the latter part of the summer running together every Friday morning. Kimmy did her long run since it was her day off from Devine's, but with Stevie's knee injury still mending, she had lost her running partner. She asked Brian first, but he claimed he was too tired from all the soccer camps he coached and summer leagues he played in. She asked Justin, who was free outside of helping his dad at the shop, because his parents couldn't afford the private soccer clubs Derek and Brian were part of, to join her instead. So every Friday morning, they met near the 97th Street Jetty and ran six miles, pushing each other to go faster, harder, their bodies glistening with sweat by the time they finished. She was always up front about it with Brian, who didn't seem that bothered, perhaps happy someone was keeping his girlfriend away from her phone, away from incessantly texting him during one of the busiest summers of his life. It was all completely innocent until their last run, when the temperature neared ninety-nine degrees by 8:00 a.m. They finished with a sprint, both their faces red with exhaustion, and Justin spoke first. "It's too fucking hot to do anything today."

Kimmy nodded, the idea of even lying on the beach unappealing. "All I want to do is strip and sit directly in front of an AC vent."

"That sounds like heaven," he said. "Let's do it."

"Strip?" she said, her brow raised, so used to Justin's crass comments she didn't even blink. He once told her her hands were so small they probably made Brian's dick look huge.

"Sit in front of an AC, perv. Stop trying to get in my pants." He gave her a friendly punch in the arm. "We can blast the air and watch a movie or something."

"I stink," Kimmy said, then bumped his side, giving an exaggerated sniff. "And so do you."

So they agreed. They would each go home and shower, then meet at Justin's.

It was her first time there alone, and she took in the scene, his house modest but cozy, couches worn, kitchen hues of yellow, proud pictures everywhere. His TV was in his room, which she hadn't expected. It was directly in front of his bed, perched on a dresser, so they each took a side, his window unit sweating on high. She gulped; she had never been in Brian's bedroom, nor he in hers. The opposite sex wasn't allowed outside of shared spaces at either the Accardi or the Devine household. Kimmy had worn her usual uniform of running shorts and a tank, and Justin was in a T-shirt and sweatpants. The moment she lay on his bed after he put the *Green Street Hooligans* DVD in the player, plenty of distance between their bodies, something changed. She knew, in that exact moment, she should go. Like, sprint out of there. Because there was an electricity, a current, pulling her toward him, one that must have always been there, sparking their close friendship despite her boyfriend, despite all the ways their personalities differed. But she had ignored it, buried it, pretended it didn't exist. Here, in his bed, it was undeniable. She gave him a side glance, his arms propped behind his head, his body flat against the bed, then found her eyes wandering south, and she immediately looked back at the TV, her cheeks hot. They didn't talk during the movie, the silence a rarity in their banter, making Kimmy all the more nervous. When Tommy Hatcher and his crew broke through the bar window more than halfway through the movie, Kimmy jumped, covering her eyes, and Justin laughed. "Wimp," he said, putting his arm around her and pulling her close, then giving her a noogie, his signature move. They settled into the position, Kimmy not pulling away, not wanting to. She rested her head on his chest, putting a hand on his stomach. He started rubbing her arm, his fingers trailing up and down. She circled her own fingers against his stomach. Their eyes were still on the movie, but Justin squeezed her closer, and Kimmy suddenly found her hand going flat, feeling Justin's chest through his shirt, the motion hungry. She tilted her head up at him and they made eye contact, unsure. He moved his hand from her arm to her outer thigh, the shock of him touching her skin enough to make her pulse all over. She pulled his right hip toward her, and suddenly he was on top, her hand on his upper thigh, just below his butt. He pushed toward her, his sweatpants against her running shorts not enough to keep her from feeling him, hard and ready. She let out a deep breath, not quite a sigh. His arms were on either side of her head, and she ran a hand up one, feeling his tricep. He pushed toward her again, and she put her hands around his neck, wanting to pull his face toward her, to make this real. But she paused, realizing what she was about to do, and dropped her hands, bringing one to her forehead, breaking eye contact. "We shouldn't," she said, but didn't mean it.

"I know," he said, still on top, still hard, still between her legs. "Fuuuuck." He rolled back to his side, both of them lying next to each other, staring up at the ceiling. By the time she got to her car, he had texted her: *download "waiting" by g love, listen to it cuz every word is 4 u.* She did as she was told, her voice caught in her throat as lyrics about maybe-requited love played from her computer speakers. Had Justin felt this way all year? How had she missed it? Because she felt it too; she couldn't ignore the inertia any longer.

She called Brian that night, her head a busy mess, and asked if they could meet, the first time they had physically been together in two weeks. They talked on a bench on Ninety-Sixth Street, right in front of the small mall housing T-shirt stores and a pizza shop. The conversation was so mundane, Kimmy hardly remembered the details. Just that they hugged at the end, a sad prolonged one of failure. Her parents were more upset than either of them. Her mom teared up, telling her baby to come in for a hug. Her dad shook his head, then said, "I liked that one." They spent the following morning tiptoeing around her, making her waffles with whipped cream and rubbing her back, adding encouraging words. She let them think she was upset, not ready to face the cold reality: she was relieved.

The ball goes out of bounds and Justin runs to the sideline across from the stands, grabbing it as the ref blows his whistle. He pauses, ball in hand, and waits as the ref hands a yellow card to the other team, his fingers gripping the shiny leather. The whole time he waits, he looks up at the stands, right at Kimmy. She feels his intensity all these feet away, staring right back. "He is totally eye fucking you," Nikki whispers, pinching Kimmy's thighs. The whistle blares, and like that, he's back in the game.

"Holy shit," Stevie says, nudging Kimmy's side. "I have never thought Justin was hot, but even I have to admit I would sleep with him after a look like that."

"Shut up, Stevie." Kimmy laughs and bumps her shoulder into hers. She agrees, though. She wants to sleep with Justin, the urgency of the feeling surprising. "Thank god it's just a scrimmage. That is not the way to win games." The three of them giggle, the flirtation of it all like sugar going to Kimmy's head. Two rows behind, Kimmy hears Katie clear her throat. She turns, and sees Katie glaring, and just behind her, Madison wears a similar look of judgment. Had they heard?

After the game, Kimmy lingers in the stands, just like she used to. "What are you doing?" Nikki asks, standing as if she were ready to leave.

"Justin asked me to meet him after," Kimmy says quietly, not wanting anyone to hear. Stevie is talking to some of their classmates,

Katie included, as the group walks toward the field, all of them used to meeting their boyfriends and friends by the locker-room door after games.

"Mmm," Nikki says, shaking her head. "No, not here. Unless you want to be the talk of the town." She grabs Kimmy's hand. "Follow me."

Kimmy hadn't thought about that, about what not just Brian would say, but other people at school. About getting a reputation. It wasn't something she had ever had to worry about, so she doesn't even know where to begin.

Nikki drags her to the parking lot, where they slide into Bev and Nikki plays Guster to calm Kimmy's heart rate. About a half hour later, the players start piling out and leaving in their respective cars. Kimmy looks at Nikki, who nods her head. "Good luck," she says. "Call me after." Kimmy squeezes her hand, knowing she will, even before she calls Stevie.

She walks over to Justin's car and leans against it, a rusty maroon sedan he had worked his ass off all summer to afford, its red like a warning she should listen to. Instead, she finds herself shyly smiling as he walks up, his hair wet from the postgame shower. The lot seems empty otherwise, and she gives him a small wave.

"Good game," she says, suddenly awkward, not sure how to act in this situation.

He's also shy, his entire demeanor new to her. They've never been in this position, one where Kimmy has finally admitted she has feelings for Justin too, at a time when they're both single, where they're allowed to explore their feelings with each other. Kimmy's heart is racing, a zillion thoughts streaming through her head. What if he doesn't feel the same about her? What if he just wants to be friends? Or what if they cross a line and it ruins their friendship? "I thought you left." He puts down his bag and opens his arms, giving her a hug. "Thanks for coming."

She breathes in his scent, a combination of Axe and cologne, his skin still hot from all the running. She presses her fingers into his back, tightening her hug. As she pulls away, she stops, her face inches from him, and looks up. *Fuck friendship*, she thinks. She doesn't care, doesn't want anything except to kiss him. He towers over her, and she locks her fingers around the back of his neck. "Hi," she whispers, smiling and arching up on her tippy-toes.

He pulls her waist closer, and they kiss, a soft gentle one that makes Kimmy almost pass out from anticipation. Her entire body tingles, and she forgets about everything, about worrying what people might think, how this might hurt Brian, how it might isolate her from her friend group. She kisses him harder, moving her hand to his cheek, and he presses his lips into hers, clutching the back of her shirt, months of anticipation charging their entire interaction. When they finally come up for air, her cheek against his, she whispers, "Do you want to drive around a little before you drop me off?"

Justin pulls back, his face slightly surprised, excited. "Yeah?" he says, his thumb rubbing the small of her back as she nods.

They park near the Point, where Kimmy climbs into the rear row of the car, pulling Justin with her, both of them fumbling to get out of their clothes, fogging the windows, rocking the car, the excitement of it all far more satisfying than the sex itself. After, Kimmy's body resting against his, her chin nestled into the crook of his neck, he whispers, "You're full of surprises, Legs." And she feels herself smile, liking this new attention. She wants to absorb him, to eat every inch of him so they're forever enmeshed, some chemical reaction making her feel like an addict. She is obsessed.

What neither of them realize is that in their blind infatuation, they didn't see Derek, mouth ajar, watching as Kimmy climbed into the passenger seat of Justin's car.

14

Beach Week 2022

DAY 3

The beach is crowded, groups of tourists and summer locals scattered for miles. Erin should be annoyed. But today their presence is the perfect distraction, her head spinning from last night with Peter. What the fuck is wrong with her? Why does she feel so horrible? He usually saves her, his presence a consistent support these past few months. But today, she feels dirty, impatient, ready to stop being his mistress; it's the first time she's really felt anxious while sleeping next to him, something about his tone during their ultimatum conversation concerning. She unfolds her beach chair, the move more aggressive than she anticipated, ancient grains of sand flying out of its crevices as it jerks open. She does the same to the second one, wriggling them both until they sit flat against the sand. She looks toward the 110th Street beach access nestled between the dunes and spots Kimmy, who Erin can already tell will look like a fitness model in her suit, despite her best attempts to hide her body with a high-waisted two-piece. Erin peeks at her own boobs and hips, their curviness feeling extra vampish in her high-cut string bikini compared to her sister's stick-thin figure. It makes her spiral even more, this idea that she's let the devil on her shoulder, the one goading her to break apart Peter's family, take full control. Would Peter like her as much if her body looked like Kimmy's? If he wasn't so mesmerized by the shape of Erin? She shakes the thought, waving down Kimmy instead. "Hey, slutface!" she shouts, and a few people on the beach turn their heads. Deflecting attention to Kimmy makes her feel better. One mom in the shade of a CoolCabana tent bristles, ushering a baffled-looking three-year-old closer. Kimmy looks mortified and picks up her pace, almost running to her sister.

"Did you really have to do that?" she asks, punching Erin's shoulder. But she's laughing, her mood light. Erin had texted her just before she got on the road from Philly at 9:00 a.m., asking if they could have a beach hang. Kimmy responded that she was walk-of-shaming from Justin's, and that she had seen Tess Cameron interviewing Madison Jensen to place a nanny. *How the mighty have fallen*, Kimmy typed. Erin started crying alone in her car at the mention of a nanny, the reminder that Peter had made a family—two young kids!—and she had not, despite her longing to. And that the nanny would likely be picked by Madison. Erin's guilt over everything that happened between her and Madison at the end of Erin's sophomore year was like a lingering headache, the trickle of pain persistent no matter how much Advil she took. Her entire drive home, she found herself tearing up on and off. When she pulled into her parents' driveway, both of them already at the store for the day, she texted Peter. *Let me know how the convo with Tess goes. Love you.* She left her phone in her room when she headed to the beach, wanting to clear her head and not spiral thinking about what Peter was doing at that very moment—if he was with Tess, with his kids, altering all their lives permanently. "God," Kimmy interrupts Erin's thoughts, "you have zero shame."

Erin puts on her best grin, hoping it hides the mess in her head. She feels held together by Scotch tape, ready to fall apart at any moment. She knows she needs to tell Kimmy about everything before Peter tells Tess, before the ripples of their decision cause a potential tsunami. She worries that Kimmy is going to judge her harshly; ever since high school, her sister has always been the sane, rational one, and here Erin is again causing chaos. After all, Kimmy is a finance superstar, whereas Erin lives with their parents and has failed at both being a wife and becoming a mother. Despite their ups and downs and glaring differences, though, Kimmy is Erin's person. She needs to vent, to quiet the nagging feeling in the pit of her stomach. But not yet, not before she and Kimmy ease into conversation; she doesn't want the reveal to feel like an affront. "I just call 'em like I see 'em," Erin says, motioning for Kimmy to sit in the chair next to her. "But please tell me you were, in fact, a slutface last night?"

"Er." Kimmy sits and leans toward her sister. She holds Erin's wrist, pulling her closer like she's the one about to disclose a scandal. "It was, like, god I don't even know where to begin. It was so much more than sex."

Erin should be concerned by her sister's earnestness, by the speed at which she's fallen back into Justin's arms, but instead she stays quiet. She's too tired, too hypocritical, and Kimmy deserves a little happiness, even if Erin doubts its longevity. She's glowing, the sun gleaming against her skin, which needs a little vitamin D after all those years in front of a computer, basking beneath fluorescent lights. Erin adjusts the arms on her chair, leaning all the way back. "Tan and talk." Her sunglasses are planted firmly on her face. She doesn't want to ruin Kimmy's bliss with her own problems; she just wants to close her eyes and listen. Kimmy reclines too, their positions just like their beach hangs in high school. The chatter of families around them hums, portable speakers blasting oldies, seagulls calling for their next meal, the ocean bursting against the sand over and over. The cacophony soothes her, at least for a moment. It's her zen, her therapy. She almost zones out, when she hears Kimmy say, "It's like all this time, we should have been together, you know? It's so right."

She nods, not looking at Kimmy. She knows, because it's what she thinks every time she's with Peter, the way he looks at her so different from how Kent did. There's a desperation, like she's the missing puzzle piece in his life. She adores being needed, especially after so many years of the opposite. Erin watches a seagull circle a kid eating a sandwich, the bird ready to swoop in the moment the kid lets down his guard. She takes a deep breath, concentrating on the action, not wanting to look at Kimmy.

"Er, are you okay?" Kimmy scooches her chair closer and flicks Erin's forehead. "Hello? Earth to Erin?"

Erin turns to Kimmy and pulls down her sunglasses, her eyes

squinting. "I heard you, idiot. But do you really think it's a good idea to get involved with Fitzy again? Honestly, I thought it was just gonna be, like, a wham-bam-thank-you-ma'am thing."

"Gross." Kimmy makes a face. "I don't think it can ever be that casual with us."

"Mmm." Erin pushes her sunglasses back on and rolls onto her back, her face pointed at the sky again.

"What?" Kimmy asks, her voice growing tense. "Just fucking say whatever you have to say. I can handle it."

Erin takes a deep breath, jutting her jaw forward before she speaks. "I'm having an affair with Peter Cameron." She can't look at Kimmy, clutching the ends of her chair's arms as she waits for a reaction.

"How long?" Kimmy is weirdly calm, but the lightness in her voice has evaporated.

"Um." Erin takes off her sunglasses, propping them on the top of her head. She cups a hand over her eyes and turns to face Kimmy. "A little over a year."

"Fuck, Erin, what were you thinking?" Kimmy doesn't even look angry, just disappointed. Erin thinks she might even see a hint of disgust. Her brows arch inward, concerned. "Sorry, sorry. I am not blaming you. Did it start in high school?"

Erin shakes her head adamantly. "He was actually, like, really particular about that."

"Of course he was." Kimmy's delivery makes it clear that Erin had definitely detected disgust.

"Why are you not freaking out?" Erin had expected a big reaction from Kimmy, whose post–high school morals sometimes err on the side of pious. "Did someone say something?" Erin feels both caught and relieved, her secret no longer just hers and Peter's.

"Sister's intuition, I guess," she says. "Tess said Peter was in Philly last night, and your coyness about post-divorce dating and the way you totally bailed on Bluefish. Well, it all clicked." Kimmy puts a hand on Erin's arm. "How did it start?"

"We hooked up once in college, but then not at all for a really long time, obviously. But the seeds were there. They always had been." A whistle blows in the distance, one of the red-clad lifeguards dramatically motioning for a swimmer to return to the shoreline. Kimmy's attention shifts toward the commotion, and Erin has a chance to really study her expression. It's pained, annoyed, worried as she pulls up her sunglasses, turning back to Erin, waiting for more. Erin lets out a fake wail, her tongue poking through her lips. "Bleh," she says, trying, like she always does, to avoid diving deeper into exploring her betrayal, her sadness, but Kimmy doesn't let her. She keeps staring, expectant. "Fine, okay. When Kent and I broke up and I moved home, I was lonely. Like, deeply, depressingly lonely. All I wanted was a family—like we have, you know?" She sees Kimmy's eyes flicker in agreement before turning cold again. "And in a matter of months that picture in my head was shattered not only with Kent, but maybe forever. I still don't know if I'll be able to have kids—"

"Oh, Er," Kimmy says, softening. "You will. There are so many options—"

"Stop, no," Erin says, putting up her hand. "I don't want to get into that right now. Basically, all you need to know is I was very, very alone. Every time I tried to FaceTime you, you were busy. Mom and Dad were, like, my only friends. And I knew Peter was occasionally in the area. I reached out, not him. I started this."

"This is so fucked up, Erin." Kimmy purses her lips, crosses her arms, then catches the look on Erin's face. "On Peter's part, I mean. You didn't start this. He did, when you were a tiny, barely teenage baby. The fact that you don't even see that is what bothers me the most."

"You don't get it, Kimmy. After Kent, after my miscarriage, I just felt empty. And Peter reignited this flame in me. Like, I needed him to pull me out of my darkness." She smiles to herself, but stops when she sees Kimmy's skepticism.

"Does Tess know?" Kimmy raises an eyebrow.

"About me and Peter? No." Erin puts her sunglasses back on.

"Okay, good. We should keep it that way. This could get really messy, you know that, right?" Kimmy leans toward Erin, her eyes worried.

"I don't care." Erin shakes her head. "I am so tired of lying. I am ready to blow this all up. Like, I just can't deal with it anymore." She pauses. "I gave him an ultimatum last night."

"No," Kimmy starts. "You didn't. Come on, Erin."

"God, let me just fucking finish before you throw your judgmental shit in my face." Erin's voice is now loud. "I don't feel good today. I feel horrible. Like, what am I doing? And what is he doing? We need to stop sneaking around. We need to just tell Tess so we can be together."

"Have you thought about anyone but yourself in this situation?" Kimmy hisses, her irritation growing. "Like Tess and Peter's kids? Or Mom and Dad and their entire business? People talk, Er. It's a small fucking town and they talk and take sides and don't want to associate with scandal."

"No one local even knows who Peter is," Erin says, her voice quiet again.

"Well, if there's one thing this town has taught me, it's that no one likes a homewrecker." Kimmy's big-sisterness is in full force. "No wonder Mom and Dad asked me to run the store. You're a mess."

Erin's face suddenly turns angry. This was the Kimmy she hated. What was wrong with her? She was always judging, always perfect, never looking at her own reflection. "How is it different with you and Justin? Same shit, different guy."

"Not the same shit, Erin. He's not married. We're not sneaking around. We're not lying. Our relationship isn't based on a dirty foundation."

"Oh, please. *I'm Kimmy Devine and I'm sooo fucking perfect*," Erin taunts. "You don't get to come home after years away and act like you are some sage with amazing relationship advice. You don't get to tell me my relationship is fucked up when you're literally diving back into the relationship that made you run away and kept you away from all of us for years. You don't get to just come and take over the store when I'm the one who's been there every single day for the past two years, who's worked my ass off helping Mom and Dad launch a fucking e-commerce store during the pandemic. When you were completely and totally MIA, mind you." Erin is crying now, her face a wet mix of sunscreen and abandonment.

"You don't get to do this, Kimmy. You don't get to be the perfect one and highlight all my flaws. I need your support, not your fucking judgment." She's almost hyperventilating now.

"Whoa," Kimmy says, rubbing her shoulder. "I'm sorry, Er. I didn't—" She closes her eyes for a few beats. "Being back here has been disorienting. In the span of a few days, it's like I never left. It's weird, how this place does that to you." She looks back at Erin. "We'll figure out the thing with Peter, okay? I'll support whatever you want to do, really. But the store. You never mentioned you wanted a bigger role there. Do Mom and Dad even know?"

Erin shrugs. "They never asked."

"God," Kimmy says, looking at her sister. "You don't have to keep everything inside for months and months and then explode. I am always here to talk."

"But you weren't, for so long," Erin says, looking her sister up and down.

"I am now, Erin." Kimmy pulls her sister close for a hug, a reminder to Erin that she's really there. For good. "It will all be okay."

Erin looks into Kimmy's eyes. And for the first time in almost three years, she actually believes it.

15

September 2006

Wisps of smoke rise from the flickering blue-orange flames at the center of the firepit. They float above a pile of artificial rocks, Nikki's worried gaze on the gas level's control button with uncharacteristic focus. She's dog sitting for a seasonal widow with a classic Rocky Cape McMansion, three floors crowded by porthole windows and WINE O'CLOCK signs. Nikki had taught her how to surf over the past few weeks—and, in turn, the woman trusted Nikki with her multimillion-dollar home. So of course Nikki invited her friends over. It was a small gathering, only a handful of kids crowding the backyard, Rocky Cape's wealthier corners no place for massive underage ragers. A harmonica run trills from a portable speaker, G. Love's *Lemonade* album on permanent repeat since it was released the month before. The houses on either side are dark, closed for the season like much of the town. It's Kimmy's favorite time of year, Rocky Cape transitioning from overrun to peaceful in the weeks before the leaves turn. She mouths "Relax" to Nikki, who's staying sober to make sure nothing insane happens, and takes a sip of the vodka Sprite filling the red Solo cup in her hand.

She hasn't hooked up with Justin since that first time a week ago, right before school started. Kimmy isn't sure what the sex meant. Are they friends with benefits? Dating? Together? The unknowing doesn't bother her, though; she trusts Justin. He's one of her best friends, the peanut butter to her jelly. (He'd dubbed that their friendship slogan the previous year; he even put a little *pb&j* in his AIM profile while she was dating Brian.) That won't vanish overnight. Their classmates, though, have other ideas.

Kimmy tried on eleven outfits the night before her first day of senior year, a ritual she'd previously left to Erin. When nothing felt right, she walked into Erin's room, hands full of camis. "Help," she said, her expression pleading. "I hate all my clothes."

Erin was on her computer, like always, and spun her chair around. "No," she said. "Last time you borrowed a T-shirt, your sweaty pits stained it."

"Er, come on." Kimmy put her hands in a praying position. "I'll wear extra deodorant. Seriously."

"Fine." Erin walked to her closet and riffled through messy piles. "This is cute, but also still you." She tossed Kimmy a black T-shirt with *Bebe* written in gems across the chest.

"This looks like it would fit Thumbelina," Kimmy said as she held it up.

"It's supposed to be tight, prude. Wear a push-up with it. It's literally the whole point." Erin walked back to her desk, eyes on her IMs. "Bye." She waved Kimmy away.

School itself was weird. She saw Brian on her walk to homeroom, a slight ache rising when she realized she couldn't just grab his hand. They exchanged polite hellos, and for a moment she felt a longing she hadn't anticipated. It immediately disappeared moments later when she spotted Justin, who pinched her side as he walked past. He texted her just before first period. *Lookin sexy legs.*

By Wednesday, though, her mood had changed. On the drive home from school, Erin, in the passenger seat, turned to Kimmy. "Did you have sex with Justin Fitzpatrick?" She asked it matter-of-factly, like she was repeating a critical event in history class.

"What?" Kimmy kept her eyes on the road. "Where did you hear that?" Her stomach dropped and she felt Erin watching her, trying to read her reaction.

"I don't know," Erin mumbled, looking out her window. Her mouth twitched, but all she said was, "Just people."

"No," Kimmy heard herself lie. "We're just friends."

She texted Justin that night. *People at school are talking. Can we keep things between us for now? Sort of worried about fallout with Brian.* Her heart raced as she texted. Why did anyone care what she and Justin did? Why was it any of their business? Still, she didn't want them ruining things with gossip.

yeah brah, he answered almost immediately. *but I stand by my earlier text sexy legsy*

You are so lame, she responded, smiling.

Now he's next to her, their thighs brushing, the atmosphere hot, dangerous, whispering like anything could happen. Tristan Prettyman's voice pours out of the speaker, her duet with G. Love Kimmy's favorite on the album. Maybe because Justin had deemed it their song after first listen. He moves his hand behind Kimmy, leaning into her as he whispers the lyrics about wasting time and finding each other. Kimmy turns to him, their noses less than an inch apart. They whisper at the same time the line about peanut butter and jelly, about all the ways they fit. She's buzzed, leaning her head on Justin's shoulder. They're not in school, not surrounded by the people who might talk. Like Derek, who she learned had started the entire rumor about her and Justin at school when he confronted Justin in the locker room after soccer practice that week, Brian by his side. "I denied everything," Justin promised Kimmy, ignoring that he had denied their relationship before she had asked him to. It didn't matter, though; she felt people's eyes on her all week, their perception shifting.

"Hey." Justin brushes her hair away from her ear. Kimmy shivers, the sensation of his lips so close to her skin making all sorts of things swoon. "Want to go for a walk on the beach?" She nods, looking him in the eyes as she puts her hand in his. He pulls her away from the firepit and toward the beach access next to the property, their friends watching, but no one says a thing. When their feet hit the sand, the sky cloudless above and sparkling with stars, Justin stops in front of an abandoned lifeguard boat; only a few more weeks left before they're put in storage for the winter.

"I've been dying to do this all night." He holds her face in his palms and leans down, his lips brushing Kimmy's. They taste of beer and salt; she craves more. She kisses back and he lifts her, her feet dangling inches above the ground. She pulls at his lip, then presses her nose against his. "Have you ever gone skinny-dipping?" she asks, her smirk glowing in the moonlight. This is what Justin does to her; he encourages an impulsiveness that borders on recklessness.

"Never with my best friend," he says, his finger weaving under the seam of her shirt. "Or at least a best friend who's this fucking hot."

She presses a hand on his waistband, sneaking her fingers between his skin and the elastic. His eyes move toward her belt loops and his fingers fumble as they unbutton her jeans, which he slides down her legs. When they're finally on the ground, Justin stands back up, and Kimmy raises an eyebrow, then grabs his waistband again and pantses him. She turns and runs toward the ocean, the cool night air kissing her bare skin. "You're gonna get it, Legs!" she hears Justin say behind her, his gait gaining. "Not so fast." He reaches for the strap of her thong, pulling her toward him, and puts his hand on the other side of her underwear, inching it down as he brings her hips into his. They kiss again and she unclasps her bra, letting it fall to the ground. Justin scoops her into his arms, walking both of them toward the ocean. When they hit the water, the chill against Kimmy's hot skin shocks her chest like sipping a Slushee too fast. She gasps, her breath short for a moment, as Justin lowers her legs into the water, which rises to her chest. She feels him hard and circles her arms around his neck, her legs around his waist, letting him slide inside. They both close their eyes, clinging to each other as Kimmy moves up and down, her chest pressed against his, their bodies shining in the moonlight.

"Oh my god," she says, her collarbone splotchy with desire. Justin makes a deep moan, and Kimmy feels him come with a telltale pulse.

"Fuuuck." Justin lifts Kimmy off and turns her back toward him. "Sorry," he says, his breath heavy against her cheek. "I couldn't help myself." He kisses her neck, one hand draped across her shoulder and cupping her breast, his fingers circling a nipple, and the other hand racing lower until it's almost inside, pressed right where it should be, Kimmy shivering from both the chill of the ocean and Justin's accuracy. There's silence, then breathless gasps, and then a singular one from Kimmy, her head collapsing back into Justin.

"This," he says, whispering in her ear, both arms around her shoulders, "has been well worth the fucking wait." She laughs, everything inside her on fire. They walk out of the water holding hands, dark silhouettes to anyone peering out from the houses hiding just beyond the dunes.

"Can you imagine if this was our life? Like, always?" she says, looking at him.

"What do you mean?" He squeezes her hand. "You wanna join a nudist colony together?"

"Stop." She swats his arm with her free hand. "I mean just together, having sex whenever we wanted, no strings, no worries. Just pure fun." A few months ago, she never would have predicted this. There's still a part of her that wonders how she's attracted to Justin, what it is about him that has her so hooked. He's goofy, ridiculous in a zillion wrong ways. But she can't help herself, something about him is irresistible. "This just feels right," she says, her voice a whisper. "And I never would have guessed it could be."

He's quiet, his hand still in hers. "You're one of my best friends, you know that."

She nods. "Peanut butter jelly," she mumbles back, her lips swollen.

"I just—" he starts, when they suddenly see a body in the distance shouting his name.

"Shit," Kimmy says, both of them scrambling for their clothes. Kimmy goes right toward the dark pile on the beach, her tank and jeans close enough she can sneak into them before they're caught. Justin's right behind her, scurrying into his shorts and shirt.

"Fitzy. Yo, where you at, man?" Ryan is on the beach, his voice growing. "Dude," he says as he gets close to the boat. "Madison won't stop calling your phone. So we picked up and she's real banged up, man, like crying and super drunk, threatening to walk over to the house. You gotta go deal with this, Nikki is freaking out. She doesn't want to draw attention or get in trouble with the owner."

"God damnit," Justin says, the moment broken.

"Madison, as in my sister's friend Madison Jensen?" Kimmy asks, no one paying attention to her. It all starts making sense, the few times she saw them together in the hall last school year, Justin's weird knowledge of chickish pop culture, his caginess when Kimmy asked him about his love life all summer, why Erin would have probed Kimmy about something with Justin. She thought he was having a fling with a shoobie, not a monthslong hookup with someone at their school. "Hello," she says. "Justin, what the hell. Are you dating her?"

"I'm coming man, just give me a sec," Justin says to Ryan, who pushes the phone into his hand, Madison's name blared across the front, a picture of the two of them on the caller ID screen. The ringtone is "Sunshine" by G. Love. Their G. Love. Kimmy suddenly feels sick, the combination of alcohol and sex and new information disorienting. What the fuck was going on? "I have to go deal with this. I—" He stops. "We've been hooking up for a while. It's nothing official, okay? It was before us, that's all." He kisses Kimmy on the forehead, his finger trailing the edge of her jaw.

Kimmy nods, wanting to believe him. But then Justin turns and runs after Ryan, and she hears him pick up the phone, saying, "Babe, slow down." His voice trails in the distance and she's left on the beach, alone.

16

Beach Week 2022

DAY FOUR

Stevie stands at the front door of the Devines' house shifting her weight from one hip to the other. It's been ages since she was at this very spot, typically reserved for those not in the Devines' closest circle. She had entered through the side door for most of her life, running up from the dock on the bay with Kimmy by her side, Erin in their wake, giggling and sopping wet, Carissa yelling at them to towel off before they tornadoed through the house. They're not those girls anymore, though; technically, they're not even friends. But they're family.

Her parents divorced her freshman year of high school. Shortly after she graduated, her dad moved to Hilton Head with one of her mom's summer friends, a widow with plenty of money, so he could continue to be little more than a mooch. Neither Stevie nor her big brother, Joey, had talked to him since he made the move. In truth, they used it as an excuse to do what they wanted to for so many years: to cut him and his coldness out of their lives. He wasn't outright mean, he was just selfish. Their success was about him and his reputation. Their mom's kindness was her greatest flaw, her inability to see how he was never thinking about much beyond himself, how his own desires drove every single decision he made. He didn't even come to her wake, sending a heinous floral wreath to the funeral home that said, simply, "Condolences." Their mom would have hated it.

It took losing her mom almost a year ago for Stevie to realize how important the Devines were in her life. After the funeral, Joey and Stevie stayed at their mom's apartment, in the space above the Flower Box, the two of them watching home videos, laughing and crying all at once. He flew back to Colorado days later, and Stevie, as executor, was left alone, picking up the pieces of her mom's life as well as that of the store. There were moments it felt unbearable, the emotional heaviness of tackling all the paperwork and legalese without her mom, her best friend, by her side. It wasn't until Carissa and Erin showed up on her doorstep, casseroles in hand, that her world felt manageable. They were here, they reminded her. They were always here for her.

She and Erin started going for short weekly walks, keeping conversation light by focusing on celebrity gossip and *Real Housewives* plotlines. They never talked about Kimmy, never went down that road, and Stevie was grateful for it. She cherished their friendship, the nostalgia that came with rekindling their relationship—it felt like a blessing to have grown apart only to grow back together, and she didn't want old drama ruining that.

Then Aaron moved back to Rocky Cape a few months ago.

He looked the same, albeit aged. But age only made his features more enthralling to Stevie, sharp and jagged, rock candy she wanted to lick. They got drinks to catch up. She couldn't believe how easy it was, how quickly they fell into a playful banter. She went down on him that night, his back arched against the slide on the Eighty-Sixth Street playground. They were too old—are too old—for that shit, but she loved it. She felt alive again, for the first time since she lost her mom.

She was surprised at the speed of their relationship, how soon he became a fixture in her life. He gave her a key to his place just as people were taking down their holiday decorations, his presence making the winter chill bearable.

Those first months were bliss. Business at the shop was slow minus the occasional winter wedding, and the club where Aaron bartended was closed, so they spent their days lazily lounging in bed, watching bad TV, wrapped in each other. She cooked for him, elaborate meals she found in cookbooks by Ina Garten and Jamie Oliver. They complained about their dads, their continued absence lingering salt in the wounds they'd already given them. They watched indie and foreign films Aaron recommended, Stevie feeling like they were a super artsy and unique duo. They were a real couple. In love.

But in June, when Stevie was in the throes of wedding season and overworked, she came home to find Aaron asleep with his phone on his lap, his head arched to the side, body slumped into the couch. The screen glowed with Instagram notifications. She hadn't realized Aaron had one, had always thought it wasn't his thing. After making sure he was fully asleep, she picked up his phone, holding it up to his face to unlock—and that's when she saw it, an Instagram feed filled with shots of girls in skimpy bikinis and thirst traps. His inbox blared red, over fifty unread notifications. He snored loudly, spooking Stevie; she dropped the phone by his side on the couch, brushing it off by telling herself guys will be guys.

Then Erin told Stevie that Kimmy was coming home. Not just visiting. Moving home, permanently. It was the first time her name had been uttered during their walks, and Stevie knew it was time to read the letter Kimmy had sent her when her mom died. It had been stashed away in a desk drawer since it arrived. The loss of her mom had felt too fresh then. She didn't want to add the stress and sadness of her history with Kimmy on top of it all. She slit it open and started reading. Kimmy had never been much of a writer, so it was little more than a collection of her favorite memories of Stevie's mom: the time she let them slide down the stairs between the Flower Box and their apartment on a sled; the time they snuck into her liquor cabinet, and when she caught them, made them a "proper" cocktail so they knew better than to drink the bad stuff; her affinity for adding chocolate chips to their freshly popped popcorn on movie nights; the way she made them flower crowns whenever they had a bad day. Stevie started crying as she read, laughing as tears wet her cheeks. Aaron walked in at that moment and asked what she was reading. When she told him, he rolled his eyes and tried to snatch it. "Why are you trying to revisit the past, Stevie?" But she held the letter to her chest, like a talisman.

Seeing Kimmy in person at Bluefish a few nights ago ripped open something inside Stevie. It seemed nostalgia had hit Kimmy as hard during the pandemic as it had hit Stevie. She felt the warmth in her approach, the way the two picked up like they had left off, save for their massive blowup. The fight Aaron had caused. It felt good, like the hole left behind when Stevie's mom died didn't have to loom so large, like she could have her sister back. When they went to the bathroom together, several drinks in, Stevie felt Kimmy watching her as they washed their hands. Boldly, Stevie turned and looked right at her—and for the first time, she saw what she had missed all those years ago. Fear.

"Aaron is not a good guy," Kimmy said, cornering Stevie. She didn't want to hear what Kimmy had to say, though, and she shook her head, wanting it to stop. "I have had years and years of therapy to process all the shit that happened in high school. Like, expensive-ass therapists. And I finally have the language and the mental capacity to openly talk about what he did to me—"

Stevie shook her head harder, turning the faucet off. "Stop," she said, quietly at first.

"You know I never would have betrayed you." Kimmy reached her arm out to touch Stevie.

"Stop," Stevie said again, this time louder. She pushed past Kimmy, out the bathroom door. She couldn't hear it, didn't want to. There had been whispers about Aaron for as long as she knew him, increasingly dark after he graduated from high school. The worst one was that, in addition to opioids, he dealt roofies for a few years. Stevie asked him about it when they started dating, hoping it wasn't true. He was honest, albeit vague, claiming he sold a lot of things he regretted, but promising he never used them himself. That forced confession gave Stevie an excuse to ignore his past, erase it. As she looked at Kimmy in the bathroom, she thought, *How desperate am I?* Despite all their years apart, she knew Kimmy, her tics and facial expressions. She wasn't lying.

Stevie rushed toward Aaron, blaming an upset stomach, then straight to her bike. She needed air. She needed to think. She pedaled and ped- aled, right to Aaron's house. When she got to his cottage, a small rental about a mile inland, she didn't know what she was looking for. Pictures, mementos, a diary. Anything to prove Kimmy was wrong. She tried to log on to Aaron's computer, but had no idea what his password was. She opened dresser drawers, carefully riffling through. She opened his closet, sifting through racks of clothes and shoeboxes on the floor. She spun around, not sure where to look next, when her eyes landed on Aaron's bookshelf. Stevie ran her hand along the spines. Hemingway, Philip Roth, David Foster Wallace. She noticed there were two copies of *Infinite Jest*—a hardcover and a paperback—which seemed odd. She pulled out the hardback, which was uncharacteristically pristine, and she quickly realized the pages were glued together. She shook the book, and something inside clattered. She lifted the front cover, and inside the book's hollowed core sat two pill bottles. Frozen, Stevie stared at them, caps still tightly closed on both. She put the book flat on the bookshelf and picked a bottle up, looking for a prescription of any kind, but it lacked a label, so she screwed it open, tossed a few pills in her pocket, and put it all back exactly where she found it.

At home, she lay in bed, looking up at the ceiling, the lightbulb in her fan flickering like it was about to go out. She pulled out her phone and texted Erin. *Can I come over tomorrow? I need to talk to you about something. Alone.*

So she's here, at the Devines', about to meet with Erin, purposely coordinating their get-together during a time when the house is empty. Of the Devine parents, but mainly of Kimmy. Stevie raises her fist to the front door and knocks three times. Almost immediately, Erin opens the door. "Hey," she says, her hair wet, likely from a swim in the bay. Bill Devine and his daughters are famous for circling it, their long arms crawling and legs fluttering as their bodies trace the edge. So much changes, yet so much stays the same. Erin gives Stevie a butts-out hug, leading her through the entry foyer. "I thought we could meet in my room." Erin turns, adding, "Kimmy's not here, but just in case . . ." Her voice trails off. Stevie nods, but Erin's back is to her as she leads Stevie down the hallway she used to know so well, the one that houses Erin and Kimmy's rooms, as well as the movie room they spent so many hours in as kids. They walk past the door to Kimmy's room and Stevie is tempted to pause, to stick her head in and see what's changed. Instead, she walks past and follows Erin into her room.

"Oh wow," Stevie says as she takes in the room, the pink ceiling and shag rug replaced with a cool seafoam green and a hardwood floor. "This is totally different."

"Yeah." Erin shrugs, her arms crossed in awkwardness. "The parentals renovated a few years ago. You know Carissa; she's never one to let things get musty."

Stevie remembers Carissa's attention to detail—how she was always tweaking the décor in the house, especially when they were teens, her need for control relegated to fabric swatches and throw pillows when the girls started thinking and acting for themselves. The memory is not enough to shake Stevie's tenseness. This feels different than their walks, the intimacy of being in Erin's room, back in this house, more overwhelming than Stevie anticipated.

"So you'll never believe this," Erin says as she sits on the edge of her bed, "but Kimmy's getting a pedicure because she has a date tonight. With Justin Fitzpatrick."

"Those two could never seem to keep away from each other," Stevie says, a little smile on her face. "Not surprised at all." Erin watches her look at the closed bedroom door. "And your parents?"

"At the Callahans' for Beach Week cocktails or something. Honestly, I'm not sure." They pause awkwardly. "So, not to be blunt, but what's up? Your text was super cryptic and sort of freaked me out."

"I'm just—" She pauses, her bottom lip quivering. Stevie suddenly regrets coming here, her sightline drifting back to the door. She is being crazy, overthinking the situation. That's all. She should just go home, make up some excuse, and speed walk to her house.

"Stevie." Erin's voice reassures her, a reminder that this isn't some random person. It's Erin Devine, the little sister she's always wanted, the person she could always share her darkest thoughts with. She won't judge, Stevie knows, and that is rare in this town.

"God, I don't even know where to begin. And maybe I'm just being one hundred percent insane." She sits across from Erin on the edge of the bed. "So I ran into Kimmy at Bluefish the other night." Erin nods, like she's already heard this. Of course she has; Stevie imagines Erin lounging on her belly across Kimmy's bed, Kimmy twirling in her desk chair as she recaps her night. When they were kids, Stevie would have been lying right next to Erin, enraptured by all of Kimmy's experience, the confidence she had when recounting a seventh-grade dance or AIM conversation with a crush. "We were getting along, really. Like old times, almost like all these years hadn't passed and none of the high school shit went down. It was nice."

"Aw, I knew this day would come. It's about fucking time." She smiles, and Stevie winces, her forehead creasing, dreading what she's about to say next.

"Okay, well hold off on popping the champs, because it sort of went south." She crinkles her nose as she takes in Erin's expression of resigned annoyance. "We had a few drinks and then went to the bathroom together, as you do," Stevie says. "And when we were in there, Kimmy sort of cornered me and got all serious and told me Aaron wasn't a good guy and I shouldn't be with him. It felt like history repeating itself."

"Okay." Erin leans against her comforter.

"I just turned around and sort of ran away from her. But instead of going to my place, I rode to Aaron's. I don't know what I was looking for, but something about the way Kimmy said things this time just felt real. Like, you don't talk about someone that way fifteen years later unless something was actually fucked up. And I thought, *What did I miss?* Because I had to be missing something. And I knew he'd be at the party all night. You know how him and Derek and all those guys are at these things. Fucking idiots."

Erin nods, sitting more upright and crossing her arms. Stevie realizes Erin doesn't actually know, though, because Erin never really hangs out with them, seems to actively avoid that crowd since moving home, now that she thinks about it. Her nerves pick up and she's talking fast, her cheeks splotchy. "So I go into his house and just sort of peruse, like blindly, I guess. And I found these hidden in a hollowed-out book." She unzips her purse and pulls out a sandwich bag with a handful of small white pills powdering the bottom.

"Oh, shit." Erin holds the bag, looking at it close. "What are these? Ativan?"

"Is that what they are?" Stevie asks. Stevie remembered Kent's start-up did something with packaging prescription pills and hoped a fraction of his knowledge had been passed on to Erin before they split.

"See these?" She points to the imprint of some letters on one side and numbers on the other. "I'm pretty sure that's what it is. Does Aaron have insomnia? Or anxiety?" Erin holds the pills up to her eyes. "It's not weird to have, but it is weird to hide them in a carved-out book."

"Not that I know of." Stevie sighs, looking up at the ceiling. "And I mean, there wasn't a prescription on the bottle. That's weird, right? Do you think he's dealing? He used to in college."

"Um." Erin puts the pills on the bed and places a hand on Stevie's. "I think you have to talk to him."

"Do you think he did something to Kimmy?" Stevie asks, inching closer. She wants Erin to say no, to tell her it's all fine, it's all in her head, that Kimmy's just overreacting.

"I honestly don't know." Erin smooths her hands against her thighs. "Kimmy wasn't herself that year, especially at the end. That's really all I know."

"The things I said," Stevie whispers, the memories rushing back. It's still seared in Stevie's head, the fight they had in the school cafeteria, the way Kimmy seemed to go blank, taking every insult as if she deserved it.

"Yeah," Erin says, raising her brows. "I'm not going to pretend you were Mary fucking Poppins."

"What do I do? Do I ask her about it again?" Stevie takes a deep breath, hoping it quells the tangled feeling in her chest. She fucked up, all those years ago. She sees it now, how her petty jealousy blinded her to the truth, to being there when her best friend needed her most.

"Um," Erin says, stumbling over her words again, "honestly, there's a lot going on in our house you don't even know about."

Is that why Kimmy moved home? Stevie wonders. How much she's missed over these past fifteen years . . . Kimmy's life a strange mystery. She wants to hold Kimmy in her arms and whisper apologies over and over and over until it absolves their past, to time travel to 2007 and right all her wrongs. She wants to be there for her. "I don't want to add to Kimmy's stress. Maybe start with Aaron and go from there? It could be nothing."

Stevie stops when Erin puts a finger to her mouth. They hear the front door open and close, then footsteps going up the stairs. They're both quiet, waiting for the door to burst open, but they only hear silence.

"Kimmy?" Erin shouts, hiding the pills under her mattress. When no one answers, she whispers to Stevie, "I'll keep these here for now until you figure shit out, okay?"

Stevie nods, swallowing hard. "This is a nightmare."

Erin looks at her. "Is anything involving Aaron, you, and Kimmy not a nightmare?"

Stevie gives her a look, then picks up her purse. "Don't tell Kimmy, please?" Stevie's eyes plead, her contrition obvious. "I want to fix this myself. To fix us myself."

Erin nods as she walks Stevie to the front door, waving as Stevie turns the corner. She returns to her room, throwing her body on her bed and digging her face into her comforter. And she screams, the sound stifled by layers of down filling.

Thanks for coming. I needed you more than I realized.

I will always be here for you. Whether you want me or not. But you shouldn't have to do this alone.

Kent's Kent, you know? I'm trying to respect all the stuff he has going on at work. I don't want to add more stress to it.

I'm not sure I would call scheduling a business trip while your wife gets a D&C the appropriate approach to handling stress. And who's worried about your stress?

You.

And I always will be. But you're allowed to have more than your family in your corner. You're allowed to let other people in. You're allowed to want more love in your cup, sweetheart.

You sound like a fucking Hallmark card. Pass me the remote. Speaking of, wanna watch Hallmark?

17

November 2006

Their medals glisten atop their bags stuffed in the backseat of Madison's car, light splintered across the highway as Madison pays the toll on the drive from Philly to Rocky Cape. Erin's hair is still plastered with glitter spray, her lips doused in bright red gloss, cheeks and muscles sore from smiling and dancing. The team's first competition of the season was in Philly that afternoon, their leotards and jazz shoes now smooshed in their bags. Madison and Erin had done a lyrical duet, their choreography practiced all fall. And it showed. They were both proud, both grinning ear to ear when they won. Neither one had parents in the audience to watch; Erin's are at a trade show in New York and Madison's are generally MIA these days. But Erin didn't care, because Peter was there.

Things had been weird ever since she kissed him three months earlier. He was always on AIM, but rarely IM'd her, the absence of their conversations like drinking caffeine-free coffee, the taste unchanged, but the buzz—the reason for drinking coffee to begin with— completely gone. She told him about her dance competition in Philly and he sent some excuse about being busy with school. She always had to IM him first, to be the one to initiate a conversation, and even when she did, his responses were short, if he responded at all. He visited the Shore the Thursday before Halloween weekend. He hadn't told Erin he'd be there, but she saw his car in the driveway, his back at the dinner table. That was the thing about beach houses, all built one right next to the other—it was near impossible to keep anything secret. Carissa said his mom told her Peter was visiting alone so he could study for his

Dental Admission Test; he needed to get away from all the senior year parties and focus.

That night, she decided to take matters into her own hands. Around 10:00, she saw the lights were on in the second-floor family room of Peter's house. The rest of the house was dark, confirming he was home alone. She saw the outline of Peter's head in the window, his hand propping it up, the glow of the TV bouncing off his face. The window of her room, which was on the first floor of her house, was in view, a downward angle from Peter on the sofa watching a movie, facing her bedroom. She turned on her light and opened her window, her boom box right next to the screen blaring Justin Timberlake toward Peter's house. She started stretching, pretending she was working on her dance moves in her room, her limbs bending as she swayed, kicking her leg on her bureau, reaching for her toes. She didn't know if he was watching, but she hoped. Her heart pounded against her skin, not wanting to look. She couldn't bear the embarrassment if he saw her and didn't like what she was doing. She was wearing a T-shirt and shorts, casual and extremely unsexy workout clothes, but she had planned to try on her costume for tomorrow's Halloween party; she was going as a sexy cat with Madison.

She walked right next to the window, her hands at the bottom of her shirt, pulling it over her head. Her breasts had grown a full size that year, pushing the limits of her C-cup bra. She knew the power they had, the way boys ogled them, but she only wanted Peter to see them. Her bra was black, and she pulled a leotard overtop, looking herself up and down, still trying to avoid looking out the window, then topping it with her kitty ears. As she posed in the mirror, she heard her phone chime.

I never took you for a black cat kinda girl

She couldn't stop smiling. He had seen her.

Are you spying on me? she typed back, walking toward the window. She waved up at him, and he waved back.

It's not my fault you don't have blinds, he wrote back.

She stood at the window, looking up at him. She put her phone on the vanity next to the window, then pulled down the straps of her leotard, inching out of it so that her bra and underwear were on full display. She took a deep breath, reminding herself that her bikinis were far skimpier and thousands of beachgoers had seen her in those every summer. Yet this felt different, the intimacy of the moment, of the fact that it was just for Peter, making it far sexier. Or so she hoped. She watched him watch her, then pulled down her blinds. Had she looked like she knew what she was doing? Because, in reality, her hands were trembling so intensely she thought her leotard would get stuck on its way down. She lay on her bed, her body warm as she grinned at her phone and "SexyBack" played—until Carissa pounded on her door. "Erin, honey, what are you doing? Turn down the music. Your sister's trying to sleep."

Her mom turned the knob, poking her head into Erin's room. "Mom!" Erin yelled, grabbing the shirt she'd just tossed onto her bed moments before and slinking into it. "Get out!"

"Did you hear me?" Carissa said, walking across Erin's room to her boom box, perched on a shelf near the window. "It's almost ten, honey. Why on earth are you blasting music?" Erin watched Carissa's eyes move from the boom box to Erin, taking in her cat ears and the leotard on the floor. "Is that what you're wearing for Halloween?" she asked, sitting next to Erin on the bed, her fingers twiddling the felt cat ears Erin had glued to a headband.

Erin nodded, sitting cross-legged while facing her mom. "Madison's idea. It seemed like an easy way to repurpose our dance gear." Her lie is transparent; sexy cat is easy, yes, but also, well, sexy. Anyone dressed as a sexy cat knows exactly what they're doing.

"You know," her mom said, "you don't have to show skin to get attention. You've got a lot more worth up here." She tapped her daughter's forehead. "And here," pointing to Erin's heart.

"Mom." Erin rolled her eyes. "That's not why I'm wearing this, god."

"I know," Carissa said, but she looked unconvinced. "I just want you to always remember that, okay? If I remember anything about being a teenage girl, it's that it was very easy to lose myself. And you have value, sweetheart. You, my perfect Erin. You, not your body, is what boys should be paying attention to." Erin gulped, giving her mom a hug, before Carissa said goodnight. When her mom left the room, Erin lay on her pillow, wishing anything her mom said was actually true, and picked up her phone, holding it overhead as she waited for Peter's next text.

Peter showed up at her competition two weeks later. She saw him in the lobby of the hotel hosting the competition; she and Madison had just performed and they were on the hunt for lunch. "Wait, is that hot neighbor?" Madison whispered to Erin, pinching her side.

"Oh my god." Erin grabbed her arm for support. "Is he here?"

"Go talk to him, idiot." Madison pushed her in his direction. "I'll get us food." She winked, then walked away, leaving Erin alone in the crowd. Madison didn't approve, despite her own taste in older guys when she was at boarding school, and the previous summer when she hooked up with several college guys who had share houses for the summer. Now that she was with Justin, though, she thought high school guys were *the best* and doled out dating tips like a hybrid of *Cosmo* and Chris Harrison. Erin walked up to Peter, tapping him on the back, her finger shaking as she touched him.

"Hi." Her voice was meeker than she expected. He turned, and before she could even react, his arms were around her, lifting her from the ground. She took in his shampoo, his hair longer than usual, senioritis at work.

"You were so good!" he said as he put her back down, beaming. "If you and your partner don't win, then I'll be convinced they paid off the ref."

"It's a judge," she laughed, thankful her face was so caked with makeup it hid her blushing.

"He's right," she heard a voice, then saw Mrs. Cameron pop up behind Peter. "Your performance was gorgeous." She gave Erin a hug too; Erin tried her best to mask her surprise.

"I can't believe you're here." She said it to both of them, her head shaking back and forth in confusion. "What a fun surprise!"

"Your mother told me you would be performing, and Peter's right around the corner—and, you know, we're only in Blue Bell, so it was an easy drive. I dragged him to come watch. We're going to grab lunch by Rittenhouse now and we wanted to see our favorite Jersey girl before," she said, squeezing Erin's arm. "And your parents tell me Peter's tutoring worked wonders." Erin forced a smile, hoping her caked-on foundation hid her mortification. Peter looked bashful as his mom spoke, his build looming over the crowd of young girls in skimpy outfits. But he had seen her dance. For now, that was enough.

"Okay," Madison asks, her hands gripping the wheel, "where's your head at?" She picks up a fountain Diet Coke from the cup holder, both of them devouring their matching large McDonald's splurges, a habit they've acquired after dance class.

"Hmm." Erin mimics Madison's motion. She bites her straw, then flicks it as she thinks.

"Hello? Not in Lady Lex," Madison says, her obsession with the blue Lexus SUV her dad got for her after his divorce matched only by her obsession with Justin and Von Dutch hats. Whenever she posted pictures on MySpace or Facebook, she always made sure the wheel logo was showing.

"Relax," Erin says, annoyed. Madison's dad got her car detailed for her every few months; what did it matter if a few drops of soda dripped? But that is Madison: spoiled and bossy, always reminding you who's in control. "I am thinking it was weird he came with his mom. Like, what do I make of that?" She sinks into the seat, putting her hands on her face.

"I mean, what were you expecting? For him to sweep you into his arms and make out *Notebook*-style?" Madison makes a grossed-out face, and Erin feels all the more stupid.

"No, but—" Erin starts. "You're the one who told me last year that older guys are where it's at."

"Um, one: Shoobies are way different than a guy who lives right next to you. And two: You are the literal definition of jailbait, girl." Madison takes another sip of her soda, the bubbles gurgling through the straw especially irritating to Erin in this moment.

"I'll be eighteen in less than two years." Erin feels defensive.

"Uh, yeah. Key detail being that you're not eighteen yet."

"Whatever. If I lost my virginity to him, I would be the happiest person in the world." Madison looks at Erin, her car swerving a tiny bit. "Whoa, eyes on the road, Madison." Erin grips the handle over her window.

"I'm just, like, shocked you would say that."

"Why?" Erin asks, confused. They talked about sex all the time. At least about Madison having sex. And Erin pretending she was knowledgeable, when in reality the most she'd ever done was kiss Alex Raffetto a few times in closets in ninth grade.

"Because it's, like, a supremely slutty thing to say."

"Says the girl who lost her v-card to a wannabe shoobie photographer she met on MySpace."

"Oh, puh-lease. That's low. You know we met at the hotel, I just stalked his MySpace. And he's only a year older than me. Plus now that I actually know what love is like, I wish I hadn't done that."

"Love?" Erin gulps more of her soda. "You're in love with Justin? Are you two even official?" She thought it was casual, that Justin was just messing with everyone—including her sister. Erin hadn't even known Madison and Justin were hooking up until rumors of Kimmy and Justin tittered through the Rocky High hallways the first week of school, and Madison started freaking out. Madison confessed it had been casual with Justin for a few months, nothing consistent, but when she spent a month visiting her mom in Florida away from him at the end of the summer, she realized she wanted something official, something real—and she let Justin know after getting too drunk a few nights after he ignored her at the season's first soccer game.

"He's basically hubs material." She takes another sip of her Diet Coke. "And yes, we're official. We've been official this whole time."

Erin says nothing. She hears mumbles from Kimmy's room late at night, and she knows who she's on the phone with. Or the way she'll quickly turn off her monitor when Erin unexpectedly shows up in her room. Kimmy refers to Justin as her best guy friend, and he refers to Kimmy as his best girl friend. But Erin knows it's more than that for Kimmy, that she isn't one to do anything half-assed. That Kimmy is hardcore in love with Justin. "I didn't realize he was your boyfriend," Erin finally says, not adding more.

"Probably because your skanky-ass sister wants everyone to think he's not." Madison sips her soda again, and for a moment Erin visualizes grabbing it from her hand and throwing it directly at her head. "Justin is my boyfriend. Mine. It doesn't matter how much Kimmy throws herself at him," Madison says.

"They're just friends, Madison," Erin repeats, but they both know she's lying. In fact, Erin is sure Justin and her sister are probably together right now. Probably not alone, but still. They're in the same friend group; it's unavoidable. Kimmy tells Erin about 60 percent of what goes on, but Erin picks up some of the scraps she leaves out, her observational skills honed from years of being a little sister. She hates being in this spot, stuck between her best friend and her sister. She hates that Kimmy has put her there. The air in the car suddenly cold, Erin shivers, her spine tense.

Madison looks at Erin again, her voice vicious: "She's obsessed with him. You and I both know it. So remind her he's fucking taken."

"I mean, she's also obsessed with granny panties, if that makes you feel better. Loves a nice, full-coverage underpant," Erin jokes, hoping to defuse Madison's hostility, to make her feel superior to Kimmy in some way so she'll lay off. Madison smiles.

"Ew, remember when she left that pair in the bathroom a few months back? They were, like, a tarp." Madison pauses, considering this information. "You're right. I'm being crazy. Justin would never slum like that."

Erin nods, whispering a "yeah," and turns up the volume, Amy Winehouse's new album playing. She looks out the window, the pit of her stomach twisted, and says nothing more.

18

Beach Week 2022

DAY FOUR

It's been fifteen years since Kimmy's been on the Rocky Cape board-walk, its half-mile stretch of wood planks nestled between wild dunes and rows of oceanfront mansions, a far cry from the bustling chaos ever present on the Oceanwind boardwalk's nearly three-mile path. There's little to do except walk, run, or ride, save for a handful of playgrounds and a shuttered shack that houses one of the Shore's best ice cream spots, an old-school arcade, and a new restaurant called Sea Salt, which replaced the pizzeria Kimmy and Justin used to frequent in high school. "Weird, right?" he says, taking Kimmy's hand as he walks her up the ramp to Sea Salt's entrance, flanked by café lights, navy casement windows, and a minimalist ocean wave sign dangling above the front door.

"Wow." Kimmy brings her hand to her chest. Much like them, the shape of the place hasn't changed, but its entire inside has matured, grown with the times. She made an effort to look effortless tonight, wearing a simple black dress that plunges in the front and back; Justin didn't have to know it cost her nearly a thousand dollars. "I sort of miss the fluorescent lighting, though. I mean, what's this place with-out a little pizza grime?" She smiles at Justin, showing her pleasure in his restaurant choice. Like most places down the Shore, Sea Salt is BYOB, and Justin promised he would come prepared. He has an in-sulated tote and a towel for a little postdinner hang on the beach. As the hostess greets them, Kimmy feels some relief at not running into someone she knows almost immediately, not wanting to have to explain herself, what she's doing with Justin. It's not that she's embarrassed; she just doesn't know what, exactly, it is that they're doing. Not yet, at least. And the only thing that could cause confusion would be a run-in with someone who would tell her parents. The Fitzpatricks are good people, in Kimmy's opinion, but they aren't her parents' and their friends' people. Words like "trashy" and "dirtbag" were tossed around by her parents when rumblings about Justin's behavior with Kimmy spread from the mouths of her classmates to teachers to parents fifteen years ago. His parents were known for hosting wild adult ragers, ones with tropical shirts and limbo and red-faced men streaking from the house to the beach; more than three adults had gotten DUIs leaving the Fitzpatricks' when Kimmy was in high school. And they were open about their weed use long before it was legal, before most of the Reagan-era War on Drugs fanatics had been sent to assisted-living centers. Bill and Carissa stomached Kimmy's friendship with Justin, accepting that he was a by-product of Kimmy's friendship with Nikki, but when they heard there was a romantic element to their relationship, that he had been stringing along their daughter for months—well, that was unforgivable. And Kimmy's parents—her mom, in particular—aren't apt to give up a good grudge.

They're sitting on the outside porch, café lights twinkling overhead. The planks are painted stripes of blue and white, a perfect contrast to the rainbow sky fading above the oceanline. Justin motions to a chair, and they sit side by side, Kimmy snaking her hand toward his, which he grasps loosely. It's amazing how quickly they revert to old ways, to the precarious nature of everything happening all at once, yet, for Kimmy, not nearly fast enough.

"You think they'll be okay if I crack open some PBRs in this joint?" He pulls her closer and smiles at the brief look of horror on her face. "Don't worry, babe. I only brought the best for you." He twists his neck, giving her a light bite on her ear before he reaches into the cooler nestled between their chairs. He pulls out a bottle of Oyster Bay, and for a moment, Kimmy almost grimaces. She was expecting, at the very least, a Sancerre; a sixteen-dollar bottle of sauvignon blanc does not elicit ideas of "the best." "This is Reid's go-to wine," Justin says as he finishes pouring. "So I was hoping it would be impressive for you too. You know that kid. He's the bougiest of the Fitzpatricks." And all of a sudden Kimmy feels a rush of embarrassment—she's not in London, at a fancy restaurant where the cheapest bottle of wine tops a hundred dollars. She's here, with Justin. This is enough.

"Did I tell you I ran into him on my way out yesterday morning?" Kimmy says as she takes a sip. The breeze is light, just enough to keep the mosquitoes and greenheads away.

Justin looks up as he finishes pouring his own glass, his reaction not what Kimmy expects. "Oh." He screws the cap on the wine bottle and he looks out at the ocean. "How was he?"

Kimmy makes a face, her lips downturned. "Fine?" She takes another sip, putting a hand on Justin's thigh. "In a rush. But it was good to see him. Tell him the wine's perfect." She kisses Justin's cheek and feels him relax. Something is going on between those two, she can sense, but doesn't want to get into it right now. It's too soon for reality to hit. He looks at her and brushes a stray hair from her cheek, the moment almost surreal. The waitress interrupts, the two of them finally breaking apart to place their orders.

When their appetizers arrive, Kimmy's already feeling a buzz, their first bottle fully poured, their second glasses half full. She takes a bite out of her cucumber crostini, whipped tahini zinging her tongue, when Justin says, "You remember that time we got drunk on your parents' boat senior year? That was a wild night."

His eyes are glittering with the memory, but it stings Kimmy for a moment. It was the last week before her parents winterized the boat, and they had all snuck out there at midnight. It was just before Halloween, the air crisp, and Kimmy wore a pair of Uggs, a jean skirt, and a long-sleeve shirt, none of it warm enough for the October night's bite. They had all been at Justin's, bumming around, and rode their bikes to the yacht club, Kimmy on the handlebars of Justin's bike, facing him, her feet perched on the riding bars. It was dark, the only thing illuminating the sky the moon and sporadic streetlights. As they cruised, Justin looked around Kimmy, his eyes on the road, then drifted toward the back of the pack, giving Kimmy a quick smile before turning his eyes back to the road. She glanced over her shoulder, trying to catch where everyone was, when she felt his fingers on the inside of her thigh, up her skirt, flicking at the edge of her thong. By the time they got to the boat, they raced to the lower cabin, where they had sex against the table while everyone else drank on the deck of the *Devine Intervention*. Two days later, Justin IM'd her apologetically, saying they shouldn't have done that, that he had a girlfriend, a label that was news to Kimmy.

"Mmmhmm," she says, swiping the corner of her mouth with her pinky, pretending the memory he recalls so fondly doesn't hurt her still. She takes another sip.

"You never had any idea how sexy you were. Still are," he whispers into her ear, running a finger along her collarbone. Kimmy finds herself turned on, but also nervous, wanting to look around to make sure no one's watching, worried what people might report back to their parents. "From girl next door to sophisticated CEO. Dominate me, boss." His finger trails lower, near the V of the top of her dress.

"Justin." She swats his hand away. "Pace yourself." She raises her eyebrows. "We have another course before you're allowed any dessert."

He clinks a glass to hers, and they slink back into conversation, catching up on life. He's a marine engineer in Florida, where he spends months at sea, then months on land before he starts a new contract. The only real issue is that there's little stability in his personal life. "I guess there was never anyone worth settling down for," he says, his eyes tearing into Kimmy. *Until now*, they say.

"I appreciate that," she says with a smile. Work has been her life for far too long—and, of course, there was no one of real interest either, no one who sparked her insides like he did. Just over Justin's shoulder, she sees the outline of the Dunes hotel. It's owned by Madison's family. Maybe it's the wine, but she can't help herself. "I also ran into Madison the other morning."

"Oh," Justin says, his back stiffening.

"Yeah," Kimmy says. "I was wearing a shirt with your name on the back, of course. Just my luck."

He laughs awkwardly, and Kimmy regrets sharing the detail. "Did she talk to you?"

Kimmy shakes her head. "Not really. She was discussing nannies with Peter Cameron's wife. He was our neighbor back in the day. Summer kid. He tutored Erin for a summer." She pauses, realizing that statement has a whole new meaning now, but doesn't get into it with Justin just yet. She takes another sip. "Whatever happened with you two?"

"Aw, Legs." He places an arm around her. "Do you really want to get into that?"

Yes, she wants to shout. Of course she wants to know what happened, all the details about why he didn't choose her. But she feels the mood shifting, so she stops. "No, no. I guess I just want to know one thing: Do you still talk to her? You've been home more than me, so I wouldn't judge." She means it. She wants to know where those two stand, considering how small this town is. Especially before she and Justin start something more serious.

"No," he says, shaking his head. "I haven't talked to her in years."

Something inside Kimmy relaxes, and she leans into him even more. She's home, with the guy who got away, and he's finally hers. What more could she want?

After dinner, they hold hands as they walk past the dunes, the moon lighting the beach. Justin pulls out the towel, laying it on the ground, then brings out another bottle and plastic glasses, but Kimmy stops him. "After," she says, taking a step toward him. She stands on her tiptoes, wrapping her arms around his neck, and kisses him, hard. His hands run up and down her dress, the material rubbing against her skin.

"You feel like sex," he says, his finger looping around the strap of her underwear.

"Sit," she says, and he obeys, his legs out. She unzips his pants, pulling them to his knees, and straddles him. When they're finished, Kimmy's hair tousled and Justin's chest speckled with sweat, he pulls his pants back up and Kimmy rests against him, both of them looking out at the ocean, Justin leaning back with Kimmy between his legs, her back on his chest, her head nestled right below his chin. They're both silent, their breathing synchronized as Justin rubs Kimmy's arm, his touch so familiar.

"You feel like home," she says, shaking her head into him even more. He kisses the top of her head, putting an arm around her collarbone.

"You've been gone for so long," he says. "I still can't believe this is real. That you're actually in my arms."

She gives a little laugh. "Same. If you told the Kimmy of, I don't know, two years ago that I'd be here, with the guy who absolutely pulverized my heart when I was eighteen, in my hometown of all places, I would have laughed in your face."

"Hey." He sits up, his face serious. "You broke my heart too. Like, we got in a fight. I was an indecisive little prick. And then you were gone. What was I supposed to do?"

"Chase after me," Kimmy says, as if that were ever an option.

"You told me not to contact you. 'Ever fucking again' were your exact words, if I recall. I just assumed you were running from me."

I was, Kimmy wants to say. *But I was also running from so much more.* How would she even start that conversation without getting way too serious way too fast, without fully scaring him away? "I was dramatic. And so were you."

"Two kids too young to realize how good they were for each other." He gives Kimmy a kiss, and her stomach flips. "You know you've always had a piece of my heart. You always will."

This is endgame, she realizes. *This has to be endgame.* She pulls his arm closer around her, not able to look directly at him as she starts talking. "So, in the spirit of new beginnings and truth, you should know something." The waves crash, almost violently. "My dad had a heart attack earlier this summer. He was diagnosed with hypertension a few years ago and obviously all the craziness with the business these past two years sort of put everything into overdrive. His doctor recommended he retire for his health, and so that's the real reason I'm home. To be there for him, for my mom, for the store. To help alleviate his workload so it doesn't happen again."

"Oh, Legs." He pulls her closer. "I'm so sorry to hear that. How's he feeling about it all?"

She shakes her head, biting her lip as she thinks about the way he's slowed since she last saw him, the extra grays in his head and the extra time it takes him to finish his morning swim. "Honestly, I'm not sure, because he's being all stoic about it, which is very him, as you might remember."

Justin laughs. "I am still terrified of your parents." *You should be*, she thinks. It won't be easy to get them to forget.

"But yeah, he seems like himself, just a little older and more obsessed with his health, which is a good thing! It's definitely not fun getting smacked in the face with your parents' mortality." She feels her eyes watering, and a tear falls down her cheek.

Justin takes a thumb and brushes her cheek dry. "I wish I didn't have to go back to Florida at the end of the week." He looks back toward the water, then at Kimmy. "I wish I could be here with you."

"So don't go." Kimmy holds his hands tighter. She turns to look at him. "Stay here. With me. Let's give this a real shot."

"I have a job." He shakes his head. "I can't just, like, quit."

"Why not?" she asks. "I have enough in savings to give you a bridge. That's all it would be. A bridge. There are so many ports in New Jersey. I'm sure you'd be able to find an amazing new contract, hopefully one that doesn't have you offshore for so much of the year."

He brings a hand to his head. "I'm just trying to process." His brow furrows and Kimmy can tell she's losing him; she can't go through that again. She straddles him again, bending her legs around him, pulling the string of her halter so it falls to her waist. She watches Justin's eyes drift down, his gaze going from worried to thirsty. "Goddamnit, Legs," he says, tossing his head into her chest. "I never could say no to you."

19

December 2006

"Erin, honey, can you grab the pizza?" Carissa asks, her messy hair sweeping across the shoulders of her oversize sweater. It's the thick of winter break, the time between Christmas and New Year's Eve as frozen as the icicles lining the edges of roofs all over town. Erin and Kimmy have spent the bulk of their break lounging in their living room watching season 1 of *Sex and the City* on DVD and a disgusting number of movies on Hallmark and Lifetime. Kimmy has been in a mood the whole time, sullen and biting one second, tearing up at a commercial about a generic couple swooning over a cheap-looking Zales bracelet the next. Erin assumed it was because Madison and Justin each added "ONE" to their AIM profiles shortly before break, Justin deleting the small *pb&j* at the bottom of his; but she also wanted to believe her sister wasn't that pathetic, so she let her stew, not asking what was up. Erin threw a remote at her earlier today when she was sniffling and, when it hit Kimmy's forehead instead of her lap, Erin laughed. Kimmy cried even harder, screaming that her sister was insane, as she ran to her room.

"Is Kimmy gracing us with her presence for dinner?" Erin tries not to sound worried as she asks, her tone the slightest bit haughty.

"Why would she not join us?" Bill asks as he nearly skips into the kitchen, emerging from hours in his man cave watching basketball. Two of the three Devine's locations were now officially closed through April, making this the start of his least stressful stretch of the year.

Erin shrugs, pulling a glove on her hand as she walks to the oven. The top rack holds a thick crust, pepperoni curling at the edges as it burrows into the cheesy center. It's so thick it looks like a cartoon, melting in real time. Erin pulls it out and feels Carissa's breath on her neck. "Oh no, honey, that's for your dad and Kimmy. This is ours." Carissa slides by her side, oven gloves on both her hands. She pulls out the pizza on the lower shelf, a sad flatbread topped with green and red peppers, a sprinkle of parmesan nearly disappearing into the sauce.

"If you were just going to get it yourself, why did you ask me?" Erin says with a bite, putting the pepperoni pizza directly on the counter. Carissa tsks as she places both on a cooling rack. "That pizza looks like one of the guys from *VeggieTales* got murdered. No thanks."

"No one is forcing you to eat it." Carissa's face is wounded. "But you did request it." She has her signature passive-aggressive tone, a slight what-do-I-know-I'm-just-your-mother vibe to it all. Erin sucks in her stomach, pulling the hem of her T-shirt past her hips. Madison had recently gone vegan after reading *Skinny Bitch*. It was just after Thanksgiving, her collarbone extra pronounced. "It changed my life, I swear," she said. She was getting ready for her family's annual holiday vacation to the Bahamas, and Erin could tell she was antsy leaving Justin for ten days, their relationship official but still shaky. She complained about how his temperament with any and everyone was flirtatious, how he had too many friends who were girls, how he was terrible with his phone, how he ditched her to smoke and play video games with Ryan and Chris—ending every tirade with a massive declaration of her love for him. Erin chalked up Madison's diet to those nerves, to thinking losing a few pounds would answer all her insecurities. But she stuck with it, giving Erin a copy just before Christmas. Every mirror suddenly felt like an assault, like it was showing all the ways her diet of cheesesteaks and chicken fingers and meatballs was making her a bloated, animal-killing monster. Carissa starts slicing, the silver disc mesmerizing as it drives through the crust, then places a piece of veggie pizza on Erin's plate. "Do you want a piece of pepperoni too?" she asks, her eyes waving a white flag. She places a slice on a separate plate. For Kimmy, Erin assumes.

"No," Erin says, taking her deflated triangle and Kimmy's juicy-looking slice to the table. She thought maybe if she too lost a few pounds she would look older, more mature. Like a college student, someone old enough for Peter.

"What's for din?" Kimmy breezes into the kitchen, her wet hair leaving a pool of dampness on her sweatshirt's hood. From her bedroom window, Erin had watched Kimmy sprint across the street two hours earlier, her breath whirring frozen clouds as her legs sliced the air with each stride. Despite her shower, her cheeks are still pink from the frigid air, but not pink enough to hide the massive welt on her forehead.

"Kimmy!" her mom says with a dramatic flair when she sees the burgeoning bruise. "What happened to your head?"

"Ask your idiot daughter over there." She glares at Erin.

"It's not my fault she can't catch." Erin bites her pizza, grimacing as she chews. It tastes like cardboard, the cheese tacky against her teeth.

"Girls, what was the only thing your mother said she wanted for Christmas?" Bill asks, shoveling three slices of pepperoni onto his plate.

"For us to get along," Erin and Kimmy sing together.

"So let's move on from whatever is going on here." Bill waves his hands in the air.

Kimmy rolls her eyes as she grabs a seat next to Erin. "You get the good pizza," Erin says, and pushes the pepperoni toward her.

"Um, okay?" Kimmy looks at Erin's plate. "Are you allergic or something? That looks disgusting."

"I'm vegetarian. I think eventually I'll go fully vegan, but I'm easing into it." Erin says it matter-of-factly, as if Kimmy is uncivilized for not doing the same. "Madison's doing it too. Like, every celebrity who looks amazing is vegan. Like Posh Spice."

"Ah, yes, because we should all aspire to look like bobbleheads," Kimmy says, dragging her pizza toward her mouth. The cheese drips, slopping against the table.

"Kimmy." Carissa appears with an empty plate, placing it under Kimmy's chin. "Must you always eat like an uncultured human being?"

"Sorry, Mom, it was a long-run day. I'm starving." Kimmy smiles and Erin knows. She met with Justin. There's no way she didn't. Kimmy thinks she's stealthy, thinks she's being quiet, but Erin hears her talking to him on the phone at night. They are hot and cold, depending on whatever is happening with Justin and Madison, but Kimmy is always there, always available. Always pathetic. "Why would you want to look like Madison, anyway? She's like a poor man's Paris Hilton."

"Who's Paris Hilton?" their dad asks, but his question goes ignored.

"God, you are so jealous." Erin seethes at her sister, her head tilted. Kimmy says nothing, just glares back.

"Erin." Bill interrupts the standoff. "The start of college hoops has me thinking we should start scheduling some tours. I have the Princeton Review book in my study. Kimmy wrote on a few pages, but it's otherwise untouched. Though I can also see if there's an updated version. Maybe you'll even want to go to Rutgers, like your sister."

Erin nods, not wanting to add much. She would never be able to get in there. They all know it, all ignore it, all pretend she is as good as Kimmy. No one really cares that Erin's an excellent painter or has the best fouetté on the dance team; in this house, this country, they care about your race times and SAT scores. So she isn't, will never be, as good as Kimmy.

"Ah, how nice to have both my babies just a short drive away." Carissa winks at Erin. Erin doesn't know where she wants to go to school yet. She's honestly not even sure where she'll get in. She finds herself struggling to pay attention in class, thinking about Peter all the time. What he is doing. When he will get back to her. Looking forward to their occasional AIM conversation, even if it is just for a few minutes every few weeks. She fills her MySpace and Facebook pages with pictures meant for him, her eyes rimmed with dark liner, her tops tight, her legs twisted in unnatural dance poses. She wants him to remember what he's missing.

"Erin," Carissa says, as if she's been repeating her name. "What do you think?"

"Sorry." Erin realizes she once again drifted away from reality while dreaming of Peter. "Of what?"

"Of doing some sort of graduation gift for Peter Cameron. He has been so good to you with all his tutoring," she says. "Did you know he graduated early? He's spending this semester traveling around Europe before he starts work in the summer. Such a smart boy."

Erin's cheeks turn a light shade of pink, her eyes meeting Kimmy's. Kimmy curls her lips inward, her eyes big, trying not to laugh at Carissa's obliviousness. Erin did know, only because they were still Facebook friends after Peter invited her to join last year, before he knew her age, when you still had to have a college email or get an invite from someone with one to make a profile. "Sure," Erin says. "Whatever you want."

Carissa raises her eyebrows. "Well, what does he like?" she asks. "You know him the best."

"Underage girls," Kimmy whispers, and Erin gives her a kick under the table.

"What was that?" Carissa asks, her expression changing.

"I said underage girls," Kimmy says louder. Retaliation for Erin's earlier dig. "Do you not think it's odd he IMs Erin, like, all the time? And he went to her dance competition? I swear he's half the reason her grades suck." Kimmy stops, then looks at Erin. "The other half being that she's stupid, of course."

"Excuse me?" Carissa says, looking at Erin, who ignores her.

"You don't need to make everyone else miserable just because you are," she says to Kimmy. "I mean, not all of us can be as gifted at keeping up our grades while spending so much time on our back. So, so sorry I'm not as talented as you, Kimmy."

"Screw you," Kimmy says.

"Back at ya, slore." Erin feels her face getting hot, pushing away from the table.

"What are you all talking about?" Carissa asks, trying to get in a word as Kimmy and Erin scream at each other.

"Enough," Bill says, pounding the table. "Enough!" he shouts again, this time loudly. Everyone quiets, including Carissa, whom their dad looks at, some sort of knowing acknowledgment between them that only twenty years of marriage allows. "No one is leaving this table." He ignores the insults, turning to Kimmy. "Peter has been nothing but a good influence on your sister. Erin, is there anything we should be concerned with about your relationship?"

Erin shakes her head no. "Good," her dad says. "And Kimmy, I don't want to know what Erin's insinuating, but I am going to strongly advise that you don't do anything that might get you a reputation."

"I don't have a reputation, Dad," she says. Kimmy looks like she's about to cry, her eyes big and wet. Erin rolls her eyes, wanting to scream *liar*.

"Good," Carissa says, looking back at Bill like she wants him to say more.

He nods. "And whatever plans you have for tomorrow night are canceled."

"Dad!" they shout in unison. Tomorrow is New Year's Eve, and both of them fully believe the mindset from *The O.C.*'s New Year's Eve episode: how you spend your New Year's Eve is how you'll spend the rest of the year. Erin is supposed to drive into Philly with some girls on the dance team and was hoping to run into Peter; she'd already IM'd him and everything. He hadn't responded yet, but still.

"You'll go to Lisa's annual New Year's party. Together." He crosses his arms, sitting back with a satisfied grin. Lisa's is the destination for local retirees who had made it their tradition for the past fifty years. It was for very, very old people.

"No," Kimmy says, shaking her head. "I already have plans." There's an urgency in her voice, and Erin rolls her eyes again. She knows Justin's having a party—and Madison is out of town.

"What are they? Being a slore?" Erin asks, taking a bite of her pizza.

"Jesus Christ, Erin." Carissa glares at her daughter. "Have you no respect for your sister? Or, quite honestly, for yourself? Maybe Kimmy's right and you do idolize Madison a touch too much. You sound just like her. The way she talked about her mother . . . ," she says, trailing off.

"How would you know?" Erin crosses her arms. "What are you, like, spying on us? Psycho."

"I've had enough of this. We both have." Carissa pats Bill's shoulder. "You two could obviously use a little sisterly bonding. You don't realize how lucky you are to have each other."

Bill puts his hand on Carissa's, nodding. "And don't even think of sneaking away from Lisa's. There are still a few of Nanny and Pop's friends who are alive and go there every year—and, of course, Lisa, who will call me in a second if you two don't show up."

Erin growls at Kimmy, who growls right back.

Kimmy cannot believe she's at Lisa's Diner on New Year's Eve. It glows like 1972, its windows decorated with tinsel and paint meant to mimic frost. She's wearing a black turtleneck and dark jeans, a look of mourning. And she feels like she is mourning. Justin is having a party tonight and half their grade will be there. Yesterday, she texted him before heading out on her long run, letting him know she'd pass his house on her route. When she got close, he met her outside, saying hi, asking again if she was coming to his house for New Year's. She knew Madison was on vacation, knew what he was asking—just before she left to finish her run, he lightly smacked her butt with a wicked grin on his face. She needed to see Justin tonight, was desperate to, had promised she would be there. But she's not. She's here, at Lisa's, the median age seventy-two, a sea of white hair and a symphony of orthopedic shoes squeaking against the linoleum floor as the jukebox plays soft rock.

"I think we may have hit the NYE jackpot." Erin wiggles her eyebrows. "I found the silver fox I'm planning to kiss tonight." She tilts her head toward an ancient-looking man slumped in his wheelchair, soft snores floating from his mouth. It's classic Erin, pretending the huge fight they had twenty-four hours earlier never happened, hoping if she smiles hard enough it will all disintegrate.

"Don't be a bitch," Kimmy whispers, hip checking her. "This is probably the most exciting night of the year for a bunch of these people." Kimmy's still mad at her but knows she has to make the best of the evening. Plus, there's something about the scene that is endearing, the middle-aged couples who brought their parents from assisted-living communities, or the cliques of locals who obviously come year after year, their comfort in the booths they've occupied every New Year's Eve for decades obvious. "Hi," Kimmy says to the host, a skinny teen who looks about their age. "We have a table for two. I think our dad made a reservation. Under Devine." She gives a polite smile, sure this kid is as miserable being forced to spend his night here as they are. He smiles back, but it doesn't seem like one of commiseration.

"Right this way." He grabs two laminated menus as he leads them to a booth. Erin trails right behind him, Kimmy behind her. She can tell Erin's being nosy and is about to ask him a zillion questions.

"Who are you?" Erin picks up her speed so she's almost right next to him. When they get to the booth, he stops and Erin almost knocks him over.

Kimmy flicks her shoulder. "He works here, Er," she says, looking at the host. "Sorry for my sister's lack of manners. I think I've seen you here before," she says, then regrets it. The last time she was here, it was midnight and Nikki almost nodded off into her burger while Kimmy drunkenly curled herself on Justin's lap and Ben twisted his lit cigarette into the plastic cushion of the booth. The host looks at Kimmy with a hint of recognition, but doesn't say anything, saving her the embarrassment. Instead he laughs, his ease with Erin's lack of personal space surprising.

"James Langley." He motions toward the table. "Lisa's grandson. My aunt runs the place now." Lisa is still around, Kimmy knows, but more in a chairwoman role, popping in to make sure all's well but hardly involved in the day-to-day of the business. James did look familiar to her; she remembered her Nanny showing them Lisa's Christmas card one year, pointing out all her handsome grandsons. He must be one of them.

"Interesting," Erin says as she and Kimmy slide into the booth. "You don't live here, though. Right? Because I have literally never seen you before in my life."

"Erin." Kimmy kicks her under the table. "You're being so rude." She just wants to get through the night. "I'm pretty sure our Nanny mentioned you. She was close with Lisa."

"It's fine," James says, turning back toward Erin. "My parents are in Doylestown. I'm at Germantown," he says, looking bashful. "On scholarship."

"That's cool." Kimmy looks at him again. She'd been so inside her own head about Justin she hadn't actually paid attention to anything

James said at first. But he seems so earnest; it is refreshing. "I ran against some girls from Germantown in States last year. Do you know Nora Green?"

"Yeah," he says. "She's a grade below me, but really cool."

"She's Kimmy's cross-country nemesis." Erin rests her chin on her hands and smiles; Kimmy sees that she knows exactly what she's doing.

"Oh." James shifts his weight with discomfort. "Well, on that note, what drinks can I get for you two?"

"Shirley Temple," they say at the same time, then giggle, forgetting their feud for a few seconds. It's their all-time favorite, ever since they were kids. "Extra, extra cherries for me," Erin says, "and only one for Kimmy. She thinks the maraschino juice clashes with the grenadine, whatever that means. She's particular."

Kimmy rolls her eyes, giving James yet another apologetic smile.

"Noted." He laughs, seeming unsure how else to react to their banter. "I'll be sure to tell the bartender to sift out the maraschino juice." He nods toward the diner counter, where a man who is very much not a bartender is pouring wine into a glass. "Gonna go put this in," he says, "but I'll be back."

"What are you up to?" Kimmy asks Erin, a bite in her tone. "You call me a slut to Mom and Dad like, a day ago, and now you want to be my best friend again? Honestly, Erin, what is your problem? You don't get to have it both ways."

This time, Erin kicks Kimmy under the table. "Can you just relax. Why do you have to be so angsty about everything?"

Kimmy huffs, pulling her phone from her bag. She had texted Justin earlier in the day wishing him a good party, but hasn't heard back. Nikki had texted her *missssss youoisdkjds* and Kimmy knows they are all definitely drunk. Kimmy flips her phone shut and sees Erin staring at her. "Who are you texting with?"

"Nikki," she says, glad it's not a lie. "She's drunk. They all are. Why do you want to know? So you can report back to your jealous little bestie?"

"Justin's Madison's boyfriend, Kimmy," Erin says, her face serious. "Like, that means something."

Kimmy looks back at her phone, avoiding eye contact with her sister.

Erin carves into her omelet, the cheese oozing from its center as she cuts it apart, her plans to go vegan on hold until Madison and her judgment return to New Jersey. "I just don't understand what's going on with you." She looks at Kimmy as she shovels a bite into her mouth. They haven't had this type of one-on-one time in ages, always distracted by boys or homework or sports or their phones. Erin isn't sure she'll get an opportunity like this again for a long time.

"What do you mean?" Kimmy says, moving around the hash browns on her plate but hardly eating. "Nothing is going on with me."

"Why do you keep lying?" Erin's voice rises. "I hear you talking on the phone at night, Kimmy. It's with Justin, right? I'm not as stupid as you apparently think I am." Once, four years ago, Kimmy called Erin stupid after she couldn't figure out how to get past level three in their Harry Potter computer game. She's never been able to fully let it go, to kick away the quiet worry that that's how Kimmy really feels about her general existence.

"We're just friends," Kimmy says, but Erin puts up her hands.

"No," she says. "No, you're not. Anyone with eyes can see that."

"What do you want me to say, Er?" Kimmy throws her fork down, her voice exasperated. "That I'm not in love with him? Or do you just want to be able to tell Madison what a ho I am?"

There are moments when Kimmy drives Erin crazy, and she does, in fact, want to call Madison and share every single suspicion she has about Justin and Kimmy, to be a real best friend and tell her that he is trouble, that she can do better. But she would never actually betray her sister like that, and anyway, Madison would never listen. She has Justin on a pedestal.

"I'm your sister, Kimmy. You will always be my best friend. Above everyone else."

Kimmy's brow turns down and Erin watches her lower lip quiver. "I am just so sad," she says, wiping the stray tears from her eyes. "Like,

I have never felt this way about anyone. Ever. Even Brian. I don't know what to do." She puts her head in her hands, her shoulders shaking. "I don't even care that people are talking or think I'm desperate or whatever. I just can't help it."

"Have you had sex with him?"

"With Justin?" Kimmy asks, stalling. Erin nods, pushing her sister. She's not sure why she wants to know, but something about having the knowledge feels better than the not.

"I don't—I'm not answering that, Er."

"Uh, so that's a yes," Erin says. Kimmy looks down at her food, tears starting to pile in her eyes. She's always moping, always crying over Justin. Erin is so sick of it. "Stop crying. Seriously."

Kimmy looks up at her. "What?"

"Stop feeling sorry for yourself. You did this to you, Kimmy. Like, I get that I'm way less experienced and all that, but sleeping with a guy who has a girlfriend is undeniably messed up."

"I know," Kimmy whispers. "I really do, and I have tried so hard for the past month or whatever. But he keeps kissing me, Er. It's like every time I'm about to move on, he does something to hook me again. Like he has a sixth sense for it or something."

"What do you mean he keeps kissing you?"

"Well, last week, for example. We were going to Derek's birthday party, which was already going to be a little awkward because Brian was there, but Justin needed a ride because his car got rear-ended the week before. So we leave the basketball game and he asks for a ride. I parked by Derek's, and he put his hand on my leg while I was driving, and then as we were walking in, he grabbed my hand and pulled me back. And just kissed me. And then was, like, *Oh, sorry, I couldn't help myself.*" She shakes her head. "Like, how am I supposed to move on when he won't let me?"

"God, Kimmy, don't be so stupid. You deserve someone who doesn't play games with you. You're such a catch. Justin, well, he's—" Erin is about to tell Kimmy that he's not worth it, that she's so much better than him, but she sees that Kimmy's sobbing, her shoulders shaking into the table. "Here." Erin slides her a piece of bacon. "A peace offering." She lifts the slice of bacon and taps it on Kimmy's left shoulder. "I knight thee the Princess of Rocky Cape, the town's most amazing, high-class lady who shall only settle for someone as wonderful as she." She taps the bacon on Kimmy's other shoulder, then head, as she talks.

Kimmy lifts her face, laughing her tears away. "You are so weird," she says. "And that's why I love you."

Erin reaches across the table, holding her sister's hand. She knows she should choose between her sister and Madison. She feels the tension every day, the way Madison is using her for information about Kimmy, the way Kimmy winces at every mention of Madison's name. But she hopes instead she can just get her sister to stop liking Justin. Or maybe for Madison to see how much of a dick Justin is. "I love you too, sis." She looks up, and their waiter James is walking toward them, notepad in hand, and she realizes she can make part of that plan come true. He's cute, in a nerdy way—a way Kimmy used to like. Brian had some of those vibes, when he wasn't leaning into his more dominant soccer douchebag bro ones. She is, after all, totally into Seth Cohen. As he reaches their table, "Dance with Me" by Orleans plays.

"Dessert?" he asks, pen to the page.

"How about a dance, Diner James?" Erin smiles at her sister.

"Oh, I don't—" James starts, his cheeks turning pink. Erin presses the tip of her shoe against Kimmy's shin, and Kimmy looks at James with a surprisingly open face.

"What's that thing Summer Roberts said about New Year's Eve?" Erin eggs on Kimmy, wiggling her eyebrows.

"You need a life," Kimmy says to Erin, but she puts her hand up for James to take. "Diner James, will you dance with me?"

He looks around, making sure he's not needed immediately at another table, then cautiously puts his paper and pen down and takes Kimmy's hand, pulling her onto the makeshift dance floor. Erin smiles as she watches them sway, the full foot between them, filled with sweetness and innocence.

Erin's phone goes off and she pulls it from her purse. A picture text of Madison sitting in a massive gold chair, her hair braided and skin golden.

Just met Ashton at Nobu. So hot, basically famous now. How's dinner with the ho? hahaha sux I bet u miss me bitch

Erin read the text again, feeling guilty for the way she had let Madison talk about her sister all this time.

Actually having an okay time. Kimmy's getting swept off her feet with a new love interest

She sends Madison a picture of Kimmy and Diner James on the dance floor, feeling proud of her interference. She pauses, looking at her phone again, then decides to just go for it. *By the way*, she types, *K said Justin tried to kiss her last week before Derek's party. Just thought you should know.* Erin knew he had told Madison that Derek's party was a small thing just for some of the soccer guys, because Madison cried to Erin about not being invited for a solid hour. She was annoyed with both Kimmy and Madison—and, most of all, Justin, who didn't deserve either of them.

Erin's heart is racing as she waits for Madison's response. She didn't want to stoke the fire, but wasn't the role of the best friend not to let your best friend get cheated on?

Lol did K tell you that? Pleasssse. She is so desperate. Hubs would never do that shit to me. She is such a liar.

Erin takes another deep breath and closes her eyes, sliding her phone into her purse. This was never going to end, was it?

20

Beach Week 2022

DAY FIVE

"Don't be nervous," Kimmy whispers to Justin, rubbing the back of his suit jacket. His jaw is tight, and she worries this was the wrong call, throwing him into her parents' world so quickly. At the same time, she had little choice after her mother's lecture that morning. Susie Reynolds had seen the two of them at Sea Salt and told her parents they were inappropriately affectionate, the vague accusation worse than specifics. "You're too old and too visible in the community for that kind of show. And with that boy, to make it all worse," her mom scolded. "If you're going to revisit that terrible road, at least do it with a little respect for yourself and this family." So that morning, they made it official: Justin would attend the party as her date.

"I'm not," he says, but she watches him rub a small trickle of sweat from the rim of his hairline, the crisp air-conditioned lobby not enough to fool his body into relaxing. Her hand is in his, but his grip is loose, noncommittal. Before she can feel insecure, Erin greets them in the hallway.

"If it isn't the evening's lady of honor," she says as she fake-curtsies. She's wearing a lime-green dress, the edges hugging her curves, the back low enough that it shows off the edges of her tattoo, a minimalist sunset she got during art school hugging her lower-left love handle. Kimmy knows she's dressed for Peter, and she did a damn good job of it. She just hopes they both keep it in check tonight.

"Hey, Er," Justin says, his arms out. Erin should hate him, but for whatever reason she's the one Devine who's refused to totally toss him off. She's always been one for second chances.

"Fifteen years and a few extra inches. You clean up nice, Fitzy," she says, loosely hugging back. She pulls away, her face stern. "So are you finally going to seal the deal and become the brother I never asked for?" Kimmy knows Erin's nervous, her jokes always frantic and completely aggressive when she's in her own head. Justin's cheeks flush, and Kimmy wants to smack her sister. "God, I'm kidding. Chill. You are going to face far more formidable adversaries than myself tonight."

As she says this, the most formidable of the bunch appear. "Hi, Mr. and Mrs. Devine. Thanks so much for having me tonight," Justin says, his hand out.

"Justin Fitzpatrick." Bill's approach is stern. He doesn't meet Justin's hand, doesn't welcome Justin with any sort of kindness. "I hope you'll be on your best behavior tonight."

Carissa walks up behind him. "Bill." She puts a hand on his shoulder, as if she's keeping her husband from knocking Justin right in the nose.

"We're not in high school, Dad." Kimmy gives him a glare, holding Justin's hand tighter.

"And yet Justin has already managed to get people talking about you," Carissa says, an eyebrow raised.

Instead of looking apologetic, Justin looks pissed. Kimmy watches his jaw clench.

"Does it really mean anything if it came from Susie Reynolds?" Erin asks, trying to defuse the tension. She turns to Justin. "She's, like, the club's biggest gossip and notoriously hyperbolic."

Kimmy sees him relax, knowing at least Erin is in his corner. "Why don't you save your lecture for after the party?" Kimmy pulls Justin closer. "Tonight is a celebration, so we're going to do just that. We're going to the bar." She turns, Erin in their wake.

"What was that? Two minutes? Might be a new record for the emergence of the judgy Devines." Erin's joking, but Kimmy notices her twitchiness, the way she's looking around the club. For Peter.

"I'm gonna need something strong to get through tonight," Justin says. "But it's worth it for you." He kisses Kimmy on the forehead. She watches her parents walk to the other corner of the club, where Mayor Kasanaar is surrounded by gray-haired men and sparkling women, all of them club members and local business owners, this party less about fun and more about business. She spots James, at the right side of the mayor, and drops the hand in Justin's to give him a wave from across the room.

"Who is that?" Erin asks, poking her in the side. "Next to the mayor. He looks so familiar."

"Diner James," Kimmy says. "Remember him?"

"Damn. He grew up." Erin cranes her neck, getting a better look, and Kimmy shakes her head with secondhand embarrassment.

"Who's Diner James?" Justin asks, and Kimmy senses something tense in his voice, something new.

"No one," she says. "A guy we met for, like, a millisecond in high school. He went to private school in Philly."

"Fancy." Justin crosses his arms, his insecurity shimmering like bad bronzer.

"On scholarship. He's not like that," Kimmy says, only to realize she's making it worse.

Erin looks from Kimmy to Justin, then to the bar. "Three espresso martinis, stat." The bartender turns and makes eye contact and it's Aaron Roop. Because of course it is. Erin and Kimmy both jump.

"Congrats," he says to Kimmy, his voice monotone. "I hope tonight is everything you want it to be." He flashes a plastic smile as he shakes their cocktails. Erin gives her a side glance, and grabs her hand under the table. Her parents had no idea of their history, no sense that he shouldn't be here.

"Why did that feel like a threat?" whispers Erin, now off to the side with Kimmy. "Did you know Stevie broke up with him yesterday?"

"What?" Kimmy wants to ask more, but they're interrupted by the Singers, who own the pancake house famous in this region. As they chat, cordial small talk and congratulations, she notices Justin and Aaron talking, as if they're old buddies—because, well, they are. Something inside her turns, an annoyance. She wants to shout at Justin, to shake him and say stop, to make him see what's going on. She always promised herself she would never be a victim, would never let this one thing define her. But here, faced with it in her hometown, with the boy who, in a way, sparked all of it, she's not sure what to feel.

Erin nudges Kimmy. "Kimmy, Mr. and Mrs. Singer were wondering what you think the best restaurant in London is?"

She's about to answer when Justin sneaks up behind her. "Hey," he whispers, pulling her aside. She mouths an apology to the Singers, promising to return. "I'm gonna sneak outside to get some air. The whole thing with your parents has me feeling claustrophobic."

Kimmy nods, understanding. She turns her face up to give him a kiss, but he's already walking toward the door.

Forty-five minutes later, Justin returns just as Bill walks to a podium at the front of the room. "Hey," Justin says, his voice husky, his jacket scented stinky-sweet.

"Did you just smoke?" she whispers, incredulous.

He smiles, his lips curling in a goofy grin. "Just a little. I needed a break." His eyes are bloodshot, glassy. Kimmy's lips tighten, the one cocktail she's been nursing since Justin's disappearance far too weak for this.

"I cannot believe you," she hisses as her dad taps the microphone, getting the sound just right. "Go to the bathroom and air out. This is not that kind of crowd." She looks around to make sure no one's staring. She sees Erin and her mom watching, but they both turn to face forward when she makes eye contact.

"I don't want to miss the speech," Justin says, but he's hardly there.

"I'll fill you in." She forces a sweet smile and gives him a kiss on the cheek as her dad starts. "Go."

He does as he's told, but not without a small sulk. Kimmy ignores it and moves toward the front of the room, where her dad's saying her name.

"Kimmy, there you are!" he shouts once he finally sees her. He's had at least three glasses of pinot, his lips a darker red than usual. He's not supposed to drink red, something about it potentially elevating blood pressure, but they all decided he could take just one night off to enjoy himself. Everyone is smiling at her, at his protégée. She shuffles forward, her chest once again heavy, her anxiety picking up. *Breathe*, she tells herself. She brings a hand to her chest, rubbing her sternum. As she does, she feels an arm wrap around one side of her waist—and another around the other. Erin and her mom. Her chest loosens, and she leans into their support, letting them hold her up.

"If you can believe it," her dad says, "it has been fifteen years since Kimmy has been home for longer than forty-eight hours. We've never held it against her. After all, she was taking the world by storm. First at Pepperdine, where she graduated in the top one percent of her class." He skates over the devastating conversation they had in late 2007, when Kimmy told him she was transferring from his beloved Rutgers to Pepperdine, his dreams for her visibly broken. She worked extra hard once she was on the West Coast, determined to prove that she didn't break his heart for no good reason. "Then Oxford's Saïd Business School, where she scored an internship at one of London's premier private equity firms. During her first five years on the job, she assisted the firm's partners with seven major deals, totaling over three billion dollars. And in 2016, she courted an esteemed chain of grocers that was struggling, and helped them realign their leadership, operations, and strategy. And, as you may have read in the *Wall Street Journal* this winter"—he pauses, taking in the nods of recognition—"Kimmy led the sale of that grocery chain to Aldi in a home-run deal." The crowd applauds, and Kimmy finds her face turning red. "Now, Devine's isn't on the market, so don't get any ideas," Bill says, the whole crowd laughing. "But we are so thrilled to have Kimmy and her brilliant mind back in our hometown—and back at the family business. Tonight is about saying thanks to all of you, our friends and partners, for being along for this ride, and toasting the next generation of it." Bill raises his cocktail. "Please, enjoy the evening. Drinks are on us!" Her mom and Erin hug her, and over their shoulder, she sees Justin sitting at the bar, alone.

"He's here," Erin whispers in Kimmy's ear, nodding toward the entrance. Peter's in the frame, wearing a navy sport coat over a teal checkered button-down, his outfit crisp but something about his general appearance disheveled, aloof. Kimmy watches him spot Erin, and his face completely transforms. It's light, happy. She doesn't know how to feel, if she should be happy for Erin or terrified.

Peter walks toward the group, and Kimmy eyes Justin in the background, wandering toward the band, his gait unsteady. They all used to get fucked up as kids, and she and Justin have had their fair share of cocktail-heavy nights this week, but they are in their thirties; she assumed that by now he too had learned when it was appropriate to binge and when it wasn't. She'd asked her mom to order two fruity mocktails when she went to the bar, hoping the mix would be sugary enough to trick Justin into thinking it was the real thing and sober him up.

"The Devine crew!" Peter says, their parents walking up right behind with hands full of drinks. "You are a sight for sore eyes." He says it to the entire family, but he's looking right at Erin.

"Peter!" Bill says, pushing his drinks into Kimmy's hands. "How are you?" He gives him a big hug. "How are Tess and the kids? We loved your Christmas card."

"Drink?" Carissa asks, offering him one of the mocktails in her hand. "I could use a little help lightening the load."

"I'm okay," he says, waving her off. "I wish I could stay longer, but with two little ones it's never easy. So I'm off the sauce tonight, mainly so the wife doesn't kill me." Kimmy sees Erin stiffen, and Peter catch her expression.

"Have this one." Carissa passes a drink to him. "They're non-alcoholic. It was supposed to be for Kimmy's prize-winning lush of a date, but I don't think he'll mind." Justin is standing right in front of the band bobbing his head alone.

"I'm right here, Mom," Kimmy says, rolling her eyes. "But it's fine." She turns to Peter. "Probably not a bad idea for you to stay sober, anyway." There's an edge to her voice, and she hopes he notices.

Peter laughs nervously as he takes the drink from Carissa. "Thanks, Mrs. Devine." He takes a sip. Just then, the mayor approaches with James. "Bill, Carissa, will you come with me to talk to Martha

Holmes? I always forget her kids' names. I need an assist." He winks at Kimmy. "James can keep you company while we're gone."

Kimmy's about to protest that she already has company, but Justin's in a trance by the band, swaying to their yacht rock jams. Just then, the band starts playing Orleans's "Dance with Me." She looks over at James. "This cannot be a coincidence."

He smiles, his hand out. "Ms. Kimberly Devine, may I have this dance? For old times' sake." Without thinking, she steps toward him, her arm around his neck and her hand in his, his palm on her waist. Despite his frame, he's surprisingly light on his feet. He leads her into a turn, spinning her out, then back in, her body bumping into his slightly.

She laughs. "Okay, Diner James. You did not have these moves fifteen years ago."

"Endless government soirees will teach you a thing or two," he says. She takes in his smell, clean and simple, like nothing more than body soap. They sway, quiet for a moment.

Kimmy sees her parents watching, Mayor Kasanaar next to them, all their faces glowing with delight. "Why am I starting to feel like this is a setup?" Kimmy asks James, nodding toward their cheering section. Still, she can't help but acknowledge the ease she feels in his arms, the lack of friction, the immediate approval from her family. Is this how a relationship's supposed to be, so full of support and excitement from those closest to her rather than worry and apprehension?

"They gotta get their thrills where they can. Though I'd be lying if I said I wasn't debating asking you out for a drink ever since the auction," he laughs, spinning Kimmy away from him, then back into his arms before she can answer. They sway again, a beat of silence, then James says, "You've had quite the decade of accomplishments. If you had told me the sad girl I met in the diner all those years ago would be one of the most successful people I've ever met? Well, to be honest, I wouldn't have been surprised."

"What do you mean?" Kimmy says, curious. "Sad? Oh god. I totally forgot I completely bawled that night."

"Yeah, but you had a fire. Even then, you were determined. To no longer be sad. It was like this push-pull between you and some larger force you just couldn't control." He steps closer to her, looking into her eyes as he speaks. "It seemed like you were stronger than it. And that you still are."

How had he known, seen all her potential, when she hadn't even realized it herself at the time? Because he is right; she is strong, every terrible event of that year thickening her skin, priming her to fight, to never let the darkness keep her from success. She tilts her head, her eyes on his, and takes in their calming blue, how they seem to strip away her bullshit tough-girl armor and see her, vulnerabilities and all. Just as she wants to hold him closer, he drops her hand. "Sorry, man," he says, raising his hands. Justin scoots between them, his footing clumsy as he puts both hands around Kimmy's waist, his hands inching a touch too low. "It was a lovely dance, Ms. Devine." James gives a dorky little bow. "And my offer stands on that drink." He then turns toward the mayor.

"Diner James with the smooth moves," Justin says, his voice mocking. "How do you really know him? Did you fuck him? Because it seems like he's way more than just some guy from the diner."

"Oh god, Justin." Kimmy makes a face. This isn't who he is. Or at least, she doesn't think so. She takes in his bloodshot eyes, his unkempt beard, the stumbling way he's leading her through the dance, and realizes she has no idea. They haven't talked in fifteen years. How much about him—the Justin of 2022, not 2007—does she actually know? She shakes the thought, though; she's known him since they were kids. Of course this isn't who he is. "I have spent a total of sixty minutes with that man in my entire life."

"In my experience, that's plenty of time for you to make yourself memorable."

She cocks her head, processing what she thinks she's hearing. "What are you insinuating?" She feels a wall coming back up, an anger she thought she'd shed.

"I don't care who you slept with fifteen years ago," he says. "Obviously." He looks toward the bar, and Kimmy follows his gaze, which is on Aaron. She swallows, knowing this is not the time or place to unpack the truth. Instead, she compartmentalizes, pushing his comment into a little box so they can get through the night and still have a future in the morning. Kimmy takes Justin's hand and drags him toward the exit before he can say anything else.

"I'm getting you an Uber." She props him on a bench near the club's valet. "I'll call you in the morning."

As they wait at the door, she sees two figures in the darkness walking toward the edge of the lawn, the moon spilling across the ocean behind them, and she knows Erin is about to have the conversation she's been dreading.

I worked here when I was about your age. Isn't that funny?

That you were ever our age? Yes. That's actually not something I can imagine.

Oh, hush. One of the chefs I worked with was still there until a few summers ago.

Then why did you never let us get cheesesteaks from here until recently?

He and a few of the other older chefs used to push the waitresses against the walls of the kitchen and try to give us hickeys on our necks. It was a game they thought was funny.

Ew, what? That's messed up.

Um, Kimmy, I believe what you meant to say is, "That's sexual assault." But yeah, Mom, that's messed up.

Back then, it wasn't. We just pushed them off and kept doing our job.

21

March 2007

The Flower Box has an eerie feel to it past dusk, the plants in its windows like looming monsters, claws out, arms creeping toward the sills. Kimmy walks past the front window, the small alley on the building's right side wet from melted snow. She's in her sweats, no makeup, her eyes shrunken from the cold. She snuck out when she got Stevie's call about thirty minutes earlier, her voice a rushed hush of excitement. *Aaron's home, he just texted me.* Kimmy knew Stevie's mom was at a conference in Philly, and her dad at a boat show in California. *He's coming over. With friends. Please come, I need you.*

Kimmy rubs her eyes, the sleep making them heavy. She has snuck out plenty of times before, always with Nikki, always to some party Justin may or may not be at. This? This felt annoying. Stevie lost her virginity to Aaron at Justin's New Year's Eve party that Kimmy hadn't been allowed to attend, the one where she was supposed to kiss Justin as the ball dropped, to start the year with him. Instead, her absence at the party drove him deeper into Madison's arms; Nikki said he spent all night locked in his room talking to her on the phone. So now Kimmy and Justin were just friends, officially. Justin told her they had to stop messing around, that he loved Madison. The reveal broke Kimmy's heart, but the "just friends" label was the only way to keep him in her life. She once again became his confidante, always there when he needed to vent about school or complain about Madison. Stevie's news about hooking up with Aaron almost felt like an affront, as if she were rubbing her happiness in Kimmy's face. But then Aaron went back to college and stopped returning Stevie's texts, only to reemerge when he was home and in need of a booty call. Kimmy didn't say any of this to

Stevie, though. Instead, she said she'd be there, their friendship feeling fraught these past few months, more and more of Kimmy's time spent with Nikki—or Justin.

She pushes the back door open, dragging her legs up each step, the store below quiet, the rest of the house on the second and third floors. She hears music and drunk laughter before she walks into the kitchen. Aaron is perched on a stool, his frame towering against the small countertop. Stevie stands next to him, a shot glass in her hand, her face frozen with infatuation as she looks at him doe-eyed. "Kimmy!" Stevie shouts when she spots her best friend, her arms wide open. She saunters over to Kimmy, collapsing into her. "Thank you for coming," she whispers, her words already slurred.

"Sup, Kimmy," Aaron says, his voice bellowing against the cottage's walls. He introduces her to the two other guys there, both in hoodies and beanies, hair sprouting from their chins and cheeks, shiny studs in their ears. Friends from school, he explains. Kimmy nods at them, wary, the whole scene feeling precarious. "You want?" He pushes a bottle of vodka toward her. Watermelon. She winces, the smell so sugary sweet it's enough to make her gag. But it's that or Everclear, she notices, the only other bottle on the island. She pours herself a drink, a mix of watermelon vodka and Sprite, and takes a sip, forcing a smile at Stevie.

"So how's college, Aaron?" she asks, making small talk as she sips her cocktail.

"It's good." His gaze is intense, more severe than Kimmy remembered. The gray in his eyes seems to pop the more he drinks, their ruddy color turning metallic as the night goes on. It makes her break eye contact, the slightest bit of discomfort creeping in. "I don't really think I'm a school kind of guy, though. Much better to learn from the school of life."

"Oh," Kimmy says, watching Stevie soak in all his pseudo intellect.

"But the drugs are sweet," he adds, "and so are my rich-ass student customers." His friends give him high fives as they all laugh.

Kimmy takes another small sip, the watermelon scent burning her nose as it goes down. Stevie leans on her elbows, her butt sticking out, her cheeks inflamed as she giggles in agreement.

Kimmy wants to be home. Wants to be warm in her bed. To be talking to Justin, his calls usually arriving at eleven or twelve, when they're both in near dream states. Almost like she wills it, her phone rings, Justin's name splayed across the front. Stevie raises a knowing brow. "Sorry, I have to get this," she says to Aaron and his friends, sneaking to the dining room down the hall. "Hey," she whispers, "I'm actually at Stevie's right now. Can I call you when I get home?"

"Shit," Justin says, his voice exasperated. "Can I come meet you there?" He sounds desperate, panting almost.

"Of course," she says, her heart racing, her mind playing a scene of him finally realizing she's the one as he pulls his car up to Stevie's house and Kimmy runs into his arms. She tries to hide her excitement. "Are you okay?"

"I'll explain when I'm there. I need you, Kimmy." He hangs up, and Kimmy immediately returns to the kitchen, grabbing her cocktail, throwing it back, her body tingling with anticipation. She loves when Justin needs her, when no one else but her can help. She can't wait to see him.

Ten minutes later, Stevie sits on Aaron's lap, his two guys friends are playing quarters, and Kimmy gets a text from Justin. *Out front.* She walks down the stairs, to the strip of sidewalk just in front of the Flower Box. She sees Justin's car, then him—then Madison, in the car's passenger seat. Kimmy pulls her parka around her body tight, looking at Justin's face for an explanation. Because there has to be one. He couldn't be this casually cruel, flaunting their relationship so intimately. When he looks at her, his face is solemn. "Kimmy." Desperation oozes from his words. She doesn't like it, doesn't want to know what he's about to say.

"What is this, Justin?" she asks quietly. Madison watches them, Kimmy knowing she is trying to lip-read everything coming out of her mouth. "Why are you here? Why is *she* here?"

"I didn't want to do this. To ask this of you. But"—he pauses, looking back at Madison, then to Kimmy—"our condom broke today, and Madison's not on birth control. We're in trouble. And Erin told Madison about one time you got Plan B." Kimmy takes a deep breath, her head suddenly spinning. She feels an anger in her chest. What the fuck was wrong with Erin? She had no business sharing that information with anyone, let alone Madison. It meant Erin had snooped around her room, probably looking for a shirt or makeup to borrow, because Kimmy had hidden the Plan B package the entire weekend she took it, until she could drop it in a trash can in the bathroom at school, where her parents—her mom, really—wouldn't find it. What Erin doesn't know, what Justin doesn't know, is that she took it after the second time she and Justin slept together. Kimmy exhales, the air from her mouth floating in a frigid cloud between her and Justin. She says nothing, secretly vowing to kill her sister when she gets the chance. "And I just—I mean, you're my best friend. I trust you with my life, right? So I thought maybe you could help us out. Because Madison isn't eighteen yet, so she can't get it herself, and she didn't want me to be seen at CVS, because you never know. So—"

"Wait, so you're both too embarrassed to go?" Kimmy asks, her arms crossed.

"It's a small town, Kimmy, and her dad's a big deal," he says.

"I'm not eighteen yet either. I'd have to go to Planned Parenthood." Nikki, almost a full year older than Kimmy, was the one who got it for her in September. "But it's okay if I'm seen there, or at CVS? If people assume I'm the town slut?" Kimmy's hissing, her voice rising. She takes a step closer to Justin, her teeth gritted. "I would do anything for you, Justin. Anything. But are you kidding me?" Her eyes are big, incredulous.

"I just—" he starts, but she sees him pause, realizing he messed up with this request. "Madison just thought—"

Kimmy looks at the car, her desire to flip Madison off so strong it takes everything to hold back. She's still watching them, and Kimmy swears she sees a sneer on her face. She looks back at Justin, both their cheeks red. "It's freezing. I'm going inside. I'll see you at school."

As she turns, Justin whispers sorry and touches her back, and she spins around. "Don't fucking touch me," she shrieks, her arms up. "Do not touch me. Do not talk to me. Do not even look at me." Tears well, then her voice drops. "Leave me alone, Justin. Please." Her tone is unkind, she knows, but she's tired, resigned.

They both pause for a moment, his mouth looking like it's about to move, but he says nothing, and Kimmy turns back inside and stomps up the stairs. When she gets to the kitchen, she takes the bottle of vodka and brings it right to her lips, wincing as she gulps.

"Oh my god," Stevie says, a cackle escaping. "Kimmy!" She slides off Aaron's lap, shimmying over to the island, then wraps her arm around Kimmy's waist, putting her mouth near Kimmy's ear. "Justin?" she whispers, their foreheads touching.

"I don't want to talk about it," Kimmy says. "Let's just drink, okay?"

Stevie nods, sliding two shot glasses in front of them. "To assholes," Kimmy says, cheersing.

Kimmy and Stevie are three additional shots in, twirling in circles as they sing the words to a song from *Rent* at the top of their lungs, Aaron and his friends slouch on the couch playing Fifa.

"Do you remember when we saw this in the theater last year?" Stevie asks, falling onto a stool against the kitchen counter. "That was, like, a big event. Everything is so different now."

Kimmy slides onto the stool next to her, wrapping her arm around Stevie's shoulders. "It's not that different," she says, but she feels it too, the shattering of their innocence, of simpler times.

"You are." Stevie's body stiffens for a moment. "You have a new best friend."

"I don't have a new best friend," Kimmy says, making a face. But she knows it's true. Her tongue feels thick and the room spins. "Nikki is your friend too."

"Only because of you," Stevie says. "And Justin. Your life revolves around him."

Kimmy pulls away, her body beating with heat. "That's rude."

"You know it's true. I get it, you're in love with him. But Kimmy, he has a girlfriend."

The room spins. "Are you trying to punish me for something?"

"No," Stevie says, shaking her head. "I'm just sad. I miss you."

Kimmy puts her hands on Stevie's shoulders and shakes her head. "I didn't realize you felt like I was MIA. Really," she says, the room still spinning. "I love you, you know that. You'll always be one of the most important people in my life."

Stevie tilts her head. "I love you too."

"Sisters forever." Kimmy leans her head into Stevie's. They clink their glasses together.

The rest of the night is in flashes.

Texts from Justin, begging apologies, Kimmy turning off her phone.

A shot glass, empty, while Kimmy brags that she's never thrown up from drinking before.

Stevie passed out on the couch, her snores loud, her shoes on, Aaron's two friends from college drawing on her face.

A pile of vomit, Kimmy's, all over the kitchen floor, her eyes teary, her chest heaving.

The ceiling, posters of Tristan Prettyman and Nada Surf swirling around her, lit only by the glow of a clock light. Stevie's bed.

Lips against hers. The taste of cigarettes. "Justin?" Kimmy whispers, her body slack from the alcohol, her vision blurred. She moans when she feels a heavy weight on her chest.

Then darkness. Total and complete darkness.

A chill wakes Kimmy, her body covered in goose bumps. She sits up, disoriented, and looks around. Her pants are crumpled on the floor, her underwear perfectly perched on top, as if both were pulled off as a unit. She wraps her arms around her chest, her thick sweatshirt still on, the confusion in her head too much, the raw ache between her legs freaking her out. The clock says 5:13 a.m., her brain muddled as she crawls out of the bed, slinking into her pants. She checks her phone, four unread texts from Justin.

legs
im sorry
come on pick up n talk 2 me
don't be mad pls ur my best friend i need u

She tiptoes into the kitchen, the damage of the night still there. She grabs a cloth and soap, scrubbing what's left of her vomit. Stevie purrs on the couch, her ability to sleep through anything ever present. The guys are nowhere to be seen, but Aaron's jacket is on the kitchen table. She lifts it up, about to put it on the couch next to Stevie, when the smell hits her. Distinct, cigarettes and Altoids, all at once. The same taste as her lips, and suddenly her stomach twists, and she runs to the bathroom, vomiting for a second time.

As she leans against the toilet bowl, her body exhausted, she takes a deep breath and knows what she has to do. Run. That's all there is. So she stands up, rinses her mouth with Listerine, puts on her shoes, and sneaks out Stevie's back door. The sun is rising, the skyline a shade of red. She starts with a jog, then a trot, then a full-on sprint, each pace helping numb her mind. She lets her feet lead her, chasing away her anxiety, taking her to the only place she knows she'll feel safe, like she doesn't have to explain herself. When she gets to the front door, she looks at her phone. It's 6:03. Still way too early, but what choice does she have? She rings the doorbell, both Nikki and her mom already up, their coffee machine gurgling. Nikki opens the door, takes one look at her, and opens her arms. She knows, Kimmy can tell. She already knows something isn't right.

22

Beach Week 2022

DAY FIVE

"You look gorgeous tonight," Peter says, running a hand down Erin's cheek, her neck, toward her collarbone.

She's glad he noticed all her effort, but she pushes his hand down, her own shaking as they make contact. "Peter," she says, taking a step back.

"I know." He lowers his head and walks over to a bench in the shadows of the uplit flagpole, America's Stars and Stripes fluttering in the night breeze. Erin stays standing, not wanting to fall into his embrace. "There's so much going on, Erin. It's more than you even realize." Her arms are crossed. "You came into my life when I needed you. When I was at my absolute lowest. When I thought I was going to lose everything."

"What do you mean?" she asks, shifting her weight to her right hip. She had always thought he had done that for her, not the other way around. His body language isn't what she hoped for, doesn't scream *I just told my wife about us and we can finally be together.* Erin swallows, her throat clicking like something's stuck inside. Her guilt, maybe, or the truth, like if she refuses to hear whatever Peter's about to tell her, time will suspend and they can go back to their affair, to their little bubble. To the moment before she gave him an ultimatum. Why had she done that?

"I lost everything. All our savings. Investing in a former Penn buddy's start-up in 2018 that totally bombed right after we started construction on the Shore house."

"Okay," she says, taking another step back, even more deeply worried about where this conversation is going. "I'm confused what this has to do with me?"

"I love you," Peter says. "I probably have since the first time I met you. But we have shitty timing."

She feels the tears welling. "What are you trying to say, Peter?"

"Tess knows. She knows about us. I came clean to her."

"You told her?" Erin smiles, their secret finally out in the open. They can be together.

"She found out before I could. Someone saw us at the Bellevue. Some-one who knows a girl named Madison Jensen. Tess interviewed her—"

"No," Erin says, her brain racing to her last Bellevue visit. She hadn't seen anyone, had she? Then she remembers the woman in the elevator, how she looked like she was about her age, how her eyes lingered a few seconds too long. It had to have been her. "Kimmy saw them the other morning. I didn't realize—" She puts her face in her hands, her worst nightmare unfolding.

"We got in a huge fight yesterday. I mean, Tess threw our kids' mon-itor at me. I'm only here to end things." Peter's face is strained and he breaks eye contact, his age showing more tonight than it ever has before. Everything about him suddenly disgusts Erin. "I can't leave her, Erin."

"You can't, or you won't?" Erin's voice is hardly more than a whisper, her surprise like a leech sucking all the passion from her expression. This is not how she expected the evening to go.

"I am in so much fucking debt. And the twins," he says, as if he has been thinking about them the whole time. "I need to fix what I broke. She's calling her parents tonight to help us figure things out, to get us back on our feet."

"So you're staying with her for the money? Not because you love her?" She pauses, hoping he'll tell her that's all, that they just have to wait a few more years.

"Of course I love Tess." He puts a hand to his forehead, wiping a bead of sweat. "She's the mother of my kids."

"I cannot believe you," Erin says, her hands adjusting the straps of her dress, his words devastating her entire sense of worth. She is not Tess, a virtuous mother. She will never be, her uterus far too hostile. "You used me, Peter. You used me like I'm some common whore." He begins to stand, but she stops him. "Don't." It all feels so deflating and sad. "Why have I never been enough for you?" she asks, the tears coming. She thinks of him, of Kent retreating more and more with each fertility injection, of her parents forcing Kimmy to upend her life abroad to run the store despite Erin being right there in Rocky Cape the whole time. Why is she never enough for anyone?

"You are, Erin," he says. "You always have been. It's just, my hands are tied. I'm married, for god's sake." He throws that at her like it's her fault, like she lured him into this situation. Something in his voice is off, the slightest bit slow. "You knew this when we started things."

"Are you drunk?" Erin asks, hoping some sort of chemical is impairing his decision making. Because this can't be her reality. This can't be how their love story ends.

He stands, then sits back down. "No," he says, running a hand through his hair. "This whole thing is dizzying." He brings the back of his hand to his head, looking at Erin with round, sad eyes.

"It's dizzying? Oh, poor you, Peter," Erin says, her face distorted with anger. "You are such an egomaniac. You never really loved me. Or Tess." Erin's voice gets louder. "I hate you." She knows how petty she sounds, but she can't help it, trying her best to control her emotion. How dare he think he can just get away with this, that he can sweep her off her feet for a year—or fifteen, really—snap his fingers, and hope it all disappears. He doesn't get to erase their passion, their love, to treat her like a mistake without feeling terrible in the process.

"Erin," Peter says, his voice soft, sad.

"You are a pathetic excuse for a human. I hope I never have to look at your face ever again. You are nothing more than a loser who ruins everything you touch. The world would be a better place without you in it." And with that, she turns and runs back toward the club, where she feels the emotion hit her full throttle. She falls onto the grass, collapsing into sobs, her shoulders convulsing with each gasp. It's not until she feels them calm, feels a familiar warmth and comfort envelop her, that she realizes Kimmy is holding her, is right there like a promise to make everything okay.

23

May 2007

"The Camerons are in town for the holiday," Carissa told Erin and Kimmy casually that morning. "I hope you girls don't have plans, because they're coming over for dinner." As Kimmy reminded Carissa that she had friends coming over that night to celebrate her birthday, Erin quietly retreated to her room, not wanting to shriek in front of her mom. She hadn't known this, the fact making something inside her turn with excitement. She and Peter hadn't talked for over a month, his postgrad travels taking him all across Europe. She missed him, missed their conversations. She was deliberate when picking out her outfit, her flowy white skirt and tight blue tank top hugging without being too inappropriate for a family dinner. As Kimmy sets the table on their back porch, Erin thinks about all the questions she wants to ask Peter, how she wants to impress him with her knowledge of Europe, despite never having visited herself. She had spent hours over the past months Googling cities mentioned in the pictures he posted on Facebook. Once he's impressed, she's sure he'll accept her invitation to join her at the Memorial Weekend fireworks tonight, their legs dangling off the dock as they watch the colors burst throughout the night sky. She places seven settings, asking Kimmy to grab the water glasses, when her mom comes out. "Honey, eight. Can you add one more?"

"For Nikki?" she asks, looking at Kimmy for confirmation.

"She's having dinner with her mom before she comes over," Kimmy says, straightening the rows of silverware Erin had carefully placed on each napkin. "Since our plans got bumped thanks to this little soiree." She rolls her eyes, a move that's become something of her signature lately.

"Peter's bringing his girlfriend," Carissa says, turning back around, not aware of the arrow she just delivered. Erin stands there, stunned. Her mom turns again. "ErBear, please honey, chop-chop. They're going to be here any second."

She goes to grab more place settings, running through all their conversations. Had he ever mentioned a girlfriend? No, she tells herself. Absolutely not. Never. She would remember.

Just then, the doorbell rings. "Judy. Phil. So good to see you!" Erin hears down the hall. She walks in and sees her mom hugging Peter's parents, her dad and Kimmy coming down the stairs joining the greeting line. She stays back, waiting.

"You remember Peter?" Judy asks, pushing her son forward.

"How could we ever forget our favorite tutor?" Bill says, sticking his hand out. "You may be the only thing that stood between Erin and community college." Erin cringes, the elitism and judgment in her father's voice gut shaking.

"And this is Peter's girlfriend, Tess." They walk into the foyer, both dressed in sharply pressed prep, his khakis stone and his collared shirt striped, her dress some swirling Lilly Pulitzer pattern Erin could swear her mother owns. She's wearing pearls, large and round in her ears.

"Hi, Mrs. Devine," Tess says, putting her hand out. "Thank you so much for having me. Your home is lovely."

What is she, from the 1950s? But as they walk toward the kitchen, Erin hides behind the counter, her shoulders feeling alarmingly bare. Why had she worn this, today? She had wanted Peter to look at her, but now she just feels slutty. Kimmy walks behind the crowd, giving Erin a look as she passes. "Come on," she says, her hand out. "We'll discuss later."

Erin never told Kimmy about Peter, but there's something in her voice that feels like pity. Like she knows about her crush. *But it's more than that!* Erin wants to scream.

They all sit, the fan on the covered porch blowing the edges of Erin's napkin. "So," Kimmy starts. "Peter, I heard you were all over Europe. What did you say, Er—Scotland? How was that?"

He looks at Erin for a moment. Was it annoyance she detected, a flash? It wasn't her fault he friended her on Facebook, that he sent her occasional emails with updates. Was she not supposed to tell anyone about them?

"Europe," Erin's dad says. "Where about? You know, we have some distant relatives in County Cork."

The conversation drones on and Erin doesn't say a thing, instead monitoring Tess's every move, trying to find a flaw she can fixate on. At one point, Peter puts his arm around Tess, pulling her close, and Erin almost chokes on a piece of shrimp. "Sorry," she says, looking across the table. "I think I'm allergic to whatever perfume you're wearing, Tess. It's really strong." Kimmy kicks her under the table, and Carissa gives them both a look. No one else seems to notice, but Peter keeps avoiding eye contact with Erin.

"Peter was in Wales, Edinburgh, and Glasgow. Right, babe?" she rubs the hand that is draped around her shoulder. "Not that I would know. As Mrs. Cameron and I have joked, Peter is the worst communicator in the world. I think he Skyped me, like, once during his entire trip." This makes Erin perk up. Peter had sent her three emails during his trip. She had sent him seven, but whatever. He had talked to her more than Tess!

"Sorry, babe," Peter says, looking back at her, their mutual use of "babe" enough to make Erin want to throw up. "They're exaggerating, though. Tess and I had a standing Wednesday night Skype date, which I made it to almost every week." He winks at Tess, and then he kisses her, right there, in front of everyone, and Erin feels her face getting brighter and brighter. Kimmy grabs her hand under the table.

"Mom," she says, interrupting the moment. "Er and I will get the salad." Kimmy pulls her sister with her to the kitchen, saving her from further embarrassment. She opens the fridge and pulls out the large bowl, greens fluffed to the rim. She places it in Erin's hands, then plops two tongs in the center. As she opens the fridge again, grabbing two containers of dressing, she turns to Erin. "He's an asshole." Kimmy shakes the Italian, the oil mixing with the orange mess. "You're so young, Er. You don't need to put up with guys like that already."

You either, Erin wants to say. Instead, she grabs the dressing and returns to the table, a smile plastered on her face.

The Devines' pool glows teal in the night air, the bay glistening in the distance. Kimmy floats on a tube in the shallow end of the pool, laughing as she watches Nikki and Ben race each other on inflatable sea horses. The floaties were new additions to the pool last summer, Bill so fed up with seagulls swooping in he grabbed five oversize floats from the store, all shaped like ridiculous animals, and connected them by string so they loomed across the water, scaring away the birds. Erin called it the Devine Family Circus. They had become something of a novelty now, every friend who visited immediately grabbing one and creating one ridiculous game after another. "Come on, Lamb," Justin shouts, his hands cupped around his mouth. "Don't let Nikki beat your ass."

Kimmy is surprised he's here. He's next to her, their legs hanging over the edges of the floats in parallel. Madison spent all of that morning on the beach, her entire body slathered in oil; now she's home with a second-degree sunburn, refusing to let anyone, including Justin, see her until it calms. He texted Kimmy about an hour before everyone was supposed to arrive, between dinner and dessert with the Camerons, asking if it was okay if he came. Things had cooled between them since he showed up at Stevie's in March; Kimmy threw herself into partying, distracting her from the emptiness she couldn't seem to shake, and for weeks only responded to Justin's texts and IMs with one-word answers, if at all. But after they were assigned to a history group project together in April, she'd opened up a bit more, their regular banter picking up again, and seeing him in person, without Madison? It makes her feel a warmth she's missed. And she knows her distance has only increased his persistence to get her back on his side. She flicks water at him and cups her own hands around her mouth. "Go, Nik!"

She reaches toward the edge of the pool, the plastic ribbed glass holding more than just lemonade. Her parents took the Camerons to the yacht club for postdinner cocktails, and Erin, Kimmy knew, was in the family room watching *Sex and the City* on DVD. Kimmy felt so bad for her after dinner she invited her to join the night's festivities, but Erin said no, her entire tone shifting from hours earlier when she was singing Ashlee Simpson in her room as she got ready. "You want yours?" Kimmy asks, her hand reaching for Justin's drink.

"Nah, I got it," he says, sliding off his tube and pushing the side of Kimmy's into the water in the process. Her drink spills on her stomach as she wobbles.

"Justin!" She lifts her hips to let her drink drain into the pool water. As she does, Justin brings his mouth to her abs, slurping the excess liquid.

"Got it for you," he says as he raises his head, spinning Kimmy in the tube. He grabs his drink, his hand still on her float, and takes a swig before placing it on the edge of the pool again.

"Stop," she says, quietly. "You have a girlfriend." She looks over to Nikki and Ben, then Ryan and Chris, all four of them at the other end of the pool. Gossip about her and Justin had simmered during the early winter months, but after her night with Aaron, Kimmy sort of lost it. She drank more, made out with randoms, took it all the way with a few. When she was feeling particularly low, she texted Brian and they started hanging out again, until Brian told her he wasn't looking for a girlfriend right now since college was just around the corner. The next day, after an extra-large mixed drink and sucking a weed lollipop with Nikki during a casual hang at Justin's, she had sex with Ethan, a junior on the baseball team who smoked with them occasionally, on Justin's futon under a ratty beach blanket, while Nikki was passed out and Justin pretended to watch a movie. The next day, he IM'd her: *Were you thinking of me?* By Tuesday, Ethan had told the entire baseball team, who told everyone at school.

So now Brian could hardly look at her. Stevie had been getting more and more annoyed with her flakiness. Derek and Katie loved blabbing to anyone who would listen that she was a drunk nymphomaniac. Her parents were worried about her disinterest in running beyond practice. Her mom had come into her room the other night and given her a weird pep talk about how wonderful and smart she was and how bright her future is. Her head was a fucking mess. So much of that mess started with Justin, culminating with Aaron. She wanted to escape, but for whatever reason, she couldn't let go of Justin, spiraling further and further into disarray. Still, she couldn't deal with any more rumors; they were eating away at her core, forcing her to drift from who she thought she was. She didn't know anymore.

"I've missed you, Legs." Justin leans his elbows on the tube. He is drunk, she can tell.

"We hang out all the time." Kimmy takes another sip of her drink, laying her head on the tube. The sky is crystal, tiny sparkles dancing as Justin spins her around. He stops the tube when the top of her head is against his stomach. He squats so his mouth is right by her ear, and a hand disappears.

"Not alone," he says, and Kimmy feels his fingers against her bathing suit bottom. She breathes in, not saying no for a moment, remembering how good they feel when there's no barrier, then snaps out of it, flipping onto her stomach so she faces him, their noses an inch apart.

"So do something about it," she says, testing him.

"What?" He stands with a confused look on his face. Kimmy slides off her tube and walks toward him, her buzz hitting as she watches the water ripple against Justin's chest.

"If you want me," she says, tugging at the drawstrings of his swimsuit, "break up with Madison." She said it, finally. After months of hoping he would come around, of pretending not to care so they can still be friends, she said it. Because, she realizes, they will never be just friends. They never were just friends. They are scientifically incapable of it. Justin puts a hand on Kimmy's side, pulling her a step closer. She looks up at him, waiting for an answer.

"I have an idea." He grins as he looks down at her. She raises an eyebrow and Justin turns toward the other side of the pool, where Nikki, Ben, Ryan, and Chris are splashing one another like kids at summer camp. "Yo, guys," he shouts. "Now that Legs is finally eighteen, wanna get some ink?"

Nikki raises her arm, showing off song lyrics she had sketched on her bicep a few months ago. "You know I'm in."

"For real, guys," he says, now addressing the group. "This is our crew. Who knows if we'll be this close ever again. Let's get something to commemorate it."

"Shit, dude. I love it. Like the *Lord of the Rings* cast," Chris says, pulling himself up out of the pool. "I'm in."

Kimmy makes eye contact with Ben, smiling as if to say, *It's okay.* He's awkward because he made a move on her last Friday when she was smooshed between him and Ryan in the backseat of Bev, taking turns sipping vodka out of a water bottle as Nikki drove them to a Disco Biscuits concert at the Electric Factory. When Kimmy patted his hand away with what can only be described as condescending affection, he stewed all night, later hissing in her ear: "I'm just confused why you won't hook up when it seems like you're game to hook up with anyone these days." Kimmy didn't respond, pretending she couldn't hear him above the psychedelic music. She hasn't told Nikki or anyone else; she doesn't want things to be awkward, to ruin the last few weeks of school by causing a fight. But she doesn't care, really. He was no different from any drunk idiot. Weren't all guys like this? She raises her eyebrows at him. "You in, Lamb?" And with that one question, she watches his shoulders relax, his misbehavior forgiven—and, likely for him, forgotten.

They race their bikes toward the closest tattoo shop, the wind in Kimmy's hair as she rides with Justin, the night feeling endless. Ben, Nikki, Ryan, and Chris crowd two chairs near the front of the shop, and Justin pulls Kimmy to his, near the back. She watches as he gets a simple set of waves on the edge of his forearm, the design they all chose. Her face gives her away, and Justin assures her it's not as painful as it looks. As the artist nears the end, Justin tells him he wants one more. He puts out his left arm and points to a spot on his bicep parallel to his heart. Kimmy watches as the artist writes a small *pb* in cursive. When it's her turn, Justin sits in a stool next to the chair. Kimmy gets the waves on her hipbone, right where her bikini bottoms stop so her parents will never see. When it's done, Justin looks at her expectantly and she turns on her side. "*J,*" she tells the artist. "I want a small, cursive *j*, right here." She pulls up the bottom edge of her bikini top, pointing to her side, aligned with her heart. As the artist sticks the needle in her skin, she looks up at Justin, and he grabs her hand, squeezing.

"I told you," he whispers, his face close to hers. "We'll always be connected."

It's not an answer to her earlier demand. It's even better. It's more than a high school label, a fleeting fling. The needle digs deeper, the pain suddenly visceral. Kimmy finds she likes it, and as she looks at Justin, she smiles. Before the artist is even done, she knows she'll end up in Justin's bed tonight.

Stevie walks up the stairs to the Devines' second floor, the house uncharacteristically empty. Erin's on the sectional, *Sex and the City* blaring from the screen. "Hey," she says when she spots Stevie.

"Where is everyone?" Stevie crashes into the couch, her brace tight as her knee bends.

"Probably having an orgy somewhere," Erin says, rolling her eyes.

"Uh, okay, perv," Stevie says, but presses. "Is Kimmy here? She knew I'd be over late because of work." Stevie puts the new fabric journal she wrapped for Kimmy by her side on the couch, the whorl of the ceiling fan shimmering against the metallic paper.

Erin shrugs. "They all left, like, a half hour ago. No idea where, but they biked." Stevie pulls out her phone, about to call Kimmy, when Erin interrupts. "Don't even bother. Kimmy was on Justin's bike. I don't know if she thinks she gets a birthday pass to be a slut, but it seems that's her plan. I'm so sick of it." Erin looks back at the TV.

Stevie hasn't even loosened her grip on the overnight bag she packed. Every year since they were seven, Stevie sleeps over at the Devines' on Kimmy's birthday. Erin usually crashes, and the three of them stay up all night eating junk food, bingeing rom-coms, and talking. "There's no way she remembered the sleepover," Erin says, scooching so she faces Stevie, her legs pulled into her chest. "But are you surprised? She has literally become the most selfish person in the world. I'm tired of defending her."

Stevie takes a breath, not wanting to pile on about Kimmy, but she feels the same.

"Did you know she had sex with Justin all throughout the fall? She told me around New Year's." Erin's mouth turns down, her disapproval palpable.

Stevie lifts an eyebrow. "It's not just Justin. There's, like, seven guys on that list."

"Wait, what?" Erin asks, confused. "Since when?"

"I guess the gossip hasn't made it to the sophs yet. Little babies," Stevie says, tickling Erin's stomach.

"Idiot." Erin smacks Stevie with a pillow, both of them laughing before Stevie turns serious again.

"She got in a huge fight with Justin in March and has been on a tear ever since. Let me think." Stevie looks at her fingers, counting. "She told me about Greg, Matt, and obviously Brian again. And then I heard rumors about Drew and Ethan. And lord knows who else. She's become so shady, it's weird. It's like she's not even herself anymore."

Erin's quiet, staring at the TV as Charlotte complains to Carrie about whoever she's dating this episode. "It's funny," she says. "In our little group I always thought she was the Charlotte." She keeps watching, suddenly zoned out. Stevie stands.

"Well, I should probably go," she says, but Erin shushes her.

"Shut up. You're as much my friend as Kimmy's these days. Want to watch *Aquamarine*?"

"I forgot my shell bra. Should I go home and get it? Oh wait, you have one around here, don't you?" Stevie jokes, referring to Erin's seventh-grade Halloween costume when she and some of her friends dressed as mermaids. Her mom wouldn't let her wear just a shell bra, so she glued it onto a white leotard and all the boys made fun of her, saying she looked like Casper instead of Ariel.

"Why must you be so jealous of how hot I am?" Erin says, hopping off the sofa and grabbing Oreos from their pantry. "Yo, girl, we going for the heavy shiz tonight." She tosses Stevie a pack of double stuffed.

"Hit me," Stevie says, and Erin hears the sadness in her voice. She wants to reach out, to hug her and say she gets it, she feels it, they're on the same page. But instead, she settles in across from Stevie and turns on the movie, her irritation with Kimmy growing. Impulsively, she pulls out her phone and texts Madison. *Kimmy's sluttiness is so much worse than we guessed*

Omg deets pls, Madison responds almost immediately. *I am so bored as I nurse my face back to health hahaha I'm an idiot*

And without realizing it, Erin yanks at the final thread that kept her sister from fully unraveling.

24

Beach Week 2022

DAY FIVE

"Erin!" Peter shouts as she sprints in the opposite direction. He stands to run after her, but feels all the blood rush to his head. He teeters, his brows stitched in confusion. He takes a final sip of his mocktail, chalking up his dizziness to nothing more than dehydration.

Or maybe it's the stress. The money, the affair, the kids and lack of sleep.

Or the drugs. He's been careful and strategic about taking them from the office, and they are tame enough. Every once in a while, he sneaks a codeine pill, just to help take off the edge. He popped one before coming here, after his fight with Tess, to help make the whole thing less painful.

Peter loves Erin. He really does, and always has, in a way he knew was inappropriate. He is intoxicated by her, the shape of her, the way she fits in his arms, the way he fits in her body. Ever since that first time, back in her dorm room, he knew he would regret marrying Tess, that he would always think of Erin.

When Peter ran into her at Devine's almost a year ago, he knew he was in trouble. He used to scroll through her Facebook and eventually her Tumblr, where she'd post dance shots in all these convoluted positions, and Peter would imagine her massive tits spilling out of the dainty top of her leotard, her back against a ballet bar and legs spread in a wide straddle as they fucked. He knew she wanted him too, but she was a minor, untouchable, which only magnified his desire to sleep with her.

When he finally got to fuck her during his bachelor party, he thought his obsession would pass, his itch finally scratched. And it did, minus checking her Facebook photos a few times a year and jerking off as he zoomed on the ones where she was in a bikini. Until he ran into her at Devine's. And she was divorced. Available.

He thought about texting her, but he would glimpse Tess's swollen belly and know he couldn't do it to her, to their family. But then the twins arrived, and something inside him broke. Instead of feeling unconditional love for them, he felt annoyed. Why did they look like raisins, and why did they poop and vomit and cry so fucking much? He spent more time at the office and at the Shore, using the construction on their house as an excuse to get away. When his buddy's start-up crashed in summer 2021, Peter lost two hundred thousand dollars in savings. His stress was at an all-time high, lava building and building and ready to explode. And then Erin texted him, and he knew she was the answer to all this. She could be his savior.

His dependency on Erin increased with each hangout. All Tess did was yell at him, her nipples bleeding and eyes ringed from exhaustion. "That's not how you change Everett's diapers. He'll poop through it. Tighter," she said as she pushed Peter to the side and yanked at the straps of the baby's Coterie. "Don't even think about it," she said, swatting his hands when he tried to sleep with her a few days after her six-week postpartum checkup. "Oh my god, Peter, are you trying to kill them?" she asked when she walked in on him feeding the babies chicken nuggets cut into fourths when they were ten months old. Erin, on the other hand, made him feel like a god. She soothed his ego with her unwavering interest, his stress with her constant reassurances that he'd figure it all out, and his dick with her mouth. He couldn't remember the last time Tess gave him head.

But then Erin got too greedy and threatened to ruin his entire world. After she gave him an ultimatum, he pulled into the driveway of their Shore house and saw Tess dancing with the twins in the kitchen, the three of them singing and giggling, a picture of sublime suburbia. What the fuck had he been doing? He had a great wife, great kids, a great life.

Tess is his best friend. The mother of his children. The loyal woman who stands by his side no matter how much he fucks up. The problem solver in their family. She isn't afraid of confrontation the way Peter is, never a coward. He walked in the door two days earlier and she asked, point blank, "Are you fucking Erin Devine?" He owned up to everything, Tess putting the twins in front of a TV, playing *Cocomelon*—one of her big no-nos; she claimed it melted babies' brains—so they could scream at each other, or really, so Tess could scream at him. But by the end, they were both calm, and Peter made promises to Tess to be loyal, be better, be honest. He never mentioned the painkillers, but he could quit that no problem. He was sure of it. At least after tonight.

But after his conversation with Erin, he is flaccid, emasculated, a broken man ruining one woman's life and working uphill to gain another's trust back. But he will. He knows he will.

He feels sleepy, the world swirling around him as he lays his head on the bench. When he opens his eyes again, the yacht club is quiet, peaceful. He shakes his head and stands up to walk to Tess. He will make it home, he will be better. He will make it all up to her. He takes out his phone, but the screen looks blurry. His muscle memory kicks in and he calls Tess using Siri on his watch. What time is it? He has no idea, his mind getting foggier. He hears her voice and starts to talk, until he realizes it's her voicemail. When the beep goes, he slurs out his apology.

"I'm so, so, so, so sorry. I don't deserve you. I don't deserve the twins. I love you. I love you. I love you," he repeats, over and over. "I'll fix this. I'll fix it." He can't hear her on the other side of the line, like his ears are suddenly filled with silence. He just wants to sleep, to find a place to rest. He sees a bed in the distance, the back cushion of a yacht, white and fluffy, a light shining down on it. It looks like a cloud, waiting for him. He walks toward it, the path bumpy, but he's close. So close. Just a few more steps.

His legs give out, the exhaustion too much. He leans into it, falling as they do, flying, free for just a moment, until the splash comes, and then nothing else.

Nikki said she thinks her roommate got roofied last night.

                                    What do you mean? Is she okay?

Well, I'm not sure. It sounds like they went out for one drink and Nikki had to, like, drag her limp body home.

                    Have they called the police? Is Nikki's friend okay? Is Nikki?

Yeah, Nikki said she took her home once she started acting odd. But neither of them saw anyone slip something in her drink, so there's not much to do. Even though they're across the country, it sort of makes me never want to go out. Is that crazy?

                        No, honey. Not at all. You can never be too careful.

That's what I thought too.

25

June 2007

"To the last day of senior year." Nikki splits the brownie in her hand into four even pieces. "One for you," she says, giving one to Kimmy, who's sitting in the front seat. Her legs are tight, sore from her morning run, her mind just as tense. She has been pushing herself harder and harder, her runs more extreme, just like her moods. Sometimes, when she has finished her ninth mile, she tries to sprint the last one, will convince herself that if she got under six minutes, everything would be right again. Justin would be hers.

"And here's one for you and you," she says, putting a square in Ben's hand and another in Ryan's, the two cramped in the small backseat of Bev.

The brownies were left over from prom. Kimmy went with Chris, and Nikki went with Ryan, all agreeing to have the best platonic, high-as-fuck night on the dance floor. Ben asked Erin, neglecting to get Kimmy's approval ahead of time. And, of course, Justin went with Madison. They took pictures in front of the bay in the Devines' back-yard, Nikki and Kimmy posing like Charlie's Angels as their corsages itched against their wrists, and the Devine parents were hosts with the most to all the sets of parents except the Fitzpatricks, whom they coolly greeted then ignored. Stevie went with some guy from Derek and Brian's soccer club, so she didn't join them for pictures; Kimmy felt a notable absence, but pushed the feeling aside with a layer of lip gloss and, once they were in the limo on the way to prom, a brownie. She felt Erin's glare on her as she ate one, but ignored it. Why was she even there, anyway? So she could keep scheming with her shitty best friend?

Kimmy and Nikki danced like they were in the front row at Coachella, their reckless grinding in stark contrast to their tulle gowns and bedazzled updos. Near the end of the night, as Kimmy was walking from the bathroom back to the dance floor, she passed Justin and he grabbed her arm. His pupils were as big as hers. "You look really beautiful tonight," he whispered in her ear, and she felt a smile take over her face. When he broke away, she made eye contact with Madison. Normally, she'd avert her eyes, pretend nothing had happened. But she felt emboldened by the pot; she kept smiling, their gazes locked.

"Aye, aye, aye," Ben says as he stuffs the entire thing in his mouth. Kimmy laughs, taking a big bite of hers. She still avoids smoking, not so irresponsible she forgot about her lungs, but edibles? They were all right by her.

"Nik, this shit is tight." Ryan's teeth are dirty from the chocolate. "You're like the Betty Crocker of the weed world."

Nikki does a fake bow, with a laugh. "Though to be honest, I can't take all the credit. This is my mom's recipe. Gotta make her proud, ya know."

The four of them leave the car, the sun bright. Nikki snakes her arm through Kimmy's, the guys strolling in behind them. As they walk up the sidewalk from their school's student lot to the entrance, Kimmy spots Justin and Madison walking toward them. She makes eye contact with Madison for a moment, the anger in her belly ignited once again. "Fucking bitch," Nikki whispers, and the two laugh, both looking her way. *Make her insecure*, Kimmy thinks. *Who cares if she knows we are talking about her.*

"Sup, my dudes," Justin says as they near, bro-high-fiving Ben and Ryan, Madison quiet by his side. She is always quiet in person, like a shadow judging everyone and everything in her path. But online, her voice is deafening, always posting pictures of her and Justin kissing, commenting on his wall, updating her status with their whereabouts and all the cute things they're doing. Kimmy wanted to defriend her, but knew that would be way worse than just muscling through her updates.

"Tweaking, man," Ryan says, popping the last bit of his brownie in his mouth.

"Damn, where was my invite?" Justin says.

"Classy," Madison says under her breath, but loud enough they all can hear.

"Would rather enjoy nature's finest than have a fucking stick up my designer-clad ass twenty-four seven," Nikki says over her shoulder, looking at Madison. "But hey, to each their own."

Justin pushes Nikki's backpack playfully. "Down, girl."

Kimmy laughs, putting her head on Nikki's shoulder as they walk into the school hallway.

There's a frenetic energy there, a freedom-is-just-around-the-corner vibe. Kimmy's homeroom is in the first hallway, so she peels off. "Bye, babe," Nikki says, blowing her a kiss. She blows a kiss back and feels Justin's eyes on her, then sees Madison's on him. She smiles back at him, the edible starting to hit.

She shrinks into her desk, her backpack melting into a pile on the floor. The room glows, that comfortable body high tingling through her limbs. The teacher isn't there yet, so Kimmy grabs some Visine from her backpack. As she starts putting a drop in one eye, Stevie sits at the desk next to her. She scoots closer, looking at Kimmy's eyes once she puts in the other drop. "Are you high?" Her question isn't accusatory per se, but Kimmy doesn't care, already vibing.

She nods, a giggle coming from her lips. "It's cool."

"Gross," says Katie, who sits behind Stevie. "So cool that you're becoming a stoner burnout. So cool." She rolls her eyes and opens a book, despite finals being over.

"Not all of us can be so pure, Katie." Katie glares at her, then back down. Their friendship had fully splintered that spring, Kimmy's behavior getting less and less predictable, her time spent with Nikki growing. She and Stevie were still okay, but something had shifted and Kimmy felt it, her secret shame an albatross following them without Stevie even realizing—and it pushed Stevie back into Katie's arms.

"So Aaron is home from school," Stevie whispers to Kimmy. "Did you know that? I guess he's having a party tonight. Wanna go?"

Kimmy looks at Stevie, her high unable to mask her disgust. "Um, no. I think I'm gonna do something with Nikki tonight, if that's cool."

"Kimmy, it's our last night of high school. We didn't even go to prom together. We have to hang out. Besides, I bet Nikki will be there."

Doubtful, Kimmy wants to say. But she doesn't. "Okay," Kimmy says noncommittally. "Let me know the plan and I'll see if I can swing it."

"I don't know why you hate Aaron so much," Stevie says. "I wanted him to take my virginity. Like, he didn't use me, okay? I know that's what you think." Kimmy says nothing. "He's a cool guy once you get to know him."

She nods, then looks forward. Kimmy can't look at Stevie, can't listen to her gush about that monster for a second longer. *He is a creep*, she wants to scream. But is he? Or maybe the truth is that she's just a slut like everyone says. She put the bottle to her mouth, asked for it by getting so fucked up. So instead she closes her eyes and lets her high take over, slouching in her chair, her head back. *Make me forget*, she wills. *Make it all go away.*

"Our final meal!" Justin drapes his arm over Nikki's shoulders as they walk toward their respective lunch tables. Kimmy follows Justin and Nikki, Stevie at her side. They sit at two of the tables on a platform at the front of the cafeteria, the four tables up there historically reserved for seniors.

"I can't believe it's our last day." Stevie looks wistfully at her tray. Kimmy nods, thinking instead about Justin. He hasn't ended things with Madison yet, has been waiting until school was officially over to avoid drama. *Tonight*, he had texted her. She was obsessed, couldn't focus on anything else. Tonight. Tonight, tonight, tonight.

She is so fixated she doesn't notice the pile of papers being passed around in the cafeteria, a wave of white floating among the tables off the platform.

"Um, why is everyone looking up here?" Stevie says, dropping her tray on their table as a crumpled ball hits her shoulder. "What the hell?" she shouts at the rest of the cafeteria. Nikki reaches for it, unfurling the ball, and Kimmy watches her expression change. Justin and the guys at the table next to them don't seem to notice, their focus on their food and one another.

Nikki looks up at Kimmy, her face concerned. They're both still high, but not like this morning, the effects near the end. "What is it?" Stevie asks, grabbing for the paper. "Let me see." Nikki moves, but not fast enough. Kimmy reads over Stevie's shoulder, taking in the crinkled message. "Who Hasn't Kimmy Devine Slept With?" and underneath, a scanned picture of her in her track uniform, her legs bare and stomach showing, with pictures pulled from Facebook all around. Brian. Justin. Ethan, plus two other guys from their class she slept with while wasted at parties over the past two months. And at the very top of the list: Aaron. "Wait," Stevie says. "Kimmy, why is Aaron here?"

Kimmy looks up, taking in all the eyes on her, her skin prickling. Not everyone is staring, not like a movie where they're cackling. It's worse, the quiet snickers and stares and looks of pity. Nikki grabs her arm, pulling her. "Let's get out of here," she says, not letting Kimmy answer Stevie's question.

"Hello," Stevie says, pushing Kimmy's shoulder. "Why the fuck is Aaron on here?"

"Come on." Nikki pulls at Kimmy's arm, but Kimmy turns to Stevie. She whispers, "I'm sorry," and Nikki pulls again.

"You don't have to deal with this shit." Nikki turns to Stevie. "You don't understand."

"You knew about this," Stevie asks Nikki, looking back at Kimmy. "Nikki knew about this? Are you kidding?" The paper's crumpled again in Stevie's palm, which is locked in a fist. "What is it I don't understand?" she asks, taking a step closer to Kimmy. "That you fucked the guy I like? That you betrayed me? That apparently everyone knew except me?" Stevie's eyes are big, her jaw clenched.

"No, it's not—" Kimmy starts, but Stevie interrupts, her voice getting louder.

"That you don't care about anyone but yourself? Oh wait, and Justin." He's watching, Kimmy realizes. Everyone is. "Hey, Justin, she's in love with you. Like, batshit-crazy, obsessive love." Stevie's voice turns lower again. "There. Finally told him." Kimmy's eyes are welling, the whole room blurry.

"Stevie, I'm sorry. I didn't mean for this to happen. I was so drunk."

"Shocker," Stevie says, then puts up a hand when Kimmy's about to talk. "You're always drunk. Always fucking someone and then crying about Justin after." She holds up the paper in Kimmy's face. "Anyone who sleeps with you should cut their dick off. That's how fucking gross you are." Stevie's crying now, her cheeks wet with tears, her eyes red with rage. "I don't even know who you are anymore."

Nikki pulls at Kimmy's arm again, and this time Kimmy follows, leaving Stevie behind. And Kimmy knows, almost instantly, things will never be the same.

Erin had been in line in the cafeteria checkout when she heard yelling from the stage, shocked when she realized it was directed at her sister. She left her tray in line, walking past the cashier and into the main seating area. "What's going on?" she asked no one in particular, when a paper with her sister's face at its center floated toward her. At first, she thought it had to be a *Walk to Remember*–style joke. Her eyes drifted over the names, but she crumpled it before they reached the end of the list. She knew who would be listed, because it's the same list she and Madison discussed days earlier. And she knew it definitely wasn't a joke, but an imitation—because only one person would have created this printout, and Madison had never been that original. Erin's cheeks flushed, the unmistakable red of knowing you majorly fucked up. She had just been venting, trying to make her best friend feel better. "Can you believe she slept with all those people?" Erin said, her eyes huge. "I told you it's not just about Justin," she lied, trying to appease Madison's suspicions about Justin's whereabouts after he didn't text her for days following Kimmy's birthday. "She also fucked Aaron Roop," Madison had said, her lips pursed. "Aaron had the guys over to smoke when he was home at some point and he told them. So Justin told me when we were fighting awhile back. I think to make the same point you did," she said, her worry lines softening. Erin wanted to stop her right there, to get more details. She couldn't believe her sister would do that—she had been on some sort of bender, but this sort of betrayal of her best friend, their sister, felt out of character. "When?" Erin asked Madison. "In March, I think," she said, waving at the air. "Justin told me about it in April, when they had to work on that history project together and started talking again. He was like, She's a slut! Stop worrying!" Madison cackled. "God, he was right."

Two days after their conversation, Madison texted Erin, asking if Kimmy had any tattoos. "Not that I know of," Erin responded, but a few days later she walked into the bathroom when Kimmy was blow-drying her hair in her bra, and Erin saw the edge of a small *j* etched below her underwire. Her heart sank; Madison would come for blood.

When Kimmy ran out of the cafeteria, Nikki pulling her arm, Erin followed, catching them just as they burst out the school's back door into the student parking lot.

Now she's in the backseat of Nikki's Jeep, watching her sister hyper-ventilate in the passenger seat as Nikki drives, her knuckles white as she grips the wheel. "I will find whoever did this and kill them," she says, her teeth snared.

Erin gulps, looking at her phone. She should text Madison, confront her. But she doesn't want a paper trail, doesn't want to be implicated in any way, because the way her sister is crying is unlike anything Erin has seen from her before.

"Kimmy," she says, leaning forward as she puts a hand on her shoulder. "It's all gonna be okay. No one will believe this list." She sobs harder, trying to say something through her gasps. "What?" Erin asks.

"They should. I am a terrible person."

"You are not a terrible person," Nikki says. "Aaron Roop is a terrible person. You don't deserve any of this shit."

Erin leans back, realizing how right Nikki is, how her own inse-curity propelled this forward. She gulps, feeling her anxiety turn to secondhand hurt, her sister deeply broken—and Erin needs to fix it. And then her hurt turns to anger. Only she is allowed to talk shit about her sister, not Madison. She had gone way too far. Erin wouldn't let her get away with it.

26

Beach Week 2022

INTERVIEW ONE

Tess Cameron sits across from Detective Ben Lamb at her kitchen table, her perfect manicure now ragged. Her face is drawn, tired. "The twins have already been napping for an hour," she says. "We don't have a ton of time, but I want to be as helpful as possible. I just want to find out what happened." She sniffles. "So can we just get started?" Her skin is tanned with spray, her teeth whitened with strips. You can see the slight signs of age, but she hides them well with good style and money. She's familiar to Ben, reminding him of so many of the Main Line locals who frequent the Shore for three months each year, then disappear back to their stone farmhouses centered on oaky acres.

Ben had talked to the Devine family this morning while his associates started meeting with everyone else who attended the party. He hadn't seen Kimmy since the summer after high school; he watched the look of surprise on her face when he walked through the front door of her house, its interior completely different than he remembered. He felt proud, being able to show her he had made something of himself, that he was more than the gangly kid who passed out early at every party and had an unrequited crush on her their entire junior and senior years. He was not only a detective, but eight years sober—and a good, loyal husband to his wife, Emily, for the past two years. "Ben," she said, giving him a hug. He felt his body stiffen, wanting to maintain some sense of professionalism, but when he smelled the scent of her perfume, the same one she wore in high school, he impulsively relaxed.

"I'm sorry we're reuniting under such awful circumstances," he said, pulling away. He looked at her parents, whom he had worked with plenty of times on petty crimes in their stores. "Carissa, Bill, is there somewhere we can all chat? I just want to get a rundown of what happened at the party last night before I talk to Tess." They nodded, leading him to the TV room at the back of the house, the ratty old sectional they used to sink into replaced by two love seats, two swivel chairs, and a Peloton in the back corner. They all sat, everyone perched near the end of the cushions, when Erin walked in, her eyes rimmed with red, the sleeves of her oversize sweatshirt wet from her chewing on them. She gave Ben a weak wave, then plopped next to Kimmy and leaned into her. They saw each other out occasionally, though Ben rarely frequented bars these days. He has his sobriety to uphold.

"It was a normal night," Bill started to say. "We only saw Peter for, what?" He looked at Carissa to confirm. "Maybe ten minutes, if that?"

Ben nodded, taking notes in the small pad in his hand. "When did you last see him? We'll check the security cameras at the yacht club later today, but they have limited scope, so who knows what they caught."

"About ten p.m.," Carissa said. "We were talking to the Singers and saw him walk outside through the back deck." She tucked her hair behind her ears, putting her hands on her lap as she looked at Kimmy. "Kimmy, honey, wasn't that around the time you sent Justin home?"

Kimmy gave her a mom a look, then addressed Ben. "Justin Fitzpatrick was my date last night." Her voice was meek, embarrassed. "He got too drunk and we put him in an Uber around ten. I didn't see Peter, though. Just Erin." Then she put her hand to her mouth as Carissa and Bill directed their attention to Erin, who suddenly sat up. She avoided their gaze, looking at Ben instead.

"You'll see me and Peter on the club's video recording around ten. Fighting." She sniffled, rubbing her sweatshirt under her nose.

"What?" Carissa asked, her face laced with confusion. "Why were you fighting with Peter Cameron?"

Kimmy put her hand on her sister's lap, and Erin sat up straighter.

"We were having an affair. Tess confronted him about it before the party."

"Oh god," Bill said, standing. "Erin, no. Tell me this is one of your ridiculous jokes." He started pacing, his hand to his head.

"I don't know, Dad," she said, her sobs starting. "I thought he loved me."

Kimmy looked at Ben, ignoring the chaos in the background. "Erin left a little after their fight. After I sent Justin home, I ordered an Uber for her too. My parents have a doorbell camera, so you should be able to confirm that timeline. If there's some suspicion she needs an alibi or whatever." Kimmy was all business, even her breathing tempered. She had always been good under pressure, at compartmentalizing whatever was thrown her way. Ben remembered the last day of school, the way Stevie screamed at her, how the guys, including him, all laughed as they held the paper with her hit list in their hands. Even then, she didn't flinch. She left the cafeteria with her head held high, the only sign of unease the look back she gave to Stevie as she walked out the door.

"Thanks," Ben said. "As of right now, it's assumed it was a suicide. He left Tess a voicemail last night, though she said he didn't sound like himself. Like maybe he was inebriated . . . ," he added, his voice trailing off.

Bill quieted when he heard this, looking at Carissa. "We should tell him," he said, and her mouth turned thin. He walked over to the wet bar on the other side of the room and picked up a piece of paper with WATCH YOUR BACK spelled out in a bland font.

"What's that?" Erin asked, craning her neck to see. Bill ignored her and placed it on the coffee table in front of Ben.

"Carissa and I found this on Kimmy's car two nights ago. When she was out with Justin." Kimmy stood and walked over to the table. Ben picked the paper up, inspecting it.

"Why didn't you tell me?" Kimmy asked, her arms crossing as her voice wavered.

"We didn't want to scare you, honey," Carissa said, stepping closer to Bill. "We thought it was a prank."

Ben observed the family, the secrets they had all kept. Small ones, but ones that might help him understand what led to Peter's death. "Did anything weird happen last night? With Peter, or with you, Kimmy?"

She shook her head. "No, the only weird thing was how drunk Justin was." She shrugged. "I mean, we literally tried to feed him a mocktail to get him to sober up."

"The mocktail," Carissa said, her eyes brightening. "You just told Kimmy Peter sounded drunk?" Ben nodded, unaware she had been listening. "Peter said he wasn't drinking. The only thing I saw him have was a mocktail. We ordered two at the bar. They were supposed to be for Kimmy and Justin, but we gave one of them to Peter instead."

"Wait," Erin said, rubbing her eyes. "Peter told me he felt weird, during our fight. He sat on the bench halfway through our conversation. I thought it was a power move, but maybe he really did feel off."

"Did you drink yours, Kimmy?" Ben asked, looking right at her.

"Actually, no," she said, her brows arched as she thought about the night. "I think maybe a sip? I honestly can't remember. I put it on a table and started talking to some people, and then I forgot about it."

Ben had what he needed, at least for now. He thanked the Devines and headed to the yacht club, where, as Erin predicted, he watched her and Peter talking to each other in the light of the flagpole. Erin then walked away, and Peter retreated to a bench, where he lay down and fell asleep for about three hours. They fast-forwarded through the recording, to about 1:15 a.m., when he sat up, his exact motions unknowable in the dark. Then he walked offscreen, and that was the last they saw.

Sitting across from Tess, Ben isn't sure where to begin. The department still thinks the death is a suicide, but something feels off, like Peter wasn't quite himself by the night's end. A sober man with an angry wife at home doesn't fall asleep on a bench for hours. His deputy had spent the morning with Tess, helping her with her kids as she got some sleep, answering any questions she had with short, vague responses. And now it's time for Ben to ask the real ones.

"Mrs. Cameron," Ben starts.

"Tess, please." She's nice, Tess Cameron. She's demanding, gets things done, but kind.

"Tess," he continues, "what's your relationship with the Devine sisters?"

"Well," she says, sighing, "I guess limited? I mean I've known them both since they were in high school. Peter's family lived next door to them in the summer. But you probably already knew that," she adds. "Anyway, I've always viewed them as family friends. And that Erin had a crush on Peter when she was a kid. That was it. Peter was always funny about that. So I would get updates occasionally, mainly through their parents' Christmas card. I knew Kimmy was this big-time finance person overseas, and Erin was married in Texas and running an Etsy shop where she painted portraits of dogs. And then I heard last summer she got divorced and had moved home."

"Did that bother you?"

"At the time, no," Tess says. "I don't think so. I don't know, really. Like I said, I didn't think much about them. Until recently."

"Recently," Ben asks. "What changed? I sense you're not a fan of Erin."

Tess shakes her head. "No, I never said that." She pauses. "Am I a suspect or something? Because as far as I know, I'm the only one here with a dead husband and broken family." Ben sees the tears in her eyes well, her lower lip quivering.

"No, you're not." He pauses, then says, "The Devines received a threat two nights ago. A sign on one of their cars that said 'Watch your back.'"

Tess's eyes open wider. "Wait, so you think Peter's death wasn't a suicide?"

Ben shakes his head. "We'll have to do an autopsy. We've learned he complained of feeling dizzy before leaving the party, so we're wondering if somehow someone interfered with his mental state."

"Like, drugged him?"

Ben pauses. "Again, like I said, we're not sure. Just trying to gather as much information as we can. But it's possible he might not have been the target. Carissa said she gave Peter his first drink of the night. She was carrying two mocktails meant for Kimmy and her date— but she ran into Peter and gave him the mocktail, because he said he wasn't drinking. So as far as anyone knew, he hadn't been drinking, making the slurred tone in the voicemail he left you all the more curious."

"You're kidding," Tess says, her mouth tight. "This is too much." She takes a deep breath.

"I'm sorry, Mrs. Cameron. I just need a few more minutes of your time." She sniffles, pulling herself together, looking at the monitor before looking back at Ben. "Can you tell me about your husband and Erin?" Ben asks. Tess says nothing. "What is the relationship there?"

She shrugs. "Honestly, I think he pitied her." There's something biting in her voice this time. Ben stays quiet, his silence egging Tess on. "And she took advantage of that pity."

"Are you aware they had been having a relationship?"

Tess looks up, her mouth small, and she sighs, her head resting on her hands. "Please," she says. "I don't want to hear any more right now."

"You didn't know?" Ben says, looking down at his notes.

"No, I did know. Not until recently. But I had a feeling something was going on. And Madison? Well, she nearly confirmed it."

"Madison? Madison Jensen?" Ben asks. "What do you mean?"

"During our coffee the other morning, she started asking all these probing questions about both Kimmy and Erin. Saying how weird it was that they both had moved home. You could tell there was some history there."

Ben nods. He knows the history well.

"So then she gets all hushed, and says, 'You know Erin's having an affair? With some older guy in Philly?' As if I would be interested in that sort of gossip. I told her I didn't know. And she added, 'Yeah, one of my girlfriends saw them at the Bellevue last night.' I guess Madison had really hated Erin, so all her college friends stalked her online years ago or something and knew her face. Anyway, it all clicked for me. It was Peter. It had to be. That's where he was staying, and Erin had been so obsessed with him as a kid, and after the twins arrived he was at the Shore house all the time. So I confronted him about it when he got back from Philly." She looks tired suddenly, all her makeup unable to hide the sadness.

"I'm sorry, Tess. We don't have to talk about this right now. I'm sure you're still in shock."

She shakes her head. "I guess I always have known, in a way. What a fucking disaster," she says, puffing air up against some wisps falling into her face. "So we got in a screaming fight about it the day before the party—about that, but also some other things. Just money stress, the normal thing." She waves the air, dismissive. "He told me he was going to end it with Erin. He promised me he would."

Ben nods, noting the mention of finances. He'd have to look into that more, but not yet, not when she was still so raw and so much was left unknown. "And did he?"

She shrugs. "I have no idea. The last I heard from him was around one, when he left the voicemail I shared with your team."

Ben has listened to that voicemail several times today; his deputy sent it to him hours ago, shortly after Tess first played it. "Thanks, Mrs. Cameron. We'll be in touch if we have additional questions. And we'll keep you updated on all the developments."

She stands up, brushing crumbs off her sweatpants. She bites her lip, her nostrils flared, then takes a deep breath. "Will you talk to everyone who was at the party last night?" Her voice quavers. "If this wasn't a suicide, I deserve to know. I deserve to know who took Peter from me. From our twins." She clears her throat.

Ben shakes her hand. "We are planning to get in touch with everyone at the party to see if there are any leads. We'll be in touch, truly."

Tess nods, bringing her other hand to his. "I know this seems crazy, but I just wanted to say, you should probably talk to Madison. She seems to be harboring a lot of resentment toward that family. At best, that means she likely knows something none of us do. And at worst, that is never a healthy thing."

Ben nods as he takes his hand from Tess. He doesn't think she's onto something, but who knows. He remembers that resentment, the evil it made Madison do.

27

June 2007

The chimes wake Erin up, the red on her clock blaring 2:54 a.m. She rolls over, hazy confusion in her movements as she picks up her phone. "Hello?" she says, her eyes still half closed.

"Look outside," she hears, and she suddenly jolts awake. It's Peter. They haven't talked since the dinner with Tess, when all of Erin's dreams about the two of them came crashing down.

"What?" Her voice is scratchy with sleep.

"Look outside," he says again, and she walks to the window, where she squints toward the backyard. It's dark, minus a few soft lights by the pool house. Then, as her eyes adjust, she sees his outline in the pool, clinging on to the side, his phone a tiny floating light.

"What are you doing?" she asks. "My parents are going to kill you."

"We're pool hopping," he says into the phone. She looks again and notices three other bodies. She can tell Peter's buzzed. "Come with us. With me," he adds quietly.

She looks at the clock again, then out at Peter. She should say no, but instead she puts her suit on and almost races down the stairs. She quietly opens the door to their backyard, Peter's face glistening with water. "Hi," he says, and she can feel his smile in the dark.

Instead of asking him about Tess, about where he's been these past few weeks, about his summer, she pulls her cover-up off and sits on the edge of the pool right next to him. "Where to next?" she asks, and he rests his jaw on her thigh. The move is sudden, it makes Erin jump. He's never touched her like this, never let himself get so close.

"You're the local," he says looking up at her. "You tell us."

"Hmm." Erin thinks, pretending this is something she's done before.

She knew a bunch of the guys in her grade did, all of them talking about jumping the fences of the beachside motels for quick dips, then sprinting away when they were spotted. "Do you have bikes?"

"Only three," Peter says, his chin digging into Erin's leg. The three other guys in the pool are splashing at one another, and Peter shushes them. She feels her insides tingle, everything on edge.

"Then the SeaView it is," Erin says. She hops up, leaving her cover-up on the lounger next to the pool, and walks around to her own bike. "Come on," she whispers, "you can ride with me." She throws towels in the front basket of her cruiser, and Peter, soaking wet, hops onto the back, his feet perched on the ride-on bars, the other guys scrambling to keep up. Erin pedals, Peter's hands on her shoulders, the streetlights striping them in and out of darkness. When the neon glow of the SeaView's sign comes into view, Erin points so they all know where to go. "This has to be quick," she says as they slow, shifting their bikes onto kickstands. It's dark, but there's a pink aura to the evening, the bright colors of the sign like a bubblegum dream.

As she talks, Peter's friends are already running toward the fence, pushing one another and giggling like little kids as they go. They jump right over in near unison, and when they land, she watches them pull down their suits, splashing into the pool stark naked. She gulps, her eyes widening. "I'll keep my suit on," Peter says, running a hand through his wet hair, his eyes not meeting Erin's.

She senses hesitation in his voice, like he wants to take it off, and wants her to strip too. "Okay," she hears herself say, her voice a squeak. She doesn't want to be the prude, she's almost seventeen, after all. But she's also never been naked in front of a guy, let alone four. There are some things she wants to save just for him. Before she can change her mind, she runs ahead and hops the fence, jumping into the pool, Peter right behind her. He treads next to Erin and she gives him a shy smile, then ducks under the water, pushing off the wall and emerging on the other side, her arms stretched along the curb as the water hits her chin. Peter swims over to her, ignoring his friends, who are taking turns tumbling down the slide, their skin screeching against the dry surface since the water's off for the night. Peter says nothing as he moves closer, and when he's finally face-to-face with her, Erin isn't sure what to do. Is he going to kiss her? Their bodies inches apart, Erin feels the water moving around his shape, but still they don't touch. "Erin," Peter says, but he's interrupted by a booming voice.

"Get the hell out of here," the night manager screams from the second floor of the motel. "Or I'm calling the cops." He moves toward the stairs, and Peter's friends all scramble, grabbing their suits and running for their lives, no time to cover up as they sprint. Erin scrambles out, jumping back over the fence and on her bike, Peter a few steps behind. She pedals as fast as she can back toward her house, her bathing suit and hair dripping, Peter's hands gripping her shoulders. After about five minutes, her adrenaline rushing, she slows and pulls into one of the parking lots in front of a beach entryway a few blocks from their house. She turns around, realizing they're alone. "Oh no," she says, "your friends." She hops off the bike, turning around to look, when she sees Peter staring at her.

"They're fine," he says almost breathlessly. Erin feels her body tingle, her breath catch. She grabs a towel and throws it at him, then wraps one around her own shoulders. She bites her lip, not sure what to say.

"You know," Peter says, looking toward the beach behind her, "I've never seen the sun rise over the ocean."

"So what are you waiting for?" she asks, holding her hand out. Peter takes it, and they walk to the beach, every cell inside Erin exploding. She still doesn't mention Tess, doesn't mention anything at all, too afraid she might pop this dream. The colors of dawn are starting to creep up, much of the sky still dark and starry. Just before the sand hardens, Peter takes off his towel and drops it on the soft ground, sitting and patting the spot next to him for Erin. She sits cross-legged and hears a slight shiver escape his lips. "Here." She takes one side of her towel and drapes it over his shoulders, their bare skin touching. He doesn't push her away, doesn't say she can't. She leans into him, and he wraps his arm around her waist, his fingers gripping the front of her stomach like he's afraid she'll float away.

"I think you inspire me to make bad decisions," Peter whispers into her ear, their body heat rising under the warmth of the towel.

"Maybe you're just not great at making good ones," she laughs, looking at him.

"Call me when you're eighteen, okay?" He's still looking at the ocean.

"I'm almost seventeen, Peter," she says, inching closer. "What's the difference in a few months? Besides," she adds, feeling her late-night Googling spilling from her lips, "the age of consent in New Jersey is sixteen."

Peter pulls his hand from Erin, returning it to his lap. She feels she said the wrong thing, but doesn't know why it's wrong; isn't that what he wanted to hear? That this—them together—is okay? He turns to face her, the towel dropping as he does. She watches him, not sure what move she should make.

"I'm drunk, Erin," Peter says, inching farther away. "Please don't tempt me. I don't want to do something you'll regret." She wants to protest, to tell him she would never regret anything with him. But before she can, he says, "You should probably ride home before your parents wake up. I'll walk back in a bit." He looks back at the ocean, his face coated with restraint. As she walks toward the dunes, she feels the tears start, her insecurity and confusion overwhelming, and she wraps her towel tighter around her body.

28

Beach Week 2022

DAY SEVEN

"I think we all need this," Carissa says as she carries four margaritas to their back porch, the entire Devine family parked at a table over-looking their bayside pool. "Spicy for you two," she says, pushing two drinks toward Kimmy and Erin, "smokey for you," she says, passing Bill a drink, "and skinny for me." She winks, and Kimmy sees her per-formance, the way she's trying her best to make them all smile, make them forget that Peter died less than forty-eight hours ago.

Kimmy takes a sip, the jalapeño tickling her throat. She grimaces and fights down a cough, and Erin lets out a small laugh. She pops a slice of jalapeño floating on the top of the drink in her mouth. It's the first time Erin's smiled in hours, and Kimmy squeezes Erin's knee and takes a deep breath, looking out at the calm bay, the sunset streaking the water's reflection with pinks and purples and oranges. "This week has been interesting, to say the least," Kimmy says, an understatement. "But it's good to be home with all of you." She raises her glass.

Bill rubs his upper arm, and Kimmy gives him a concerned look when they make eye contact. Is she seeing things? Paranoid? He brushes it off, turning to Carissa. "Though maybe only one of these for each of our girls," Bill says, "since their decision making of late seems to be questionable." He raises an eyebrow.

"Bill," Carissa warns, her eyes weary as they drift to Erin. The police are still investigating Peter's death, but as far as the Devines are aware, it was either a suicide or an unfortunate accident. Tess has organized a funeral in Philadelphia for the following Sunday, and Kimmy knows Erin can't go, that if she does Tess would likely call security on her. The mistress doesn't get to say goodbye to him in front of his wife, his kids. The mistress doesn't get the comfort of closure. Kimmy feels the entire family's anxiety, yet her mom's going above and beyond to quell it, much like she used to do before hurricanes, making virgin piña coladas and hosting dance parties in the living room with the girls while Bill boarded the windows.

"So, Dad," Kimmy says, changing the subject, "what's the game plan for the two of us at Devine's?" She thought maybe talking about work, about the future, would get Erin's mind off Peter. She didn't need to be the singular CEO, and after talking to Erin she decided to pitch him an idea: the two of them as co-CEOs. She hadn't mentioned it to Erin yet, but thought she'd like the surprise. Plus, she's anxious to map out their exact next steps. After Carissa told them about Peter's death, Kimmy texted Justin. He called her almost immediately, apologizing nonstop for his behavior, for all the things he said. He wanted to make it up to her, to show her he was serious about his feelings. She asked Justin to make a decision about their future, Peter's death coupled with her dad's health troubles making her realize how short life is, how they shouldn't wait fifteen years again to try to make something work. They decided: when he gets back to Florida today he'll sort through his affairs and figure out his plan to move back north—to Rocky Cape, to Kimmy. So Kimmy needs to know what, exactly, her role will be at Devine's.

"What do you mean, honey?" her dad asks, his eyebrow raised. "You'll take the reins." He takes another sip. "And Er will keep doing what she's doing, but in a much bigger way."

"So Kimmy's my boss?" Erin rolls her eyes. "Typical."

Kimmy, uneasy, looks at Erin, then back at her dad. "Seriously, Dad, I don't want this decision to impact our family. The whole point of me coming home was to be together," she says, feeling like she fumbled her pitch already. "I had an idea. Er and I as co—" she starts.

"Girls, Bill, can we talk business after dinner? Please?" Carissa interrupts, putting a hand up. "It's a gorgeous evening and we're all together. Let's talk about anything else. Anything."

"Okay, Mom and Dad," Erin says, looking at them. "Why don't you tell me how you really feel about me and Peter? About how I've always been such a disappointment and I continue to be." Erin's voice grows louder, her eyes daring.

"Erin, honey, that's not true," Carissa says.

"Oh, really? So why is it that even though I've been in the weeds of the business every day for the past two years, and I'm the only daughter who's been an actual entrepreneur, you are giving Kimmy all the responsibility? God, how do you not see that that's how it's always been?"

"Erin, we've been very proud of you over the past two years," Bill says, rubbing his arm again. "But I'm not sure I'd equate running an Etsy shop with being a founder. I know you had a front-row look at it all thanks to Kent—"

"So typical," Erin says, looking off at the water. "All you do is minimize me. Always. It's just not fair. None of it is fair."

Kimmy wants to defend Erin, but she often struggles with Erin's woe-is-me soliloquies. She loves being a victim, something Kimmy has adamantly avoided her entire adult life. Her dad is right; Erin has no sense of what it takes to run a real business. She's long been the white space to Kimmy's numbers-backed strategies. Together, though, they could be an exceptional team. She's about to tell her dad this when she sees him clutching his arm even tighter. "Dad, are you okay?" Kimmy asks, giving her mom a look that says *Watch him*.

"Yes, fine," he snaps back. "I must've pulled something swimming this morning. Like your mother said, can we just discuss this later? It's been a stressful few days." He looks at them both, a pained smile on his face. "When people ask where my high blood pressure came from, I tell them I have two daughters." He's been telling this joke since they were teens, a true dad classic he uses to alleviate tense situations. But something feels off about the delivery, his face more tired than usual.

Erin rolls her eyes again. "Good one, Dad," she says, "but someone's actual death isn't something to joke about." Her phone buzzes and Kimmy watches her expression change as she reads the screen.

"What?" Kimmy asks, trying to get a look. She's been waiting for Erin to have a full-blown breakdown about Peter's death, for the shock to wear off and reveal the deeper sadness, the kind that crushes your soul. Every time Erin has gotten a text over the past two days, she's tried to get a glimpse, to see if the final trigger is in a little blue bubble waiting to destroy her sister. "Is it about Peter?"

Erin holds her phone to her chest, shaking her head. "Don't worry about it," she says, avoiding Kimmy's eyes.

"What is it?" Carissa asks, craning her neck toward Erin's phone. "Is it the detective?"

"Er, just let me see." Kimmy puts her hand out, assuming it's a comforting message from Stevie trying to make Erin feel better, something Erin worries will spin Kimmy into an annoyed spiral. Instead, when Erin passes the phone to her sister, Kimmy sees at the top the name Reid Fitzpatrick, Justin's little brother. *I like Kimmy too much to watch my idiot brother mess with her again*, the message says. *He slept with Madison on Sunday, literally the day before the auction. I love him, but he's an asshole. Kimmy deserves better.*

Kimmy's chest knots, and she drops the phone. "What is this?" she asks, not wanting to believe what she just read.

"Who is it?" Carissa asks, her neck still craned, Bill hardly paying attention.

Kimmy stares at the message and hears Erin say, "Dad, you look, like, really gray. Are you okay?"

But she keeps her eyes on the screen, her hurt completely consuming. How could he do this to her—again? And how had she been so stupid not to think he would? "Did you know?" Kimmy asks Erin, her brow furrowed.

"Know what?" Carissa asks, but both girls ignore her.

Erin looks like she's just been slapped. "Are you serious? How on earth would I know? We're not all conspiring against you or something."

"Carissa," Bill says. Carissa, blurred in the periphery of Kimmy's gaze, is now facing Bill, her hand on his forehead; Kimmy pays no notice.

"You still hang out with Stevie," she spits at Erin. "What's keeping you from hanging out with Madison too? Maybe you're all planning to gang up on me again."

"Oh my god," Erin says, throwing a Tostito at Kimmy's face. "Grow the fuck up, Kimmy. Not everything is about you. I just lost one of the most important people in my life, and you think I'm busy gossiping about you behind your back? You are so fucking self-centered, it's unreal."

Kimmy inhales sharply, gritting her teeth so she doesn't say what she's really thinking: *Is Erin serious?* Peter was a creep, plain and simple. A creep who spent almost twenty years fucking with his sister's head. *That's not love*, she wants to scream, loud enough to drown out the concern she has that her situation with Justin isn't so dissimilar.

"I mean, who cares if Justin slept with Madison before you got home. He hadn't seen you in fifteen years. What did you expect?" Erin's glare narrows on her sister. "Oh wait, I know—that he was just waiting for you all these years because you can't imagine someone not being obsessed with you."

"Girls," Carissa says, trying to calm her bickering daughters, but Kimmy, who feels transported back to 2007, hardly hears her mom. "I didn't think he was waiting for me all this time." A part of her, bigger than she is ready to admit, had hoped he had been, though. Kimmy looks down, her vision blurring at the realization the past week has been one massive mistake, like she's immersed herself in a rerun of her teenage years' soapiest moments. "I just can't trust him."

"No shit, Kimmy," Erin says, loud now. "Did you really think something real could happen with him?"

"Girls!" Carissa's voice cracks, and both Erin and Kimmy whip their heads toward their mom, whose hand is under Bill's armpit, pulling him up from his seat. "Your father and I need to go to the hospital. Now."

"Carissa, I'm fine, really." His fingers are pressed against his chest, circling his sternum. "It's probably just heartburn from the margarita."

"I'm not taking that chance. Not again," she says, and he acquiesces, shaking her hand off him as he walks to the car, their practiced emergency routine in action.

"Wait, what is happening?" Erin asks, the color draining from her face.

"Your father's having chest pain. If you two weren't so busy being wrapped up in your self-created drama, you would have noticed." Carissa looks to the car, where Bill shuffles into the passenger seat, then back at her daughters. "You two are adults now. Please, for the sake of us all, start acting like it." She shakes her head, her jaw jutting in annoyance, but it softens as she sees their worried expressions. "I'll text you once he sees a doctor, okay? I'm sure he'll be fine. It will all be fine." Carissa turns, leaving Kimmy and Erin alone by the bay.

Erin's on the couch, watching *Gilmore Girls* as an escape. Anything to make her forget reality. Peter's dead. Her dad's in the hospital. How had so much gone wrong so quickly?

"Hey," Kimmy says, plopping on the sectional next to her.

Erin looks up, but says nothing.

"I'm sorry," Kimmy says, bending first, which is a rarity, her stubborn need to win bleeding into their everyday arguments far too often. "I guess Justin still makes me crazy. And I know you have a lot going on."

Erin raises an eyebrow. A lot going on? *No shit*, she wants to yell as she shakes her sister, but she doesn't have the energy. "Mm-hmm," she mumbles, not wanting to start a fight. "I'm exhausted, Kimmy." She throws her head back, her inhale deep, and brings her hands to her eyes, rubbing to keep the tears away. "I'm so fucking exhausted."

"I get it, really," Kimmy says, inching closer.

"Do you?" Erin brings her legs to her chest, curling into a ball as she looks at her sister. "You're so good at compartmentalizing. At keeping your emotions tight and orderly. I mean, Christ, you can even be around Aaron Roop with civility, which is something I could never do if I was you."

Kimmy tilts her head to the side, a look of confusion sprinkling her expression. "What do you mean?"

Erin gulps, worried she said too much. "Stevie told me about what happened to you. That he . . ." She pauses, not wanting to say the word. "That he raped you."

Kimmy breaks eye contact with her sister, tucking her legs under herself, her nostrils flaring as she looks toward the TV. Erin wants to put a hand on her sister, to share comfort in any way, but feels nervous to do so, Kimmy suddenly looking like she might shatter if touched. "This thing that happened to me when I was seventeen? It doesn't get to define me." Kimmy looks back at Erin, her irises glowing like they're on fire. "He does not get that power."

"But Kimmy," Erin says, her forehead wrinkled in concern, "why didn't you tell me? Or, like, the police? Why did you hold on to this for so long?"

"God, Er." Kimmy's almost laughing, like Erin told a ridiculous joke. "Have you lived under a rock the past decade? So much has changed, but so much hasn't. Who would have believed me back then? Don't you remember Kristen Weninger—she was two grades above me, I think." Erin shakes her head; the name sounds vaguely familiar, but Erin can't place her face. "She blacked out during senior week and was raped by Mikey Brown, that guy who was the town's big football star. Remember him? And I don't really know the details, just that her friends told her to report it, and then a bunch of the guys in her class who were at the party talked to the police and listed every person she'd been with that week, how much she drank, what she wore. Like, grade-A slut-shaming. Mikey went to college on a scholarship, and I honestly have no idea what she's doing now."

"Fuck," Erin says, biting her lower lip. "I hate people."

"Yeah," Kimmy says, putting a hand on her sister's knee. "I had that story floating in my head after Aaron, so I pushed away the idea that he raped me. I chalked it up to being too drunk and just blamed myself for a long time. But then I started going to therapy and learned about dissociation and consent and all the ways I exhibited behaviors of someone who was sexually assaulted. And some of the media changed the way it covered those types of situations, so people changed their perceptions too. Not all people, obviously, but enough. And I began to heal."

Erin places her hand atop Kimmy's. "I'm sorry you didn't feel like you could tell me."

"I knew I could, Er—you're my person, always." Kimmy smiles, bringing her sister into her arms for a hug. They embrace, and Kimmy whispers into her hair, "I just didn't want to burden you."

Erin feels the weight of high school, of the last few years, of this past week collide, every muscle in her body giving in to her sadness. She lets it cloak her, weaving across her muscles like a river cleansing her of all the shit that's built up. The mistakes, the loss, the reframing of a relationship that consumed almost half her life. "I'm so sorry, Kimmy. I'm just so sad."

"Hey," Kimmy says, pulling back. She puts her hands on her sister's cheeks, rubbing under her eyes with her thumbs. "You will feel better. I promise. Your trauma will always be a part of you, but it only defines you if you let it."

Erin sniffles, shifting so she's leaning back against the corner of the sectional. She digs a hand behind her back, pulling out a bag of Milanos. "Want one?"

Kimmy dips a hand into the bag, the cookie like a peace offering. She takes a bite and sinks next to Erin, who puts an arm around her. "You know you deserve better than Justin, right?"

Kimmy closes her eyes and lets out a frustrated sigh. "I am just too old for this kind of drama."

Erin agrees, which is why she's going to start her own fresh chapter, one without any of the men from her past in it. She's decided she'll give Kent what he wants so they can finally, officially, be divorced. She will agree to destroy the remaining embryos they made together, despite her worry that she'll have even less of a chance of having kids without them. She can find a sperm donor, she can do IVF again. She doesn't need Kent, or Peter, or anyone to pursue her dream of having a family of her own. She just needs a plan and a little science.

She's about to tell Kimmy when their phones vibrate, a text from their mom. *EKG normal, false alarm. Need to stay for some monitoring but dad's okay. Love, mom*

"Thank god," Erin says, both of them visibly relaxing in the wake of the news.

"You know, before everything happened with Dad," Kimmy says, grabbing another Milano, "I was going to ask him if we could be co-CEOs."

"Oh my god," Erin says, squaring her shoulders toward her sister. "Is there ever a second of any day you're not thinking about work? Cold-hearted CEO bitch."

"Fine," Kimmy says, rolling her eyes. "I just thought it was a good idea! And maybe when Dad gets home we can talk about it with him. Honestly, I don't want a super-intense job again. I want a life. I thought with Justin, but now I think with you and Mom and Dad and just in general."

"Are you sure?" Erin asks, trying to mask her smile. She needs this all more than Kimmy even realizes.

"Yeah," Kimmy says, giving her a nod. "Plus, I think it will be really fun working together. Side by side, just like the old days." As she says this, Kimmy's phone rings. Erin sees Justin's name flash across the screen.

"You should talk to him," she says, nodding to Kimmy's phone. "Just ask him for the truth. Your gut will know what to do from there."

Kimmy nods, and stands. "Love you, sis."

"Always," Erin says.

Kimmy sneaks back to her room to take Justin's call. She nestles into a corner of her bed and presses accept. "Hey," she says, her voice small. *Stay strong*, she tells herself.

"Hey, sexy," he says, and she can hear the smile on his face. "Landed, like, an hour ago, but I'm missing you already."

"I need to ask you something," she says, the hand holding her cell phone shaking. "Did you sleep with Madison this week?"

"What? No," he stammers, his tone changing. "I mean, yes. I did. But it was before you. Before I even knew you were coming home." He takes a deep breath. "It meant nothing. It always means nothing with her."

"Do not—" she starts, her voice rising. Then she freezes, the déjà vu of the moment hitting. "What do you mean it always means nothing?" He sighs. "Do not do this to me again, Justin. Do not lie. Do not." Her whole body is shaking now.

"Legs, come on. We've hooked up a few times over the years, when I'm in town and we're both single," he says, like it's nothing.

"You lied to me," she says, her arms crossed, the knot in her chest tightening. "I asked you outright about her. You said you don't talk."

"I didn't predict this for us. I didn't think my past with Madison was still a big deal." She hears a rustle and knows he's running a hand through his hair. "Come on," he says. "Calm down. You're getting all high school on me again."

"High school?" she repeats, her eyes lit with rage. "Are you fucking joking?" Her hand on her temple. "God, I'm such an idiot," she whispers to herself. She feels the rage, the pent-up anger that never left.

"You still there, Legs?" Justin asks, unable to come up with much more to say.

"I can't do this, Justin," she whispers so quietly she's not sure he hears her.

"What do you mean?" he says, his tone changing. "I'm about to upend my entire life for you. How is a one-night stand that happened before we got together, mind you, enough to change all that?"

She realizes she was right; she doesn't know him, not this version. She thinks of his behavior at the yacht club, what he said about her and Aaron, the chip on his shoulder about Diner James. Who is he beyond the borders of Rocky Cape? When he's out at sea? Has he had other serious girlfriends? Lovers? Dramas? She knows nothing at all. And what do they even have in common besides the uncontrollable desire to sleep with each other? She can't even remember the last time she listened to a Phish or Slightly Stoopid or G. Love song, those jam bands such a core part of her memory of their senior year—but no longer her taste once she left Rocky Cape. There is one thing she does know when it comes to Justin. "I can't trust you."

"You can't trust me?" he asks, a hint of anger in his voice. "What the hell does that mean?"

"It just feels like you haven't changed at all." Her anger turns to a resigned sadness.

"God, Kimmy," he says. "Do you think I've just been sitting around for fifteen years doing nothing but thinking about you? I have a fucking life without you. A good one. And I'm willing to scrap it all to chase you here, to give us a chance. Finally. Isn't that what you said you wanted, for me to chase you?"

"I know, I didn't—" She's not sure what to say. That it was all a mistake, a dream that could never actually be reality? Her parents hate him, think he was trash when they were in high school and will always be trash. His ex, the one who made Kimmy's life a literal hell, still lives in their town and would be a lingering presence. And he'll always be the catalyst of the worst memory of her life. There's just too much history, too many cracks in their foundation.

"You can't just come back into my life after all these years and try to control the outcome, to clean up a messy situation with all your fucking money so it fits your definition of acceptable."

"That's not what I'm trying to do," she says, pulling the phone away from her ear.

"Oh really? You want me to quit a job I worked my ass off to get so I can, what, come home and marry you?" She can almost feel his spit through the phone. "Classic Devine move. Your family wants to control everything. The town's politics, the way people run their businesses on Main Street, even who you love."

"You're seriously trying to turn this around on me and my family, Justin? I asked you a simple question, and you lied. You didn't even have to. You chose to, like it's pathological or something. How fucking stupid did I look wearing your shirt the other day? You wonder why my parents hate you?"

"Jesus Christ," Justin says. "Who cares? Who fucking cares what people think? Why does that shit matter so much to you?"

Kimmy swallows, her jaw jutting. "You've never had to worry about that. You don't get it, Justin. What all those rumors did to me, to my sense of self. The Facebook messages Madison and her friends sent me calling me a skank. The way their words ate away at my worth. The friends I lost."

"We're thirty-three, Kimmy," he says, trying to calm her. "It will be different this time. We're grown-ass adults."

"I know," she says, her lips quivering, "but for whatever reason, it doesn't feel like it. It's like we're in a time capsule. And honestly, I can't do it again, Justin." She feels her eyes watering. "I have worked too hard to go back. I just can't." She wants to bury her face in his chest and take in his smell, his heft, but she can't. She stiffens, knowing she needs to cut this off, for good.

"So that's it?" he asks. "You're going to just run again?"

She shakes her head. "I'm not running. I'm staying right here. Just not with you." She's finally realized this place is about so much more than Justin, that it doesn't always have to be tied up with memories of him and Aaron and the few terrible months she had at the end of high school.

"I guess it's your turn to break my heart, huh?" he says, and she hears the cocky smirk on his face. She fights back tears; she knows he'll always have a part of her heart, some of the most vibrant memories of her life tied to him, intertwined with some of the worst. How funny to end their big love in such a small way—by phone—yet again. But maybe that's always been the only way, the physical forever clouding her judgment. Because she's ready to put a cap on this portion of her heart, to lock the memories in one valve so the others can beat stronger, harder, as they make new, untainted ones.

We were all in this small karaoke bar near our office in the City. It was maybe six of us. I wasn't even that drunk, but my boss was.

What happened, honey? Did he hurt you?

No, not at all. He put his arm over my shoulders a few times. I didn't think anything of it at the time, but I just found out some guy in the office is telling people I'm sleeping with him and that's why I get on all the good deals.

Can you report him?

No, no. I don't want to make it a thing. I'm going to keep my head down and work hard, same as always. I just needed to vent.

You don't always have to be so strong.

But I do. I'm not sure there's any other way.

29

July 2007

Erin listens to Brad Richards go on and on about his routine for waxing his surfboard, the party around her buzzing, everyone still covered in sand after watching the Fourth of July fireworks on the beach. They're at a junior's house near the edge of town, the place packed with her classmates. She knows Kimmy's at Justin's, both of them ditching any after party to hang out together. She feels a pang of jealousy, but also annoyance. She watched her sister long for him all year, heard her sneak out all those times, knowing where she was going. Watched Justin fuck with her head. She wasn't thrilled they were together, but also knew Kimmy was leaving for Rutgers in about three weeks, and Justin would start at University of Florida soon after. So who cared? Let her live out her fantasies until reality and running practice hit her in the face.

Her phone buzzes and she looks down. A picture of a plant from Stevie. "This is cocaine!!!" she writes, which makes Erin laugh. She's hiking Machu Picchu, Erin knows; she hadn't told her sister they still talked, and neither had Stevie. But why should Erin have to lose one sister over the other's mistake? She starts typing back, looking at her phone, when she trips over something. "Watch it," someone slurs. She looks down, the bedazzled phone in the girl's hand unmistakable.

"Hey, Madison," Erin says, and Madison looks up. Her eyes are black with mascara, tear-streaked and bleeding glitter.

Madison rolls her eyes, pulling her legs into her chest. She pats the spot next to her. Erin pretends she doesn't see, but Madison grabs her leg. "Sit," she says, pulling.

Erin obliges, worried she doesn't have near enough alcohol in her system for this conversation. "Did you know they got matching tattoos?" she says, looking blankly at the wall across the way.

"Who?"

"Who do you think, idiot?" Madison snarls, a bottle of Goldschläger in her hand. She swigs, the flakes floating as she flips the bottle. "He's *my* boyfriend, yet he won't answer any of my texts and they're getting matching tattoos?" She wipes her eyes, only making it worse. Erin says nothing. "Were they fucking the whole time?" Madison asks, looking right at Erin. The cinnamon on her tongue stings Erin's nostrils.

"I don't know," Erin mumbles. She heard Kimmy on the phone until 3:00 a.m. more nights than she can count, knowing there was only one person on the other side of the line. Maybe they hadn't physically been together, but wasn't the alternative worse?

"Bullshit," Madison says. "You are probably so happy about this. You've always been so jealous. Of me. Of your sister. Chasing after some college guy who wants nothing to do with you."

The last comment hurts, Erin still feeling raw from her last interaction with Peter. He texted her the next day, thanking her for "being such a good friend," as if he hadn't gawked at her body, as if nothing had almost happened. "You're fucked up, Madison," Erin says, ignoring her comment. "You don't know what you're saying."

"I can't believe you thought this whole time that you had a chance with Peter," she slurs.

"That's not true," Erin lies, and stands. "Anyway, he has a girlfriend. So who cares—"

"Once again, bullshit!" Madison dings her hand in the air. "You care. Or, wait, I should say you don't care. Because your whole fucking family is full of homewreckers. You're a bunch of desperate homewreckers." She takes one more swig, and Erin watches her face twist as it goes down, knowing what's coming next. The puke is projectile, splattering the wall.

"What the fuck?" someone yells. Erin grabs Madison's arms and lifts her limp body once she takes a break.

"Come on," she says, worried Madison will puke on herself again.

"Why does he want to be with her?" Madison whimpers to herself, sloppily wiping her mouth as Erin pushes the two of them through the crowd. When they're outside, Madison leans her head into Erin's shoulder. For a moment, it's like old times, the two inseparable again. But then Madison says, "He added that stupid pb and j thing in his profile. Two days ago," she says, crumbling on the sidewalk. School had been out for less than a month, and shortly after their last day Madison left for Florida to spend three weeks with her mom, per her parents' custody agreement. Erin hasn't talked to her at all since the flyers circulated, and she's guessing Justin hasn't either. "He won't answer any of my texts or calls. He's going to break up with me. I know it."

"Madison, let's get you home," Erin says, her buzz near gone at this point. "You know the police patrol the streets like crazy tonight. You can ride on the back of my bike home."

Madison trips, bumping into a bush lining the sidewalk. "The list was supposed to end it. But it backfired," she says, as if she's alone. "It backfired." She looks up at the sky, waving her hands as she sobs again.

"You made those flyers about Kimmy?" Erin asks, as if she didn't already know.

"Please," Madison says, swinging her tiny purse on her wrist. "Your sister deserved it. She fucked my boyfriend. She fucked her best friend's crush. She fucked, like, half the class. It's not like it was a secret. I mean, you're the one who told me."

Erin had watched Kimmy cry the week after those flyers were shared, her reaction scaring her, making her worried about what her sister wasn't saying. Kimmy had stayed in bed the entire time, shades drawn, comforter pulled up, while the rest of the senior class partied and celebrated graduation. Every time Erin went in to talk to her, she was motionless. It was only when Justin showed up one afternoon, their parents not home, that she emerged, her mood changed, Justin always the perfect distraction. Madison fishes her car keys from her purse, holding them out as she presses unlock, searching for her car despite it being right in front of them. Erin was planning to give her a ride, to make sure she made it home in one piece. But the fact that Madison feels no remorse—nay, feels glee over all she did to Kimmy—sets off a force in

Erin that makes her completely snap. The anger at Peter. The anger at Madison. The protectiveness she feels toward her sister. No one messes with her sister. Madison pulls open the door to her car, sliding into the driver's seat. "Bunch of hoes," she slurs again to herself, her keys turning in the ignition as she slams the door.

"Drive safe," Erin says as she pulls out. She estimates it's a twenty-minute drive home, Madison's house on the other side of the island. Once she's just out of view, Erin pulls out her phone and presses *67, not even sure if it will work—but at this point, she doesn't care—then dials.

"911. What's your emergency?"

"Hi, officers? I'm so worried about my friend. She's so drunk," she fake-sobs. "She wouldn't listen to any of us and got behind the wheel. She's probably on Ocean Boulevard now, in a blue Lexus SUV. Please, someone go help her. I'm so scared she'll hurt herself."

And then Erin hangs up, smiling as she gets on her bike and pedals home.

30

Beach Week 2022

INTERVIEW TWO

"Why am I here, Ben?" Madison asks, her lips twisted in an expression of annoyance. "I'm only doing this as a courtesy. But, like, what the fuck?" She drops her carryall on the table, her sharp nails grasping at the inside searching for something. She pulls out a tube of gloss, slathering it on her lips, which she then purses again.

"That's what we're hoping you can tell us, Madison. As you may have heard, Peter Cameron died after the Devines' party at the country club—"

"It's a yacht club," Madison interrupts. Ben looks up from his notes, eyebrows arched. "I'm just saying, if you're going to take notes, make sure they're factually correct. Like, there's a golf club and then there's a yacht club. Setting is important." She shrugs, her own vanity enough to trump whatever bad blood exists between them all.

"Okay," Ben drags on. "Well, we have reason to believe Peter Cameron was accidentally drugged, and the drugs were meant for one of the Devine girls. Were you at the event at all?"

Madison shakes her head, the condensation from her iced coffee dripping on the table. "No," she says. She pauses, takes a sip. "Like, I would prefer to not run into the Devine sisters—one ruined my life and one stole my boyfriend. Bygones, and all that, but like no thanks."

"Right," Ben says. "About that. You do have a history with both of them, do you not? And I assume you're aware Kimmy's been spotted with Justin again."

Madison nods. "What do I care, Ben? I'm not some lovestruck sixteen-year-old." She takes another sip. "I could give a shit if those two want to relive their youth. I have bigger things to worry about, like building a multimillion-dollar childcare business. Puh-lease."

Ben thinks of how to phrase his next question, his words cautious. He's still friends with Justin, knows Madison and Justin hook up occasionally when home. Or at least used to, always after a big night out. He never understood it, what Justin saw in her over Kimmy. "And you're sure those feelings aren't still there?"

She stops, cocks her heads. "Justin is my comfort food, okay? He's cozy and all that, but he's bad for me. He makes me fat and lazy and foggy-headed. Like, when I saw Kimmy the other morning in his shirt, I had to laugh. Even after all these years, she's still lapping up my sloppy seconds." She cocks her head to the side. "And anyway, after high school I actually hated Erin way more than Kimmy."

Ben stops writing, looking up from his notepad. "And why's that?"

"My DUI? The one that, like, flipped my entire fucking world upside down? I know it's not on my record anymore—thank god I was a minor—but I also know you know about it. It's why I was sent to Florida to live with my psychotic mother. It made me, like, a total outcast in the middle of nowhere America for what should have been the best year of my life. Justin was literally the only good thing that whole year." She takes another sip of her coffee, and raises one brow. "Who do you think called the police when I started driving home?"

"Erin?" Ben asks, leading.

"Bingo," Madison says. "Trust me, if it was like 2008 and we were in this situation, I probably would have done something insane. But I swear, it wasn't me. Anyway, I have an alibi. I grabbed cocktails at the Dunes with Maggie Fisher. You can probably get video footage of me walking by the hotel, and I'm happy to provide any time stamps from my phone or car if needed. Actually . . ." She pulls out her phone and pulls up a picture. "See, Maggie and I did a selfie." The time stamp says 10:17 p.m.

Ben nods, knowing he's grasping at straws with her. "We'll look into it, thanks." He organizes his notes, about to put them in a manila folder, when Madison reaches across.

"Hey," she says, her voice softer. "I know she's your friend, but you need to look into Stevie. From what I've heard, that's the real story, especially now that she's with Aaron."

He nods, knowing she's right, thinking about the conversation he had with Justin when he called him that morning, about how Aaron slipped him half an Ativan while they smoked weed outside, a little something to take the edge off the night. It's why he got so fucked up so fast. Ben knows he has to call Aaron, to get him in to find out more. But he's starting with Stevie. The girlfriends always know more than their boyfriends realize.

August 2007

"Do you think Mom's totally freaking right now?" Erin laughs as she looks at Kimmy, her life jacket piled in the back of her kayak. She speeds her paddle, aligning with Kimmy. "'You girls always leave me out,'" Erin mocks, pretending she's Carissa.

"Aw, don't be so mean." Kimmy passes Erin the end of her paddle, and they both lie down, each holding a side so they can float together. "All she wants is for us to be together. I think every parent has a hard time sending a kid off to college."

"You don't always have to be so diplomatic. Sometimes she's just plain insane." Erin turns to her side, facing Kimmy. "Though, I'll admit, this time I agree with her sentiment. What am I supposed to do without you?"

"Stop." Kimmy closes her eyes as she tilts her face to the sun. "You're going to make me cry. And you promised me you wouldn't today."

"I know. I just can't believe you're really leaving." But Erin can, of course. It is the only option, after the past few weeks they'd had.

The police had found Madison in her car, slurring expletives when they pulled her over. She was arrested for driving under the influence and had to stay overnight in jail, her dad out of town for business. She sent Erin a simple text the next day. *You are a fucking snake*. Erin didn't respond, didn't want to implicate herself. Instead, she pressed delete, her hand shaking as she did.

Days later, Kimmy came into her room with tears in her eyes. "Fuck Justin Fitzpatrick." She lay on Erin's bed, curling herself into a ball in her sister's arms.

Erin didn't know what to say. Kimmy rarely cursed, rarely cried, rarely showed this type of upset so openly, yet all of June she had turned into an emotional mess. "What happened?" Erin asked, hopeful. She prayed it wasn't her fault.

"On my birthday, he promised he was going to break up with Madison. Like, we got matching tattoos." Kimmy lifted her shirt, the tiny cursive *j* on her rib cage bared. "So we've been hanging out while Madison was in Florida. He promised, like really promised. So I thought it was fine—like, different this time. And then the past few days he went totally MIA. And I know she got back this week. And I just called him, like, demanding an answer. And he said Madison got in some major, life-changing trouble, and he had to be there for her. Something about a DUI and her having to move to her mom's in Florida. Of fucking course she'll live two hours from UF." Exactly where Justin was starting in the fall. Kimmy looked up at her. "You don't look surprised."

"I'm the one who tipped off the cops," Erin said, her eyes big. "Please don't tell Mom and Dad. I don't want to cause more of an issue."

"Erin, what the hell? Why would you do that?"

"She was saying all this messed-up stuff about you. That she was the one who made those flyers at school, and I saw how it crushed you. And . . ." Erin pauses. "I didn't want to tell you this at the time, but I'm the one who told her about some of the other guys. Stevie came over on your birthday and was all upset and complaining about how self-centered you'd been—and honestly, Kimmy, you can't deny that. Like, the three of us always celebrate birthdays together. And you just ditched us, and I was angry about that, and about Peter, and about all of it, so I gossiped with Madison. It was stupid and careless and I'm so, so, so sorry."

Kimmy gulps, then looks away. "You and Stevie spent my birthday talking shit about me?"

"You weren't even there. You ditched us for Justin. And Nikki. Like always."

Kimmy blinked at Erin, then took a deep breath. "I don't even know where to begin." Her voice wavered, and she got up and walked out of Erin's room, back through their shared bathroom, and slammed the door to her room.

Erin stood up cautiously and followed, her ear to the door. "Kimmy?" she said, her voice almost a whisper. She turned the knob and walked into her sister's room. Kimmy was curled in the fetal position on her bed sobbing. Erin felt her own eyes welling, her guilt pouring out like a monsoon. "Kimmy, I'm so sorry. If I could take it all back, I would. I'm so, so sorry." She curled up next to her, putting her arms around her sister's waist. They shook together.

"How could you do that to me, Er? How?"

"I don't know," she said, crying just as hard as Kimmy now. "When that flyer came out I realized I messed up. And I wanted to get back at Madison. To make things right. Looks like I can't even do that without fucking it up."

Kimmy broke away from Erin, turning to face her. "You called the police on Madison for me?"

Erin wiped her eyes. "Of course, Kimmy. I'd do anything for you."

Kimmy sat up, holding Erin's wrist. "Do you remember when you got caught in that rip tide when you were, like, seven?"

Erin nodded, though the memory was hazy. She mainly remembered the speed at which everyone on the beach got small, the eerie calm she felt as she followed the instructions she had been taught since she was four—"If you get caught in a rip tide, swim sideways"—and the gumball SpongeBob Popsicle she ate after she made it back ashore.

"I have never been more scared in my life. I mean, you were right next to me body surfing, and then you weren't, just like that. My memory of it all is so vivid because it was so terrifying." She paused, sniffling and wiping away her tears. "But then you saved yourself. Like, I was sprinting after you not sure what to do, and you somehow swam your way out of that current. It was unreal. And it made me realize what I already knew—you're so strong, stronger than me. And I think I need you more than you need me."

"Kimmy," Erin said, putting a hand on her sister's back. "I need you too. Don't you remember? You're the one who taught me what to do in a rip tide." She thought back to the hours they spent in the bay as kids, Kimmy's favorite game Lifeguard, because she could boss Stevie and her little sister around. She'd pace across the lower dock, whistle in hand as she created fake scenarios—shark! waterspout! rip tide!—and shouted commands to them both to help them survive.

"Oh my god," Kimmy said, wiping her tears as she laughed. "I forgot about Lifeguard. I was such a psycho."

"Still are," Erin said, tussling her sister's hair. "But a psycho I love."

Kimmy shook again, another sob. "I've already lost Stevie. I can't lose you too. Even though I hate you right now," she said, and laughed. "You're my sister, and that means more than anything else. Always." As Erin held her, Kimmy drew her face back, her thoughts still spinning. "Wait, so if you didn't tell Madison about Aaron, who did?"

"Justin. Like, months ago," Erin said, not realizing the impact of her punch until she saw Kimmy's face fall, the realization that he had never been on her side. It had always been about Madison.

They crafted a text for Justin. It was eviscerating, a string of one-liners about his narcissism, his pathological need to chase what he couldn't have, and his delusion that he was somehow better than Kimmy. The text ended with a simple request: to delete her number, to leave her alone, and to never, ever reach out again. There was no turning back once Kimmy pressed send. And then, together, the Devine sisters deleted Justin Fitzpatrick's number, and therefore his existence, from their lives.

Erin and Kimmy promised each other they'd spend the final two weeks of Kimmy's last summer home together. They moved their shifts around so they would be at Devine's together, getting in fake water-gun fights with each other and playing puppets with the hermit crabs when the days were slow. They finished all six seasons of 24 available on DVD, plowing through it every night. And they kayaked. Every single afternoon, right after they got off work. Kimmy left for college tomorrow. Tonight was their last ride.

"I need a fresh start." Kimmy props up on her side, mirroring Erin. "You know I do."

"But do you have to leave us all behind in the process?" Erin can feel a tear welling. She couldn't imagine Rocky Cape without Kimmy, her identity in this place completely entwined with her sister's existence.

"I'm not, god. I'm just going to college. Stop being such a drama queen." Kimmy throws the sunscreen at Erin's stomach. "I'll obviously visit. Just wearing a hoodie and sunglasses the whole time so I can avoid the entire world."

"At least you won't have to worry about running into Madison," Erin says with a smile.

Kimmy smiles back but says nothing, and Erin realizes it's still raw, Madison's name still a sting for Kimmy.

"I'm sorry," Erin starts, but Kimmy stops her.

"It would have ended up this way regardless. I've thought about it over and over and over. Like, ad nauseum. And it's just who Justin is. He loves the chase. And that's all I was."

"I don't know about that," Erin says, raising an eyebrow. "You were way more to him than a chase."

Kimmy shrugs. "What does it matter? I'm nothing to him now." She rolls onto her back. "Speaking of a chase. You need to keep me updated on the neighbor."

Erin gulps. "Peter?"

"Yeah, dummy. I'm not blind. I see how you adore him," Kimmy says, laughing.

"He doesn't view me like that," Erin says. "I mean, he has a girlfriend. We're just friends."

"Good thing he doesn't or he'd be in jail," Kimmy says, splashing Erin with her oar. "Just be careful with him. Something about him feels like trouble."

"Thanks for keeping me safe, O strong big sis!" Erin teases, sticking out her tongue. "Seriously, though, we don't even talk anymore. He's starting dental school and is busy with life. I wouldn't worry about it." There's a sadness in Erin's voice, one familiar to Kimmy. Romantic defeat. She doesn't push it, though.

"Whoa," Erin says, breaking the moment. "Kimmy, look." She points out toward the horizon, the sun lowering and setting the sky ablaze.

About fifty yards away, a crew of dolphins flip around. It's breathtaking, and Kimmy feels her eyes watering. She will miss this place so much. "Stevie would love this," Kimmy says.

"You could reach out," Erin says, her eyes hopeful.

Kimmy ignores the suggestion, pausing for a moment as she looks toward the horizon, then says, "Race you back to the dock?"

Before Erin can answer, Kimmy's paddling, and then Erin is close behind, the two of them navigating the reedy swamps of the intercoastal area together, weaving through the uneven currents as they head back to the bay where their house sits. As they pull in, Carissa and Bill are sitting on the dock in two Adirondack chairs. Carissa stands and waves, and Bill puts down his drink, ready to give the girls a hand out of the water.

32

Beach Week 2022

INTERVIEW THREE

"Hey, Stevie." Ben opens the door to his office. "I know you were working a wedding on Saturday night, so I'm sorry we still have to ask you questions." He feels awkward, pulling out the chair on the other side of his desk for her. She sits without comment, looking around at his office, taking it all in. He rarely invites friends to work, just in case a situation like this were ever to arise. Church and state, and all that.

"I know why you called me," she says, her eyes on Ben, taking a deep breath. "It's about Aaron, right?"

Ben cocks his head, not wanting to give too much away. "Why would you think that?"

"He raped Kimmy. Did you know that?" she asks, her tone accusatory.

Ben tries to hide the surprise on his face. He remembered Aaron telling them he "nailed the class princess" as they passed around a bong, Justin's face white as he pretended not to care and Ben's green as he processed this reveal. He remembered thinking Aaron seemed like an odd choice for Kimmy, and her somewhat going off the rails the rest of the year. And he even remembered hitting on her and failing, massively. But he didn't remember anyone ever uttering the word *rape* when it came to gossiping about Kimmy's exploits. "What do you mean?" he asks, his tone even.

"In high school. When they slept together? It wasn't Kimmy's choice. Kimmy was so drunk she was almost unconscious. I watched her puke three times that night." She takes another deep breath, regret drawn all over her face. Ben feels a knot in his stomach, thinking of the flyers that circulated that last day of high school, the way they all laughed at Kimmy, joked about the list of guys she "took down."

"I didn't know that, no," he says, breaking eye contact with Stevie. "How did you find this out?"

"At Bluefish the other night, Kimmy told me. Well, to be accurate, she said he was a bad guy. That was it. She was sort of cagey about it, but the way she said it scared me a little. Like, it was so urgent." She looks off, then back at Ben. "I called Nikki Ritter the other morning. Completely out of the blue, but I thought if someone would know, it would be her."

"And she verified that it had happened?" Ben asks, his heartbeat picking up.

"She said Kimmy never told her outright, but she ran to Nikki's house the next morning and she had never seen Kimmy like that, so she always assumed something real fucked had happened."

"Okay," Ben says, waiting for Stevie to spill more.

"So I confronted Aaron about it, the day before the party. And he, like, lost it on me. Told me Kimmy was a cunt, that she was a liar, blah blah blah. And that girls like her always think they're so much better than guys like him but they always get what's coming. It was sort of unhinged. So I told him it was over. The whole interaction just made me super uncomfortable."

That's not enough to arrest him, Ben thinks. "Do you think he was planning to harm her at the party?"

Stevie looks up at him, her eyes big. "I didn't tell you the weirdest part. He has a drug stash. I don't know what they are, but they're hidden in a copy of *Infinite Jest*, of all things. I found it a few days ago. I took these as proof." She holds up a ziplock bag with pills sprinkling the bottom. "But as far as I know, he doesn't have a prescription."

Bingo, Ben thinks. "Okay, we're going to have to check this out," Ben says, standing up from his desk. "For your own safety, I'm going to recommend you hang out here until we find Aaron."

Stevie nods, her eyes widening. "Did he do something to Peter?"

"We're not sure," Ben says, but he feels a theory forming. "It will be weeks before we have autopsy results, but the drugs alone are important to check out."

Stevie goes into an interview room, officers bringing her coffee as Ben sits back down at his desk and makes two calls: the first to a judge for a search warrant, and the second to Aaron himself.

I want passion in my relationships. Why do you have to be so judgmental about that?

I'm not being judgmental. I'm trying to share some wisdom from someone who's experienced a bit more life than you.

I don't want to spend every night of my life falling asleep on the couch while my husband does the same as we watch *Law and Order*. I want intense need. Like, the rip your clothes off need they have in *The Notebook*.

First of all, that's not real. Second of all, the couple in the end was quite different from the one in the beginning, don't you think? Because that's what real love looks like. It grows into something deep, supportive, quiet, stable. It's about partnership. What you're talking about? That's not healthy. Being elated about your relationship one day and crying hysterically the next, over and over and over again? Also not healthy.

Whatever. Like you would know.

You'll see, honey. You'll see.

33

February 2024

Ben rubs his eyes, taking a final sip of coffee as he looks at the clock. It's 9:27 p.m., the snow just starting to stick. It's calm, the scene outside. He loves the Shore in the off-season. No tourists, no gimmicky sales tactics on Main Street, no chaos. It's just the locals, the people he's known his whole life. The same people he has to tell that one of their own will be in jail for a very, very long time.

After Stevie shared her version of events, they searched Aaron's apartment and found a stash of benzos. He claimed insomnia, but when Ben pushed him on what Stevie had said—that he was pissed because she ended things after Kimmy told Stevie he raped her, he got defensive.

"Is it true?" Ben had asked him, himself trying to calm his voice. He had laughed when the flyer went around, thinking it wasn't anything more than a bunch of names on a bathroom wall. "Did you rape Kimmy Devine?"

"Isn't there, like, a statute of limitations on that shit?" he joked, looking at the other officer in the room, who didn't smile. "But no, I didn't rape her."

"Why would Kimmy hint at that? And why would Nikki explicitly tell Stevie you did?"

"Am I supposed to know the inner workings of the head of a crazy cunt and her friend?" he said suddenly, his voice raised. "She's just making shit up. She's never liked me, and she doesn't want me with Stevie. She's obviously stuck in the past. Why else would she start fucking Fitzy again? It's like she's got all these itches she has to scratch. A little bitch mutt with fleas she can't shake."

Ben tried his best to stay composed, to not punch Aaron in the nose right then and there. How had he never noticed what an asshole he was? Or maybe he chose to ignore it, just to keep his head down and not rock the boat, not chase away the one party house they could all rely on. Ben pivoted. "We're going to run your prints through the system, just to rule out anything in the case."

He watched Aaron shift. "What the fuck, man. How can you just do that? Those pills are legal."

"We'll call your doctor as well. Like I said, this is just procedure. Do you have a contact number for them?"

"I want a fucking lawyer," he said as Ben turned. "I want a fucking lawyer."

They didn't have much. At that point, Ben's best theory was that Aaron was pissed at Kimmy and tried to drug her and Justin to—what?—embarrass them? And the delivery got twisted. Tess was adamant it wasn't suicide, that it couldn't be, but they wouldn't know for sure until they got the autopsy's toxicology report a few weeks later.

Aaron was charged with possession of a controlled dangerous substance with intent to distribute and held at Mercer County Corrections Facility, where he received a court-appointed lawyer and an uphill battle ahead of possible conviction—which only grew steeper when Peter's tox screen showed he had codeine and lorazepam in his system at the time of his death. "I've never even seen that guy," Aaron continually repeated during subsequent questioning. "Seriously. Take my DNA, do whatever. I didn't give him drugs. I've never even met him." So they collected his DNA and added it to Aaron's profile.

Unable to quiet the nagging in his gut ever since Stevie told him Aaron raped Kimmy, Ben asked the forensics lab to run Aaron's DNA through the state database, and two days later, Ben's jaw almost dropped when he saw the results. Aaron Roop's DNA was a near perfect match with three rape cases from 2008, 2010, and 2016, all in various college towns in New Jersey. The first two victims had flunitrazepam—or roofies—in their system at the time of the rape, and the third had lorazepam.

Still, it wasn't as if they were able to wrap things up with Aaron overnight. Tess's face lost color when Ben told her the results of Peter's tox report, knowing it wasn't suicide, but it wasn't entirely someone else's fault. She didn't want Peter's death associated with Aaron—and it was proving difficult to conclusively prove he was involved since no one witnessed Aaron handing Peter a pill—and Tess didn't want her children to associate their father with opioids, so she stopped pressing and agreed it should be ruled as an accidental death.

Tess sold their Rocky Cape house in the meantime, and she and her toddlers moved in with her parents on the Main Line. Ben coordinated with the various detectives overseeing the rape cases beyond Cape County's borders. After months and months of officers gathering supporting evidence and the victims having to rehash one of the worst nights of their lives, including identifying Aaron in physical and photo lineups, a conviction was announced that afternoon: seventeen years in prison.

It has been a long year, Ben's autumn a whirlwind of information and research and emotional whiplash catching up to him. But finally, finally, he hopes, these women have all gained peace. And maybe, just maybe, he thinks as he looks at his wife's most recent text—an ultrasound of the baby girl who's been growing in her the past twenty-two weeks—he's made up for his own sins.

Epilogue

September 2024

The balloons bob in the wind, dancing back and forth against the backdrop of the bay. "Congratulations," they spell, their metallic sheen scattering the sunlight across the deck. We're retired. Bill and I, officially. I can't believe it, the freedom we feel. So many years of sweat, of stress, of highs and lows. And now calm.

Kimmy hugs me, her arms tight. "Love you, Mom." She's had three glasses of rosé already, which I normally would yell at her about if it weren't for the recently placed diamond on her left ring finger.

"Carissa, congratulations," James says, his freckled smile always a delight. Such a handsome boy, that James.

"Kimmy's taking work off our hands, and you're taking Kimmy off our hands!" Bill quips, his dad jokes at an all-time high when he's excited. And he is, about all of it.

"God, Dad," Erin says, a piece of cake perched near her mouth. "You sound like you're straight out of a 1920s movie. 'Oh, here's a dowry too!'" Bill has no idea, but after getting a sperm donor and going through a round of IVF, Erin is seven weeks pregnant. She stuffs the piece into her face, her hormones and hunger at extremes, and smiles at both of us. I know she can't resist our banter. Stevie's by her side, in her rightful place as our adopted daughter. I only wish her mom were here to see that our girls had reconciled, that they're once again inseparable.

It's just the six of us, no one wanting to jinx the celebrations with a big party, especially after what happened the last time. Poor Peter Cameron, may he rest in peace.

But this is how it should be. The Devine family. Together. In Rocky Cape, the place that is as much a part of our DNA as we are in one another. And Kimmy and Erin are running Devine's—a company that is their inheritance, that should stay in our family for generations to come—together as co-CEOs. It's what my girls deserve. To be happy, in their home, without bad men trying to bring them down.

Two years ago, we were ecstatic that Kimmy had returned. There were so many moments during her career in finance where I sensed she was flailing, was working toward some impossible, emotionless goal. *And for what?* I always asked. But she dismissed my worries, my questions.

It wasn't until I overheard Stevie and Erin talking in Erin's room—I had forgotten my phone when we went to the Callahans' Beach Week cocktail party and snuck back home for a moment—when I realized what it was Kimmy wanted. Fuck You money. Freedom. Power. Over Aaron Roop, a barnacle on this town, a blemish in my daughter's history. My heart broke at what I had missed, at the signals she worked so hard to hide. My brain started spinning; he had to be dealt with, and it couldn't be that hard to frame him, right?

The next day, Susie Reynolds waltzed right up to me at the club and loudly blabbed that she saw Kimmy with Justin Fitzpatrick on a date. I almost spit out my grapefruit crab avocado salad, the tiny bit of microgreens dangling from my lip. "Excuse me?" I had asked, sure she had to be wrong.

"His hands were all over her derrière, Carissa. We saw them at Sea Salt last night. Like they were teenagers." She lowered her sunglasses. "I just thought you should know."

How had my precious Kimmy come so far only to revert to one of her worst mistakes, the one who catapulted her into a series of her darkest decisions her senior year? *No*, I decided. *Not again.*

I thought about discussing it with Erin, or with Bill, but I knew I had to end this myself.

I made sure Aaron was working the party, telling the manager he was friends with the girls. Not a lie, I suppose. And then I snuck into Erin's room, searching for the drugs I heard her and Stevie talk about. I took two pills from a ziplock hidden between Erin's mattress and bed frame. I didn't know enough about these things to know if this would do the job, but I took them with me to the club that night. When we went to order a round of drinks, I grabbed Kimmy and Justin's order with Bill getting the others, and I dropped two in the glass I planned to give to Justin, watching them sink and dissolve. My plan was to get Justin messy enough that Kimmy would see his true colors, and then claim Aaron was trying to drug Kimmy. Two birds, one stone.

As we walked toward the group, I realized just how drunk Justin already was and I worried I might kill him. I hesitated for a moment, thinking I would just dump the drink, and then Peter showed up. We all waved, excited to see him, but he only had eyes for Erin—and it all clicked. Another part of their childhood I somehow overlooked. How long had something been going on? Didn't he realize how fragile she was right now, getting over a miscarriage and a divorce? Wasn't he married, with kids? Once again, I decided absolutely not.

I thought about all the conversations I had with my girls over the years about men ruining women's happiness, smearing their names, traumatizing their sense of self. I had found a good one, Bill's kindness and patience and loyalty like a salve to all the tumultuous relationships of my teen years and early twenties. My girls deserve that sort of partnership, that abundance of love. What they don't know is that one of my classmates took advantage of me at a party in 1971 and I got pregnant. A girlfriend drove me from New Jersey to New York, and I got an abortion, worried the entire way that I was either going to get arrested or die. But I didn't; I was able to move on from one of the worst things that ever happened to me and build a beautiful life. I spent decades playing by the rules, being a good wife, a great mother, an American Dream of a woman—and I have loved the role with all my heart. Yet just before Kimmy moved home, I watched the country erase decades of progress, and the fear that consumed me all those years ago returned—it had spent so much time simmering in my depths, though, that it had turned into anger. When I learned what Aaron Roop did to Kimmy, and that my darling Erin had been brainwashed by a, what do the kids call them—a groomer? Well, my outrage bubbled over. These men controlling us with their flippant rules, their greed, their insecurity about their own inadequacies. We should be able to control our own destiny, not them.

I handed Peter the glass, no hesitation. I'm not even sure what I expected—something similar to my plan for Justin, perhaps? To show Erin the clown he truly was, a sad man drowning in a midlife crisis—one who's willing to drown her with him. He gulped almost all of it within five minutes, and then I saw him and Erin head outside together. And then he was gone.

I was horrified when I heard about his death the next day, especially when they thought it might be suicide. But I also felt relief. He's gone, he's out of their lives. No more grooming my precious little baby.

And then Justin self-destructed. That boy really could never keep his cards straight, poor thing. He learned the hard way it's never a good idea to dip your toes so intensely in the past.

And Aaron? That was the easiest part. Before the party, I brought Bill a piece of computer paper that had WATCH YOUR BACK printed on it in an inconspicuous font. "I found this on Kimmy's car last night," I told him.

He took the paper, looking worried. "Should we call the police?" he asked.

I shook my head. "Let's just get through this party tonight and we can chat with them tomorrow." Though I knew if we did call the police, that Ben Lamb would be on our side. He always had a little thing for my girls. They used to call him a Laurie, like that character from *Little Women*. It didn't matter which Devine sister he got, he just wanted to be part of the family.

And that was that. Bill told Ben about the letter when he first reached out to us, which led Tess to think Peter's death was not a suicide, which led them to Stevie, who led them to Aaron. How was I to know he was a serial rapist? Karma, I suppose. My action may not have stirred up a nation, but it made a lifetime of difference for my girls—and that's really all that matters to me.

So now all the bad boys of Rocky Cape are gone. Dead. Jailed. Discarded. And we're here: happy, wholesome, able to enjoy this evening with our whole hearts.

Because, finally, my girls are home—with no skeletons chasing them away.

Acknowledgments

Rip Tide is ultimately a book about family—and I am the luckiest for being born into mine. Thank you, Mom, Dad, Kel, and Jen, for embracing my sass, encouraging my storytelling, and loving me even when it was easy not to. You never gave up on me despite the many moments I wanted to give up on myself, and I can't imagine a life without your unconditional love. If we can survive the era of at least one Leahey sister reliably crying while eating a support Bloomin' Onion at MCO's Outback Steakhouse (c. 2007–2013), we can survive anything.

Thank you to my editor, Sarah Stein, and the entire HarperCollins team for continuing to take a chance on me; it's been such a dream to collaborate again and again. Thank you to my agent, Michelle Brower, and the brilliant Trellis crew; your partnership means the world and has been such a clarifying light in a notoriously opaque industry. And thank you to Alice Lawson, Stephanie Glencross, Crystal Patriarche, Taylor Brightwell, and Grace Fell for all you've done to share *Rip Tide* with readers across the globe. It takes a village, and I'm happy you're mine.

Thank you to the many friends and fellow creatives who answered all my spiraling texts, embraced my phase of sending at least ten Y2K memes a day, and read early drafts as I worked on *Rip Tide*: Lina Patton, my better half and forever first reader; Avery Carpenter Forrey and Carola Lovering, who have made creative life in the 'burbs more vibrant than I ever imagined; Kristin Zimmerman, my third sister and most trusted fact-checker of all things aughts; the Unyoungs—Sheila Yasmin Marikar, Brittany Kerfoot, and Liz Riggs—for being the ultimate cheerleaders; Alli Hoff Kosik, for your friendship and excellent editorial eye; the 2023 Rowland Writers Retreat cohort, whose work inspires me to always bring my A-game, professionally and personally;

and Annabel Monaghan, Jillian Medoff, Katie Gutierrez, Daisy Alpert Florin, and Jenny Hollander for sharing your valuable time and such kind words.

Thank you to Seven Mile Island, New Jersey, for being a summer home to my family for most of my life. From breakfasts at Uncle Bill's, to crab-trapping off my grandparents' dock, to listening to Hanson while my sisters and I painted our unfinished attic and covered holes with posters of the Spice Girls, to riding a mini plastic roller coaster into the Hoy's pool, to cheering Kelly on when she kicked butt as a WCBP lifeguard, I have nothing but the most wonderful memories of the Shore. And thank you to my 34L girls, Emily Rarig Duca and Jenn Johns, who filled my teen years with so much laughter, top-notch sing-alongs, and the absolute best hugs; I'm so fortunate to still have you in my life.

Thank you to the many amazing teachers who keep my unruly boys entertained and educated all week so I can write. And to Bama and Papa—for your loving childcare, yes, but also your infinite support. I pinch myself every day that I have such incredible in-laws.

And, of course, thank you to my husband, Pat, who has given me two priceless gifts: the space to pursue a creative career, and our boys, who are my everything. I love you three and our 6:00 a.m. cuddles (smelly pup included) more than words.

About the Author

COLLEEN MCKEEGAN is the author of *Rip Tide* and *The Wild One*. She was previously an editor at *Marie Claire*, where her work was nominated for a National Magazine Award, and her writing has appeared in *The Cut*, *Elle*, *Glamour*, *Bustle*, and *Fortune*. A native of Allentown, Pennsylvania, and a graduate of Georgetown University, Colleen lives with her family in Westchester, New York.